The Guardian's Son

Also by Anita Tiemeyer

A Brother for Sorrows

The Guardian's Son

Anita Tiemeyer

Shawm Publishers

This book is a work of fiction. Any reference to historical events, real people, or real places is used factiously. Other names, characters, places, and events are products of the author's imagination, and any resemblance to actual events or places or persons, living or dead, is entirely coincidental.

Genre: Historical Fiction, Family & Relationships

World War II, 1939-1945 Germany – Fiction
Holocaust, Jewish (1939-1945) – Buchenwald– Fiction
Concentration camp – Fiction
Psychology – Fiction
Post-traumatic Stress Disorder (PTSD) – Fiction
Catholicism – US – Fiction
Judaism – US- Fiction

Geographic: (N.Y.) – History – (1945 -1965) – Fiction

LoC: PS3620.A31 T2021 , DCN: 813.54TIE

Paperback: ISBN: 978-0-578-92295-9
eBook: ISBN: 978-0-578-92296-6
LCCN: 2021910686

Cover art by Ghislain Viau
Layout by Kim Autrey
Author photograph by Demico Southern

for Donna

Religion is like a pair of shoes . . . Find one that fits you, but don't make me wear your shoes.

--GEORGE CARLIN

In order to have faith in his own path, he does not need to prove that someone else's path is wrong.

--PAULO COELHO

CHAPTER ONE

Major Grayson Pierce counted the feet. He counted forty-seven in this pile, divided by two, that made twenty-three bodies, plus one that either was missing a foot or hidden under the other corpses. Frenzied insects hovered over the bodies, fighting for tasty spots of spoiled flesh. The army surgeon watched a nasty horsefly land on a hipbone, where it stayed for several seconds biting into the grey skin. He brought his hand up to his mouth and swallowed hard, forcing down the K-rations he had eaten earlier.

As soon as the 120th Evacuation Hospital unit members got out of the ambulance trucks, they stumbled, almost falling. They held their sleeves to their noses and breathed through their mouths in a useless effort not to choke on the foul air. Hundreds of people accosted them, babbling in unrecognizable foreign tongues. The mass of men and boys of all ages seemed untroubled about the shocking cornucopia of death that lay around them, nor were they bothered by the open sewer smell that permeated every molecule of air. Their weak, broken-toothed grins strained their sunken cheeks, and they lethargically rubbed their hollow chests. They took doddering steps through the rivers of urine and excrement. Claw-like hands fearfully stretched out to touch the new visitors.

The medical teams tried to tell the starving inmates that food and water were coming from the nearby town of Weimar. However, they did not understand English, and the confused camp survivors begged with wailing voices. The stronger ones became angry and impatient, and they pushed forward like ravenous animals. More army trucks barreled through the entrance, their tires bumping over railroad tracks. They were surrounded by the hoards even before they stopped. Desperate hands snatched boxes of paper-wrapped K-rations in fiberboard boxes. The inmates immediately tore them apart, and the food disappeared. Then, almost at once, vomit dripped to crusted, bare feet. Tiny stomachs made by weeks and months of starvation could not handle the pork loaves and dry biscuits and candy bars. To the soldiers' horror, some upright "cadavers" promptly collapsed and succumbed to the overwhelming bits of nourishment. Others, too weak even to ask for the boxes, sank into the mud, resigned to join their limp, pathetic friends.

More American troops and Red Cross vehicles entered the camp. Among the supplies, the soldiers distributed U. S. government-issued woolen blankets, soap, cigarettes, and first aid kits. The men and boys walking about on stick-like legs clutched their new gifts with unabashed glee. Army personnel helped more prisoners out of the endless rows of wooden, crude barracks. One would be shocked seeing the curved hip bones and complete spinal columns poking through translucent skin. They walked tentatively, holding on to sturdy arms with brittle, shaking fingers. Other, more healthy-looking men also stepped out. Although in better physical shape, the dull hollowness in their eyes revealed the hardships they had endured at Buchenwald.

American General George S. Patton of the United States Third Army had been so outraged at this gruesome spectacle that he ordered residents from Weimar to visit. The inmates gawked at the long lines of unhappy townspeople who had to look back at them. Well-furred, coiffed women in high heels tried not to stare at the naked men. But what else could they look at except the piles and piles of inert bodies with frozen gaping mouths and stiffened limbs? Men in suits and hats reluctantly entered the sheds near the crematorium. They hurried out with grimaces on their white, "innocent" faces.

Major Pierce looked on at this bizarre tragedy, staying out of view of an army journalist's camera as he shot pictures of this bitter spot of Germany's Black Forest. Taking off his Red Cross army helmet, he turned back toward the brick command headquarters building, guarded by a single, leafless tree. He walked past the prisoners' canteen, the so-called infirmary, the whipping posts, the gallows, the pathology building.

Smoke drifted out of a square-sided smokestack of another windowless brick edifice. The army doctor considered what could be burning. He walked closer and noticed tiny bits of rock falling from the sky like raindrops of a light shower. Examining a fallen pebble, he realized it was human bone. He dropped it and looked at the chimney again.

Watchtowers interspersed the twelve-foot electric fence that surrounded the entire camp. Many bodies lay along the fence, inmates who had tried to either escape or kill themselves on purpose. Major Pierce imagined them being picked off by the sharp-eyed snipers in the towers. The army doctor bent down to examine the entrance wounds in the back or behind the ear. He stood and nearly lost his balance bumping into a corpse whose left eye socket was empty, the intact right eye watching him.

This perverse version of Dante's Inferno couldn't be real! How could any place like this exist on earth? Was this the Hell foretold in the book of Revelation? Was this the dwelling place of Lucifer himself? The doctor closed his eyes, his big body weaving in nauseous vertigo. He wanted to put all this horror out of his mind. It was too much to comprehend. He could not bear to look ahead of his own feet.

Then it came to him. God had wanted him to be here. It had not been enough just to follow the American troops across western Germany with his evac hospital, taking out shrapnel and setting broken bones and amputating limbs. His true mission emerged before him in this vile, polluted camp. *For I was hungry and you gave me food, I was thirsty and you gave me drink, a stranger and you welcomed me, naked and you clothed me, ill and you cared for me . . . And the king will say to them in reply, 'Amen, I say to you, whatever you did for one of these least brothers of mine, you did for me.'* Matthew 25: 35-40.

Major Pierce gathered his courage and walked deeper into the camp, gingerly stepping over some tangled barbed wire and approaching countless rows of long, poorly built wooden shacks. A few members of the army medical staff caught up with him. Behind them appeared an emaciated, bearded prisoner of indeterminate age, dressed in frayed striped pajamas. "Wenig Lager, Juden hier," he called, waving his hand. Major Pierce turned to meet his grizzled face.

He understood the word "Juden" and surmised that this place was where the Jews had been imprisoned. He allowed the chap with the crude yellow star sewn on his filthy shirt to lead him on.

The strange prisoner stopped at a lone body lying face down near the fence. With his heart pumping fast, Major Pierce inched closer. He saw bloodstained tears in the black and white striped shirt. Healed-over scabs spotted the feet as meager, blood-soaked strips of cloth had not protected them.

He crossed himself and whispered, "Lord, have mercy." Surrounded by a few orderlies, he crouched, and with clammy hands, he gently pushed the body over on its back. The slice in the poor man's neck was so deep and so wide that it appeared he had a second mouth. The oddly bent right arm flopped in the mud, most likely broken. Dried blood spread in the soil around the man's head. A thin layer of black hair covered the victim's skull, and several days of beard dirtied his jaw. A brutal scar ran down his left cheek, jagged and red. The dark brown eyes staring directly at the doctor made him swallow with unease. Dried blood stiffened the shirtfront. He counted fourteen stab wounds. The yellow Star of David sewn on his shirt also had been ripped by stab wounds. Five numbers stitched on a black strip above it read: 72001.

Despite the horrific sight, Major Pierce calmly tried to imagine the head and body as a living, walking human being, a handsome man with wide-set eyes, a sturdy, straight nose, well-formed lips, and a smooth, angled brow. The intelligence in this man's face would make one speculate that he might have been a gifted academician, a successful businessman, maybe even an attorney. Whatever his life pursuits had been before this camp, his demise epitomized the loss of an entire civilization. Major Pierce mourned him. He crossed himself and whispered, "O, Lord, grant this man eternal rest. And let perpetual light shine upon him. May he rest in peace. Amen."

He looked away to quiet his thumping heart and then returned his attention to the body. Because of the unique brutality of this man's death, he decided he would search for his identity. Looking at the nervous inmate who stood by, he asked, "Who is this man? Why did he die like this? Who cut his throat?" The other man shook his head and stepped back, holding out his hands as if warding off some evil spirit emanating from the body.

"Name? What was his name?"

Worriedly shifting his eyes, the inmate finally said, "Kaufmann."

Major Pierce memorized the number on the right front side of the striped shirt. Knowing the Germans' obsession with documentation, he hoped to find the prisoner's name somewhere in the mountains of abandoned files in the administration building. He knew that he would have little time. Too many starving, diseased people needed him. Maybe a few of the stronger prisoners could help him look for the paperwork if he could communicate with them.

Again, he looked at the number on the bloodied shirt--the only clue. Impulsively he unbuttoned the shirt and took it off, revealing a mass of black hair on the chest, stiffened with dried blood. He gave it to an orderly. "Go put this in my medical bag."

The scrawny inmate touched the army doctor's arm and motioned him to follow him again. They walked through the rows of barracks. How many hundreds of men and boys had been crammed into these buildings, which were nothing more than sheds, with no adequate light or heat or ventilation or simple toilet facilities? Major Pierce cringed at the thought of entering one of them, afraid of what hideous scene he might see.

The prisoner stopped at a barrack and opened a door barely hanging on its hinges. A youthful, pimply-faced medic followed him inside. After a moment, he called, "Major Pierce! I think there's something in here!"

Rushing into the shack, the stench of human waste hit the doctor's face like an unexpected slap. Light from the opened door revealed empty, rough-hewed wooden beds, little better than racks, stacked to the ceiling, lining both sides of the long room. In the middle, a narrow, painful-looking board with cut-out holes sat on top of metal buckets filled with decomposing excrement.

The inmate stood at the south end of the stinking room. He pointed to the first tier of wooden slats. "Er ist innen dort."

"I think there's someone under there," said the corpsman eagerly. "I heard a noise under the boards."

By this time, more medics had come into the barrack, wide-eyed and silent as they looked around. Their army-issued handkerchiefs did little to keep the putrid smell from their nostrils.

"Flashlight?" Major Pierce asked, glancing at the men behind him. Someone handed one to him, and leaning over, he waved it through the bottom wooden planks. He got on his knees and pulled away a loose board. The miasma of old urine made him want to gag. But he clenched his jaws and pulled harder. "Help me get these out," he ordered.

The enigmatic inmate nodded excitedly. "Ya! Ya!" He clapped his hands once.

Two other orderlies crawled next to the wooden rack and pulled the boards in which bent, rusted nails protruded as if they had been pried apart several times. Behind a split board was a shallow depression in the black soil. They moved so Major Pierce could examine it with the flashlight.

Determined not to let go, he pulled out the little boy.

"Bring a blanket!"

The army surgeon cradled the trembling child to his chest as he backed up and stood. He saw the Star of David on the boy's soiled, oversized shirt. As he saw the number sewn above the star, his breath stopped: 72003.

"Der ist sein Sohn. Sein Name ist Joseph." The inmate jerked his thumb over his shoulder. "Kaufmann." He nodded again, putting on a gratified smile.

Major Pierce turned the child's pallid face. Red, pus-oozing sores dotted his lips and cheeks; lice crawled down from his thin, black hair into his collar. His pitiful legs hung over the army doctor's arms like green branches of a young tree. The doctor's face fell with compassion as he gazed into the child's stoic, brown eyes. Did he see in the child's face the acknowledgment that now that he had been discovered, the end of his life was at hand?

As Major Grayson Pierce walked out carrying the child, he tried to think how he could get back to the headquarters building without the boy seeing the corpse lying so close to the fence.

CHAPTER TWO

The powerful black car rushed almost too fast for Joe to take in the green pastures dotted with black and white cows through the half-opened window. He sat in the big man's awkward lap, an arm as heavy as a log pinning him down. He had tried to sleep earlier as the car motor hummed, but the man's deep, gravelly voice kept him from dozing. To pass the time, he gazed at the trees, the wire fences, and the occasional farmhouse whizzing by. The early July sun hovered over the distant soft hills.

The car slowed and turned right onto a black-topped road, passing through a commanding gate built with white stone blocks. The vehicle moved leisurely enough for Joe to see rows of giant trees lining both sides of the road, their branches hanging over to make an unbroken verdant canopy. Then, as he turned his eyes forward, he caught his breath. He saw a fairy castle in the distance.

Shaded by more trees just as big as the ones along the driveway, the castle built of limestone blocks stood three stories high. On top of the steep, multi-colored slate roof, Joe counted four brick chimneys. Unlike the square brick chimney of the crematorium building at the camp, no stinking smoke or ash spewed out, polluting the sky.

A large, grey stone fountain bubbled with water in front of a set of iron-molded windows. Joe imagined putting his fingers in the splashing cascade. Yellow, purple, orange, and pink flowers he had never seen before grew in the front, nestled under the sculpted bushes. On the east side of the manicured emerald lawn, vivid red roses grew in a raised bed. Giant clay planters filled with more red, pink, and white blossoms sat on both sides of a pair of knotty, mahogany front doors with arched beveled windows. Above the doors was a half-moon window, catching the last sun rays of the day.

When the car stopped at the stone porch steps, the big man opened the door and motioned for Joe to get out. At once, three women dressed in flower-printed dresses and matching beads emerged from the front doors. The tallest of them hurried a bit faster, her heels clacking as she descended the long porch. The second one with white hair walked somewhat slower with the help of a wooden cane. The third lady brought up the rear, sporting the oddest color of red hair Joe had ever seen. His heart thumped with dread as they advanced toward him. However, inexplicably, they seemed not to have seen him as they went to the big man who was paying the driver.

That was Joe's cue to stay hidden behind the black car. But, alas, it turned around and rolled away, exposing him. Where to hide! A careful study of this enormous place was in order. All around the castle beyond the expansive lawns, a high black iron fence interspersed with stone pillars looked as insurmountable as the camp's wicked electrified fences. However, along this fence, thick-branched evergreen trees created a virtual wall of greenery. These trees would be excellent places to hide in if he could make it from the driveway. He knew he could outrun the old women, but he'd need a good head start on the man with the very long legs.

The big man called him to come closer. Joe stepped forward but kept his head down. He listened to the women titter like songbirds in the same confusing language he had heard from the big man and the car driver. Thankfully, they didn't look at Joe even as the man directed their attention to him. All they wanted to do was talk excitedly with each other and with him. After several minutes of boisterous chattering, the three women turned away and walked back toward the castle's magnificent entrance.

Suddenly, Joe heard a high-pitched squeal. Out of nowhere, a small girl with blonde pigtails and wearing a red gingham dress ran to the big man. She leaped into his arms, shouting and laughing, and he swung her around and kissed her cheeks. Joe figured she was his daughter. He looked back again at the trees and fence on the west side. But before he could sprint toward them, he was dragged by the hand up the steep porch steps. The little girl took her father's other hand and skipped along. At the front doors, he said something to her, and she disappeared.

Joe stepped through the double doors into a foyer that looked as big as the courtyard in front of the camp's main building. He waited, his eyes on the black and white-tiled floor. Other than indistinct voices coming from somewhere else, everything was quiet. Out of the corner of his eye, he saw a small table against a wall. On it sat a delicate silver vase filled with fresh flowers. What he thought was a telephone rested beside it. Bravely, he looked up at the soaring, wood-paneled ceiling. A colossal light fixture with hundreds of blazing glass pieces hung in the center, throwing fragments of rainbow colors on the walls. But he didn't have time to study it. The big man stood over him.

"Go ahead." The man pointed to the next room. As Joe held back, the man walked to the living room threshold. "Looks the same as it always did, Joe," he said, hands on hips. "Like a funeral parlor." He took Joe's hand and took him into the room. "You stay here while I get the suitcases and take them upstairs." He went out the front doors.

As quietly as he could, Joe walked carefully not to put footprints in the thick, powder-blue carpet. In the middle of the cavernous room were two blue couches with matching pillows facing each other. Joe would not try to test the plump cushions. A set of rose-patterned winged-backed chairs sat in quiet repose to his left, paired with glossy wooden end tables displaying tiny ceramic statues that looked as if they would break if one stared at them too intensively.

A rocking chair stood next to a brass floor lamp, its overstuffed seat and back covered in deep purple velvet. Fussy carvings of flowers and leaves decorated the oak trim. This piece of furniture had to be the throne where the queen of the castle sat. But he didn't see a throne for the king. On another table, Joe stared at a lamp whose base was a pink angel posed in flight, its mouth gaping in a silent call to the heavens. A faded portrait of a mysterious man in a long, fuzzy beard and mustache paired with another one of a dark-haired, stoic-faced woman hung on the floral wallpaper above the oak wainscoting. They seemed ready to pass judgment on Joe as he looked up at them. The perfect stillness in this room, the orderliness, the pristine furniture, the dustless air resembled a stage set for a play that would never begin.

Uncertain as to what to do, Joe eased himself on the edge of one of the sofas. Suddenly, he saw a grey cat jump up on the other end. He watched as it sat and licked its paw. Then it looked up at him in surprise. With black pupils growing larger and tail twitching, it laid back its ears.

Joe wanted to pet the cat, and so he leaned over.

"Hissssss!"

The cat struck its needle-sharp claws on Joe's nose and raked them down to his lip. Then on sprightly paws, it leaped off the sofa and bolted out of the living room.

Joe did not cry out. He felt a sting under his nose and put the back of his hand up to it, coming away with thin, red-tinged snot. He looked where the cat had run. He wanted to put his damp hands on it and stroke its soft fur. Since he didn't have a handkerchief, he wiped the blood from his upper lip with his new white shirt sleeve. He slid off the sofa and went to the enormous fireplace. He wasn't tall enough to see his injured lip in the gold-framed, beveled mirror hanging above the stone mantle. Kneeling before the closed glass doors, he peered at the empty, ash-tipped fire grate and blackened cinder block walls. Nothing here appeared dangerous, not like the crackling ovens whose fires threw out reeking fumes and pieces of human bone. This fireplace, which seemed only to burn wood, was cold and inert.

On top of the mantle sat a square, black clock: 6:45. Joe studied the creamy lions' heads attached on the sides and the gold pillars on the front panel. Then he caught an image of himself in the glass door of a large corner dish cupboard. His button-down shirt hung in folds over his navy pants. But what captured his attention was seeing his reflection for the first time. It was a little boy he did not know.

"I see you've met Mr. Henry."

Joe turned around to look up at the man standing next to him dressed in a mint-colored shirt and poker green silk tie. His hand rested on the waist of his gray slacks. He held a thick, black book in his other one. Joe tried to remember the man's name, but his mind was blank.

"He's a nice fellow, but you have to let him get to know you. Pretty soon, he'll be sleeping in bed with you." The man with the high forehead bent his never-ending legs, cracking his knees. Joe smelled an oily sweet fragrance from his coffee brown hair combed so neatly that no strand dare wander out of place. His friendly grey eyes bore into Joe's brown eyes. In a tobacco-scented whisper, he said, "But during the night, he might try to steal your breath!"

The back of Joe's neck tingled. He did not know any English to understand what the man said, but it sounded scary. However, seeing his face pull back into a broad smile allowed him to exhale.

After putting the black book on the side table in the foyer, the man led him into the generous-sized half bathroom. He picked him up and sat him on the edge of the white marble-topped vanity. Joe clutched the edge to keep from falling. After rolling up his shirt sleeves, the man opened a cabinet door under the sink and took out a small cardboard box, a paper sack filled with cotton balls, and a brown glass bottle. He washed his hands using a bar of pink soap in a dish and dried them on a white towel that hung on a silver towel bar. Joe studied the man's hands. They were wide and soft, with black hairs behind each knuckle and nails clean and neatly trimmed. On his left pinky, he wore a gold ring with a ruby jewel. Joe wanted to touch the twinkling stone.

The big man prattled on about Mr. Henry. "Mildred, my sister, got Mr. Henry from a dealer in Rochester. She wanted to keep Irene occupied while I was in the army. Irene is the little girl you saw in the driveway." He held an alcohol-soaked cotton ball midair. "He's a purebred Russian Blue with papers. That makes him think he's extra special."

Joe concentrated on a painting of ivy and pink roses hanging on the wall while enduring the stinging dabs on his nose and upper lip. With growing apprehension, he thumped the heels of his brand new, Poll-Parrot shoes against the vanity. Too many distractions came all at once—the cold, wet cotton ball, the acrid alcohol smell, and the man's too close face. He tried to still his trembling by folding his arms across his stomach.

"All done. Keep this bandage on for a little while."

Joe immediately touched the annoying paper the man had stuck to his lip, and he started to peel it off. But his hand was pulled away. "What's this on your sleeve? Is that blood? Don't let your Aunt Mil see that. She'll hit the roof."

As the man set him on the floor, he halted and then lifted Joe, bringing him close. "Welcome home, Joe," he whispered, kissing his head. He touched Joe's face. "When these spots on your cheeks fade, I'm going to take you to New York City to get some professional portraits done. Those guys are better than the amateurs in this town are. Now let's see what Rose has made for dinner."

Putting Joe on his feet, the big man took his hand. On the way to the living room, he picked up the black book on the foyer table. Joe wondered what it was about. He remembered the volumes his mother had brought him from a library before the camp. His father had helped him learn to read from those books. Would this man help him, too?

In the next room, Joe's eyes widened. Heavy, gold curtains framed the large bay windows, and green and white-striped plants hung from brass chains hooked into the high molded ceiling. Behind a pair of leather, nailhead armchairs stood a giant grandfather clock, its brass pendulum swinging soundlessly inside the glass door. He observed the washed-out flower paintings that hung on the lavender walls. Small wooden tables, bookshelves, and tall cupboards displayed cut-glass candy dishes, painted trays, and dainty flower vases. All invited small curious hands to explore and accidentally drop to the floor. But that would have to wait as Joe was pulled through the room. He glimpsed a wide hallway and an enormous, spectacular staircase to his right, complete with varnished wooden balusters and matching handrail. Could he climb those red-carpeted steps to see what more treasures he might discover?

They moved on into what looked like an eating room, dominated by a massive dark cherry table on top of a crimson and gold Persian rug. Above it hung a complicated light fixture that looked like the one in the foyer. A silver bowl overflowing with purple, red, and yellow flowers took center stage on the table. Two white candles in brass holders kept a vigilant watch on both sides. The table was a dazzling vista of elegance that Joe had never seen in his short life.

Filling the water goblets was a slim young lady in a black maid's outfit with a white apron and collar. She wore a white maid's cap on top of her tightly braided hair, held in place with bobby pins. Her narrow, acned face opened when she saw the big man and Joe.

"Dr. Pierce. It's so good you're back." She set the glass water pitcher on the table.

"Thank you, Anne. Have we got a place for Joe?"

"Yes, sir." The maid looked at Joe and gave a shy smile. "He'll sit right here next to you on the end." She pointed to a high-backed, Victorian-styled chair for Joe to take. He climbed in and sat on his knees so he could better see what was on the table. In front of him were two gold-rimmed white plates, the smaller one on top of the other, gold flatware, and a linen napkin rolled up in a gleaming gold ring. Completing the setting were two more small matching plates and three long-stemmed glasses precisely arranged on a white placemat. At each of the other five chairs around the table lay an exact copy of this place setting. Next to the centerpiece stood a little white pot of jam and a stick of butter on a plate.

Joe would have been overjoyed to eat the butter and jam mixed together. He reached out to poke his finger in the butter but stopped. He looked around the table for his tin bowl. He had to have his bowl and a spoon for the soup, just like in the camp.

"Put your feet down," the big man whispered, straightening his legs. He took out a gold cigarette lighter from his shirt pocket and lit the candles. Joe drew back his hands.

"Just add a bit of olive oil in the water to keep the spaghetti from sticking together."

"That's what I told her."

"Poppycock! You don't need olive oil. You just need to watch the pot and swish the spaghetti around. The oil would make the sauce slide right off. That's what Rose told me."

"Then, next time at the meeting, *you* tell Emily."

The two elderly women he had seen in the front of the house waddled into the room, clicking their low, wide-heeled sandals on the polished wooden floor. The one with white hair walked a bit unsteadily with that mean-looking wooden cane. The other woman with the odd-colored hair followed her. They rested their plentiful derrieres in the chairs and removed their napkins to put in their laps.

The third, somewhat younger woman who had approached the big man first in the driveway entered after them, advancing in the manner of a visiting Nazi big shot. Now that Joe could see her up close, she looked a lot like the man with the same rectangular face and prominent chiseled nose. But her eyes were as lifeless as a dead fish under furrowed, severely plucked eyebrows. Brown and yellow-striped combs restrained her ash-blonde hair away from her stony face. Her mouth was a red line, embellished by a fleshy mole on the right side. When she sat across from him, Joe prayed she wouldn't look at him. He tried his best to make himself smaller.

Joe observed the big man talking to the little girl in the blonde pigtails who had just sat on her father's left side. She giggled like a toddler as her father leaned over to kiss her silly red mouth. Joe's face became hot. He wiped more snot from his nose and touched the paper on his lip. He hoped no one would notice it.

"Here we go!" sang a petite, corpulent woman in a black dress and white bib apron as she burst into the room. She banged a swivel door that appeared to lead to another room, possibly a kitchen. She set an enormous platter of steaming beef in front of the man's plate. After taking a worried look around the table, she scuttled away. Joe figured this breathless woman must be the cook. Anne, the young maid, returned with a silver tray laden with yeast rolls and, using silver tongs, placed one on each small plate. Her smile now gone, she moved with the efficiency she had been thoroughly trained to use. She put the tray next to a silver coffee and tea set on the oak sideboard and took a wine bottle. After filling the goblets, she went back through the swinging door.

The man stood. "Now it's time for the blessing,"

When Joe saw the women and the little girl rise, he also got out of his chair. They touched their foreheads, chests, and shoulders as they bowed their heads. With tightly closed eyes, knitted brows, and hands pressed together, the big man spoke with intense emotion.

"Bless us, O Lord, and these thy gifts which we are about to receive from Thy bounty. We give You thanks, our Father, for the bread and water You have put on our table. We are not worthy of Your grace and beg for your blessings in this time of great suffering. Look after the members of this household, our parish, Immaculate Conception, the community in which we live, and the world that has been so devastated by war. Help us live our days with thankful hearts and loving ways. Under Your watchful eye, let our family walk in Your footsteps. Through Jesus Christ, our Lord, amen."

At the end of the prayer, Joe noticed that they again touched their foreheads, chests, and shoulders. After sitting, he watched with great interest as the man speared a chunk of meat and put it on his plate. Then he cut it into smaller pieces and put a fork in Joe's right hand.

The cook and the maid returned with bowls filled with mashed potatoes, creamed peas, buttered cabbage and onions, and parsley carrots. A particular delight was a bowl of sweetened cooked apples. Joe inhaled the cinnamon aroma, and he despairingly watched the woman with the mole on her face pass it to the elderly, white-haired woman at the other end of the long table. The cook put a gravy boat of hot brown gravy right beyond Joe's plate. As he watched the cook and Anne serving the food, he decided to make friends with them.

"Rose, you've outdone yourself," said the man, grinning and surveying the spread. He took each bowl of vegetables and put a small spoonful on Joe's plate. Then he piled the food on his own plate.

Oh, das ist irh Name, Rose. Wann warden diese Apfel herumgehen? Joe looked forlornly as the old biddy handed the bowl of cooked apples to the other antiquated woman with the absurd-looking hair.

"I hope it meets your expectations, Dr. Pierce. After all, it is your homecoming." The cook gushed and fidgeted with her apron. "The salad is coming." She followed Anne back into the kitchen.

Joe sat on the edge of his chair, hands tucked under his thighs, his legs vigorously swinging underneath. What a feast! The meat lying in its salty juices smelled heavenly, and it would taste so good with the gravy on it. He waited while the adults and the little girl shoveled it all in their mouths. This meal had to have been what it was like in the SS officers' quarters, all that bountiful, rich, delicious food! But he knew it was only for these strange people sitting around the table. At the camp, neither he nor any others could ever dream of such a banquet. A vision of two starved youths slurping what pretended to be broth out of a tiny, beat-up metal bowl came into his mind. He had been hiding under some tarps at the time, his stomach growling and his mouth watering as he spied on them.

The man pointed to his plate with his table knife and said something. But Joe just looked at it, swallowing saliva. Somehow his fork landed on the rug beneath the table.

The old woman with the funny hair sitting on Joe's right spoke. "Rose had to save her coupons for a month to get that roast at Knight's Meat Shop. The butcher said he just got it in this morning," She cut neat pieces of greasy fat around the meat and popped them into her mouth. "Umm! The flavor is divine!" She closed her eyes, working the fat in her mouth with pleasure.

Joe studied this lady. She had a heart-shaped face and two double chins, all framed by frizzy, ginger-colored hair. Her crystal-white glasses with gold etching caught the light from the chandelier. Dark reddish rouge smeared her loose cheeks, and her eyelids repeatedly batted as if she was trying to knock off the clumps of blackening on her lashes. Her flamingo pink lips wiggled as if they had a life of their own. Maybe she was a clown. Joe had seen a picture of one in a library children's book his mother had brought him. She certainly seemed to know how to make herself up as one.

"Yes, Aunt Elvie, the roast turned out exceptionally well this time," said the stern-looking woman with the dead fish eyes. "It's a matter of roasting the meat slowly, you know."

The clown lady sighed. "Must be. My roasts always come out overdone and tough."

"Daddy, don't forget to try the cabbage," the little girl blurted out, proudly waving her spoon. "I grew it myself."

"Did you enjoy growing your Victory garden, honeybun?" The man looked at her lovingly.

"Yes, but it was hard work. I had to go out and pull weeds every day."

After taking a swallow from her wine glass, the dead fish-eyed woman said, "Eat up, Grayson. You're as thin as a scarecrow. Didn't they feed you in the army?"

"Yes, Mildred, but I had to spend a lot of time on my feet. Don't worry about me. Rose's cooking will fatten me back up." He pointed to Joe's plate again with his fork and nodded to him.

"The beets are about ready for harvest, and we're overflowing with tomatoes," Frau Dead Fish Eyes said. "Irene, you are going to help Rose can them." Authority rang in her voice.

The little girl with the luminous grey eyes and pigtails made a face. When she saw Joe watching her, she stuck out her tongue at him. Then she pointed at him and tapped her upper lip. She covered her mouth to keep from laughing out loud.

Wheels of retribution turned in his seven-year-old brain.

Frau Clown said, "So, Grayson, tell us about your little boy."

The man put down his fork. "Well, Aunt Elvie, Joe is originally from Germany, and I brought him back from a Catholic orphanage in Switzerland. Irene, he's your new brother."

Joe understood the last word, "brother," and heard the girl's name, "Irene." *Denken Sie Doran, Irene ist ihr Name.* Did he hear the clown lady's name? *Evie? Elsie?*

"Uh-uh. He's too skinny." The little girl dropped her spoon, apparently finished with her meal. She hadn't even touched her cooked apples.

"Yes, he looks quite like a ragamuffin, Grayson," remarked Frau Clown, looking at Joe as if for the first time. "He needs a haircut."

Frau Dead Fish Eyes took her first official look at him. "Is that a bandage on his lip?"

Irene squealed in laughter. "Eat your mashed potatoes," her father said sharply. To the disdainful woman, he said, "Yes, Mildred. That's a bandage. He met Mr. Henry earlier."

Just before Joe reached for a bit of meat, Frau Dead Fish Eyes startled him by dropping her knife with a clatter. "He didn't tease him, did he?"

Joe immediately pulled back his hand.

"Of course not! Essen Sie, Joe."

"Well, he looks like something Mr. Henry dragged in from the backyard."

Joe was aware of the big man's growing annoyance by how forcefully he turned pages in that black book next to his water glass.

"He needs a haircut." Frau Clown said again. She replaced her sparkly glasses with cheap-looking half-glasses that hung on her chest. She blinked as if the new glasses were ineffectual. Squinting, she said, "What are those spots on his cheeks?" She replaced her glasses and went back to her creamed peas.

The big man looked down as if sorting out the answer in his head. "They were insect bites, and they're just taking a while to heal." He looked again at Joe's untouched plate and pushed it closer to him.

A smear of cream sauce graced her first double chin. "Insect bites? My goodness!"

"Grayson, where has this child been? Where did he come from?" Frau Dead Fish Eyes demanded.

All the while, Joe looked at the congealing food on his plate. His mouth watered. When could he start grabbing some to stuff under his shirt? He would need to save some of it for later. Rose, the cook, had set a brimming glass of milk on the far side of his plate. But he would, without a doubt, spill it if he tried to take it. He sighed.

The man said to the cook who had appeared again, "Would you bring one of Irene's baby cups of water for Joe? He shouldn't have milk with the pot roast."

"Very well, Dr. Pierce." Rose, the cook, looked about the table to see who else might need more water.

"And, Rose, let's make a date to go to the Cornell library. We need to do some research on Jewish dietary laws. I want you to learn to prepare kosher meals for Joe. Anne will need to learn, too." He stopped to think. "Hmmm. I also need to contact the rabbi at that synagogue. Beth-El, I think it's called."

The lively, diminutive cook beamed. "Oh, yes, Dr. Pierce! I'm ready to help!" The cook was so full of manic joy she went to Joe and impulsively gave him a wet kiss on his bug-bitten cheek. Joe met her buried, hazel eyes behind her thick smeary glasses. He suddenly envisioned the other overweight lady who had been so good to him and his father, bringing them food at night.

"Jewish dietary laws? Kosher meals? What's this all about?"

Joe recoiled at this sudden outburst from the far side of the table. The old biddy angrily set aside her wine goblet. Joe had forgotten about her. Did he see white steam come out of her nostrils?

Anne appeared with another opened wine bottle. As she filled the glasses, the old biddy said, "Anne, remove the centerpiece. I need a better look."

The flowers vanished.

The big man said, "Mother, in the letters I sent you, didn't I tell you he's Jewish? It's not kosher for Jews to eat meat and dairy products at the same meal."

The dragon woman worked some food in her wrinkled mouth and glowered. "Well, he's in a proper Christian home now, and he needs to eat real food."

"Daddy, what does kosher mean?" asked Irene, holding a roll dripping with strawberry jam. She swung her legs incessantly under the table just as Joe did.

Her father replied, "Kosher is the term Jewish people use to describe how they prepare their food. It means that they cook their food in a certain way to make it proper to eat according to their religious beliefs."

"How do you know about that? Did he tell you?"

"I read it in a book. Now, stop asking so many questions."

As the others returned to their food, Frau Dead Fish Eyes wouldn't give up. "Grayson, you didn't answer my question. Where did this boy come from?"

The man splashed wine when he set his wine glass down too fast. "Mildred, I told you in my letters that he came from Germany. He's an orphan, and I've brought him home to be my ward. I don't understand all the confusion. I assume you read my letters explaining all this, right?"

"You brought him back to be placed in an orphanage here in the States! How splendid of you, Grayson!" Frau Clown smiled, showing crooked, fragile teeth. She feigned pity. "There must be so many orphans over there in Europe after the war. It's so sad."

Joe saw a sliver of gold outlining her front tooth. Wouldn't the Jewish dentist have loved to pull that one for the SS guards' collection?

The man's voice tightened. "No, Aunt Elvie. He's not going to an orphanage."

Frau Clown turned to the white-haired dragon lady. "Nina, perhaps you could help find him a home. You know so many good people right here in Ithaca." Back to Joe, she puckered her wormy lips as if she was trying to kiss the air. "He's such a sweet little boy."

Frau Dead Fish Eyes jumped in. "He only said he was bringing home a little boy. He said nothing about what he was going to do with him."

The man gripped his knife and fork in his big surgeon's hands. "I told you exactly what I was going to do with him. I am his guardian. He is now a member of this family. I can't help it if you didn't bother reading my letters carefully." He sliced his roast beef vigorously enough to scratch the plate under it.

The hoary lizard lady glared at everyone except Joe. She angrily set down her wine glass as if it were a gauntlet. "Grayson, you can't just bring a child into our home without knowing anything about it or where it's from! We cannot have another child in this house. This is entirely unacceptable."

The man threw down his gauntlet in the form of his fork on his plate. "Mother, *it* is a little boy, and his name is Joe Kaufmann. His father is dead, and his mother was nowhere to be found. I have decided to be his guardian and rear him until he is of legal age. I just said that not one minute ago. I've phoned Al down in Washington, and he put me in touch with lawyers in Albany to get the paperwork for citizenship started. I already completed the guardianship papers while I was in Washington. He's here to stay." He returned to his pot roast.

His mother, Nina Cassandra, narrowed her rheumy eyes. "Then you got your brother involved, too."

"Well, that makes everything more complicated, doesn't it? Did you know about this, Mildred?" Without thinking, Frau Clown slathered butter on her roll that she had already buttered.

Before Mildred could answer, Grayson, pointing his knife at his mother, snapped, "If you choose not to accept it, then that will be your problem to deal with. I have always wanted a son, and I knew when I saw this kid, he would be mine." He pressed his napkin to his mouth and attacked his cooked cabbage.

The dragon lady chewed her pot roast, her jowls working under loose skin like a well-oiled pulley. Threatening anger rose around her like an aura.

Frau Dead Fish Eyes took another slice of pot roast and a dollop of mashed potatoes. "I hardly know what to think. It's going to take some time to get used to the idea of having another child in the house. This is just another example of you acting on impulse without any regard to how it might affect anyone else."

The man put down his fork and exhaled noisily. He took another gulp of his wine.

During the tense conversation, Joe slouched as far as he could, staring at the plate in front of him. Since he had heard his name from the man, he figured they were arguing about him. Nevertheless, the food still smelled good, and he was starving! Timidly, he picked up a morsel of cabbage and put it in his mouth. It tasted salty and oily, much like the cabbage given to him by his father when he had returned from the camp kitchen where he had worked. That nice lady had always given Vater something to eat at the end of his workday in the camp kitchen. She had been the head cook for the SS officers, and the food had been the leftovers from their meals. He brought it to Joe back in the barrack. He had hidden in that dirt hole behind the board slats and had to eat it fast before the other prisoners knew what was going on. Those treasured moments had been so fleeting!

The silverware was there, but it was too shiny to touch. Bravely, Joe took a dripping handful of creamed peas. The white sauce slid down into his shirtsleeve. As he was about to put them in his mouth, Frau Dead Fish Eyes shrieked, "Why aren't you using a spoon, young man?"

Joe immediately dropped the peas and drew back his hand. Terror blazed through his small body.

The man said, "Mildred, let him eat. He doesn't understand what you're saying."

"His table manners are atrocious! Where did he live, in a pigsty?"

Punishment was imminent.

"Don't worry about that now. Before you teach Joe correct manners, he's got to learn English. I have this dictionary to help us teach him." He tapped his black book. Again, he pointed to Joe's plate and nodded.

"Can he speak, Daddy?" asked the little girl.

"Of course, my dear. He just doesn't know any English. He knows German because he's from Germany. You've seen that country on a map, haven't you?"

Joe looked down as he knew to keep his eyes to himself. This whole scenario was just a deception. He knew what would happen to him, just like what happened to everyone else in the camp. Who amongst these strangers would be his executioner? Except for the little girl and possibly the clown lady, anyone at this table would be capable of carrying out his inevitable fate.

In the meantime, he would have to figure out how to get back into this room later to steal the rolls. Who knew when he would eat again? He remembered how knots of starving men had fought and killed each other over a piece of moldy black bread the Nazi soldiers had thrown at them. The cruel guards and even the kapos had laughed at them. He decided that he would sneak back to this room when everyone went to bed to steal the leftover food. But he would need to find a good place to hide it.

He noticed an odd figurine tacked up on the wall above the sideboard. A painted, naked man with shoulder-length brown hair and droopy eyes looked upward, his flame-red mouth slightly open. He had some odd-looking prickly head covering, and a narrow swatch covered his private parts. Thin, muscled arms stretched horizontally on a stick. The legs were tightly bound, one foot on top of the other, making his extremities form a "t." Gruesome red marks that looked like blood dotted his feet and palms. Did this figurine suffer in the camp, too?

"Here," the man said, offering a roll to Joe. Before eating it, he broke it in half and put part of it into his pants pocket for later. He would eat just enough now to stave off the hunger pains.

The old biddy's surprisingly sharp eyes caught him. "Now, see here! Don't put that roll in your pocket! Grayson, how you could bring this child into my house with such horrid table manners!"

Joe flinched. He dropped the roll on his plate.

Grayson said quietly, "Let him keep it." He pressed a small black button on the wall next to the dish cabinet.

Anne appeared at once.

"Coffee, please, my dear."

She turned and left.

Frau Dead Fish Eyes put her knife and fork on her finished plate and dabbed her non-existent lips with her napkin. "Well, if he's here to stay, he's going to need clothes. I'll look for a sale in the paper on children's clothing at Holly's. He's going to need underwear, pajamas, and some pants and shirts. I don't know what size he wears. He's awfully small. Then we'll go to Rothschild's to get him a suit. But we'll have to go the day after tomorrow. Helen Schlazier and I are going to work at the bake sale for Catholic Daughters of America downtown." She ignored the clicking forked tongue at the other end of the table. "Ithaca Engraving will get his name engraved in his missal. We need to do it right away so it will be ready for mass on Sunday. I should make a list."

Rising, she went to a small writing desk that stood in a corner and found an envelope. She looked at the paper inside. "I still have the latest letter you sent while you were in Washington." She put on her half-glasses which had hung by a gold chain around her neck. "I hope they'll have his name spelled correctly. What's his name again?"

Swallowing the last of his mashed potatoes, the man said, "Kaufmann. Joseph Kaufmann with a 'K' and two 'ns."

The little girl giggled. "That's a funny name."

The man said, "Irene, stop making fun of your brother." To his sister, he said, "You think of everything, don't you?"

"What do you mean?" Frau Dead Fish Eyes asked. "Are you referring to his missal? What's wrong with that? We have to get him ready for Sunday mass right away."

"Daddy, may I be excused?" Irene tried to look bored.

"No. Finish your peas." Frau Dead Fish Eyes pointed to the little girl's half-eaten food. "And no dessert until that plate's clean." She put the letter back in the envelope and put it into a drawer. Then she searched for her notepad on top of the desk.

Irene wrinkled her nose. Joe thought he understood what had just been said, and he'd like to help clean her plate. He noticed the girl crossing her arms and pouting.

"Who's ready for dessert?" The cook's voice rang as she burst into the dining room. "I baked a chocolate cake just for the occasion!" She looked to see what plates to remove.

"I am!" Irene jumped up.

Just as Frau Dead Fish Eyes opened her mouth to scold her, Joe took advantage of the moment. He grabbed a slice of beef and a handful of cabbage and carrots and hastily stuffed them under his shirt. The potatoes and gravy were too soft to take, so he took a partially eaten roll from the man's bread plate. He sprinted through the grandfather clock room and into the living room. He stopped in the foyer, debating whether or not to make a run for it out of the castle. But, alas, the front doors were too heavy to pull open quickly. He frantically searched a place to hide.

He was good at finding such places. He could anticipate when a guard was about to turn his head in his direction, and he would fly quicker than a sparrow to hide in a stack of discarded empty barrels or under a truck. One time he had to bury himself under a pile of corpses. They were as heavy as tree trunks, and because they were a few days old, they had stunk like old, uncooked meat. Pretending to be a baby rabbit (he had learned about animals in his mother's books), he had stayed motionless until after dusk. When it was dark, he had heard slow footsteps. He had peeked out between some heads. There in the dirt were his father's feet wrapped in torn strips of bloody cloth.

Joe opened a closet door. He slammed it shut after he went in and immediately knocked into a cylindrical metal thing with a cord wrapped around it. He sat on a pair of boots and some other stiff shoes with thin, metal blades on the soles. He shook on the inside from hunger; his heart pounded. He ripped off that embarrassing sticky paper. The food began to seep through his shirt, and he unbuttoned it. Then he ate. It tasted wonderful!

He knew he had to be quiet in this black place. Was there a way he could lock it from the inside? He smelled some unusual clean odor, not unpleasant. When he lifted his head, he brushed against some coats and a soft, furry wrap. He held his breath so he could concentrate on listening. Agitated voices told him he wasn't entirely safe yet. He licked some beef drippings off his collar. Then he began sucking on it, just as he did on his other shirt in the camp. It helped him cope with that dreaded sinking feeling that made his palms sweaty. His stomach cramped and growled. He was so tired of being hungry! Tears came into his eyes.

The door creaked opened. Joe braced himself. He blinked his eyes to rid the tears, and he started buttoning his food-stained shirt. He backed up against the wall.

"Joe?"

It was the big man's guttural voice. In the light from the opened door, Joe saw the darkened hulk get on his hands and knees and stretch out his hand to grab him. But the big man caught only air.

"Ouch!" Something cracked under the man's knee.

"What was that?" someone called out.

"I think I just broke a mothball." Groaning, he touched Joe's shoulder. Despite Joe's stifled protests, the man pulled him out into the foyer by his gooey sleeve. Once on their feet, the terrifying man dragged him by the hand into the living room. He almost put Joe on the couch but went on through the clock room and into the dining room. "Let's go in the kitchen to wash your face, Joe."

But Joe would have none of it. His gut told him bad things were in the room he thought they were going, perhaps knives or needles and syringes filled with poison. Having heard the cook say, "Doktor Pierce," he knew now that the man was a doctor. This supposedly nice, friendly man would lay him down on a table and stick sharp, painful things into his chest, into his heart. He had heard the other prisoners whispering about what went on in the infirmary. He had seen the dead bodies carried out.

He set his feet firmly on the Persian rug and pulled back to break this monster's grip on his hand. Almost losing his hold, the man said, "What's the matter, boy? We're going to get you cleaned up. There's some dessert waiting for you."

Joe's resistance did not waver. He decided it was time to fight. When the man picked him up and carried him, he screamed as loud as he could. He beat on the two-legged beast's shoulders and tried to get in a good position to bite him, preferably on his neck or face.

"What's that noise about?" the old queen bee shouted from another room. She and the clown lady entered the dining room to see the commotion. "Grayson, can't you keep that child quiet?"

"Goodness, he's worse than a toddler!" declared the clown lady.

"He's just upset," Grayson said flatly, steadfastly holding on to Joe.

The lady with the fleshy mole on her face followed him. "Why don't you put him up in his room and shut the door? He can have his temper tantrum in there without bothering the rest of us."

In the colossal-sized kitchen, lined with cabinets, dishes, sinks, and all sorts of pots and pans, Joe gave up screaming and melted into genuine crying. Through his tears, he saw the two ovens built into a red-brick wall, much smaller than those in the camp but still capable of burning dead people. Collapsing in the big man's arms, he didn't have any more strength to fight for his life. His life was over now.

When the man sat with him in a kitchen chair next to the aged, weather-beaten worktable, the sympathetic cook held a damp washcloth to wipe his face and hands. "Oh, the poor thing! He's so scared."

Joe felt his shirt being removed, leaving him naked and defenseless. The remaining roast beef and soggy vegetables dripped down his pants. When the food fell to the floor, he tried to reach down to get it, but the man wouldn't let him. Someone wiped his cheeks with a cloth.

"Now, now, you're okay, Joe. I know you're scared. We're going to have to get you into a clean shirt." The man gave the soiled garment to the cook for the laundry. It was white no longer.

Standing in the doorway, Frau Dead Fish Eyes snapped, "Is this how he's going to act, like a three-year-old?"

"He'll be all right. He's had a long day, and he's tired." The man rubbed Joe's back.

In his peripheral vision, Joe saw Frau Dead Fish Eyes raise her hands and leave. His crying turned into whiney moans as he tried to soothe himself, pressing his face into the man's chest. Where was his shirt collar?

The man eyed the chocolate cake on the kitchen counter next to a pitcher of milk. "Anne, bring me some napkins and a slice of that cake. And a glass of milk, please. The kosher meal can wait." The big man spoke to Joe. "Shhh, shhh. It's okay. You'll be fine, boy. Nothing bad is going to happen."

Joe did not understand the man's slow words. His insides shook so uncontrollably from terror that he thought he would vomit. His throat caught when he tried to gulp, and he couldn't catch his breath. He did not meet the big man's eyes. As he had learned in the camp, he stood a chance of being overlooked by avoiding eye contact. But no such luck here. He sat still as the man hugged him. He smelled the familiar tobacco scent on the man's shirt, and he closed his eyes. He could not comprehend what was happening to him. What did it mean? He knew that it was just a matter of time. The ovens were waiting for him.

The smell of chocolate made him open his eyes to see the cupcake decorated with white icing and tiny chocolate chips on a plate looming in front of his face.

"I baked some cupcakes with the leftover batter. I thought Irene and Joe might like them," said Anne.

"Well, well! Thank you, Anne. You just might get a raise for that ingenious idea." The man gave a laugh, nearly loosening his grip on Joe.

Joe grabbed the treat and stuffed as much of it as he could into his mouth. He forgot his tears. The man laughed again. "Here's some milk to wash it down." And he drank and drank. The man took the napkin from Anne and wiped the dribble from his chin.

Anne took the empty plate and the glass, but not before she stroked Joe's head. The man carried him back through the living room to the half bathroom to use the toilet and clean off his pants. Then they went out into the foyer. Joe saw the man ascend that awesome staircase. His legs gave out, and he crumpled to the floor. Moments later, the man returned with a clean, white shirt. Still wary, Joe listened to the man's small talk as he put it on him. Finally, the man proclaimed, "There! Now you look like a new man!"

Joe breathed deeply, trying to stop shaking. Perhaps he would get a reprieve. The big man, Grayson, patted his shoulder and kissed his cheek.

CHAPTER THREE

Grayson led Joe by the hand up the grand, two-tiered staircase to the little girl's room. Joe glanced back as he heard faint music coming from another part of the castle.

Irene sat cross-legged on her bed, a white paper crown on her head and a silver baton in her hand. A menagerie of stuffed animals held court around her.

"Sweetheart," said her father, guiding Joe into the room. "I've got to talk with our womenfolk. Will you keep Joe entertained up here?"

"What am I supposed to do with him?"

"Don't you have a stack of board games stuffed in your closet?"

Irene shrugged.

Grayson rummaged through the bottom nightstand drawer next to her bed. "Here. Start with your coloring book and your crayons. And try to get him to say a few words in English." He hesitated before shutting the door.

Irene got off the bed, her crown carelessly falling to the floor. Stepping up to him, she put her fist on her pushed-out little hip. Shaking the metal baton in his face, she said, "You'd better mind what I tell you." After dropping it on the banana-yellow carpet, she grabbed the coloring book and a fistful of crayons from the nightstand drawer and sat at a child-sized desk in the corner. Pretending to ignore him, she began coloring a unicorn.

Joe looked around, amazed at this magical room. A frilly yellow canopy topped her white bed, and two nightstands with yellow ceramic lamps sat on each side. A bookcase, a brown and white rocking horse, and a polished cedar chest crowded the room. Messy finger paintings and crayon drawings hung on the walls with tape, and a mountain of clothes buried the white dresser. The little girl had enough dolls and toys scattered about to fill a toy store. Joe thought her bedroom befitted a princess, so she must be very rich and important.

Abruptly, the girl went to the door. She opened it a crack and listened. After putting her finger to her lips to keep Joe quiet, she removed her shoes and soundlessly padded out of the room. Joe followed and sat next to her halfway down the oak stairs on the landing. Irene pressed her face between the decoratively carved balusters, her face contorted in concentration. Joe strained his ears, listening to the voices coming from a far-away place. He did not understand what was being said, but he noticed that the little girl sat motionless as she listened. She put her right hand up to her head and began twisting a lock of hair. He scooted a little closer to her.

That far-away place was the music room, named for the eight-foot Bosendorfer grand piano that stood before the floor-to-ceiling west windows. The dragon lady's mother had received it from her husband on their twenty-fifth wedding anniversary when they had lived in Syracuse. She had been a fairly accomplished pianist. Upon her death in 1879, the piano needed a new home. The music room was explicitly built onto the seventy-five-year-old mansion to accommodate the glorious instrument. Silver-framed pictures on an old, fringed shawl adorned the closed lid. In the spring and summer, crystal vases of cut flowers from the gardens around the house filled the entire room with scented air. Tonight, vases held bouquets of roses, salvia, daylilies, dahlias, and marigolds. On rare occasions, Mildred might tickle the Bosendorfer's ivory keys as long as no one else was in the room.

In addition to the piano, a floor model, 1940 Philharmonic, "Gothic Grande" cabinet console radio with remote control took its place on the north wall, guarded by a six-foot Ficus tree. A brick fireplace with an iron tray of wood sat on the east wall. Above it hung a famous painting by Renoir, *Two Young Girls at the Piano*. At the south end of the room, French doors opened to the garden room, a glorified screened-in back porch filled with white wicker furniture, and a jungle of houseplants. On the east wall stood Mildred's ebony desk, decorated in gold leaf and complemented with a matching straight chair. Here, she kept meticulous household records and organized her schedule for her volunteer and fundraising activities. Her mother, Nina Cassandra, had her own walnut, drop-lid desk near the French doors, a Christmas gift from her husband years ago. A glass cabinet on top housed her bone china knick-knacks. Two roomy couches covered in a red, pink, and green peony pattern took center stage in the room, and a green and yellow-striped velvet fainting couch stood in a corner that no one ever laid on. Decades-old parlor palms accented the room, and small folding tables between the west windows and the Bosendorfer were just the right spot for Mildred's cherished African violets. And in another obscure corner stood a four-foot-tall Victor Victrola, with a 78-rpm recording of Caruso singing *Celeste Aida* (Heavenly Aida) by Giuseppe Verdi lying on the turntable under the closed lid. The old-fashioned musical shrine was never played but not forgotten.

The music room was the family's favorite and most used room. Friends gathered here for garden club meetings and canasta card games. Before the war, Grayson had enjoyed relaxing in his recliner after a long day at the Tompkins County Hospital, relishing his quiet time with his newspaper, a tumbler of whiskey, and his pipe. On Tuesday evenings, his closest friend and colleague, Dr. Morey Allen, and his wife Alice came over for a game or two of bridge. The radio played almost constantly, tuned to daytime soap operas, late afternoon serials, and short comedies such as Ma Perkins and Fibber McGee. On Ithaca station WHCU, local celebrity Jack Deal played his organ and told funny stories. CBS News was announced on the hour, and on Sunday evenings, the Pierce family listened to wonderful performances by the New York Philharmonic Orchestra.

Tonight, while Grayson was upstairs with the children, the women had migrated to the music room like penguins with bellies full of fish. Anne followed with their coffee and chocolate cake on an engraved, silver-plated tray. As was the drill every evening, the radio was tuned to the New York City station, WNBC. Mildred worked on her to-do list as she sat at her desk. Aunt Elvie pondered her *New York Times* crossword puzzle. And the queen bee, Nina Cassandra, sat on her throne, an antique Lincoln rocking chair upholstered in garnet linen. She dabbed her turkey-wattled throat with a perfumed kerchief as she rocked at full tilt. Her dessert sat untouched on the small Pembroke table next to her.

Finally, stretched out on the silk-woven Oriental rug under the piano in all his two-foot glory was Mr. Henry, his tail twitching, his high-set ears turned back, and his avocado green eyes round and alert. A pink string of yarn lay dead under his front paw.

Grayson entered the room and stood at the opened French doors, enjoying the cool evening air drifting in, cherry-sweetened tobacco smoke lingering from his pipe. Cicadas sang in the backyard oaks, and fireflies occasionally punctuated the deepening night. When the doctor looked down, he noticed Mr. Henry crouching next to him on the parquet floor, surveying the darkened porch, his compact body taut as a drum. Grayson slid open a screened door to let him out.

"I will never understand how you managed to get him out of that horrid war zone." Mildred set her mouth firmly as she put down her pencil and notepad and moved to one of the sofas. The light from a Tiffany table lamp haloed her well-defined profile. She pulled a canvas bag out of a magazine rack. In it was her latest cross-stitch project, a rose garden with a white gate centerpiece. She laid out embroidery skeins and rummaged through her bag for a packet of needles.

"The grass needs cutting," Grayson replied blandly. "Will you call the gardener tomorrow?" When he turned back, Mildred saw his tired face and put down her needlework. He laid his pipe in the stand-alone ashtray, and sat in his well-worn soft leather recliner and put his feet on the ottoman. He rubbed his forehead. "I had to go back to get him. He had no family, no one to look after him. I was terribly worried about him."

The waning sunlight from the windows behind the piano cast shadows into the music room. Aunt Elvie picked up the remote and turned off the radio. She went back to her crossword puzzle but kept raising her bespeckled eyes to check on the other family members.

"Grayson, we have not been prepared for this new predicament." Nina Cassandra picked up her knitting, which she kept in a basket on the floor. But she looked at it with disgust and put it back. "This is a serious matter. It's not fair to us to have to contend with this impossible arrangement. What were you thinking? Did the Army addle your brain?"

"Of course not, Mother. I knew when I saw that kid that I would take him. I didn't want to talk about his situation at dinner in front of him because I don't know how much English he's picked up. I couldn't risk getting him and Irene upset."

"Upset?" Nina Cassandra's voice raised an octave. "What about us? He's turned this whole house upside down! Gracious! Stuffing all that food under his clothes and running into the closet like that. There's probably a trail of it all over the living room. Thank goodness the cleaning ladies will be here tomorrow. What would make him do such a thing?" She stopped rocking and leaned forward, lowering her voice. "Was he abused?"

Grayson held his emotion. "You have no idea." He met her colorless eyes. "I found him at a Nazi concentration camp."

"You mean the place where all those Jews were supposedly killed?" Aunt Elvie asked. "We read about those places in the newspaper!" Excitement made her a little breathless as if she were sharing a secret. She remembered her cake and began eating it. Suddenly, she stopped, her fork clattering on her plate. "I went with Sadie McNaughton to the movies in May. We saw *Picture of Dorian Gray*. Such a marvelous film with George Sands and Donna Reed. I believe Angela Lansbury was in it, too." She sipped her coffee. "But those newsreels nearly ruined our enjoyment of the film! It was scandalous. It was so embarrassing to see all those naked bodies up there on the screen. People walked out. Sadie said those films were just play-acting, something put together out in Hollywood. 'It's the government behind it,' she said. 'They're trying to scare us about the Germans!' " She went back to her cake.

Grayson blinked. "No, Aunt Elvie. Those weren't movies made up in Hollywood. It was real."

"Oh." Aunt Elvie burped.

"The camp where I found Joe was called Buchenwald. It was a slave labor camp. The prisoners were worked to death rather than outright murdered as the Jews were in other camps. It was one of the largest in Germany. There were many other camps, mainly in the east. In Poland, there was a huge death camp called Auschwitz."

Mildred looked at her brother. "Death camp?"

He nodded. "I've heard about thousands, tens, or even hundreds of thousands murdered, gassed to death, and their bodies thrown into outdoor pits and burned. It's impossible to imagine such wholesale slaughter. There's no comprehension of it.

"You remember I got assigned with the 120th Evacuation Hospital down in Mississippi? I wrote to you from Guroch, Scotland, last December, and later from LeHavre, France. We were following Patton's Third Army. It was the big push to Berlin, you know. In April, we went east into Germany, first to Frankfurt and then on to Ettersburg."

He regarded the women. They probably had no idea where any of these European cities were, nor would they care. He took a deep breath. "On April eleventh, two Russian prisoners who had escaped from the Buchenwald camp alerted a reconnaissance party from the Ninth Infantry battalion. It wasn't on their route to stop in that area close to Weimar, the town nearest to the concentration camp. The army went into Buchenwald the next day, and then we went in a couple of days after that. Our commander, Colonel Buck Williams, and several of us officers entered first to see the place. Then we went back to bring in the ambulances and the relief trucks."

His voice caught. "There were hundreds of starving, wretched people from all parts of Eastern Europe and even Russia. They had no food or water, barely any clothes, living in shacks. Some Polish prisoners, Communists, seemed to be in charge. I believe I heard some of the prisoners call them kapos. They were a rough bunch. We had to work fast to start triage, but many were too far gone to save. In about three days, we had brought the death rate down from a hundred per day to fewer than thirty. There was the threat of typhus, and some auxiliary units sprayed DDT to stop it. Still, some caught the disease and died." He hesitated, thinking about the mounds and mounds of skeletal remains. "I-I won't upset you ladies with the details of what all I saw. God, I'll have nightmares the rest of my life."

"I just can't imagine such a place!" Aunt Elvie remarked, looking at Mildred.

"How did you find the imp?" asked Nina Cassandra in a harsh voice.

"His name is Joe, Mother! J-O-E! He has a name!"

Nina Cassandra scowled and began rocking again.

On the staircase landing, perhaps because of the satisfying fullness of the cupcake in his belly, or the swishing of Irene's hair, or the disembodied voices downstairs, Joe began to get sleepy. He laid down, cradled his head in his arms, and fell asleep. He did not know that the little girl beside him gazed at his long, black eyelashes, his small, red mouth, the fading brown spots on his cheeks, the cat scratches on his lip. She wanted to stroke his silky black hair.

Grayson's deep-pitched voice softened. "There was a prisoner, a Jewish fellow, who led us to Joe. He was in a hole under some slats in the barrack where the prisoners slept. Lord, the smell in there! No outhouse ever smelled that bad. I had to pull out the boards to get to him. He was in bad shape, ear infections, lice crawling out of his hair, malnourished, dehydrated. Those marks you saw on his face were mosquito and horsefly bites. There were plenty of 'em. He was so weak he couldn't stand.

"I treated him at the mobile hospital unit in one of the Nazis SS barracks until we had to move on. The French Red Cross was there, and I met a priest who was taking children to an orphanage in Zurich. His name was Father Courtenay Bertrand. We talked and planned that no matter where Joe ended up, we'd stay in contact until I could come back to get him.

"I had to go on with my unit to Cham and the Dachau concentration camp. It was more of what we had found at Buchenwald. But we had more equipment and supplies by that time to function as a real hospital. Of course, the war was over by May seventh, and by the first week in June, we headed back to the U. S. to Virginia."

"Yes, yes," Mildred said impatiently. "We know all about that and how you returned to Mississippi."

"Louisiana. Camp Polk, to be exact. After I was discharged, I hopped on a transport plane at Barksdale Air Base in late June to go back to Europe. In the meantime, Father Bertrand and I had exchanged letters so I could keep up with Joe's recovery at the orphanage."

"Yes, and instead of coming home to be with your own family and your daughter, you went right back to that—that orphanage or whatever it was to chase after the kid!" Nina Cassandra stopped rocking again, her eyes hard as iron. "How could you do such a thing? The priest had charge for it. *Your* responsibility was to be here and tend to your own flesh and blood!"

Working his jaw, Grayson said, "I found Joe and brought him home. I will always be in debt to Father Bertrand."

"Didn't you say something about that town, Weimar?" Mildred asked. "What about the townspeople? Wasn't there anyone there who would take him?"

"You don't understand, Mil. Do you think any of the townspeople would be willing to take care of one Jewish boy? There were hundreds of boys of all ages, all orphans. Weimar is a small town. There would be no way it could absorb that many children. Besides, with their attitude, they certainly wouldn't be willing to take in any *Jewish* kids. You have to remember that the Germans wanted to get rid of these people! And they did! If we hadn't come when we did, all those destitute, helpless people would have been dead . . . and so would Joe."

Grayson waved a dismissive hand. "Those people from Weimar claimed they didn't know about this place. Of course, they knew! Through a translator at the camp, I talked to some prisoners who said they had been forced to walk to Weimar and other towns to work for the German war effort. They worked as slave laborers in munitions factories, on railroads, in mining camps. The townspeople either condoned it or looked away. At the very least, they knew the camp existed because they could smell it miles away." Grayson kept to himself that after leaving Buchenwald, the mayor of Weimar and his wife had slit their wrists.

"Did I tell you General Patton himself was there? He came about the same time we had arrived, and he was so infuriated with what he saw, he forced the people from Weimar to come to see the place. It got the attention of the press, too. They came with their cameras and took pictures of all of it. They even had movie cameras filming the whole sorted mess! Those were the newsreels you saw at the movies, Aunt Elvie. Well-fed, well-dressed German townsfolk had to look at stacks of cadavers. It almost turned into a farce, all that sensationalism."

"What about this child's parents? How do you know he is an orphan?" Nina Cassandra clasped her arthritic hands.

"I know what you're asking, Mom." Grayson shifted in his chair. He crossed his ankles and loosened his tie. "I never saw his mother, but I know for certain that his father is dead. I found the paperwork and some other evidence to prove it." He slid off his tie. "But I've locked all that away, and I will say no more about it. It's a closed subject, and no one in this room is to question Joe about it . . . *ever.*"

His strict tone demanded silence from the room. He rose to pull the chain to start the wooden fan hanging in the center of the ceiling. His shirt stuck to his back with perspiration.

Mildred folded her cross-stitching cloth. "When is he going to be ready for school? We don't even know if he can read! I'll have to call Sister Mary Harper to let her know that we have another child to enroll."

"Joe isn't going to Immaculate Conception. He'll go to the temple school if they have one there at Beth-El, maybe after Christmas."

"What?" Aunt Elvie dropped her pencil.

Mildred said, "Grayson, you must be joking. That boy will be attending Immaculate Conception. How could you possibly think otherwise?" A look of disgust at her brother's idiocy crossed her face.

"He's not going to school until he's had time to adjust to our home and learn English first. And we're not going to push him. There's not enough time between now and when school starts in September. Besides, I will rear him as a Jew, and he will receive education in Judaism."

Nina Cassandra almost shouted, "Grayson, how can you not bring him into the Church? I'll not have that little—little pagan worshiping that nonsense in this house! He's going to Immaculate Conception with Irene, and that's it!"

"The boy was born into a Jewish family who is now dead. I won't rob him of his heritage by pushing the Catholic Church down his throat."

"No!" Mildred set down her cross-stitching. She stood before her brother, pointing her finger at him. "This child *will* be converted and baptized! If he's not, he'll be shamed and ostracized his entire life! The Jews are responsible for putting Christ on the cross! They chose *not* to believe in Jesus as the Messiah. That's why they have been punished throughout history!" Her head shook in her passion. "And if that doesn't matter to you, then think about his soul. His spiritual well-being is in your hands, Grayson! Without bringing him to our Lord Jesus Christ, he will be lost to Satan. He will be cursed forever. Is that what you want? If you love that boy, you will do the right thing!"

Grayson never took his eyes from his sister's as he rose. He replied in an even-tempered voice, "I am going to call Sam Greene tonight. He's in the hematology department at the hospital. He'll put me in touch with the right people at that synagogue."

Mildred looked daggers at her brother.

"Now, I'm going upstairs to check on the kids. It's too quiet up there." He left the room.

CHAPTER FOUR

Joe woke up, feeling Irene's hand stop on his head. Upon hearing her father's final words, she released her grasp on his hair and fled, leaving Joe sprawled on the landing. He laid his head back down on the red-carpeted floor and closed his eyes. But warm, burly hands worked under his side and lifted him. Someone carried him up the second set of stairs. He opened his eyes as Grayson entered a bedroom and put him down. Now he was wide awake.

A delicate lemon scent lingered in the room. Joe's feet crunched on the freshly vacuumed pine green carpet as he stumbled into the voluminous room. He saw his reflection in the rectangular beveled mirror attached to the oak dresser. Next to it stood a rocking chair with a cane seat, ready for an occupant. The four-poster double bed was so vast he knew he would get lost if he climbed into it. Fat, lacy white pillows and a blue and green plaid blanket lay on top of the navy bedspread. He ran a finger along the edge of the matching nightstand illuminated by a peacock-decorated Tiffany lamp. Next to it sat a plastic table radio with white buttons. Hanging on the wall opposite the built-in closet was a painting of a New England farm scene of a red barn, a rail fence, and a couple of sheep. Above the bed's oak headboard hung another "t" shaped set of sticks with the same sad-looking man mounted on it.

A double set of windows with opened cerulean brocade curtains caught Joe's attention. Looking out, he could see the tops of the elm and maple trees and the black iron fence interspersed with columns of the same limestone that matched the gate. Beyond it, points of streetlights dotted the blackness.

There were two more doors. One led to the bathroom on the right, and the other would be Joe's new hiding place: the spacious walk-in closet. When he opened the doors and looked inside, he saw it filled with winter coats, woolen sweaters, shoes, boots, stacks of blankets, and a tower of boxes. It had the same oddly pleasant smell as the closet downstairs. He couldn't reach the string to turn on the light bulb, but that was all right. Joe thought about the bleak, urine-stained corner of the narrow barrack he and his father had slept in along with the other pitiful, cranky prisoners. In his mind's eye, he saw the drafty plank walls covered with black mold and the remains of dead flies and moths in spider webs hanging from the low ceiling. And permeating the air the nauseating smells of excrement and sweaty bodies.

But this new sleeping room was tidy and bright. After everyone had gone to bed, he would go into the closet, rearrange the stuff, shut the door, and wait; wait until someone would come and rescue him. Joe would soon be back home to the attic above the dressmaker's shop on Bornne Street, or so he hoped.

The big man helped Joe take off his shirt and pants. In his underwear, he used the toilet and brushed his teeth as the black-robed women at the orphanage had taught him. At the bed, Grayson pulled back the bedspread and motioned him to hop in. The door opened just as Joe started to climb in. Irene stood in her one-piece, Jack-in-the-Box print pajamas, holding a stuffed yellow and brown teddy bear.

"I brought Pammy for him," she murmured, her chin down.

"Why, that was very thoughtful of you, Irene." Grayson smiled at his daughter. "Go ahead and give it to him."

Somberly, Irene held out the bear. Joe looked at Grayson and then took it, holding it to his chest. "Danke," he whispered.

"What'd he say?" asked Irene.

"I believe he said 'thank you' in German. Say 'you're welcome.' "

"You're welcome . . . Joe."

A phone's far-away ring woke up Joe as he lay in that gigantic bed. The alarm clock on the nightstand displayed the time: 12:30. He heard voices and doors opening and closing. A toilet flushed, then water ran and stopped. Someone stomped down the stairs rapidly. Grateful for the tiny nightlight behind the rocking chair to help him see about the room, he dragged a heavy wooden chair to the windows and climbed up to see the black driveway. Leaves danced on the tree limbs in the wind. In the distance, a dog barked once.

A rumbling from below drew his attention. When the humongous black car backed out, it stopped with the motor still running. Joe caught sight of the big man getting out, leaving, and then swiftly getting back in. After the car turned around, it rolled up the long driveway toward the gate. The big man seemed to be in a hurry as he gunned the engine. The red tail lights disappeared.

Panic clutched Joe's heart. Was the man leaving for good? Was he abandoning him in this sinister castle with these unpleasant, domineering women? What should he do? How could he escape?

He went inside the closet and closed the door. Making a nest of flattened shoe boxes, he lay on his side and drew his knees to his chest. He tried not to make any noise as he cried.

CHAPTER FIVE

"La—la—la—la—la!"

The singing increased in volume, coming toward the bedroom door. As soon as Joe opened his eyes to the total darkness of the closet, he heard clinking sounds and then clattering, as if plates had been dropped to the floor.

"AAACCCKKK! Call the police! Call the fire department!"

"What's wrong? What's happened?" Joe heard another female voice from the hall. He thought it might be Frau Dead Fish Eyes. He wished he knew what they were saying.

"The little boy! Joe! He's gone! Mr. Henry must have eaten him!"

"Oh, calm down, Rose. He's around here somewhere."

More doors, near and far, opened and closed, as well as drawers opened and slammed shut. Joe heard a high-pitched giggle which he knew belonged to the little girl. He also heard a "meow." His old adversary, Mr. Henry, had surfaced.

"He's in here, Aunt Mil."

"Shhh! You'll wake your father."

The closet door creaked open. "Joe, are you in here?" Frau Dead Fish Eyes, smartly dressed this morning in a pale melon-colored suit and her hair swept up in a French bun, pulled the light cord. "What on earth are you doing in here? Did you sleep in here all night?"

As Joe's heart raced, she grabbed his wrist and dragged him into the bedroom.

"Here. Let's wash your face and get you dressed. You need to look presentable when your father sees you." She walked hurriedly into the bathroom, not letting go of his wrist.

A new version of a concentration camp was about to begin.

Grayson's sister, Mildred, loved taking on a new project, especially one that seemed likely to fail without her supervision. Her tenacious commitment, determination, and organizational skills would out-pace the most seasoned political campaign manager. Her drive came from her visceral need for absolute, unmitigated control. Her commanding leadership talent proved her ability to get others to do what they were supposed to do to get the job done. To her credit, she had raised hundreds of dollars for various charities toward the war effort in the past four years. But with the war over, she needed a new mission. Now she would focus her efforts on this child who had unceremoniously arrived at the Pierce home. Assuredly she'd be able to mold him in a way that would live up to the Pierce family's distinguished reputation in the community. So far, that had eluded her with Irene. However, from observing Joe's antics at the dinner table, discipline was what he needed most. Pragmatism was Mildred's watchword. There was so much to be done with him!

After breakfast, all the ladies, including Irene, Rose the cook, and the maid, Anne, sat at the dining table. The women had gathered to come up with a plan to deal with this most perplexing set of circumstances. Mildred acknowledged Joe was here to stay and that her mother and aunt had better accept it. "This child is our top priority. We have to attend to his needs and get him prepared for school."

"Yes," the old woman, Nina Cassandra, agreed. "But I think you're in for far more than you realize."

Mildred waved her pen like a wand. "Today, we will get Joe started on his English lesson. Aunt Elvie, can you find some of Irene's old spelling books and some blank paper and crayons? Irene, you help her. I'm sure if you take a snow shovel from the garage and dig through that avalanche of papers on your desk, you'll find something." She didn't notice her niece making a face. "Appointments have to be made for him to get a haircut and to see the dentist. Anne, will you do that? Just call that barber Grayson goes to—Mel's Barbershop. He's in the phone book. Dr. Bernhardt's dental office phone number is in my address book on my desk. I'll take care of ordering his missal and getting a copy of *Saint Joseph's Baltimore Catechism* at Charzan's."

Aunt Elvie spoke timidly. "But what about Dr. Pierce's plans for his—"

"Don't worry about that. I'll handle Grayson. We'll just keep it all under wraps."

Joe listened from the family room sofa, trying to understand what was being said. Suddenly four tiny pressure points landed in his lap. Mr. Henry pushed his square head against his chest, purring like a tuned-up sports car. Joe stroked his back and tail and endured his front claws as he kneaded his arm. A truce of sorts had been reached.

The discussion ceased as Grayson descended the stairs in his bathrobe and messy hair, appearing as if he had had a rough night. He poured himself a cup of coffee and grabbed a slice of coffee cake from the sideboard. "I've got an appointment with the rabbi at Temple Beth-El this afternoon for him to see Joe. Mil, please see that he's ready." Before heading back upstairs with his cup and coffee cake, he added, "If you are starting his English lesson, my dictionary is on the table over there." He waved his coffee cake toward the black book on the dining table. Irene followed him upstairs.

Mildred scowled at her brother when he turned his back. She motioned Joe to come into the dining room. "Aunt Elvie, you do his English lesson this morning. I'm already late for the bake sale," she said as she pulled on her white summer gloves and donned her matching white hat. She picked up a foil-covered plate on the table. Without saying "goodbye," she left.

After the others disappeared to tend to their own business, Aunt Elvie remained at the table, and Joe sat next to her. He realized he need not be afraid of this amiable woman, even though she looked like she had slept in her clown makeup. And her frightful reddish hair stood on end all over her head except in the back where it was completely flat.

Soon Grayson came down again, dressed in a lightweight, sand-colored suit, followed by Irene in play clothes. Apparently, she didn't "find" any of her old spelling books. She asked her father if he could take her to "Mollie's house," and out the back kitchen door she ran before he could reply.

To Joe and Aunt Elvie, Grayson said, "I'm going to the hospital, but I'll be back for lunch, I hope. I need to see if I still have an office. It might be a janitor's closet." He spoke to Joe. "We'll visit with someone this afternoon you'll be glad to see. Mind your elders. Goodbye, Joe." He leaned down and kissed Joe on top of his head. "Don't work him too much, Aunt Elvie." He grabbed his keys, his hat, and his sunglasses and pushed through the kitchen door, making it swing wildly.

"Whatever you say, Grayson!" Aunt Elvie called forlornly as he hurried off. After hearing him close the back kitchen door, she sighed. She glanced at the thick, black book lying on the table and then looked at Joe. Then she got up and wandered around the dining room, looking and looking. She went into another room. Joe heard something fall like a stack of papers and her subsequent mutterings. Upon returning, she sat with a half-sized sheet of blank paper and a pencil in her hand. She examined the paper as if she had never seen it before in her life and had no idea what to do with it. Giving Joe a forced smile, she cleared her throat and pointed to a short-stemmed, depression glass bowl filled with stewed prunes on the dining table. A silver dipping spoon floated in it.

"That's a fruit compote bowl. It was given to me by my Great Aunt Nora as a wedding present. My, let's see. It's at least fifty years old. Aunt Nora was my grandmother's sister, who married James Westin. He started a small furniture company, but it didn't last. I was told he didn't have a head for business." She pressed her lips, shaded today in a pale tangerine color. Her lipstick matched the color of her beaded necklace. Her earrings seemed about to drop out of her flabby earlobes.

She wrote in flowing cursive, *fruit compote bowl*. Leaning over to watch, Joe knew the letters but didn't know the words except that they must mean the bowl. He had no idea what else she was saying. He wanted to take her pencil and copy the words. Frau Clown did not look at him but flitted her delicate eyelids. She wrote the words to the items on the table: the salt and pepper shakers that sat next to the porcelain sugar bowl, her coffee cup and saucer, her cloth napkin, and the pair of crystal candle holders that had replaced the gold ones from last night. Joe was eager to follow and learn. He wanted to say the words aloud and practice writing them. However, she did not even allow him to hold the pencil. She seemed relieved whenever Rose or Anne walked past, giving her the excuse to speak to them. Twice she went to the sideboard to fill her coffee cup and cut another small piece of iced coffee cake. She didn't offer any of the cake to Joe. After about fifteen minutes, she heard the grandfather clock in the family room chime.

"It's ten o'clock. Time for Arthur Godfrey." She left the table, taking the pencil with her to go into the music room to turn on the radio.

Joe studied the paper and debated about looking for another pencil to copy the words. He looked at the small, neat desk in the corner but didn't see any writing instrument, although there might be one in the drawer. He folded the paper and put it in his pants pocket. He heard the cook and her young teenaged helper talking in the kitchen and the old, white-haired dragon woman conversing on the phone in the foyer. Her voice, so brusque and impatient last night, was now pleasing and sweet. He had no idea where "Mildred" or the little girl was. With a big sigh, he sat.

CHAPTER SIX

The square, blond-brick building stood in a placid, shady neighborhood just a few blocks from downtown Ithaca. The brick-red slated dome on the roof blazed in the early afternoon sun.

Rabbi Passow met Grayson and Joe at the front door. "Shalom!" the scraggy, hollow-faced man said, smiling and showing stained, slightly crooked teeth. His thick white hair blew out of place in a sudden wind gust.

Grayson shook hands with him. "I'm Grayson Pierce. This is Joe Kaufmann. Thank you for seeing us, Rabbi Passow."

"It is my pleasure to welcome you and Joe. We'll go through the sanctuary to my office."

They walked through a darkened foyer and into a high-ceilinged sanctuary filled with straight rows of wooden seats. Joe looked with amazement at the rectangle, yellow stained-glassed windows. Down in front, a wooden podium stood on a raised platform with a plaque with carved Hebrew lettering fastened on it. Behind it was a rectangular table covered in a red cloth, papers, and books lying on top. High on the back wall behind the table was the ark, with a compartment that held the Torah. A brass lamp on a chain hung on a hook over it. On both the east and west walls were large gold metal plaques etched with names of past and present congregants. An American flag on a brass pole stood on the left side of the sanctuary.

The rabbi led them down the center aisle to a side door on the west wall. "This way, please." He held out his hand to his guests.

The tiny room overflowed with books, newspapers, binders, and other office paraphernalia. "Let me move these papers, and you may have a seat." The rabbi picked up some newspapers and files from two cloth-covered folding chairs and put them on top of a wooden filing cabinet.

As they sat at a round table, Joe's heart jumped at the sight of the shiny brass Star of David hanging on the wall. He reached out to touch a blue glass menorah on the window sill, but Grayson gently pulled him into his lap. Joe put his hands on the table and looked at the other items--a plastic cup full of pencils, a notepad, several shabby books, and an ashtray full of cigarette butts which the rabbi moved to his overloaded desk.

"Have you been at Beth-El long?" Grayson asked.

"Only three years," Rabbi Passow replied as he sat opposite of the other two. He interlaced his fingers in his lap and crossed his bony knees. He looked at Joe, still smiling. "This is your new boy?" He had a slight European accent.

"Yes," Grayson replied. "Joe is my ward. I'm his guardian."

"You mentioned that over the phone. May I ask why you're not adopting him?"

"I want him to keep his surname. His father died in the Buchenwald concentration camp. Unfortunately, I never found out what had happened to his mother. Joe must keep his heritage and honor his parents."

Joe pricked his ears at the word, "Buchenwald."

Rabbi Passow still kept his respectful smile. His face was so wrinkled there was enough skin to make a new one. His filmy, brown eyes were set deep underneath his unkempt brows.

Grayson said, "You've heard about the concentration camps?"

"The information we have received has been mainly from the newspapers and radio. I fear the worst has yet to come out. Many of our congregants had relatives in Europe. For the past several years, they simply stopped communication with them, as if they'd just vanished. It's bad, very bad."

The conversation stalled. The two men watched Joe pick up a pen and playing with it.

The rabbi spoke. "You mentioned you were with the army in the European theatre. What unit were you with?"

"I was with the 120th Evacuation Hospital. We were following the Ninth Division that moved across southern Germany under Patton's Third Army. We were there to take care of wounded soldiers, but when we discovered the camp, we had to treat starving prisoners." Grayson hesitated and then spoke carefully. "We found Joe hiding under some wooden slats in one of the prisoners' barracks. It's difficult to talk about."

"Of course."

Grayson's eyes softened as he looked at Joe. "You see, I'm a widower. My wife died when my daughter was born eight years ago. I've always wanted another child, and God made it possible with Joe."

Rabbi Passow nodded with understanding. Both men observed Joe taking a piece of paper and writing on it. "He's a lefty," Grayson commented.

After finishing his scribbling, he pushed the paper toward the rabbi.

Rabbi Passow said, "It's a name: Yosef. And he wrote it in Hebrew! Look!" He showed it to Grayson.

"Good heavens," Grayson said as he studied the unfamiliar marks.

"This is his Hebrew name. It means 'supplanter' or 'held by the heel.' There was a famous first-century teacher who was also a rabbi by that name. Perhaps Joe's parents thought he might become a rabbi or a teacher." He spoke to Joe in German. "Konne Sie Ihren deutschen Namen noticien? Can you write down your German name?"

Joe wrote "Joseph Kaufmann" and continued writing.

Grayson said, "This is fortunate for me that you know German, Rabbi. All I have is a dictionary, and I barely know how to use it."

"I'm second-generation German, and I learned from my parents in Brooklyn." The rabbi studied Joe's paper. "He knows Yiddish, too. Here he wrote, 'I am a little boy.' " He turned back to Joe. "Now, write down how old you are. Sind Sie wie alt?"

Joe drew a large but neat "7." Grayson hugged his small shoulders and took the paper. "I'm going to keep this." He folded it and put it in his breast pocket. "Please, continue."

Leaning closer to Joe, Rabbi Passow said, "Do you know who I am? Wissen Sie, wem ich bin?"

Joe looked up at him. "Are you a rabbi?" he asked in German.

Matching his language, the religious man replied, "Yes. My name is Rabbi Passow. Joe, do you know where you are? Why you are here?"

Joe shook his head.

Rabbi Passow got up. "Ah, let's try this," He searched in the overloaded bookshelves. Returning to his chair, he laid an open volume of the *Encyclopedia Britannica* on the table. They resumed in German, with Grayson looking on.

"Here is where you came from. This is Germany." He pointed to the European country and then the blue expanse to the left of it. "This is the Atlantic Ocean, and over here is the United States. Dr. Pierce brought you to this country, America." He went back to get another volume. He found the page he wanted and said, "There you are, in New York. You live in Ithaca, New York."

Sitting motionless, Joe studied the map in the first book, running his finger along its edge. He had never seen such a strange picture with blue parts and beige parts and all that compact, busy printing everywhere. He didn't recognize the name "Germany." He looked up at the rabbi, worry shadowing his face. "I am not home here. Will I get to go home?" he asked.

Rabbi Passow replied in a tender voice, "No, Joe. Your new home is here."

Joe's mind bubbled with questions. "But *this* is Germany? Here?" He pointed to the map again.

"Yes. And there is France and Italy and Russia, and up here is England. Have you heard of those places?"

Joe shrugged. He wasn't sure of anything anymore.

The rabbi went on. "These are all different countries of the world. You know about the war, Germany against these other countries, don't you? The war is over now, and this country over here, the United States, helped defeat Germany and bring down the bad people."

Joe's legs swung wildly as his brain worked on this. He was completely unaware that he was hitting his guardian's shins. Somehow his collar had slipped into his mouth, and he sucked on it nervously.

"Dr. Pierce knew that you needed help, Joe. He knew you were alone, and he brought you to his home to be part of his family."

Letting go of the collar and stopping his restless legs, Joe locked eyes with Grayson. His guardian held his breath.

Joe could not stop his tears from running down his cheeks. He brushed them away and faced the rabbi again. "I want to go home."

"Where was your home?" the rabbi asked.

"Berlin. But we had to hide in the attic."

"How long did you hide?"

"A long time."

"Will you allow Dr. Pierce to take care of you?"

Swinging his legs again, hands clutching the big book, he said, "I'm afraid." The collar went back in his mouth.

"Afraid of what?"

Joe cast down his eyes. Saliva saturated his collar. He murmured, "I'm going to die."

"Die? What do you mean?"

"I'm going to be shot and burned up like everybody else."

Rabbi Passow's face blanched.

"What? What did he say?" Grayson demanded.

Rabbi Passow spoke solemnly in English. "He said he will be killed."

"Oh, my God!" Grayson shook his head and crossed himself. "No, no."

Joe stopped swinging his legs.

"Dr. Pierce, let me go on."

After putting Joe on his feet, Grayson stood and faced the window, hiding his filled eyes.

Returning to Joe, Rabbi Passow put his hands on the boy's shoulders to keep his attention. His German words were rapid and terse. "Joe, you need to listen to what I'm telling you, and you have to believe me. You are not going to die. No one is going to kill you. Remember, you are not in Germany anymore. Jews are safe here. I'm here. This place, this temple is for Jews to worship God, to pray, and to celebrate our holidays." He pointed to Grayson. "This man saved your life. He is not going to kill you. He loves you, Joe. I know you had a family who loved you very much, but they are with God now. Dr. Pierce is your new family."

Joe stared at the heavy book in his hands.

"Tell him he will stay a Jew, just as he was with his mother and father," Grayson said in a cracked voice.

Rabbi Passow looked at the big man. Then he repeated the words to Joe.

He turned around. "I want to bring him to your temple services if you'll allow me to sit in."

"Your attendance will be most appreciated, Dr. Pierce. And I commend you, sir. Not every Gentile would be so willing to accommodate a child with such challenging issues." Returning to Joe, the rabbi said in German, "I will help you say the Kaddish prayers for your family. You will come to this temple called Beth-El for Shabbat services. Have you been to a temple before?"

Joe shook his head again, not looking up.

"Well, here, you will be welcome. Dr. Pierce will bring you on Friday evenings, and he will stay with you through the service. Afterward, you and Dr. Pierce can come to our big dinner we have downstairs. There will be lots of good food. Then we will sing, and dance and everybody will have fun. We want you to be part of all that. We are your new community, Joseph. There are people I want you to meet, and some of them have children your age. They would love to play with you. And you can attend Sunday school classes to learn more about Judaism. And when you are twelve, we will begin preparing for your bar mitzvah. Do you understand?"

"Are you sure I will not end up like the other boys?" Joe's voice was weak with trepidation.

"No, Joe. You will live. You have a new life here in this country."

The heavy book Joe was holding slipped to the floor.

"Joe, do you know any English?"

Although Joe heard the question, he sat on the floor on top of the encyclopedia book and did not answer.

Grayson put his big hands under his arms and pulled him up. "He's getting tired. Let me ask you. Is there a Jewish school he can attend other than your Sunday classes?"

"Unfortunately, no. We have no primary school. The children go to the public schools."

"I want him to attend your Sunday school, then. He's probably had very little education in Judaism beyond knowing Hebrew. But he needs to get settled first in my home."

"Please let me know if there's anything I can do to help Joe. I would be honored to teach him. He's been through much more than either of us can know. He's a smart little boy." Rabbi Passow retrieved a black satin yarmulke from a storage closet and gave it to Joe. "Put this on your head, Joseph. It's a way for you to show respect to God."

Joe put the skullcap on the back of his head. He said, "Danke schon, Rabbiner." He wondered if the rabbi would also give him a yellow Star of David to pin to his shirt.

When they walked back through the sanctuary and into the foyer, Rabbi Passow took Joe aside. He crouched to meet his liquid brown eyes. "Joe, do you understand that you have a new home and a new family?" Joe nodded. "You will learn English, and you are obligated to respect and obey Dr. Pierce just as if he was your own father. Do what he tells you, and you'll get along just fine. Agreed?" Joe nodded again. "Okay. Shabbat Shalom, my little friend." The rabbi drew him to his chest and hugged him.

CHAPTER SEVEN

After leaving Temple Beth-El, Grayson took Joe to Woolworth's Five and Dime store downtown. In the toy section, Joe's energy perked as he looked at all the multi-colored marbles, board games, puppets, stuffed animals, and all sizes of springy balls. Shelves and bins overflowed with toy trains, metal cars and trucks, spinning tops, dollhouse kits, miniature guitars and bells, tin airplanes and boats, dolls of every size, and even Jack-in-the-Box sets. This abundance of toys even surpassed the staggering amount in the little girl's room.

The big man pointed to a jigsaw puzzle of four kittens snuggled in a straw basket. Joe nodded, and Grayson took it. On the way to the cashier, they stopped at a glass counter that displayed nuts and candy. Inside the case, a light bulb warmed the trays of cashews, peanuts, almonds, walnuts, and bridge mix. It all smelled heavenly.

"Would you like some nuts?" A young woman wearing an orange smock stood behind the counter.

Joe thought he understood, and yes, he wanted some nuts. He looked up at Grayson.

"Say, 'Yes, please.'" Grayson put his hand on Joe's shoulder and guided him closer to the counter.

"Ya, bitte," Joe said to the woman.

"Say, 'Yes, please.'"

Joe put his fingers on the counter edge. "Yes, please."

"Good! Now, what kind do you want?" Grayson pointed to the nuts.

Joe selected the almonds and the cashews. The woman put them in two paper sacks and weigh them on a white scale. She marked the prices on them and handed them to Grayson.

As they stood outside on the sidewalk under the store canopy, Joe devoured the nuts. He loved the salty flavor. When the paper sacks were empty, he wished he had saved a few for later. He and Grayson sat on a bench, watching pedestrians walking by and cars moving slowly up and down the street. Just as he had observed from the small window in the attic, the people appeared much like the Berlin residents, carrying shopping bags or rolled-up newspapers under their arms. Out of the blue, Joe heard a loud bang like a gun going off, and he instinctively clutched Grayson's sleeve. He looked for the dreaded dark green trucks with the swastikas on the doors. When the black-shirted Gestapo carrying rifles emerged from the vehicles, people fled in terror. But here, there was no chaos, no screaming, no women dragging frightened children.

"All done?" Grayson threw the sacks into a trashcan. He put on his sunglasses and took Joe's hand. "Come along. Let's go home."

"Hello, Rose," Grayson said warmly as he and Joe entered the kitchen.

Rose stood at the ancient work table, stirring cookie dough in a large blue bowl. She pushed her streaked glasses up on her short, red nose. "Oh! You're back so soon!"

"We had a good visit with Rabbi Passow. Joe will be going to Temple Beth-El for their services on Friday evenings. They always have a big get-together after the service, so you won't need to set a place for us for dinner. We've been invited to share their meal."

Rose wiped her hands on a dishtowel. "Yes, sir. I'll mark the calendar."

Grayson pulled out the paper Joe had written on from his breast pocket. "Joe wrote his name while we were there."

Rose looked at the scrap. "Oh, my goodness!" She crossed herself and then put her soft hands on Joe's cheeks. "How wonderful! You can write your name! I'm so happy for you! Maybe you'll make some friends at your new church!"

Joe gazed back at the woman's round, washed-out eyes behind her Coke-bottle-bottomed glasses. Her face was flushed, as she had been exerting herself in the humid kitchen. Tight, gray pin curls on her head quivered. He smelled a sweet odor on her breath. He loved her.

"What are those other marks?" she asked, examining the paper again.

"Hebrew. He's more educated than we thought." Grayson stuffed the paper back in his shirt pocket. "Joe, where's your skullcap?" He pointed to the top of his head.

Joe pulled his yarmulke from under his belt and put it on his head.

Seeing Joe's new kippa, Rose asked, "Where did you get that cute cap?"

"The rabbi gave it to him. It's the head covering Jews wear during their services." He looked around. "Where's Irene?"

"Here I am, Daddy." The little girl hopped into the kitchen. "What did you bring me?"

"Nothing this time, sweetheart. I bought a new jigsaw puzzle for Joe, and I want you to go with him out on the back porch and show him how to put the pieces together."

Joe stood with the cardboard box in his hands. He didn't like the change in Irene's face and the way she crossed her arms. "Do I have to?"

"Yes. Go on. I've things to do in my study, and I can't look after Joe right now." He left the kitchen.

"Okay, c'mon," Irene said, sighing. She grabbed the box from Joe and went out the kitchen door to the screened garden room.

Joe followed her reluctantly. He sadly realized the puzzle wasn't really for him.

Although shaded by maple and tulip trees, the screened-in back porch was warm. They sat at the glass-topped wicker table. Irene tore the seal off the box and studied the lid before choosing pieces to put together. Joe watched as she tried one piece after another. But when he put his hand in the box to take some pieces, she slapped it and snapped, "No! I'm doing this!"

Knowing not to argue with the little girl, Joe wandered around the porch, looking at the houseplants and the birds at the birdfeeders hanging on the low tree branches. He decided he was thirsty from eating the nuts, and he went back into the kitchen to get Rose's attention.

While Rose gave him a glass of water and tried to get him to speak some words in English, Joe heard a door slam. Grayson's stern voice rose from the porch. Irene responded with high-pitched whines. From the kitchen window, Joe and Rose watched the father bending over his daughter, shaking his finger and talking sternly. Then he saw Joe and motioned him to come back out to the porch.

"Your guardian wants you, my dear," Rose said. "You'd better give me the glass."

Upon entering the porch, Joe shyly edged his way along the screened windows. Irene turned her head away from him.

"Sit here, Joe," Grayson said, pointing to a wicker chair. "Irene will share the puzzle with you. Show him, Irene."

With simmering abnegation, Irene dropped a handful of puzzle pieces in front of Joe. He began fitting them together while maintaining a safe distance. Grayson went back inside to continue working at his desk.

CHAPTER EIGHT

Joe and Irene accompanied Aunt Mil on a shopping trip on Thursday. Frau Dead Fish Eyes searched the boys' section at Holly's Clothing Store for some better-fitting clothes for Joe. He cooperated, never complaining or fussing when she held up a shirt on him or had him try on a pair of little boy's trousers in the dressing room.

Irene sulked. Keenly aware of her resentment toward him and not knowing what to expect from her, Joe kept his mouth closed, and his eyes turned aside. He hung back from the woman and the girl, listening to their constant arguing.

"Why do we have to go to Charzan's? I'm getting hungry!" Irene whined.

Standing in the women's lingerie department, Aunt Mil inspected girdles hanging on a rack. Without looking at the girl, she replied, "We've got to order his missal so he'll have it for mass on Sunday."

"Aw, who cares?" Irene pawed through a bin of half-priced brassieres.

Her aunt ignored her.

Irene took a bra out of its package and held it up to her chest for size. "Will you get a book for me while we're there?"

"Irene Donovan Pierce! Just because we go to the gift shop doesn't entitle you to have something on the spot. Now put that bra back!" Frau Dead Fish Eyes moved on to the slips, checking prices.

Joe watched Irene put the brassiere back on top of the stack. He wished he could understand the conversation. All he knew was that Irene was unhappy, and that was irritating Aunt Mil.

They moved on to men's underwear. Having helped Rose do the laundry, Aunt Mil knew that Grayson needed new shorts and undershirts. His days in the Army ruined his old ones. She firmly believed in sturdy underwear. She chose a package of men's briefs.

Undeterred, Irene pleaded, "Can we leave now?"

"That's enough! If you keep it up, I'll think again before allowing you to attend Mary Gable's birthday party tomorrow."

"But I already have her present wrapped! Oh, please, let me go!"

"Then be quiet! I've had enough of your attitude! You are nothing but a spoiled brat!"

Joe did not understand what the tall, angry woman just said, but he could tell it hurt the little girl. She began to cry.

Aunt Mil forcefully shook the girl's arm. "Stop crying and act your age!"

Irene stamped her foot. "Why are you buying all these things for him and not for me? That's not fair!"

Glancing behind her and seeing another woman customer nearby, Mildred took Joe and Irene hurriedly toward the women's restroom. She gave Joe the packages and told him to stand right inside the door. Under no uncertain terms was he to leave that spot. She pushed Irene farther into the restroom.

In the still, cool room, a faucet dripped in one of the sinks.

Frau Dead Fish Eyes put her face inches from Irene's. "Listen to me. That little boy just came out of a terrible place in Germany. He had no bed, no food, not even a blanket. The good Lord gave your father the compassion to rescue him and bring him into our home. He is a member of our family, and he deserves every bit of comfort you have enjoyed your entire life! You stop thinking only about yourself, you ungrateful child!

"When we get home, you are to march up to your room and get on your knees and beg Christ for forgiveness for your selfish insolence!" Frau Dead Fish Eyes picked up the packages Joe had dropped and pushed open the restroom door.

The little girl followed with tears dripping onto her blouse. Back out in the store, Irene looked frigidly at Joe. He met her eyes and felt his face drain of blood.

They made one last stop before heading back to the castle. Charzan's Gift Shop and Book Store stood behind Immaculate Conception Parish on West State Street. While browsing the shelves of small animal statues, pen and pencil sets, cards for every holiday and occasion, plus a whole lot of other knick-knacks and curiosity items, he saw his aunt in a corner talking to a sales clerk. They bent over stacks of books on a table. Besides the Bibles and missals, his eyes widened at the sight of the abundance of nearly naked figurines on crossed sticks, in different sizes and styles hanging on the walls. There were also paintings of the same bearded man, clothed in muted colored robes, and statues of overweight toddlers in haloes and sporting wings. Shellacked woodcuts of curved writing in yet another unfamiliar language hung on pegs, and tiny, beaded bracelets with tiny metal t's were displayed in a lighted glass case. It was a most peculiar shop. He almost lost Frau Dead Fish Eyes when he discovered that she and Irene had left while he studied a portrait of a mournful-faced young woman with a blue veil on her head and a baby in her arms. He heard his name and rushed out.

Back at the Pierce mansion, the blonde-headed girl disappeared upstairs, followed by a decidedly put-out Frau Dead Fish Eyes with her packages. Relieved yet cautious, Joe wandered around the family room. Carefully stepping around the snoring old lizard lady slumped in an armchair, he tip-toed to a henna-colored set of books on a built-in shelf along the wall. They looked identical to the ones in the rabbi's office. He selected a thin volume and opened it. "Florida" was printed on the top of the page. He studied the pictures of what he figured out was the blue ocean. He tried to pronounce some of the words in his head. He put the book back and picked out the "D" book. But "Deutschland" wasn't in this book. He kept glancing toward the chair to see if the old queen bee would wake up. Replacing the volume, he looked at more books on other shelves. They were all different sizes and colors, many of them so beat-up the covers were coming off. He wished he could read them all! Books had been scarce luxuries when he was hiding in the attic with his mother and father. He loved reading over and over the ones his mother brought him. He even read the occasional newspaper given to his father from the family who lived in the back of the clothing shop where his mother worked. But these books were in the same language as the book the rabbi had shown him. He knew he had to learn this language--English! He sat on his knees. Choosing a thick book, he turned one page at a time, looking at the pictures and reading the captions underneath, working out the words and how they matched the illustrations. Some words were similar to German, but the grammar and the sentence structure were different.

Where was that black book the big man always carried around? Joe had seen him dig into it whenever he tried to translate a word to him, like toothbrush or lamp or shoes. He wished he had his own Worterbuch. He decided his next goal would be to find that black book after hunting for his next meal.

****

" 'Alice was beginning to get very tired of sitting by her sister on the bank, and of having nothing to do; once or twice she had peeped into the book her sister was reading, but it had no pictures or conversation in it, "and what is the use of the book," thought Alice, "without pictures or conversation?" ' "

In the family room on Saturday evening, Joe sat in Grayson's lap, and Irene sat next to her father, leaning into his shoulder. Grayson had chosen Lewis Carroll's *Alice in Wonderland* to read aloud to Joe. But he read too laboriously for Irene, who knew the story practically by heart. "Why are you reading so slowly?" she asked impatiently. She took another handful of popcorn from her bowl.

"I'm reading to Joe, honey. I want him to hear how each word is pronounced. Why don't you read the next paragraph?" Grayson turned the book to her. "Now, listen, Joe." He gently tugged Joe's earlobe.

Irene put her finger under the next line and read aloud quickly as if she had read the passage a hundred times before. Joe glued his eyes on the page, taking in each word's pronunciation even if he didn't catch the meaning.

" 'So she was considering in her own mind (as well as she could, for the hot day made her feel very sleepy and stupid) whether the pleasure of making a daisy chain would be worth the trouble of getting up and picking the daisies, when suddenly a white rabbit with pink eyes ran close by her.' " Irene giggled. "A white rabbit, Joe." She pointed to the ink drawing of the famous white rabbit in the waistcoat and cravat, looking at his pocket watch.

Joe nodded with enthusiasm. "Vite rabbit," he said. Yes, he knew what a rabbit was, even if it stood on its hind legs and held an umbrella under its foreleg.

The story reading went on for a half-hour. As the room darkened in the waning sunlight, Irene grew as sleepy as Alice had been. But Joe wanted to continue. He occasionally interjected to repeat a word or two that went with a picture. But too soon, all the popcorn had been eaten, and he had swallowed the last drops of the brown-colored bubbly drink called "Coke." Aunt Mil, who had sat with them throughout the evening, said it was time for bed. Disappointed, Joe watched the man close the book. He made sure to know where he put it back on a shelf of the wall bookcase.

"I'll be there in a minute to hear your prayers," Aunt Mil said to Irene as they climbed the staircase. She followed Joe into his room and shut the door.

Joe's heart jumped a beat. Before he knew it, the towering woman stood in front of him, opening a brown paper sack. Holding up the Mickey Mouse and Dagwood-printed pajamas, she said, "These should fit you." She began unbuttoning his shirt.

Joe was used to Grayson helping him change his clothes. But he didn't know about this scary lady. Was she preparing to stick him in a pot? She stood over him in the bathroom, pointing to use the toilet, to wash his hands and face, and to brush his teeth. The kind women in the black and white robes had taught him this routine at the orphanage. When he climbed into bed, Frau Dead Fish Eyes had a brown, leather-bound book in her hand. It was different from the big man's book. Sitting next to him, she took a pen from the nightstand drawer and marked a passage.

She peered through her half-glasses. "You will learn the Lord's prayer, here in Matthew, chapter six, verses nine through thirteen. Follow my finger. 'Our Father, who art in Heaven, hallowed be Thy name . . .' "

Joe leaned closer, listening carefully to the woman's sedate voice. The red-polished fingernail rushed from one word to the next, and the tiny print proved difficult to read. Although he tried to concentrate, a powdery fragrance from her face distracted him.

" 'But deliver us from the evil one. Amen.'" She turned to the cover of the book. Below the letters, M-I-S-S-A-L in gold lettering, was his name, Joseph Kaufmann, 1945.

"Joe, I want you to read in your missal every night before you go to sleep. I'll keep it in my room and bring it to you. This will be our private time together, just you and me. No one else needs to know about it."

She stood, holding the book to her bosom. Joe knew exactly what she meant. Cold, black eyes almost softened. She leaned over and put a hand on his head. Then she turned off the Tiffany lamp and left the room, leaving the door ajar.

****

"What do you mean he's not going to mass with us? I went to a great of deal trouble putting a rush on his missal—"

"Joe will stay home with Rose while we're at the parish. That's why she went to mass tonight. She will watch him tomorrow morning. I told you the first day I got back that Joe is keeping his Jewish religion. *I* went to a great deal of trouble sitting with Rabbi Passow at Temple Beth-El discussing getting him ready to attend their services and their Sunday school. When he's—"

"I don't believe it! We had it all settled that this little boy is going to be converted. I'm already preparing him."

"Well, Millie, you can just stop it. I'm in charge of rearing him, including him learning Judaism and taking part in their activities. I've already spoken to Sam Greene at the hospital, and he's more than willing to have Joe in his family's holiday celebrations. He's got a boy Joe's age, and I want him to play with him. Joe probably had no experience being around kids his own age, and he needs to learn how to socialize. That's going to be important when he starts school at East Hill Elementary after the first of the year."

"What? He's going to Immaculate with Irene. We had that decided before."

"No, he's not."

"Grayson, if this child is going to part of this family, he's going become a Catholic. That's it."

"This discussion is finished, Millie."

"We'll see about that!"

CHAPTER NINE

He almost got caught, but the guard chasing him stopped at the voice of another officer calling him. Joe dove behind some acid-smelling barrels stacked next to the water tower. He tried to breathe through his nose to stay as quiet as possible. Trains rumbled in the near distance, bringing another load of prisoners through the main gate. He looked up at the pale sky, dotted with white puffy clouds. Oh, how he wished he could fly to them and float in the sun's glowing rays.

He heard a footstep. A shadow passed over him. His breath stopped as he saw the black hole of a rifle pointing at him. He heard a click, and he began to scream.

Joe found himself under the bed, pushing as tightly as he could against the wall under the antique oak headboard. When the door squeaked open, letting in diffused light from the hallway, he saw cruel black leather boots. Unyielding fingers pulled his arm. He couldn't pry them off. Still, he squirmed to get away, but the brawny, wide hands held him firmly, drawing him to a warm, terry-clothed chest. The same hands encircled his head, stroking his damp hair and dry lips kissing his fevered cheeks. He heard low-toned murmurs in his ear. But his terror so overwhelmed him that he wetted himself.

It was the third time this week that Joe's nightmares had awakened him. The reveries occurred as predictably as going to the bathroom in the morning. Even falling asleep was impossible because his imagination would exaggerate his memories, frightening him. He saw shadows of Nazi swastikas bouncing on the walls and Nazi flags waving in the dresser mirror. They were here in his room. He was sure of it. He wanted to get inside the closet to hide, but fear numbed his legs and kept him under the bed.

Grayson could barely cope with the horrible memories himself. Like Joe, sleep often escaped him. He could still hear the truck engines idling as the loose-limbed bodies were swung into the beds. The stench of the putrefied flesh and the brooks of excrement and urine permeated his room. In the darkness, he saw the skeletons who could still sit upright in the mud. Images of unbelievable barbarity leaped into his mind's eye: the skin clinging to the charred ribs, still smoldering in the crematorium ovens, the dried blood on the metal hooks screwed into the top of the opposite wall, the gallows with the hangman's nooses ready for the next prisoner. Outside near the administration building, tables had been filled with glassed displays of split human heads, a lamp with the "professionally" constructed shade of human skin, the preserved human lungs and stomachs, the square tattoo portraits on dried human skin that would decorate a wall.

He remembered watching the throngs of reporters and photographers, so eager to take pictures that they had turned the scene of this human tragedy into a macabre circus. They even got in his way as he hurried to the next warmed-over "corpse" who needed triage. From General Omar Bradley to Joseph Pulitzer to Senator Ken Wherry from Nebraska and all their entourages, the famous visitors had made good on the publicity of Buchenwald. Yes, the absolute brutality of the Nazis needed to be put on center stage for the whole world to see, lest it would not be believed. But how many times did the corpses need to be rearranged for their photo opportunities? No amount of repositioning of the feet or arms or heads would lessen the barbarity done to these victims. Where had been the respect for these unfortunate, innocent souls? It was enough to give Grayson a constant headache.

Often, after tending to Joe in the dead of night, he took his dog-eared New American Bible and sat in the family room to read, the lamp on the end table turned low.

CHAPTER TEN

At the medical office building next to Tompkins County Hospital, Mrs. Florence Beck, Grayson's secretary, had straightened and dusted his office and had put a stack of surgical consultations on his desk. Grayson already had patients eager to see him before he had come back to Ithaca. After sitting to peruse the paperwork, he first looked up at the paneled wall. Beside his Cornell University School of Medicine diploma and a framed board of certification document, three imposing men in nineteenth-century suits stared back at him--his father, Dr. William Riley Pierce, his grandfather, Dr. Seymour Horatio Pierce, and his great-grandfather, Dr. William Henry Pierce. There was a spot left on the wall for his portrait which would be hung after his demise.

Grayson half-listened in the physicians' lounge with an untouched paper cup of coffee as the other doctors gossiped. If anyone asked him a question, he would give a short reply with a tight smile. No, he hadn't heard from Jim Manning. He had been in another evac unit during the war. Yes, the Pierce women were glad to see him. His brother, Al, was still in the army in D.C., shuffling legal papers around on his desk. What about the budget for the rest of the year? Any changes foreseen now that the war was over? The hospital needed a new X-ray machine. The New York State Board was coming in a few weeks to do its annual inspection.

As much as he enjoyed being back at work, Grayson's eyes blurred from lack of sleep. It was difficult to keep focused on his patients' complaints. He was glad no one pressed him about the details of his overseas experience. And always pushed to the front of his mind was Joe.

****

Grayson sat on the locker room bench in his scrubs, too tired to change back into his suit after the three-hour liver surgery. He thought about Margie. Eight years had passed since her death. Why was he thinking about her now? His throat constricted. Shutting his eyes, he saw in his mind the harshly lit waiting room where he had paced and paced.

****

Margie's spotting had started about six weeks before her due date. Her obstetrician, Dr. Dwight C. Hall, had put her on complete bed rest. He was an experienced, well-respected physician at the Presbyterian Hospital in Manhattan. When her labor began a few weeks later, Grayson drove her to the hospital almost at the speed of light. When Dr. Hall examined her in the ER, his finger came away with too much blood from her vagina. Already, Grayson knew what was wrong. Her condition was called placenta previa. The placenta covered her cervix instead of being at the top of her uterus. At once, the nurses rolled her away to the operating room. Time was short to get the infant out. Grayson had been banished to the waiting room.

Almost two hours later, he saw the other obstetrician, Dr. Calvin Judd, walking toward him. Blood saturated his surgical gown as if someone had thrown a bucket of it on him, even drenching his shoes. His ashen face bore defeat. Grayson pushed the doctor out of his way.

He saw the thoroughly soaked sheets and fresh blood dripping from the sides of the operating table. A nurse's back was turned; her white hose and uniform covered in scarlet from the fall she had taken on the slick floor. He stayed on his feet only by holding on to the edge of the table.

Margie's sweet face was now fixed and empty of color. Her once luxurious, thick, blonde hair was in tangled disarray around her head, strands stuck to her damp forehead. Her stunning pale blue eyes were half-lidded, the breathing tube yet to be removed from the perfect lips he had kissed so many times. Grayson lifted the sheets. Flaps of her abdomen were spread apart by clamps.

His grief rang throughout the universe.

Grayson, we'll get her back together. Please.

Where's the baby?

She's fine, Grayson. She's in the delivery ward.

****

Dr. Morey Allan entered the locker room. He and Grayson had been good friends since their undergraduate days at Cornell University. "You all right, Grayson?"

Grayson did not meet the other man's eyes. He hesitated before answering. "I-I've had a lot on my mind."

Morey opened his locker. "You seem quiet lately. You haven't been the same ol' Grayson since you got out of the army."

Grayson stared at the row of gleaming sinks in the adjoining bathroom. His voice faltered. "It was a terrible time."

"I heard you brought back a little boy."

"Yes."

"Well, you don't seem all that happy about it. I'd think having a new kid would be cause for celebration." He put on his white medical coat and searched for his stethoscope. "When are you going to bring him around so we can meet him?"

Grayson held back. "It's . . . it's not been easy. He's having a tough time adjusting." He gathered his clothes.

Morey shut the locker door. "Say, listen. I need to go. Don't forget about our golf game on Saturday. And are we still on for bridge next Tuesday?"

Grayson did not reply.

CHAPTER ELEVEN

The sun glowed in the cloudless sky, warming the pleasant day. White sand spread all around the railroad tracks. Joe lay on his stomach between the tracks. He thought he had a blanket covering him, but he wasn't sure. With his head turned to the right, he studied the thumb-sized round piece of wood lying next to his hand. He pushed away the piece of wood with his forefinger, wondering why he was so focused on it.

Now he lay on his back. The train rushed over him with an ear-deafening roar, and he calmly viewed its mechanical underside. Complicated steel parts worked seamlessly together like a giant clock to keep it going at full speed. Joe didn't wonder why this great engine running over him did not mutilate him. If he stayed perfectly still, the train would pass over him.

He stood and squinted in the blazing sun's reflection on the white sand. The azure sea threw its foamy tides. A Nazi flag slapped against the flagpole in the turbulent wind. He saw a simple white house with a red brick chimney in the distance. A black-haired man walked away from it, wearing a black and gray striped camp uniform, complete with the cap. He seemed to be waving. But just when Joe thought he recognized the man as his father, the figure became too small again. Joe wanted to run to him, but he couldn't move. His feet were stuck. His hand clutched the edge of the white sheet, and he pulled on it. He didn't want to lose sight of the man, but he had to deal with the sheet.

Joe realized he had pulled the sheet off his bed, dragging the mattress with it. As he backed up, his bare foot hit the wall. A sliver of dim light glimpsed through the closed curtains.

Grayson had finally drifted off to sleep after two hours of tossing in his bed and kicking the bedspread to the floor. The bedsheets lay in a crumpled pile at the end of the bed. Earlier, the muggy July night had made him open the curtains and raise the windows, but the light from the distant street lamps bothered him.

His door squeaked open, and someone jumped onto the bed. He awoke with a snort.

"Daddy!" Irene whispered loudly. She climbed on his stomach and pushed his shoulders.

"Honeybun, what are you doing out of bed?" he whispered back.

The diffuse light from the window framed her head. "I heard a noise coming from his room."

"What sort of noise?"

"Like a monster hitting the wall."

"Oh." Grayson put his head back on the pillow.

Irene pushed her hands on his shoulders again. "C'mon, Daddy. I'm scared."

Groaning, Grayson got up and sent Irene back to her room, reassuring her he'd take care of the noise. In his slippers, he shuffled past the other bedrooms where logs were being sawed to Joe's room. He rubbed his eyes and scratched his jaw, trying to ready himself for what new havoc awaited him.

When he turned on the nightstand lamp, he saw the mattress halfway off the box springs and the sheets and pillows on the floor. Clothes lay scattered about, and the new Chutes and Ladders board game he had just bought for Joe had been tossed all over. Joe stood between the bed and the dresser, the usual dark stain on the front of his pajama bottoms. If Grayson didn't get angry with him about the mattress, Joe knew Frau Dead Fish Eyes would in the morning. He'd have to straighten up his bed, but maybe the big man, Grayson, would help him.

Grayson put his fists on his hips as if to chastise him. But, instead, he took Joe's hand. "Let's go." They walked into the bathroom. The nightly ritual began. Joe's nightmares would awaken him, his pajamas soaked with urine. He would start crying. Grayson would come and give him a bath. Sometimes if she heard them, Rose would come up from her downstairs bedroom in her bathrobe and hair curlers. She would remove the soiled sheets and wipe down the plastic mattress cover. A clean set of sheets would be put down, and Joe would be put back in bed wearing fresh pajamas.

Tonight, because he did not awake screaming, Rose stayed asleep in her comfortable bed. After filling the tub halfway with warm water, Grayson sat on the toilet seat, unable to keep his eyes open. Joe daintily got in and began washing. His yellow rubber duck sat on the ledge next to the Luster Cream shampoo bottle. He tried to remember his strange dream, but it had evaporated in his brain.

After he finished his bath, Grayson lifted Joe out of the tub, pulled the plug, and began rubbing him dry with a large Turkish towel. The big man sat on the white and blue-tiled floor and pulled Joe to his chest. "Joe, you've got to start sleeping through the night." He looked into Joe's face, seeing his sunken eyes and purplish circles under them.

Grayson's body shook. He let go of Joe, who promptly landed on the unforgiving tile floor with a thud. Despite the painful tingling of his bumped elbow, he wrapped the towel around his waist and stood. He saw tears coursing down his guardian's cheeks. He put his hand out and touched Grayson's shoulder.

"What can I do with you?" Grayson shook his head. "How can I make you understand?" His voice cracked, and he lifted his full eyes to the high plaster ceiling.

Pointing to his head, Joe answered, "Ich kanne nicht die Munster in meinem Kopf loswerden!" He felt bad that Grayson was so upset. He didn't mean to cause so much trouble. If only he could get rid of those Nazi monsters in his dreams!

Leaning back against the tub, Grayson closed his eyes. Joe tore off some toilet paper and clumsily wiped the man's cheeks. Then Grayson hoisted himself up. He followed Joe back into the bedroom. Not finding any clean sleepwear, he put him in undershorts and a T-shirt. Too tired to straighten the room, Grayson led Joe back into his own bedroom.

After the huge man lay on his back in the continent-sized bed, Joe scrambled on top of his chest. At the camp, in the drafty barrack at night, Joe's father had laid on the outer edge of a rough-hued bunk, and Joe had to lie on top of him because when the prisoners crammed into the slatted beds, there was no room even for a small boy like Joe. And as he did with his father's prison shirt, he unbuttoned the top two buttons of Grayson's pajama shirt and laid his left ear against his hairy chest so he could listen to his heartbeat. He fell asleep.

CHAPTER TWELVE

After his guardian had left the mansion early the following day, Joe was at once accosted by Frau Dead Fish Eyes.

"We'll start with simple sentences," she said, putting a slender book in front of him as they sat at the dining room table. She laid his newly engraved missal within easy reach and ignored Grayson's German-English dictionary that he had pointedly put next to her plate of buttered toast earlier.

"The sentence begins, 'Who made us?' Now you fill in the blank." She put her finger on the horizontal line under the sentence.

Joe looked at the words, at the woman, then back at the page.

"Well? Pick up the pencil and write the answer."

Joe sat motionless. He knew he was supposed to do something but was at a loss as to what. He fearfully glanced at the dictionary on the sideboard.

Impatiently Frau Dead Fish Eyes put the pencil into his right hand and slapped the page. "Write the answer. Look here. There are the words at the bottom to choose from."

He slowly moved the pencil into his left hand and began copying the word 'Lamb' on top of the line.

"No! That's incorrect! The answer is 'God!' God made us. We are created in His image. It's as plain as the nose on your face." She took his pencil and erased his marks. Seeing her point to the correct word, he began writing again.

"Why are you using your left hand?" She grabbed his pencil and put it into his right.

Joe's letters were shaky as he tried to write frantically. But being forced to use his right hand made things worse. He simply could not concentrate from lack of sleep. If he only understood the meaning of these words, he could easily figure out the correct answers. This lesson book looked like a religious text. It had pictures of a bearded man in white and red robes, looking somewhat like the half-naked figurine glued to the sticks and hanging on the dining room wall. The words "Jesus Christ" appeared often. Was that his name?

Tears blurred Joe's vision. He had to please this horrible lady, or else she might stick him in the kitchen oven. How regrettable that his first guess was wrong, making the woman lose her temper. At the very least, she would beat him, probably using that old dragon lady's evil cane. Her swift admonishment would make any Nazi guard puff out his chest with pride. The guards always had been eager to use their rifle butts or their jackboots to strike any prisoner who didn't do as they were told fast enough.

Joe endured the woman's nerve-racking lesson through two more pages, and then mercifully, she closed the book. When he took it along with the dictionary to study in his room, the madwoman snatched them away.

Joe needed that dictionary badly. One time he had gone into Grayson's room, looking for it to steal. He found it lying on top of the chiffonier, just out of his reach. As he stretched up to grab it, the two cleaning ladies, Phyllis and Val, walked in. The noise they made, akin to birds alerting each other of an approaching cat, brought up Frau Dead Fish Eyes from the music room.

"You bad, bad boy! Do you think you can come into your father's room without his permission? You have no business in here."

Frightened but determined, Joe pointed to the book. "Ich wunsche das Buch."

"You won't be speaking in any foreign tongue in this house, young man." Frau Dead Fish Eyes pushed the book farther back on the chiffonier. "Now, you will not touch that book as long as you're in this house. It doesn't belong to you, and we both know you would tear it up as you do with everything else you lay your hands on." She stopped to catch her breath. "Mercy, sakes alive! I don't know what

I'm going to do with you. How am I ever going to straighten you out?" She pushed him roughly toward the door. "To your room with you," she said, gesturing down the hall.

Joe sat in front of his toys and stared at them, trying to make sense of it all. He already *knew* how to read and write. His father and mother had taught him when they had lived in the attic. Why is that ugly witch making it so complicated?

A red and yellow-painted metal clown holding a tiny drum and wooden sticks lay a foot away. He took it and, without thinking, broke off the sticks.

He noticed Frau Dead Fish Eyes never brought out that religious book when Grayson was around. Moreover, she always had an eye toward the family room windows while she gave the lesson as if watching for him. Why she did that was a mystery. Grayson never tried to teach him from the workbook or even bothered with his missal. Unfortunately, the big man wasn't around very much to help him. He would often come home well after Joe was in bed in the evening and be out the door before waking in the morning. And if he had to leave during the night, he would still be sleeping when Joe rose the next morning.

During the day, there were ample places to hide from the old busybodies. The castle was immense, with two sets of staircases, a full basement, an attic, a four-car garage, a parlor, a library, a study, the music room, the living room, the family room, the kitchen, storage rooms, and too many bedrooms and bathrooms to count. The ancient bovines were slow and not given to bending over, so he easily could slip under a bed to get away from them. Of course, they would call for him (usually to come out for a writing lesson), and Rose, the cook, and Anne, the maid, would be engaged in the search. And the little girl would be dragged in from her outside playtime. At first, she enjoyed looking for him, thinking this was a game of hide-and-seek. But when it began occurring several times a day, she grew tired of it and complained. There were many shouts and threats, but if he stayed put, the women would eventually give up because some other activity pressed them.

When he did make himself available to the old broads, curiously, they wanted him to disappear. "What do you think you're doing in here?" demanded the old matriarch, Nina Cassandra, when he had followed her into the music room one morning. He had been extremely interested in the lively dialogue coming from the radio. He knew this could help him learn English. "You don't belong in here. Out!" She shook her cane at him.

Aunt Elvie sat on the couch; her crossword puzzle book opened in her hand. "Oh, let him stay, Nina. He's not bothering anything."

"He's bothering me. This is a private room. I want to enjoy my shows, and I can't if I have to watch to make sure he doesn't break something. He's already broken all the toys in his room." She lowered herself with effort into her Lincoln rocker and hooked her cane on the arm. "Why Grayson keeps buying him things is pure stupidity. Just a waste of good money."

"But that's what little boys do. Didn't your kids break their toys? Mine did. It's just their age." Aunt Elvie reached over to grab the remote from the coffee table to turn up the volume on the radio.

Hence, Joe had to sit on the floor just outside the doorway to listen. In the evenings, however, Frau Dead Fish Eyes made him sit in front of the radio to listen to music. And it was marvelous! He wanted to clap his hands to the beat and sing along, but the woman would not allow it. That was okay. He secretly tapped his toe inside his shoe.

And at the times when the music room was empty, he would crawl over to the piano and pet Mr. Henry, whose habit it was to lay under it. At least *he* didn't seem to mind if Joe was around.

One quiet afternoon, when everyone was out of the house except Joe and Aunt Elvie, he saw Frau Clown sitting at the dining room table with a palm-sized deck of thick cardboard paper with numbers and faces printed on them. Taking a chance (although this resident of the castle seemed harmless), he cautiously eased himself into a chair to watch as she laid them out in seven rows face down except the top one. He had never seen such strange pieces of thick paper before. They were decorated with hearts and kings and queens and red diamonds and black clover leaves. Frau Clown drew three cards from the stack in her hand, and after careful inspection, she lay one down at the bottom of one of the rows. However, sometimes she just put the cards behind the others and made an unhappy face. Joe soon figured out that a black card and a red one were put down in the vertical rows. Four single cards labeled with A's in the corners lay above the rows, and the woman added one card at a time that was a consecutive number if she drew it from the cards in her hand or from the end of the rows.

Frau Clown hummed to herself, paying no attention to Joe, who got up on his knees to see the cards better. Without thinking of Aunt Elvie's reaction, he pointed to a card that needed to be put on top of the diamond stack. Without so much as a bat of her copiously blackened eyelashes, Frau Clown placed the card on top. She passed through her stack until there were no more cards to be played. Sighing, she swept up the whole deck, shuffled them, and laid them out again.

Joe figured out that this was a game that needed only one player. He began to see patterns emerge to arrange the cards. But there didn't seem to be a finish to it. Cards still lay in the rows. Maybe the game would be won if all the cards would eventually be stacked in the four heaps above them.

Joe did not know precisely how much time had passed. But the game took a dramatic turn when four paws landed right in the middle of the rows. Cards flew. Joe burst out laughing, and Frau Clown joined him.

Mr. Henry decided to sit on his haunches and bathe his nether parts. Peals of laughter ensued. Then he put down his hind leg and looked directly into Joe's eyes. *Who are you lookin' at?*

Joe was happy that he had found a game he could play with at least someone in the castle. But alas, that little girl to whom he had some attraction was no playmate. "Get out of my room!" she would shout at him if he loitered in the doorway. He wanted to play with her, even with her dolls, and with her neighbor friend, Mollie Eggars. If she fought with the other girl, which happened almost every day, he learned in short order to stay out of her way. When no one was looking, she liked to push him and hit his arms with her fists. He did not fight back for fear of getting into trouble. Never once did she attempt to teach him any English words. She was a miniature version of Frau Dead Fish Eyes—always angry.

On the infrequent evenings Grayson was home before Joe and Irene had gone to bed, he would take them into the family room and ask Irene to pick out a favorite book. Then he would have her read a portion of it aloud to Joe, interrupting her often to translate a word for Joe, using the dictionary.

"This is boring!" she snapped as she finished a sentence about the fox and the woodcutter, one of the characters in *Aesop's Fables*.

"Settle down, Irene. Joe, can you say 'fox?'"

Before he repeated the word, Irene shut the book and slid off the couch. "I'm not going to do this anymore! It's no fun, and I hate him!"

"Irene! You are acting very badly, and I don't like your attitude."

"See if I care!" She threw the book on the floor and stomped off toward the stairs.

Joe knew not to follow her.

Mealtime was another battlefield. Joe finally used the silverware (yes, he had used spoons and forks while living in the attic) but was forced to use his right hand, at least when Grayson wasn't around. At lunchtime, the syrupy canned peaches missed his mouth and landed in his lap. When the fruit slices then dropped to the exquisite Persian rug, all hell broke loose. He wanted to pick them up and eat them, but that was forbidden. He was sent to the kitchen to get a washcloth. He got the idea to stash the peaches into his pocket while pretending to clean up the rug. Since he was under the table, nobody bothered to watch him.

Enough food faux pas and subsequent reactions from fanatical women made him change tactics. He became selective about what he would eat. If he couldn't pick up the food securely with his fingers, he would not touch it. Since nearly all the food was cooked, he went hungry. Even when Grayson spooned the rice and the gravy onto his plate to accompany the baked chicken, he did not pick up an eating utensil. However, as much as his stomach grumbled and his mouth watered, the risk of spilling the food wasn't worth trying to eat it with his right hand. Rolls, bread, pickles, and raw vegetables were the only permissible food to be taken by the fingers, as Aunt Mil admonished him. Her dead-fish, stony eyes missed nothing.

His guardian noticed what he thought was his lack of appetite. "C'mon, Joe. Your food's getting cold." He would point to the boy's full plate with his fork. But Joe only sat. Nina Cassandra would say, "When he's hungry enough, he'll eat. Don't upset the rest of us worrying over that spoiled tyke." And Grayson would glare at her.

The only substantial food he ate was the occasional peanut butter and jelly sandwiches Rose gave him in the afternoon as a snack.

However, this had to be done covertly because some old broad would come in and shout, "Don't give him that sandwich, Rose! You'll spoil his appetite!"

Joe's next step took courage. One night when everybody was asleep, he soundlessly sneaked his way down the staircase. Enough light from the windows allowed him to negotiate through the family room, the dining room, and into the kitchen. There in the garbage pail, he found his meal. The bottom of the tin can still had sauce from the pork and beans; banana peels had the end of the sweet fruit still attached; egg whites pooled in the broken shells. There was even the heel from a loaf of bread inside the wrapper, stale but still edible. Gathering as much as he could, he stole back upstairs and closed his bedroom door quietly. The best place to eat this food would be in the closet.

He wished there had been a butter wrapper for the bread. But he would search tomorrow night. He hid the cheese wrappers, the chicken bones, the vegetable cans, and the apple cores in a corner in his bedroom closet. To be safe, he covered it all with a spare blanket. This was a bountiful meal compared to what the prisoners got.

While chewing on potato peelings and drinking the salty drops of juice from the green beans can, he remembered the good-natured, fat lady who had brought food to him and his father at night behind the kitchen building. Occasionally, an overweight man came with her. Joe had figured that he was her husband. But unlike the friendly, generous woman, the fat man was as threatening as a snarling guard dog. Joe feared him greatly. But after about eight months, the woman had stopped coming, and he and his father had begun to go hungry. Here in this castle, the garbage can in the kitchen was always overflowing with abundant food. His stash in the closet would keep him alive indefinitely.

It came into his mind that he had another reason not to eat the food at the dinner table besides running the risk of a scolding for bad manners. If he ate the food presented to him, he would gain weight. Without a doubt, the people in this dastardly citadel were trying to fatten him up before slaughtering and cooking him in that oven. He would not give them that opportunity. The sight of the wall ovens in the kitchen gave him his resolve.

CHAPTER THIRTEEN

The Pierce household was visited three times a week by the two cleaning ladies, Phyllis and Valerie. Nina Cassandra had hired them away from their custodial duties at one of the elementary schools with enticements of better pay and a free lunch. Joe knew them as his betrayers.

The two garrulous traitors had discovered Joe's food collection when they had cleaned his room and had noticed a foul odor coming from the closet. The ruckus they raised brought Joe and the rest of the house up to his room. Frau Dead Fish Eyes and the old biddies cackled about the stench and the very real possibility that vermin and roaches might stake a claim in his closet. Joe screamed and fought with every ounce of strength he had with the cleaning women as they pushed the soup cans and the eggshells and the grapefruit rinds and the bloodied butcher's wrapper into paper sacks. A key was found to lock the closet door.

And when he got his dressing down from that absolute fury who was Aunt Mil, the two other women, the nasty old biddy and the clown-face woman, supported her like a Greek chorus. It gave them great pleasure to throw more firewood on the already blazing roar of yelling and upbraiding. After that, the fuming woman with the dead fish eyes told him to stay in his room. "There will be no supper for you," she snapped.

Joe knew now he faced starvation. His tears dotted the carpet as he hid under the big double bed. He hoped that after they shut the bedroom door, no one would bother him. Frustration and rage gave way to bottomless despair. There was no place else in this room where he could hide the food. Real hunger made his stomach hurt. When the hot summer sun sank into the night, darkening the bedroom, Joe stayed under the bed curled as tightly as Mr. Henry, who lay beside him.

Oh, how tired he had become of the never-ending search for food. This reminded him of the fights he had witnessed in the camp. The other prisoners sometimes killed each other for any morsels of food, spoiled or otherwise. There wasn't even any clean water to drink. It had all started when the heavy-set lady stopped coming at night, bringing leftover food to him and his father. His father had become frantic, begging the other prisoners, even the new arrivals who had exited the trains.

Rumors had been rampant about the enemy from both the east and the west approaching the camp. Joe had heard that the Nazi leaders argued whether to abandon the camp or move the prisoners out and liquidate the place, killing all those unfortunate enough to be left behind. They knew they were losing control. The immediate future was uncertain for all. Survival became tenuous as discipline broke down; masses of prisoners were pushed together and forced to walk out of the camp to destinations unknown, while at the same time, more prisoners poured in from the eastern camps. And everybody, *everybody* wanted food.

At night, Joe thought how much he missed the attic and his mother and father. He never minded having to stay quiet, especially during the day. His mother had brought food, although meager sometimes. He and his father depended on his mother, Ina, who could move about in downtown Berlin to pick up what food she could.

No one had suspected she was a Jewess. Her Germanic looks made her appear anything but. Thick, shining blonde hair fell in soft waves around her shoulders; her startling sea-blue eyes were intelligent and cheerful. Her high, prominent cheekbones, strong chin, and softly curved jaw, the flawless complexion of her perfectly symmetrical face, and her tall stature--all gave her the appearance of a perfect model of Aryan womanhood. Her voluptuous figure certainly would have caught many a male eye on the streets of Berlin.

Joe's mother was a seamstress and had a good job working in the clothing store downstairs. She had a creative eye to make simple toys for Joe when scraps of material were available. Sitting on his father's lap, Joe would play with his stuffed dog or silly gingerbread man. What he remembered best about her were the cherished books she brought. She had borrowed a library card from her employer and checked out as many as she could. Reading proved to be no challenge for Joe. With patient guidance from his father, sitting on the rough wooden floor in a cramped corner, they read together in low voices. At first, Joe followed each word with a finger, but soon he could read complete sentences and paragraphs. His mother brought him more advanced books in many subjects, and he learned everything from the anatomy of a flower to arithmetic to long-dead great German authors. His father, noting his son's natural intelligence, taught him to write in German and Hebrew and a little bit of Yiddish. The only problem was finding enough paper for him to practice his spelling.

Joe found it harder and harder to remember what his mother and father looked like, and that distressed him. If he couldn't remember his mother's face, did that mean she was gone forever? He wouldn't think about what had happened to his father at the camp.

His seven-year-old body collapsed in weary grief under the double bed. He wanted to go home! He wanted to feel safe and loved and full from a warm meal. But it just wasn't going to happen, he concluded, as he looked beyond the iron bed frame to the bottom of the antique oak dresser. *Why, oh, why did they lock that closet door?* That was the only refuge he had in this awful place!

There was no recourse except to get out of this fortress. But how could he escape without getting caught? He could not go through the back kitchen door without someone seeing or hearing him. There was a service door right outside Rose's bedroom, but he would have to go through her room to get to it. And because the humongous front doors were locked every night, he wasn't sure how he could unlock them and pull them open. Even the garden room wouldn't work because he would have to go through the music room, and there was always some fat lady in there. In the evenings, somebody always locked the French doors, and who knew where the key was?

Crawling out from under the bed, Joe paced like a caged animal, not knowing what to do. He kicked aside his ever-growing collection of toys, already broken in past episodes of bitter vexation. He stood on a chair and stared out the big window in his room and wondered what it would be like to jump out of it. He studied the metal latch at the top that locked the inside panel and the screen behind it.

CHAPTER FOURTEEN

When Grayson came home late that evening, he had barely put his hat on the small telephone table in the foyer when his womenfolk descended on him like hungry vultures on deceased prey.

"Grayson, I hope we never have another day like today."

"Yes, we had a terrible time!"

"We are simply at our wits' end."

"Please! I've been on my feet in surgery for the past ten hours. Let me sit for a moment. Where's Rose? I need a drink."

Mildred folded her arms in high-minded anger. "Never mind about that. You've got to do something about that child! He's been very naughty today."

"Where're the kids? Did you have them stay up for me?" Grayson walked into the family room, taking off his coat and tie and tossing them on a chair.

"No. I've sent them to their rooms. They both have tried the patience of saints today. We've been waiting for you to come home to deal with them."

He opened the walnut-veneered liquor cabinet and poured himself a whiskey.

Rose appeared. "I'll take your dinner out of the oven, Dr. Pierce. It will be ready for you in five minutes."

"I'm warning you, Grayson. This arrangement is getting worse," Mildred said, looking down at her brother from her high horse.

"He's been keeping garbage in his closet," Aunt Elvie added with certainty.

"What?"

"Phyllis and Val found a whole mountain of garbage in his bedroom closet. The smell is how they discovered it." She nodded to Mildred, expecting confirmation.

Nina Cassandra followed him to the sofa, using her cane for support. "Grayson, you have a serious problem with that naughty little whipper-snapper, and you'd better face it." She shook her cane at his back. She turned to Elvie. "I think he's got mental problems, don't you agree?"

Elvie murmured, "Maybe he does."

Mildred kept going. "He's out of control. Lord knows what he'll do next! It's a good thing we have him locked up in his room."

Grayson turned to his sister. "What's this about garbage in his closet?" Taking a large swallow from his shot glass, he looked around the room for his pipe.

Mildred raised and lowered her hands for emphasis. "It was a mess! Banana peels, eggshells, coffee grounds, beef bones, empty fruit cans, butter wrappers all piled up as if he was hoarding it. And he's been doing it for some time because so much of it was spoiled. It's a wonder it didn't draw cockroaches or, worse, mice. But we got the closet cleaned out and took the sacks away to the dumpster. It took all afternoon. Why he did it is beyond my comprehension."

Elvie said, "The fuss that child made! He screamed and ranted and cried as if we were taking away his only source of food."

Grayson drained his glass. "But that's just the point. You *were* taking away his food." He got up to refill his glass. He thought better and poured another whiskey into a bigger tumbler.

"Nonsense!" spat Mildred. "There's plenty for him to eat. He gets three square meals a day. Can we help it if he's so ill-mannered that half the food ends up on the rug?"

The other two matrons nodded in complete agreement.

As he drank a liberal amount of liquor, Grayson looked at this trio of well-bred, proper New England women. They stood before him in their sturdy heels with age-spotted hands clasped under their significant bosoms, righteous scowls on their resolute faces, expecting a satisfactory solution to this problem that was turning into something more than an inconvenience to their pursuit of peace and personal comfort.

"You don't know!" Grayson set his glass firmly on the coffee table. He stood, wiping the back of his head, anger rushing through his exhausted brain. "I've tried to tell you before. Joe came from a concentration camp. He was starved. There was no food for him or anybody else. He had to save what little he could find because he didn't know when or if he would ever eat again. He still thinks there's not enough food for him. He doesn't understand yet that he doesn't have to worry about that anymore. Did you think to try to explain that to him?" He remembered what Joe had told Rabbi Passow. Joe thought he would be killed and thrown into the crematorium ovens sooner or later. This little boy still thought his life was threatened. Should he tell these women that?

"Grayson, that's ridiculous," said Mildred. "We don't need to explain anything to him. He sits at the dinner table with us at every meal. He's offered food all the time. He knows he's not going to starve."

Grayson got into her face. "No, he doesn't know that, Mil. You haven't the slightest clue as to what's going on in that little head of his. Can't you see how afraid he is? He's too scared to pick up a spoon because he knows you'll shout at him for using his left hand. He doesn't understand what you're saying, but he hears your tone of voice. Even I get scared by it. For God's sake, leave him alone!"

Grayson glanced toward the dining room. Rose stood patiently with her hands holding the top of his chair, waiting to serve him his dinner. Ironically, he went to eat his meal.

The women followed him. Watching him put a corner of his cloth napkin over his collar, Mildred said, "This arrangement with the boy is impossible. The food in the closet is just another example of how unmanageable he is. I'm trying my best to make him behave, but I can't get through to him."

"Well, are you trying to teach him some English? Are you using the dictionary?"

Mildred waved her hand dismissively. "He doesn't sit still long enough even to pay attention. He runs and hides, and we can't find him half the time. We have to get Irene or Anne to look for him."

"Well, I can't say I blame him. Sometimes I'd like to run and hide from all of you, too." Grayson dug into his meatloaf.

Nina Cassandra said in a steely voice, "Grayson, your sarcasm is tiresome, and it isn't helpful. You treat ragamuffin as if he's royalty, showering him with all those toys, and you don't punish him when he needs it. If he screams and cries at night, let him. You don't need to sit with him. He'll eventually fall back asleep. You're spoiling him, and he's learned he can manipulate you and get away with it! He needs to know who's the boss. He needs some good old-fashioned strict discipline and a healthy dose of religion, just as I did with the three of you." She looked at Mildred as if expecting her to say something about Joe's catechism lessons he seemed unable to learn.

Her grown son shook his head and put down his forkful of macaroni and cheese. "And you think he'll learn to settle down with a ruler slapped on his hand and a stick on his backside? You think he's acting like this on purpose? That he's some devious little kid who likes to wake up screaming in the middle of the night just to annoy you?" He put his hand to his forehead. To Rose, he said, "Do we have any bicarbonate of soda?"

Rose hurried back into the kitchen.

"No, but I know how to rear kids, and you can't let them control you by giving in to them." Nina Cassandra settled herself in a chair next to Grayson and pointed an arthritic, bejeweled finger. "I reared the three of you, didn't I? And no thanks to my bleeding-heart husband."

Mildred turned to her. "Now, Mother. Don't bring up Daddy again."

Nina Cassandra ignored her, focusing on her son. "Now, see here, boy. I'm telling you that you have to be firm with that child, or else he's going to be serious trouble down the road. You don't want a juvenile delinquent on your hands, do you? How do you expect he'll get along in school? Why, the sisters at Immaculate won't put up with him squirming and running around, hiding in closets and under desks. Mildred's doing the best she can by trying to get him to read and write a little. But mercy! He fidgets like the Devil's breathing down his neck."

Grayson's fork shook as he shoveled more meatloaf into his mouth, barely chewing before swallowing it. "I remember how you came after me with your flyswatter, Mom. Perhaps I needed it at times, but Joe's circumstance is different." He gulped the glass of fizzing baking soda.

Mildred said, "Grayson, we don't know anything about this child's background. How do we know if he's had any schooling? What if he didn't get good parenting when he was a baby? I'm beginning to wonder if perhaps he might be mentally . . . you know, mentally . . ."

"Retarded?" Grayson snapped. Frowning, he burped.

"Perhaps, or at least slow for his age. Have you considered that?"

The big man stared down at his plate, then back at his sister, his eyes intense with umbrage. "There's no way I can make you understand."

Mildred lowered her tense voice. "Grayson, maybe *you* don't understand. When you came back from Europe, you brought a little boy without letting us prepare for him. Then when you went back to work, you gave us the responsibility of taking care of him, and we are at our wit's end with him. You need to be here with him."

"I say you need to act like a father to him!" declared Nina Cassandra. She knocked her cane on a table leg sharply.

"I *am* a father to him! Can I help it if you disapprove? Where's Joe now?"

"He's up in his room," said Mildred.

"Since when? Has he eaten supper tonight?" Grayson looked at his watch. It was after nine o'clock.

"No. I told you he's being locked in his room." Mildred straightened her back and looked at her brother defiantly. "I told him he would get no dinner tonight as punishment for the mess he made in the closet."

"Oh, for Christ's sake!" Grayson stood, throwing down his napkin. He mentally kicked himself for not fully comprehending what his sister had said earlier about where Joe was. Damn, he was worn out!

"There's no taking the Lord's name in vain in this house, boy!" shouted Nina Cassandra. She impatiently pounded her fist on the table to get Grayson's attention as he gave Rose terse orders to prepare a plate of food for Joe.

"Here," he gave the cook his plate. "Take the rest of my food. Let's not let it go to waste."

Leaving the agitated mob in the dining room, he carried the tray up the stairs with Rose behind him with a glass of water. He knocked gently on Joe's door and then unlocked it. When he turned on the lamp on the dresser, he saw that the bed was empty, the pillow fresh, and the bedspread neat and unwrinkled. He willed himself to remain calm.

Joe squinted in the light. He had crouched between the bed and the wall, pressing his face against it, drawing up his legs, and wrapping his arms around his knees. He saw the big man put the tray on the bed, and Rose put the glass of water on his nightstand.

"Ah, pal, what are you doing in the corner like that?" Grayson said in a soothing voice. He took Joe under his arms, lifted him, and put him on the bed. "I bet you're hungry." He couldn't resist giving him a noisy kiss on his cheek.

Rose smoothed Joe's hair as he looked at the meatloaf with the catsup dressing sweetened with brown sugar, macaroni and cheese, and the buttered lima beans. He almost grabbed the food with his hands. But his guardian caught him and put a fork in his left hand, and Joe began eating. He saw the small china cup of fresh strawberries and grapes and ate those, too. Then he drank the water.

"Rose, I need to look in on Irene. I'll be back in a minute."

"Yes, Dr. Pierce. Joe's such a sweet boy. I'm so glad he's eating."

"Rose, you love it when everybody eats your cooking." Grayson gave her a weary smile.

Irene was asleep, so her father did not wake her. He went to Mildred's bedroom door and knocked. He entered. His sister sat at her vanity in her bathrobe, a new jar of Pond's cold cream opened before her. She raised her eyes in surprise to see his reflection in the beveled mirror.

His eyes were hooded, and his voice was as still as a deadly, spring-loaded trap. "You will never withhold food from my child again. You will not punish him for anything you think doesn't conform to your idea of correct behavior. Whatever he does, you will wait until I get home and tell me about it, and I will take care of it. The same goes for Irene. You said she was sent to her room for punishment too. Why? What did she do?"

"I witnessed her slapping her little friend, Mollie Eggars. They were fighting over their dolls, and Irene lost her temper. On top of that, when I confronted her about it, she lied about it. I sent the other little girl home, and Irene was put in her room and made to pray for her sins. She will go to confession on Friday."

"Did she have her dinner?"

"No."

Grayson clenched and unclenched his hands. "Mildred, I repeat. You are not to discipline my children. What Irene did was wrong, and I will talk to her about it, but you stay out of it. Do I make myself clear? From now on, *you stay out of it*."

His sister frowned, then replied, "Very well, Grayson."

Back in Joe's room, he asked Rose to make up another tray for Irene. He knocked on his daughter's door and heard sobbing. He found Irene clutching a pillow to her stomach as she sat against the headboard of her bed. She wiped her nose and averted her red eyes from her father as he sat next to her. Grayson turned on the lamp on her nightstand.

"I heard you had a rough day."

Irene lowered her face to hide it, her blonde locks falling over it. She hiccupped.

Grayson rubbed her arm.

"I hate her! She's so mean to me!"

"I've spoken to Aunt Mil. I know her side of the story. Would you like to tell me yours?"

Sniffing and wiping her nose on her pajama sleeve, Irene replied, "Mollie Eggars was going to tear the arms off my Henrietta. She's my favorite doll, and I couldn't let her do it. But she wouldn't give her back, so I had to slap her."

Her father worked out his answer in his head first. "Irene, it was wrong for Mollie not to give Henrietta to you, but it was more wrong for you to hit her. You are not to slap or strike anyone."

"Well, I got my Henrietta back! It worked!"

"Didn't Aunt Mil see you?"

Irene crossed her arms and lowered her chin. Her mouth twisted in the same way he had seen in his own mother.

The door opened, and Rose came in with Irene's tray. Irene began with the strawberries, using her fingers to pick them up.

"You will not use your hands to settle differences with others, my dear. And lying to your Aunt Mil about it is inexcusable. I will not tolerate it. If it happens again, you will regret it. My bite will hurt a lot more than Aunt Mil's. Do you understand?"

Irene refused to look at her father, focusing on the meatloaf. She stopped, holding her fork. "Why is he here?"

"You mean Joe?"

She nodded.

Grayson thought. He had never explained to her how or why he brought this new little boy into their home. He realized he should have discussed this with her sooner. Inhaling deeply, he said, "I found Joe while I was in Europe with the army. He was in a very bad place, and he needed help to get out. Look, you have a playmate now if you just give him a chance."

"But he gets everything. You're always buying things for him. And you keep reading to him and doing things for him." She tasted the lima beans and made a face.

"That's because he needs to learn our language to get ready to go to school after Christmas. When he came here, he had nothing. He had no clothes or toys or even a pair of socks for his feet."

"Aunt Mil called me a spoiled brat!"

"Your Aunt Mil thinks anyone who has more than a toothbrush is a spoiled brat. Honey, if you think about it, knowing what Joe didn't have when he came into our home should make you appreciate all the things *you* have. You've never been without clothes or a warm bed, and you have plenty of dolls and toys. Can you imagine not having any of that?"

She looked down, uncomprehending.

"Honeybun, just because I buy things for him and pay attention to him doesn't mean I don't love you. Nothing's changed about how precious you are to me. We have to fill Joe's room with toys and clothes and warm blankets, just like we've filled this room." He stroked her thick, glossy hair. He loved caressing her locks. "I will always love you, Irene."

"Do you love Joe?"

Grayson nodded. "Yes." He saw her confusion. "Sweetheart, if I say that I love Joe, that doesn't mean I love you less. Think about God's love. His love is for everybody. There's no limit or boundaries. That's the love I have for you both. I hope in time that you'll learn to love Joe, too. But in the meantime, you are not to be jealous of him, nor are you to act out on him."

Irene moved the tray aside and climbed into her father's lap and comforting arms. "What was the bad place that he came from?"

Grayson sighed. "It's best to talk about that when you're older."

"Daddy, did God tell you to bring Joe home?"

Grayson answered, "Yes."

"Why?"

"Because he needed help, Irene. God wants all of us to help those who are less fortunate. That is Christ's teaching to us, to clothe the naked, feed the hungry, and give shelter to the needy. Do you remember Father Byrne talking about that in his homilies?"

"Yes. Is that why you're a doctor? To help sick people get better?"

"I thought you already knew that, Irene. But, yes, I want to make others feel better. So did your grandfather and your great-grandfather. It runs in this family, being physicians."

"Can I be a doctor when I grow up?"

Grayson eyed his daughter with mock suspicion. "Don't you want to find an upstanding young man to marry and have a family?"

"If I do that, I wouldn't have time to help other people like you do. I want to do what you do."

"If you feel that strongly, you could take your vows and become a nurse at a Catholic hospital."

"I'd rather be a doctor."

"Training to become a doctor takes a long time. It's difficult work and demands time and dedication. You'd face an uphill battle, working side by side with mostly men. Not many women become doctors."

"Will you help me learn?"

"Yes, if you really want to try. You'd better think about it some more. There's plenty of time before you decide what you want to do with your life."

"Maybe I can practice on Joe."

Grayson chuckled. "I'm not sure about that. The main thing is that you know why you make decisions about your life. Your grandmother and Aunt Elvie and Aunt Mil and I want you to be a good person. Don't lash out when something doesn't go your way or when somebody doesn't do what you want him to do. Serving others, helping people is what the Church teaches. When you do that, you are serving God. Charity and selflessness are values you have to demonstrate to be a good Christian. That is following in Christ's footsteps." He smoothed her cheek. "And you have to control that temper of yours. You're not a very patient little girl. Okay?"

Soberly, she nodded.

Grayson stood. "You finish your dinner and set the tray outside the door. I'll tell Rose to come by later to take it back downstairs."

"Daddy, I'm sorry about hitting Mollie."

"Well, let's hope we don't get a phone call from her mother. You will apologize to Mollie tomorrow, and you will go to confession on Friday to tell your transgressions to Christ and ask for His forgiveness. Your actions were more than a venial sin. You will say the Act of Contrition to Father Byrne and receive your penance."

When she started to protest, he said. "I'm telling you that's what you will do. And you will say you're sorry to Aunt Mil."

All right." She acknowledged defeat in her doleful face. Her father left her room.

CHAPTER FIFTEEN

Tuesday, Four-forty-five. He'd have just enough time to make it to confession before Father Byrne left the parish. After parking his Lincoln on Geneva Street, Grayson Pierce entered the narrow foyer, patting his breast pocket for his rosary. He removed his summer fedora and walked into the cool, dim sanctuary. Dust motes drifted in the yellowed light from the tall, stained glass windows. A slightly overweight young mother dressed in a tight suit and hat briskly walked past him toward the parish entrance, not meeting his eyes. Her small daughter almost had to run to keep up, her quick footsteps echoing in the aisle.

After anointing himself with holy water from the marble basin, Grayson slowly walked down to the first pew. As he had done for nearly forty years, he genuflected and moved sideways into the left side pew which bore a brass nameplate, "In memory of Dr. and Mrs. Seymour H. Pierce." He pulled down the kneeling bar and positioned his substantial body. He crossed himself and closed his eyes to put himself in a contemplative mood. Then he sat back in the pew and gazed at the stained-glass image of St. George on the left. He knew the widow who had donated this window. He remembered removing her husband's cancer-ridden right lung, blackened from decades of smoking. She had been grateful that her beloved had survived the surgery. But he had died three months later.

After a few minutes, a man he did not know left the confessional booth on the right side of the altar. After looking around to see if any parishioners were still waiting to see Father Byrne, Grayson stepped forward and went into the confessional, shutting the rickety wooden door behind him. He dropped his knees on the red velvet kneeling bar and faced the shoulder-high partition. A wooden, fleur-de-lis-patterned screen separated him from the priest. Crossing himself, he said, "This is Grayson Pierce. Bless me, Father, for I have sinned. It has been more than four years since my last confession."

Grayson knew he should have come to confession as soon as he had come home three weeks ago. After his first mass upon arriving back in Ithaca, he had shaken hands with Father John Byrne but had said little. He assumed Mildred had told him about his new little boy. He had procrastinated about seeing the priest, not wanting to mention the issue of Joe's religious upbringing. But here he was, nonetheless, nervous and feeling vulnerable. Cynically, a bitter memory came into his head of asking the army chaplain to press a wad of sponges into the stomach of a young infantryman to staunch the bleeding while he dug for shrapnel.

"Welcome back to Ithaca, Grayson. I'm glad to see you again at Immaculate Conception."

"Thank you, Father. I know I should have come to confession sooner. I have many venial sins. I have taken the Lord's name in vain too many times to count. I reneged on a promise I made to a colleague about attending a luncheon in Statler Hall at Cornell. I just didn't feel like putting on a fake smile and pretending to commiserate with the other doctors." Grayson shifted uncomfortably. He bravely looked through the screen, barely seeing the priest's fair, sloe-eyed face. "I'm sad all the time. And tired."

"I understand, my son. It's difficult to adjust to a normal routine after being in the army for so many years. It will take time for you to feel like yourself again. Do you have anything else to confess?"

"No. But I need your guidance. This may take some time to explain."

"We've got all the time you need, Grayson. I believe you're the last parishioner. Is that right?"

"Yes. There's no one else in the sanctuary. I . . . there's discord in my house." He fretfully ran his fingers through his coffee-brown hair. "I've fought with my sister and mother, and I've been short with my daughter. I feel I'm losing control."

"Go on."

"This little boy I brought back from Germany, Joe. He's turning into more than we can handle. He came from the Buchenwald concentration camp. I found him under one of those wooden beds in the barrack, in a hole." He closed his eyes, giving in to the sadness inside his chest as he saw the little boy in his mind's eye. Then he opened his eyes. "He was malnourished and sick." The big man let out his breath and forcefully relaxed his broad shoulders. "Father, you don't know what I saw. In that despicable hell on earth, I thought, how could God allow it? How could He let so many innocent human beings suffer and die? It's beyond comprehension."

The priest waited.

Grayson moved to a folding chair next to the kneeling bar. "Father, when Margie died, God closed a door on me. We had planned to have a big family. I love children, you know. Seeing that little kid was God opening a crack in a window. I fell in love with him the moment I looked into his face. Christ gave this child to me, Father, this one little boy out of hundreds of orphans. I wanted to help him, give him food and water, and medicine. I wanted to give him a chance to survive!"

The priest intoned, "Christ teaches us to give of ourselves to the less fortunate. Isaiah 58:7: 'Share your food with the hungry, and give shelter to the homeless. Give clothes to those who need them, and do not hide from relatives who need your help.'"

"Father, I could do this for him. There is so much I can offer to him. Money is no issue. I have plenty of room in my house. I have the means to provide for this one sweet, cherished soul." He interlaced his fingers tightly around his knees.

"I met a priest from the French Red Cross while we were at Buchenwald. We actually conversed in Latin. He agreed to take care of Joe while I went on with the evac hospital. We left Buchenwald and headed east to Cham, the next town near the Czechoslovakian border. I gave the priest money to help not only Joe but the other orphans, too.

"We had stayed in touch through letters after the war when I had gone back to Mississippi with my unit. He sent me pictures of Joe to show how he was recovering in the orphanage in Zurich. In late June, after our evac unit was deactivated and I was out of the army, I hopped an army air transport plane back to France, and I went on by train to Zurich. There was Joe, looking much better. I was grateful for the care he had gotten at the orphanage. The nuns had been good to him. Joe looked like a real little boy."

He put trembling fingers on the flimsy screen and saw the priest's fixed profile. "But since he's been in our home, he acts like a little fiend. He destroys his toys and tears up his room. When I read to him in the evening, he does pay attention, and when my sister, Mildred, has him listen to music on the radio, he seems to enjoy it. But other times, he fidgets and cries, and now he trembles in my arms like he's scared to death. He's a sharp kid, and I know he can learn, but he's got too many emotional problems. All Joe wants to do is run and hide, and in my house, there're plenty of places where he can. He thinks he's still in Buchenwald.

"I can't make my sister or my mother understand that. They don't have any patience with him. He doesn't eat at the dinner table, maybe because he's too scared or thinks the food's not for him. I can't find the right words to convince him that he can eat the same food as we do. Because of that, he's losing weight. That worries me, Father. I can't bear to see him go hungry. His health is not good.

"At night, he wakes up screaming from nightmares. He wets his bed several times a week. I haven't been able to sleep through a whole night." Grayson tilted his head and began wringing his hands.

"The worst part is I can't communicate with him. He's so traumatized that he can't focus on learning English. And I have so much trouble with the German language that I can't say he's safe and doesn't need to do all these things. We went to Temple Beth-El for their Friday evening service a couple of weeks ago. Maybe it was being around so many people, but he just lost it and started bawling. He was so frightened I had to take him out. He may have had no experience in a Jewish temple before he was at Buchenwald. But I also think that seeing all the Jewish symbols and knowing that he was among Jews might have reminded him of his family who had died, and that's too upsetting for him. He's not ready to meet new people and make friends. Father, I feel helpless as to what to do."

"Why haven't you brought the child to Immaculate Conception to teach him how to pray to the Lord to help him?" asked Father Byrne.

Grayson exhaled slowly.

"You will not bring him to the Church?"

"No." Grayson hesitated and then bravely said, "I am raising Joe as a Jew. That is his heritage and his identity. I respect his family and their religious beliefs."

There was silence. Then Father Byrne said, "If you stand by your decision, are you prepared to take responsibility for this child's soul? Grayson, I want you to reflect more on this. Pray to God and open your heart to hear Him. 'People were bringing even infants to him that he might touch them, and when the disciples saw this, they rebuked them. Jesus, however, called the children to himself and said, "Let the children come to me and do not prevent them; for the kingdom of God belongs to such as these . . . I say unto you, whoever does not accept the kingdom of God like a child will not enter it." '

"God's hand has passed over this child through your rescue from that terrible place, my son. He led you to him for a reason. It is your task now to allow that reason to unfold as you rear him. But for his path to lead to Heaven, you are obliged to teach him to live his life in Christ."

Grayson shook his head. "I've been through all this with my family, Father. My sister, Mildred, and I have had some terrible arguments. She keeps claiming that he'll end up in Hell, that Satan is waiting for him if he doesn't convert to Catholicism. But I told her he already had visited Satan in that concentration camp! Joe needs our love and support, not threats or bullying."

Father Byrne leaned closer to the screen. "Grayson, your intentions were pure when you chose to save this little boy, but it appears you were unprepared for the consequences. Your family is only expressing what they feel is right for the child. Remember that and try to keep your emotions in check when you talk to your sister. Children do not need to hear raised voices.

"I feel your distress about dealing with this child, but I also feel your love for him. Build on that love. It is Christ's love you are trying to instill in the boy. Have patience with him, just as Christ has patience with us. Can you do that?"

"Yes, Father. I will try harder."

"Do not lose faith in the Lord. Let Him into your heart to strengthen you, to give you courage and hope."

"Yes, Father."

"My son, are you truly sorry for your sins? Do you admit your culpability for the unhappiness that has befallen your home?"

"Yes, yes."

"And do you seek forgiveness for your transgressions?"

"I do."

"For your penance, you will say the rosary and make the solemn Act of Contrition."

Grayson kneeled on the bench again and took out his rosary beads. Putting his hands together, he began. "O, my God, I am heartily sorry for having offended Thee . . ."

CHAPTER SIXTEEN

It had started as a miserable day. Joe got out of bed with a headache, a sore throat, earache, and sniffles. Mr. Henry jumped off but didn't slip through the door yet. He slept with Joe regularly, even when he had tossed around in his bad dreams and often ended up on the floor. As Joe went to the bathroom to pee and wash his face, he remembered Grayson had tried to tell him about an appointment with a doctor, using the black book to find the German words. Joe knew the word "doctor," which raised the hair on the back of his neck.

The appointment today was with Dr. Ted Abernathy, Irene's pediatrician. He was a 1932 graduate from the Cornell School of Medicine and had interned at New York City Presbyterian Hospital alongside Grayson. Tall, lean, and balding prematurely, with thin, cold fingers and a gaunt face, he nonetheless had a toothy smile for his young, anxious patients. However, he met his match with Joe.

The nurse finished taking Joe's vital signs and weighing him. He started crying as soon as Dr. Abernathy walked into the exam room. He retreated into a corner behind the exam table and bravely pleaded his case in fast German.

"I know what you're going to do to me. You're one of those Nazi doctors who do medical experiments. I saw the prisoners going in, and they came out on stretchers and went straight to the crematorium. You're going to take out my stomach or try to infect me with dirt or germs. I heard all about it from the other prisoners. You'll cut off my head and slice it in half, and put it in a glass. I know about these things. They did horrible things to prisoners. Please don't do that to me!"

The two men stood speechless. Joe crouched on the floor and wrapped his arms protectively around his knees. He hid his beet-red face, breathing fast.

Grayson said, "God, why did I leave that damn dictionary at home!"

"He said something about the Nazis, and I think he's talking about prisoners and heads." Dr. Abernathy put down his clipboard. "I studied a little German at Cornell."

"Oh, he's talking about the Nazis, all right. He's afraid we'll hurt him as they did to those helpless inmates at Buchenwald. They were absolute monsters with their medical experiments. I had the great misfortune of seeing the results."

Joe squealed as Grayson picked him up and set him on the exam table. "Joe, Dr. Abernathy is not going to hurt you. Get that out of your mind." He lightly tapped the side of Joe's head. "Nicht schaden. Verstehen?"

Joe wrenched Grayson's hand off his arm, and looking right, saw an illustrated poster of a human body showing muscles, arteries, and bones. God in Heaven, they were planning to skin him! But he didn't have any tattoos. He had heard the stories about the Bitch of Buchenwald, the commandant's wife. She had had a taste for "fine art," especially that which adorned the inmates' arms and chests. She had loved their handiwork so much she had them killed to remove their tattoos to hang in her living room. She had used their thumbs as light switches.

Grayson used both hands to keep Joe on the table. The big man got close enough to his face for Joe smelled his sour tobacco breath and a musky perfume odor from his hair. He held Joe's arms while the other doctor looked up his nose, down his throat, in his eyes, and his ears. Then he had to push him to lie down for Dr. Abernathy to thump on his chest and press that cold metal disk on his belly. Joe nearly shook the exam table with his trembling. "Let's see what his temp is." The doctor looked at Joe's chart. "Temperature's up a bit. His throat is pretty red. I want to order a throat culture."

"Joe, please, simmer down. The doctor is going to help you feel better. Nothing's going to hurt." Grayson stroked his head.

Joe sat with his knees tightly closed. His stomach quivered.

Dr. Abernathy said, "Grayson, he's not doing as well as we'd like. The lab should tell us what's going on with his throat. It may be strep. There's fluid behind his ears, too. With his weakened immune system, this could develop into something worse. I'll prescribe penicillin, and I want to see him again in a week. Call me right away if he shows any allergic reaction to the penicillin." Closing the chart, the pediatrician put his pen in the breast pocket of his white coat. "But what concerns me more is his weight. He's lost four pounds, and that's not good. Is he not eating? Any diarrhea or vomiting?"

Grayson folded his arms. "No, he's just not eating."

"No appetite? Or just doesn't like the food?"

"It's . . . no appetite. We're having trouble adjusting at home. He doesn't sleep well. He has nightmares about the Buchenwald camp."

Dr. Abernathy studied Joe. "His color is pale. Perhaps some B-12 and vitamins will help. If Joe loses any more weight, we may need to hospitalize him. Failure to thrive is what I'm going to put down as his condition for today." He opened the chart and wrote more notes and then sat on his wheeled stool. Grayson also sat in a chair. Joe poised himself to jump off the exam table. Grayson held onto him by his knee.

"To be honest, Grayson, he's in bad shape. Grayson, I know this may sound a little unconventional, but just observing him and listening to what you're telling me about his problems at home, with the nightmares and the lack of appetite, he's showing signs of depression."

Grayson nodded. "I never thought children could be depressed, but I guess I was wrong."

Joe slid off the table and sat on the floor next to Grayson's feet, exhausted.

"Does he have trouble concentrating?"

"He can't concentrate at all. According to my sister, he spends a lot of time under his bed. And he was hiding in his closet until I put a lock on the door. I've been so busy catching up with my own patients that I don't spend as much time as I should with him. But when I do, he acts the same way with me. Trying to teach him English is just impossible because he's so fearful all the time. However, he does seem to enjoy me reading to him. He likes books. Do you think he might be mentally disabled? Should we talk to a child psychiatrist?"

Dr. Abernathy answered with sincere care on his face. "Yes, I think so. I wish I had some answers for you, Grayson. Despite how he's behaving, I think there're some smarts between those ears. Let me make a call to the psych department at Presbyterian Hospital in New York. They have a children's wing, and maybe they'll have some advice."

"Please, do, Ted. I'm willing to try anything. I wish there was some medication to help relax him. We've got to get him to eat and get a good night's sleep."

Rising, the doctor said, "I'll let you know about the throat culture, hopefully later today."

After setting a follow-up appointment, Grayson and Joe left the medical office. On the way home, they stopped back at Woolworth's to get more nuts, and Joe cooperated by eating a few walnuts. Grayson said, "Good boy, Joe. I'll add nuts to Rose's grocery list."

Dinner started as a sedate, funereal exercise. Rose had made a simple meal of turkey and dumplings, cooked dill carrots, succotash, and a gelatin salad with fruit. Nina Cassandra and Aunt Elvie ate with their usual piggish gusto. Between bites, they discussed how the garden phlox was holding up along the front porch and the organist's recital coming up at the parish this coming Sunday afternoon. Frau Dead Fish Eyes checked on the children out of the corner of her eye as if daring them to display bad table etiquette. Grayson pushed around his dumplings more than putting them on his fork. His tension headache overpowered his appetite. Girding his emotional loins, he said, "Honeybun, what did you do today?"

Irene shrugged. "Nothing." She stared at her plate glumly.

"Oh, now that should have made for a long day."

"What did you say about your little friend, Mollie?" asked Mildred.

"I forget." Irene took a bite of her gravy-coated turkey and put down her fork. "I'm done. Can I leave?"

"Now, look here," said Mildred. "Since you didn't finish your plate, you'll be hungry in an hour and will be begging for some cookies or something else that won't add any nutrition to your diet."

Irene eyed her father for help.

"Irene, try a little more." Grayson looked to his left to see what Joe was doing.

Joe liked Jell-O. This serving had pineapple bits and maraschino cherries in it, and it was easy to chew. Sliding it down his sore throat would feel good too. Looking at it, he forgot his self-imposed finger food rule and used his spoon to cut into the cherry gelatin—bad mistake.

Frau Dead Fish Eyes reached for his hand. "Your right hand! Use your right hand! Must I always remind you?"

Grayson grabbed Joe's hand away from her. "You'll do no such thing! He eats with his left hand! I told you to leave him alone!"

Mildred threw knives at her brother with her eyes.

"You two! Stop that right now! I won't tolerate this arguing!" the old biddy shouted from the far end of the table.

Grayson returned volleys at both women. "He's left-handed. Stop living in the dark ages and accept it. He's got to eat, and he has to do it any way he can. Can't you see he's been losing weight?"

"As I've said before, when he's hungry enough, he'll eat." Nina Cassandra spoke to Elvie. "Pass the succotash, will you?"

"Maybe he has a tapeworm. I've heard that will make you lose weight." Elvie lifted the gold-edged china bowl and handed it to her sister-in-law.

"Aunt Elvie, please! Not in front of the kids," said Grayson.

"It's the devil's hand," Mildred muttered under her breath.

"Mil, that's an old superstition. He'll use his left hand for anything he wants, whether it's using a spoon or holding a pencil or wiping his butt."

"Grayson! For shame!" The queen bee almost rose out of her chair.

"There's no more discussion about it."

Joe's stomach was so tied up in knots he knew the Jell-O wouldn't stay down, so he put down his spoon. All this uproar made him want to crawl under the table.

His hope for a calmer evening was further dashed when two of Grayson's doctor friends, Morey Allen and his wife Alice, and Stan Madison and his wife, Beverly, came over to meet him. Even though his head and his ears hurt, he had to stand politely while the guests fussed over him. He wanted to go to bed, or preferably under it.

After about an hour of conversation and listening to *The Victor Borge Show* on the radio and eating Rose's world-famous cherry pie with vanilla ice cream, the visitors left. The day was mercifully over, and it was time for bed.

If Grayson was still working at the hospital and Mildred was out of the house, Rose cheerfully volunteered to help Joe get ready for sleep. She loved to read to him while sitting in the rocking chair and did not teach him any English words. Joe would be so tired that he would just lie still with his eyes closed. He didn't mind if Irene came in to listen. Nina Cassandra and Aunt Elvie never offered to put him to bed, nor would they be inclined even to say good night to him or Irene. They declared their child-rearing duties were long behind them, and they deserved their rest.

The white and blue ceramic tiled bathroom had two doors, one to Joe's room and the other to Grayson's. This room was always spotless. Grayson's only uncompromising demand was that the bathrooms and the kitchen be kept clean. Mildred made sure that the two cleaning ladies scoured these rooms to a surgeon's operating theatre standards. White lace curtains over the small window above the tub were routinely taken down and laundered, and the sink and the floor were thoroughly polished. Even Joe's rubber duck, Herr Ente, got a weekly soak in a bleach solution. Tonight, an unopened bottle of Kreml shampoo stood on the ledge, and a new bar of Ivory soap sat in the built-in wall tray. Herr Ente sat with sightless red eyes on the tub shelf, preparing to be drowned.

On this humid evening, guardian and ward climbed the stairs to Joe's bedroom. After laying out his Winnie-the-Pooh pajamas and turning back his bedspread and bed sheet, Grayson led him in his undershorts into the bathroom. Joe got a clean bath towel and washcloth from the closet. Grayson started the water and held out his hand to get the temperature warm but not hot. He knelt at the tub with his shirt sleeves rolled up and his back to Joe. He put the plug into the drain, and the tub began to fill.

Joe stopped and looked at Grayson's back, towel in hand. Voices whispered in his stuffy, aching ears, ethereal and ominous. He wiped his runny nose with the back of his hand and rammed his fingers in his ears, trying to clear them to hear better.

"Come on, Joe. Put the towel down and get in."

Joe did not move.

The SS officer's steel-gray wool uniform was well-fitted and immaculate from his hat with the silver eagle's wings and death's head, Totenkopf, insignia sewn above the shiny black brim down to his gleaming, knee-high black boots. His thin leather strap fitted diagonally across his broad chest and hooked to his belt with the buckle showing the ubiquitous Nazi swastika. His riding crop, an indispensable piece of equipment, was tucked under his belt conveniently on the left side. The Iron Cross and other medals hung on his coat breast pockets; the shoulder boards with silver pigtails indicated that he held an important rank, as did the decorative trim on his sleeves. He wore a swastika armband.

The tub nearly overflowed with gallons of soupy excrement. It was the same human waste as was in the open pits behind the barracks. Joe knew what else was in those god-awful trenches. How many countless times had he seen an unsuspecting man relieving himself at one of those nasty pits only to be pushed into it by an SS guard. As the poor man scrambled to get out, the Nazi would kick him again in the head and laugh. This appalling scene would go on until the guard grew bored, and then he would tell another prisoner to hold the ill-fated man down beneath the surface, drowning him in the muck.

That would not happen to Joe. He would die by any other means before suffering that humiliating death. He began shaking. Before realizing his mistake, he looked directly into the SS officer's large, clear, grey eyes.

"Joe, what's the matter with you? You look like you've seen a ghoul." The big man rose and went to him.

The shining black boots made for putting bruises on rib cages moved too fast. As Joe backed up toward the door, viselike hands caught him and lifted him high. But, by God, he was going to fight. Taking the Nazi behemoth by surprise, he kicked him as hard as he could in the groin with his heels, and the hands immediately loosened. For good measure, he bit down on the meaty web between the brute's thumb and first finger.

"Damn! What's gotten into you, boy?"

Joe dropped to the floor, but the monster overtook him. Screaming like a banshee, he fought, swinging his fists and kicking, flailing vainly in the air. Into the tub he went. He slipped, and his head went under. Panicked that he would be held down, he grabbed the edge and pulled himself up, splashing the Nazi. Hoping to blind him, Joe pushed excrement in his face and then slid out and headed toward the door.

"Millie! Millie! Come up here! I need your help! Now!"

Joe's hands were too slippery to turn the glass doorknob. Fast, thumping feet hit the carpeted stairs, and the door burst open.

"What's going on here?"

"Get him! He's gone crazy!" Grayson crawled about the floor on his hands and knees, reaching for Joe with a bleeding hand.

Mildred couldn't catch him either. He quickly went around her and dove under the bed. Breathing hard, he pushed himself against the wall.

"Grayson, what in the world is happening? Why is your shirt all wet?"

Her brother stood and pushed wet hair out of his eyes. He barked, "Something got him spooked, and I couldn't get him to stay in the tub. C'mon. You get on the other side of the bed, and we'll coax him out."

Grunting as they got down on the carpet, they peered at Joe, who had tucked himself under the headboard.

Trying to calm his breathing and his heart, Grayson forced his voice to a serene tone. "Joe, you can come out now. You don't have to have your bath tonight. There's no reason to be scared." He bent his head to catch Joe's eyes.

Silence.

"Joe Kaufmann, you get out from under this bed. You've been a very disobedient boy, and you'll get into worse trouble if you don't mind us!" said Mildred.

"C'mon, boy. You're sick, and you'll get cold from being wet. You need to get into your PJ's." Grayson's annoyance rose despite his effort to keep it under control.

Joe's heart knocked in his chest.

Grayson and Mildred got on their knees as if in prayer and faced each other across the bed. They waited. After a few moments, they wearily got to their feet. Grayson wiped his face and looked at his injured hand.

Mildred went into the bathroom. "What a mess in here! There's water all over everywhere." As she began mopping the floor with a bath towel, Grayson tended to the bite on his hand. It alarmed him that Joe had broken the skin, drawing blood. A human bite could become easily infected, so he cleaned and bandaged it carefully.

"What happened to your hand?" Mildred saw the bloodied cotton balls in the plastic wastepaper can.

"Joe bit me." Grayson shut the medicine cabinet mirror with a bang. "I'm losing it with him. The patience of Job is what I need." He met his sister's eyes. "And I don't need any advice from you."

Joe heard the two sets of feet walk out of his room, but the door was not closed completely. In his nakedness, he lay on his back, looking at the underside of the box springs.

He didn't have the English words to tell the big man that he feared being thrown back into that sickening tub of human waste. It was just another particularly sickening act of cruelty. He knew it was his vision of the Nazi officer that made him fly into a panic. Why did he fight his guardian? What he feared most was the tone of voice he had heard. His guardian, his sole advocate in this crazy place, had lost his patience with him. Joe didn't understand what he meant by the word "Job," but his point was clear. The man who had saved his life was done with him.

This scene in the bathroom and constant harassment from the people in this evil castle was driving him to the brink. He began to cry. He couldn't go on like this. The camp experience had not ended when men with big red cross symbols on their helmets had loaded him into that noisy ambulance truck. Buchenwald went with him in his mind and his heart. The memories had clung like the scabs on his face. Picking them off made the bug bites bleed again, like the flashbacks he tried to pick off his heart.

Frustrated rage made him beat the carpet with his fists. He so much wanted to tell off the lot of them! They never allowed him to explain his side of things, for example, the annoying hassle of the reading and writing lessons with that impossibly demanding woman. He could already read and not just those simple two or three-word sentences out of some child's religious book. He could read adult books and newspapers. And if he had that black book, he'd soon show that witch he could copy words even in cursive and answer questions and fill in the blanks. But the time he had touched the dictionary as it lay on the end table in the living room, all three of the old bovines had torn into him as if he were about to break a priceless crystal heirloom. Confused and frightened, he had raced into the basement to hide between the furnace and the cinderblock wall. When he had caught his breath and had begun thinking, his fear evolved into no less hatred than what he had felt toward the villainous SS guards.

He had no one to communicate his feelings. The frustration and anger and resentment had turned inward into a mud hole of misery, numbness, and emptiness, just like the eyes of the prisoners who came back after working in the quarries for twelve hours straight if they were lucky enough to come back at all. The mire of debasement was a polluted, stinking morass that sucked in one's feet and soul. There was no way to get it off, no clean water to wash away the despair, the hopelessness, the suffering, the blood pouring from bullet wounds of the men who ran toward the barbed-wire fences.

Death. What a respite that would be! Joe always wanted to sleep; he was always tired. What relief it would be to go to sleep, never waking to face another day. But the dreams came at night, torturing him. The only proper rest he would get would be to be dead. That would solve his problems. No more screaming, no more pushing him to eat, no more baths, no more hearing the gunshots, no more seeing the prisoners falling over during roll calls in the middle of the night. And no more trying to remember the faces of his mother and father.

As he thought more, he realized how he was never welcomed here in the first place. This was it. He had to get out of this barbaric place once and for all.

CHAPTER SEVENTEEN

Joe woke up to complete silence. After a few moments of listening, he slowly crawled out from under the bed and saw a faint light from under the bedroom door. The alarm clock on the nightstand read 12:22. He put on a pair of undershorts and cautiously tiptoed out of the bedroom. Joe knew all the adults were heavy sleepers. But he needed to know who was still downstairs with that light on. He silently stepped down to the bottom of the staircase to see Grayson in his undershirt sitting in his favorite easy chair in the family room, reading his New American Bible. As quietly as he could, he went back up and soundlessly shut his bedroom door.

Joe locked the bathroom door that opened into Grayson's room. He searched the bathroom closet first. There were stacks of towels and washcloths, boxes of tissues, toilet paper, first aid supplies, lotion bottles, toothbrushes, wrapped soap, a small rubber hose with a bulb at the end of it (who knew what that was for), and a whole lot of dusty things that had not been used in ages. Then he went to the medicine cabinet. Grayson kept his razor there, a small cardboard box of razor blades, Burma Shave Cream, plus an unopened tube of Ipana toothpaste, Tussy deodorant, Listerine mouthwash, a hairbrush, a tin of aspirin, and a couple of combs. Joe picked a metal comb that had a long, pointed handle. It might work.

He padded into his room. Quietly dragging a chair to the window, he stood on it and unlocked the latch, and with force, pushed up the front panel. The evening summer warmth blew in gently. Below was the driveway, lit by a penetrating security lamp attached to the side of the castle. The ageless white oaks in the expansive front yard would be the only witnesses to his next undertaking. A full, ivory moon hung in the star-filled night sky.

Grayson sat in his leather easy chair, his Bible in his lap, his eyes closed tightly, and his hand on his high, strong forehead. "Dear God, please give me guidance on what to do with Joe. I've lost my temper with him, and I feel I've come to the end of the road with him. I want so much to help him, but I can't reach him. Please give me the strength to keep trying to connect with him. Show me how I can make him understand. Take away his fear and mistrust. Please get him to eat. Comfort him when he has nightmares. I will do anything to make this child whole and happy. Tell me how I can touch his heart. I beg You to give me the courage to mend this child, my ward. In Christ's name, amen."

Grayson crossed himself and opened his eyes. He turned to the Book of Psalms.

Before beginning his work, Joe knew the comb would not complete the job. He needed something bigger and sharper. The alarm clock had a glass cover on its face. Joe took it into the closet which had been carelessly unlocked and shut the door. Wrapping lots of sweaters around it to muffle it, he struck it once on the wooden floor. He waited to hear any sound outside the closet. Hearing nothing, he unwrapped the clock to see that it had a nice crack in the glass. Using one of Grayson's razor blades, he worked it apart from the frame in two big pieces. Perfect!

Back at the window, he stopped again and thought. He pulled out a pair of pants and a T-shirt from his dresser drawer and laid them in the rocking chair. Standing on a straight-backed chair, he began the tedious task of quietly punching a hole in the screen with the comb handle.

Grayson found the verses that comforted him. "Hear me, Lord, and answer me, for I am poor and oppressed. Preserve my life, for I am loyal; save your servant who trusts in you. You are my God; pity me, Lord; to you I call all the day. Gladden the soul of your servant; to you, Lord, I lift up my soul."

Once the metal wire broke, Joe used his fingers to loosen and tear apart the webbing. The hole became as large as a fist, although his fingers were getting scratched. He'd have to hurry for fear of losing his nerve.

Grayson brought the Bible closer to his face to read the small print in the weak light. "Lord, you are benevolent and forgiving, most loving to all who call on you. Lord, hear my prayer; listen to my cry for help. In this time of trouble I call, for you will answer me."

Now it was time for the broken piece of glass. Joe had to be careful because his hands were slippery from the blood oozing out of his fingers. First, he would cut the screen wide enough to push out his clothes, and then he'd slip through. If he put on his clothes and then jumped, they would tear and make too much noise on the jagged edges. If he survived the leap to the ground, he'd have them there to put on hastily so he could run away. Where he would go, he'd figure out later—so commencing with the piece of glass . . .

"Be my rock of refuge, a stronghold to save me. You are my rock and my fortress; for your name's sake lead and guide me . . . Into your hands I commend my spirit; you will redeem me, Lord, faithful God."

Grayson heard something. He jerked up his head and waited. Then he heard it again. As if God Himself had touched his shoulder, he sprang out of the chair, his Bible dropping to the floor. His feet moved like the wings of Mercury as he dashed up the stairs, three at a time. When he opened the bedroom door, he shouted, "Joe! No! Joe!"

He saw him squeeze through the broken screen and disappear.

"Noooooo!"

Grayson banged on Mildred's door. "Millie! Wake up! Come downstairs!"

Her door opened immediately.

"Joe fell out of his window!"

"Oh, good God!"

Grayson turned on the front porch light and ran barefoot in the wet grass to the mock orange bushes under Joe's two-story bedroom window. "Joe! What did you do? Why?" He pushed aside the stiff, thick branches. Joe was buried in the middle, face down, inches from the woody crotch of the main limb.

"My baby, my baby!" Grayson couldn't yet put himself in his doctor's frame of mind as he carefully gathered Joe and lifted him out of the foliage. "Mil, get a blanket! He's not got any clothes on!"

Lights turned on from inside the mansion. Nina Cassandra and Elvie hurried out as fast as they could in bathrobes, slippers, and curlers to investigate the commotion.

"He fell out of the window," said Grayson, laying Joe carefully on the grass. The boy did not move.

The two old women looked up at the thirty-foot-high window. "Grayson," said Elvie, "it looks like the screen is torn."

"Did he tear up my window screen?" griped Nina Cassandra.

Elvie pointed to the grass near the bush. "Look. Here are his clothes. He must have thrown them out before he jumped."

Grayson glanced up and then turned back to Joe. He examined him with urgency, searching for broken bones and tender swelling, any signs of internal bleeding. At least his ward was still breathing.

Mildred came back with a blanket. Grayson took it and tenderly wrapped Joe. "Mother, call the ER and tell them we'll be there in five minutes. And call Ted Abernathy. I don't care if you wake him up. Aunt Elvie, can you get a shirt for me? And my shoes? Hurry!"

The elderly women turned back to the front porch. Irene stood in the doorway in her pajamas.

Under the porch lamp, Grayson saw plenty of bleeding scratches on Joe's face, chest, and shoulders. "Mil, my bag's in the study."

Mildred knew exactly what he meant. Grayson always kept a fully packed medical bag in his study for emergencies. When she returned, he took out his stethoscope and listened to Joe's heart and stomach.

Although he seemed not to have broken any bones, internal injuries were a real possibility. Getting him posthaste to the emergency room could be a matter of life or death.

Grayson hurriedly put on his clothes and ran to the four-car garage at the back end of the driveway. Jumping into the Lincoln, he gunned the accelerator and then screeched to a halt for Mildred to get in carrying Joe. On the way to the hospital, Joe woke up, moaning in pain. Grayson was somewhat relieved. That was a good sign. Mildred cradled Joe, his hemorrhaging face on her chest, his lacerated fingers clutching the collar of her robe. He looked into her eyes. He knew who she was, but her long face was blurry.

After being rushed into the ER on a gurney, the overhead lights made Joe squint as a sheet wafted over him. The slamming doors and the loud, terse voices confused him. He tried to shut it all out, but people kept telling him to do things like open his mouth or eyes or wiggle his toes. The chilly room smelled like something too clean, too nauseating. He couldn't stop vomiting. His body hurt so badly that he yelled out when rubber-gloved hands pushed him roughly to his side. Too many faces, both male and female, loomed over him, talking fast all at once. Turned on his back, more hands poked his chest and stomach, no matter how much he put out his injured hands to push them away. He clenched his jaws to keep from crying out as needles jabbed his deeper cuts. Tears of pain streamed down onto his pillow.

He stoically watched the doctor make the stitches with fragile black thread. He didn't understand why he could not feel anything. He noticed bulky white bandages taped on his face and arms, and knees. Stinging antiseptic was mercilessly rubbed into his lesser scratches. His whole body throbbed, but the worst was in his groin. A sticky gloved hand on his private parts made him jump.

The bed began to move. Joe didn't know that he was being wheeled swiftly into an elevator. His nausea and retching started again, and the hands turning him on his side again made him cry out once more. Someone shoved cold metal pan under his face, and he heaved again and again.

After spending time on a flat, metal table and a noisy, monstrous machine hovering over every inch of his body and making a loud, clanking noise, Joe was rolled back into the emergency room. A nurse gave him a shot in his right buttock, and he thought again that he was going to die, even if she didn't push it directly into his heart. It didn't matter that his guardian gently stroked his head, and Frau Dead Fish Eyes stood next to him, shaking her head with discountenance. But before he could come to terms with his demise, he lost consciousness.

CHAPTER EIGHTEEN

A white curtain surrounded Joe's bed. His discomfort now came from something sticking right below the crook of his left elbow. He couldn't feel the rest of his body. A big clear sticky paper held something sharp in place that was buried deep in his arm. A plastic tube from it snaked up to a glass bottle half full of a clear liquid that hung upside down hooked to a pole. This needle hurt, so he pulled off the tape and ripped it out. Blood spurted down his arm, and he gathered a fistful of his sheet with bandaged hands around his elbow to stop the flow. The needle continued to leak under the sheet. Cumbersome white dressings were everywhere, on his legs, chest, hips, and shoulders, even on his face. His nausea was gone, but he couldn't focus his eyes. Gingerly, he touched the string bow behind his neck that tied the gown he wore. Where could he find his clothes and get out of here?

The curtain suddenly drew back, and an overweight nurse who looked positively poured into her white uniform stood looking at her clipboard with a pen in her hand. Joe covered up his arm and the bloodied sheet.

"Well, Mr. Kaufmann, how are you doing? Are you awake or still sleepy? Any nausea?" Peering through her cats-eye styled glasses, she met his unfocused eyes. "Yes, you're awake. I bet you're nice and sore. Took a tumble, didn't you? Well, you're going up to the third floor where it's quiet. You'll sleep better there, and in the morning, we'll feed you a big breakfast!"

Joe caught the gist of some of what she was saying and hoped he'd be able to get to the breakfast before she did.

The nurse looked up to check the glass bottle. She took his temperature and pulse (he gave her his other hand sans needle puncture) and then left. He began to feel dizzy, and he closed his eyes.

"Ah, Joe, did you pull out your line?" asked Dr. Abernathy. He discovered the leaking tube when he saw a big damp spot on the sheet.

Joe lay in bed in his private room on the third floor. When Dr. Abernathy and a nurse tried to insert another needle, he squirmed and fought them weakly.

"Joe, this is just a saline solution. You're dehydrated, and this is going to help you feel better." The doctor pointed to the new full bottle hanging on a pole.

But Joe shook his head. He refused the cup of water as well. He saw Dr. Abernathy talk quietly to the nurse, and she nodded, writing in his chart. It didn't look good. He went back to sleep.

Grayson kept wringing his big surgeon's hands and tapping his sockless loafers on the linoleum floor, his eyes never leaving his ward's face. Joe's lips began to swell, and deep red lines from the bush's woody branches crisscrossed his cheeks and forehead. More superficial scratches marred his throat and upper chest. Bandages covered his many stitches. Grayson hated to see the restraints on his small wrists. That would upset him far more than the needle in his arm. He pulled back the sheet to look at Joe's torso and legs. The bush got him royally in his crotch, thighs, and knees. Bath time would truly be an adventure now.

In walked Mildred, Nina Cassandra, Elvie, and Irene. The old bovines crowded around Grayson, cooing and patting him. They seemed barely interested in Joe. Irene cried, "Daddy!" and clutched her father around his waist.

"My sweet Irene!" he whispered and picked her up, hugging her tightly. His kisses on her lips and face were as wet as the tears filling his eyes.

The little girl turned in his arms to look at Joe. "Is he okay? What are all those scratches and Band-Aids on him? What happened to him?"

"Now, that's enough." Nina Cassandra started to pull her out from Grayson's arms.

"No, Mother. We can't have any secrets here." He set down his daughter, and she grabbed the metal railing of Joe's hospital bed and gazed at her brother. "He had an accident up in his room. He's just sleeping. He'll be okay."

"I brought his clothes," said Aunt Elvie. She laid the garments in a visitor's chair. "How bad is he?"

"He has some pretty deep scratches and bruises and cuts that needed stitches. But no broken bones." Grayson shook his head with visible emotion. "God held out His hand to catch him . . . in the mock orange bush."

"Yes, indeed. We should go to the chapel and have a prayer service to give thanks to the Lord," said Mildred. "I'll call Father Byrne. We'll arrange to have it tomorrow morning. Grayson, you look exhausted. Why don't you come home and get some sleep?"

"No. I've got to stay here with Joe. He's going to be out of his mind when he wakes up and realizes he's in restraints."

"What are those for?" asked Irene, pointing to the leather straps.

"My dear, he pulled out the needle that puts saline solution and other nutrients into his vein. See, it's right here in his arm."

"So, he's dehydrated?" asked Mildred.

"And malnourished. Dr. Abernathy wants to keep him a couple of days to get him eating as well as making sure he's on the mend from his . . . fall."

The women clicked their tongues. They tried again to persuade Grayson to come home with them, but he wouldn't. With Irene in tow, they left, their hearts a bit heavier now that they were forced to actually think about this little boy who had nearly lost his life under their own roof.

The drive home was without discussion. Nina Cassandra reviewed the state of affairs in her mind. *Grayson said that the child was dehydrated and malnourished. My goodness, that sort of thing happens to children in poverty-stricken countries like India or Africa. I never thought the boy was that ill, that under-fed. What is the matter with him? Isn't Rose's cooking good enough for him? She lays out a feast for him three times a day. He's just stubborn, that's all. Crazy little Jew-boy. Strange habits he was taught over there in that foreign country. Is it my fault he won't eat and use proper table manners?*

And destroying my window screen. Who's going to pay for the repair? Perhaps the little hoodlum needs to do some chores around the house to make up for the wanton destruction he's caused. He'll be punished for sure.

But a more worrisome thought came into her sixty-eight-year-old mind. What would the ladies in the garden club say if they knew she allowed this child to do such a crazy thing as jump out a two-story window? Indeed, they would read about his admission to the hospital in the *Ithaca Journal*. Whether this child's mishap could be kept out of the paper was uncertain. Her friends would want to know why he had been admitted. Such goings-on were their favorite topic of conversation—who had been admitted to the hospital and why; who had been released and who had died. And since Nina Cassandra's son was a surgeon at Tompkins County Hospital, why, she was practically in charge of the institution herself and therefore would know everything that went on. Grayson did his best to keep quiet about his patients, never mentioning anyone by name. But Ithaca was a small enough town that Nina Cassandra and her friends at the beauty shop could figure out who was getting a gallbladder operation or a hysterectomy. But Nina Cassandra knew she had to anticipate the inquiries about this embarrassing debacle and decide on an appropriate explanation. Sunday was only two days away, and she would have to answer to her friends at the parish.

Nina Cassandra could not suppress that worm of discomfort--the realization that this child jumped out of a second-story window of her home and almost died. Would someone call the police? Would questions be raised about how the boy was being taken care of?

Between all the adults in the Pierce mansion, seven children had been reared. Yes, this child came out of suspicious circumstances. He had been a challenge at best and a train wreck at worst. Even Nina Cassandra, the matriarch of this family, couldn't help but feel an uncomfortable twinge of guilt that she could not rationalize away in her mind. When it was all said and done, she was the final word for the family. She had the responsibility of the affairs of the Pierce clan.

And this little boy had brought her to her arthritic knees without the first blink of an eye. Not unlike her son, she began wringing her hands.

CHAPTER NINETEEN

Joe came back to the Pierce home after three days of near force-feeding and an I.V. line in his arm. He had a total of forty-one stitches over the front of his body. Grayson would check them in the coming days and remove them as the cuts and scratches healed. Joe could barely make it to the bathroom.

His guardian gave strict orders to both family and staff that Joe was never to be left alone, day or night. Mildred made out a schedule and taped it to a cabinet door in the kitchen. Even Irene was assigned time to spend with him. Meanwhile, she went to work drawing get-well cards for him while he slept.

A grave and subdued aura lingered in the Pierce mansion. The radio stayed off. Voices spoke in hushed tones. Rose did her cooking and other chores as quietly as she could. She was so worried that she went upstairs and cracked open Joe's bedroom door to look in on him every twenty minutes or so.

****

Grayson put his mighty surgeon's hands on the edge of the porcelain kitchen sink, staring out the window at the wrens and cardinals happily indulging at the birdfeeder that hung on the redbud tree. But his attention was not on the birds. He rapped his heel impatiently on the floor.

Mildred sat at the old, scuffed kitchen work table, finishing her toast and coffee. She opened the fashion section of the Sunday *New York Times* and began reading.

Grayson turned around and folded his arms across his expansive chest. "I've been an idiot. Just a big, fat idiot." He shook his head in disgust.

Mildred put down the paper, took off her half-glasses, and looked up at him.

"I've mishandled this whole situation with Joe, and I should be taken behind the garden shed and whipped. God, I've been such a fool! He's been suffering since the day I brought his home, and I've just been blind to it."

"We all have, brother."

Grayson hesitated as if the words were too difficult to speak. "Mil, I think he was trying to kill himself."

"But he threw his clothes out first. He was trying to run away."

"What's the difference? He believed he was trapped here. He had to get out anyway he could, and he was willing to risk hurting, even killing himself to do it. What does that say about me being his guardian? That kid deserves a better parent than what I've been to him."

"It's not just you, Grayson. None of us have been able to handle him."

Grayson ignored her last words as she implied that this circumstance was Joe's fault entirely. "I was too eager to get back to work. I already had a waiting room full of patients before I even knew when I'd be coming back."

"Grayson, that only shows what a good doctor you are. People in this town trust you over all those other quacks who pretend they know how to use a scalpel. The Pierce reputation goes back a long way, you know."

"Yes, but I've screwed up my priorities. I have to make it right. I *will* make it right." He looked toward the kitchen door. "Mil, where is Rose? I've made my decision on what to do, and I need her help."

Not only did Rose come running up from the basement (she had been folding clothes), but Nina Cassandra, Aunt Elvie, and Irene also gathered around. Anne, Rose's young helper, was watching Joe.

"When Ted Abernathy sees him in a couple of weeks and thinks he's well enough, we're going on a long trip. I'll be taking Joe up to Bowman Lake State Park, maybe Lake Erie. We might even visit Niagara Falls. Rose, I want your help in getting ready for it."

"What?" shouted the Greek chorus.

"Oh, can I go, too, Daddy?" Irene begged.

"No, I'm sorry, my dear. This trip is going to be just for Joe and me. We need some time together by ourselves. Besides, you've got to go to school in a few weeks."

"But--"

"That's it, Irene. I'm not going to change my mind."

Nina Cassandra twisted her mouth in predictable disapproval. "Grayson, this is out of the question. He's not well enough."

"That's why I'm going to have Ted Abernathy check him out first. Joe's on the mend now. The twenty-four-hour watch stays in effect until we leave. I'm going to rearrange my surgery schedule and pawn off my patients to the other surgeons." He looked at his sister, who was busy studying Joe's "watch" schedule on the cabinet door.

"How long will you be gone?" asked Aunt Elvie.

"At least two weeks, maybe longer. I'm going to focus on teaching him English, and this trip will be as long as it takes to accomplish that. There'll be no distractions from you womenfolk." He was aware of the staring female eyes. "Don't worry. I'll send you all postcards and call you from time to time."

****

Grayson and Mildred stood in Joe's room while Joe was downstairs holding the cat and watching Rose and Anne rush about with last-minute preparations. Mr. Henry purred and kneaded his sharp claws into Joe's shoulder. Nina Cassandra rocked with disapprobation in her Lincoln rocker in the music room, and Aunt Elvie sat on the couch watching the commotion.

"I hope we haven't forgotten anything." Mildred touched the starched pillowcase on the bed. She went to the high bureau, opening the top drawer and looking in. "Have we packed enough underwear and socks?"

Grayson stared at the closed window, the torn screen behind it. "If not, we'll just buy more along the way. We'll be hitting some towns, Albany or Rochester. Since I'll be teaching Joe English, we'll go to the libraries there where there'll be no distractions."

"I still don't think this is a good idea. What if he tries to run away again?"

"My legs are longer than his. I think I'll be able to catch him." He took his sister's arm and turned her to face him. "This trip is necessary, Mil. I've given this a great deal of thought since his accident. There's too much upheaval in this house and too many people trying to boss him. He needs the attention of one adult, not four. I am the most important person in his life, and I intend to make him understand that."

He stepped back and looked around. "In the meantime, I want you to redecorate this room."

"What? There's not a thing wrong with this furniture. It's a wonderful guest room."

"That's just the point, Mil. It's a guest room, not a little boy's room. Go through your decorator magazines and find what's in fashion for little boys' rooms. I don't care about the expense. Get every piece of wood out of here. Repaper the walls, take out the carpet, and put down throw rugs, lamps, animal pictures, bookcases, anything that will make this a real kid's room. And, of course, get the screen fixed."

He turned toward the door and then stopped. "Oh, by the way, take down that crucifix. I plan to purchase a Star of David knickknack to hang there if I can find a temple or synagogue." He met Mildred's offended eyes. "And remove his missal from the bottom drawer in his nightstand. I'll find a Jewish missal or whatever they call it." His look of finality made Mildred keep her mouth closed.

Nina Cassandra held back her son as the rest of the family went out the front doors to the wood-paneled Ford Super Deluxe station wagon parked in the driveway. Grayson followed her into his study. She took a banker's yellow envelope from the middle drawer of his cherry wood desk, which had been acquired right before the start of the Civil War by Grayson's grandfather, Dr. Seymour H. Pierce. It was overloaded with piles of folders, papers, pens, a wire basket full of bills, a telephone, a phonebook, a small tin bowl of rubber bands, a red glass paperweight, and several moth-chewed books, some opened, others closed. The two cleaning ladies, Phyllis and Valerie, grudgingly had to pass over this mess when they cleaned the room.

"What's this?" Grayson looked inside the envelope to find several large denominations of bills. He counted three hundred dollars.

"It's for the child." Nina Cassandra tightened her grip on her cane.

"But--"

"Don't argue with me, boy. You know how I hate it when you waste my time questioning my motives. Now you go on. He's waiting for you in the car."

Awkwardly, Grayson pecked his mother's creased cheek and said, "Thank you." Nina looked as uncomfortable as he did and turned her face away.

CHAPTER TWENTY

They made good time driving east from Ithaca to Bowman Lake State Park. Grayson rolled down the windows and let the warm summer wind blow through the station wagon. Joe looked out at the fields and farmhouses and the trees and hills. He had not been on a trip since arriving at the Pierce castle six weeks ago. He had had no idea where he was going then, either.

After paying the entrance fee at the park gate, Grayson drove on, passing small cabins, picnic tables, playground areas, rough-hewed camp signs, and on the right, a line of pine trees that partially blocked a large lake. Joe's interest rallied. He would love to stop and look at the water. Moving on, he observed some couples sitting in lawn chairs around smoking cookout grills. The meaty smell made his mouth water. But the car kept going. It turned south on a gravel road at a two-way stop sign. Joe saw a green and white road sign but couldn't make out the English words.

"We're going to a trailhead where we'll set up camp," Grayson explained.

Joe frowned. He was baffled.

After several minutes of driving, Grayson stopped the car off the road at a secluded spot. "Yes, this is the place." He turned off the engine and peered through the windshield. "Here's where my dad, my brother Al, and I came for our hiking trips when I was your age." He smiled at Joe. "We couldn't talk my mother or Millie into coming with us. They said it was too far away from a bathtub. Ha! Ha!" He climbed out of the car, and Joe followed suit.

The campsite was a circular, bare dirt site sheltered by wonderful-smelling pine trees. In the middle lay a pile of softball-sized rocks, ashes, and burnt wood. Brown pine needles littered the ground. Ubiquitous knotty roots made walking difficult.

Joe kept looking back at the car as they walked on. When the big man took out a knife from its leather sheath hanging his belt, his heart leaped with sudden fear. He hadn't noticed it before. The man used it to cut short tree branches into smaller pieces. He put some unwieldy brush in Joe's arms to carry back to the campsite. He piled all of it over the old burnt wood and rocks. Then he went to the back of the station wagon and took out an ax.

Joe looked at the nearby tree stands. He had overheard some east European prisoners talk in their broken German with his father about what had happened to the people of the other towns when the mobile killing units, beweglishe Totungmaseinheiten, had swept through three years prior. They said the Nazis and the local police had marched the Jews into woods like these. After being forced to dig large, deep pits, they were then ordered to remove their clothes. Then the obedient victims had waited at the edges of the muddy chasms. They had fallen face-forward after the bullets had entered their backs.

The similarity to this place made Joe tremble. He frantically looked around. He didn't know these woods, and the man did. Where could he run to escape? The sound of the ax hacking tree limbs made him think of human limbs being chopped. He shut his eyes tightly and put his hands over his ears to stop hearing the whacks.

The man seemed to ignore him. The gigantic brute gathered an armload of cut wood and walked back to the campsite. He dumped it alongside the rest of the kindling. A rustling in the trees made Joe look up to glimpse a flock of screeching blackbirds taking flight.

"We'll make a fire when we come back from our hike." Grayson walked back to the car to put away the ax. He put on his weighted knapsack and locked the trunk. "Let's go, partner."

Joe wanted to know where they were going and what was in the big man's backpack. He still had that sinister knife on his belt. He had plenty of firewood, plus matches, and even a small can of kerosene in the back of the station wagon. The fire would soon be blazing. Instead of being given a mercifully quick bullet, he would fall victim to the knife. This place in the woods was right. The opportunity was right. The weapon was right. No. This was how his father had been murdered.

Unshed tears made Joe's throat tighten. The Nazi monster's hand compressed his like a vise. He had no choice but to let this diabolical titan drag him deeper into the shadowy, ominous forest. No one would see him. If he cried out, no one would hear him. Even when he tried to hold back, his legs kept moving. The gigantic, evil Nazi cannibal looked down at him every few steps, smiling and saying something. But Joe's ears roared.

When his feet tripped over a tree root and his knees hit the dirt, Joe began to sob. When the bearish hand loosened, he wanted to get up, but he was too afraid to move. He braced himself for the inevitable.

Instead of the giant's blade, he saw the razor-sharp knife on his father's neck as he was pushed down to his knees. Joe heard the agonizing, guttural sounds he made as the blood began to pour out. Everyone—the newly arrived women prisoners in their headscarves, their children still in their winter coats, the camp-weary, dirty, unshaven men in their black and gray uniforms—no one would step in to stop this savage act. They just gawked with the perverse curiosity of medieval villagers watching a beheading.

Joe shook so badly he couldn't breathe. Big hands lifted him and went forward.

Finally, the walking stopped. Everything was still. Joe put his hand weakly on the man's collar, his face buried in his sweaty neck. He waited, shaking uncontrollably. The prisoners did this during roll call in the dead of night or twice during the day. They just waited. The SS guards, in their long overcoats and boots and riding whips and military hats and swastika armbands, would pass through the lines, impulsively choosing their prey. On occasion, a foolish prisoner would fall on his knees and start weeping and begging for his life. His quick death by a Lugar pistol would be a reminder to all others that only strict discipline would keep them alive . . . maybe.

Joe did not think the man had a pistol. The brute's hands were lethal enough. Still, the knife would be more efficient. He was nothing more than a quick morsel to this leviathan. "Bitte. Bitte. Mach schnell."

The man pushed him back to look into his small, tear-streaked face. All Joe saw was the firm mouth, the straight, oily nose, the black sunglasses.

Grayson put him down and took the dictionary out of his knapsack. He turned several pages. "Sagen mich. Sie angst haben? Talk to me. Are you scared?"

Joe nodded.

He searched for another word. "Warum?"

Joe's face melted in resignation.

"Warum? Why, Joe?" Grayson waved a hand at the woods around them. "It's beautiful out here. The sun is shining, and we're taking this nice walk. There's a waterfall on the other side of that hill. Can you hear it?" He rubbed Joe's arm. "What's wrong, kiddo? You're shaking like a leaf."

"Sie warden mich toten."

Grayson shook his head, not understanding.

Joe grabbed the dictionary and impatiently turned pages. He pointed to the word 'Totung,' drew a finger across his neck, then pointed at the sheathed knife. He waited while the man studied the word and its English translation.

Grayson sat on a log and put Joe in front of him. He took off his sunglasses and tightly held Joe's shoulders. He shook his finger sideways. "Joe, Ich nicht tote Sie. I am not going to kill you. Do you understand? Verstehen?"

Joe squinted as he faced the westward sun. Even though Grayson was using improper German grammar, he understood what his guardian said. But he didn't believe him.

"Ich nicht toten Sie. Ich liebe Dich. I love you, Joe." He went back to the dictionary. "Halluzination?" He tried to use the German pronunciation. "Von Buchenwald?" He showed the word "halluzination" to Joe. He pushed pages in the dictionary again. "Blitzruckseite? Are you having flashbacks?"

Still not wanting to give up believing what would be his inevitable fate, Joe rattled off in German, "But we came out to this forest where there's no one around, and you have a knife on your belt, and you'll cut my throat, and then you'll take me back to the camp and build a fire and cut me into pieces and cook me over the fire and eat me.

You even brought the matches and oil to light the fire. You'll bury my bones, and nobody would ever know what happened to me, and you'll go back to the hospital and keep doing your medical experiments. You want to kill me because I'm a Jew!" He cried and cried, letting his absolute terror engulf him.

Grayson answered, "Joe, I'm not going to hurt you! I have no idea what the hell you're saying, but you don't have to be afraid!" Sweat streaked down under his sunglasses, dripping off his jaw. It was blazing hot this afternoon. "My, my, goodness. What can I do?"

Joe allowed Grayson to gather him up and press his still underweight, tender body firmly against his chest. He kissed his wet cheeks and stroked his black, silky hair. "How can I make you understand? Lord, please, give me some inspiration, some guidance to reach between this kid's ears to make him understand that he's safe with me! He doesn't have to be afraid anymore!"

As the man turned to face the overlook, Joe wondered for a split second if he was going to throw him over the edge. But the powerful arms held him fast, and Grayson rocked him. Joe buried his face into his guardian's neck. His sweaty palms slipped from the man's neck.

"I'm so sorry that you're scared, Joe. I didn't mean to upset you. I'm so very sorry. We came out here to have some fun and enjoy the woods and the peace and quiet, but I guess we're not ready to do that yet."

Joe mustered enough strength to have another go-round with his crying. Tension exploded into screaming wails. But he did not try to get out of Grayson's arms.

"C'mon, Joe. You let it out. It's all right to cry. You have a lot of frustration and anger to get out of your little body. I've been there. Sometimes I want to cry so bad I can't stand it. Out here, nobody's going to care if you cry. You can scream your sweet little head off if you want to. Maybe I'll join you."

Joe choked on his sobs. Tiredness overwhelmed him, and he collapsed and closed his eyes. He was unaware that his guardian carried him back to the campsite, his mouth hanging open just enough for his saliva to slip into his guardian's collar.

CHAPTER TWENTY-ONE

The twigs cracked and popped, and embers glowed in the dying fire. Joe thought he was going to be sick after eating his fourth, slightly burned marshmallow. He reached for the metal thermos of water and waited to burp. The supper of roasted hot dogs, carrot sticks, apple slices, and Rose's Toll House chocolate chip cookies made a satisfying meal. Eating out here in the woods with the mosquitoes and the fireflies was so much more fun than sitting at that dining room table with the old cows.

After waking up earlier, Joe had found himself on top of a sleeping bag. Grayson was busy poking at the fire. Strangely, he was no longer afraid. Now, with the bluish sky darkening behind the pine trees, he nestled himself in Grayson's lap, watching the fire and listening to the crickets.

While gently stroking his small arm, Grayson spoke in his cavernous, gravelly voice. "Joe, I want to tell you some things even though you may not understand it all right now."

Joe looked up to his guardian's heavy-lidded eyes reflecting light from the expiring fire. Grayson leaned over to lie on his side on top of his sleeping bag, and Joe lay down with him to listen.

"When I saw you at Buchenwald, I heard God's voice in my mind. He had closed a door when my Margie died, but He opened a window in you. As the saying goes, the Lord moves in mysterious ways." He cast his eyes benevolently. "Joe, I'm taking care of you as my son. But you had a father, and I know he loved you very much. I'm just taking his place to help you from here on. I'm going to rear you, protect you, educate you, and then send you off into the world so you can find your own place in it."

Joe recognized the word "father." Laying his head on Grayson's chest, he whined in German, "Ich vermisse meine Mutter und Vater. Ich machte nach Hause gehen und mit ihnen sein." I miss my father and mother. I want my parents.

Grayson raised himself to his elbow and reached for the dictionary. Thumbing through the pages, he found the words. "Yes. You want your mother and father. Trauern. Bereiten Kummer."

Joe hung his head. Yes, grief. That was a good word to describe how he felt.

"That's okay, Joe. That's okay. You have to grieve." Turning back to the dictionary, he said, "Joe, Erlernen Sie, mir zu vertrauen. Learn to trust me."

"Ich weis nicht was zu denken." I don't know what to think. "Ich weis nicht, Grayson." He tapped the side of his head. His hand found its way to his knees to scratch his healing scabs.

As Grayson took his hand away, he said, "That's fine, boy. You don't have to think about anything right now. Let's just go to sleep."

Grayson rested his head on his knapsack and gathered Joe into him, spooning him to his stomach. Joe heard his slow breathing. He assumed the man was going to sleep. Grayson's forearm rested like a heavy tree branch over his side, his silver wristwatch ticking with a lightness of insect footfalls. Joe saw again that gold ring with the ruby inset, a tiny bit of sparkle in the moonlight. It didn't look like a wedding ring. He would ask Grayson about it at another time. For now, he closed his eyes. His brain was too muddled to plan an escape. In this place, breathing in the faint arboreal pine scent, the cicadas singing in the black woods, he would sleep a dreamless sleep, a son cradled in his guardian's arms.

CHAPTER TWENTY-TWO

The number one priority was to get Joe conversant in English. Grayson knew that under the paralyzing fear, the anorexia, and the sheer lack of a good night's sleep was the frustration of not being able to communicate what was going on in that cute little head.

After studying the road map for an extraordinarily long time, he pointed to their destination. The next stop on their journey was Albany. With an inquiry at the local chamber of commerce, Grayson would find a bookstore and the county library. He put the dictionary on Joe's lap before starting the car. He knew what Grayson wanted him to do. But he looked up two words first.

"Ich benotige Papier und Bleistift. Paper und pencil, bitte, um, please."

Grayson nodded. "Okay. We'll buy some paper and pencils and some crayons, too, when we get to Albany."

"Danke schon. Thank you." Joe commenced reading the dictionary.

Grayson smiled at his ward. Somebody had taught this young man proper manners even before Mildred had gotten ahold of him.

****

The diminutive wooden child's chair creaked with protest under Grayson's butt. His knees were up to his chin. Groaning, he gave up and sat on the floor and put his elbows on the three-foot-high table. Toddlers and preschoolers ran about, pulling down picture books from the shelves along the walls and tearing out the pages. Ignoring them, Joe flipped through a pitiful book with poorly illustrated pictures of a dog and a little boy running after it. He tried his best to be patient as Grayson pointed to the two and three-word sentences in English, asking him to read them aloud.

But this was boring. These books were for babies. What he wanted to tackle were the volumes like the ones his mother had brought him. However, here in this library, they would be in English. Joe wanted to go to the adult sections on the first floor

"Gerkommen mit mir." Armed with his own German-English dictionary purchased earlier at a bookstore, Joe got up and pushed his guardian to rise also. Annoyed that Grayson took so long to get his bearings, he grabbed the big man's hand and pulled him out of that noisy children's room. They went up the stairs, carrying the paper, the pens, the pencils, and the dictionary.

Joe began in the first section: literary fiction. Only tall enough to examine the bottom three shelves, he searched and searched, hoping to recognize a title or an author. In the 'H's," he found Herman Hesse. He would be a challenging author to try to read in English. Looking further, Joe saw a sign above one aisle with the word "Mystery" printed in large black letters. After finding that word in his dictionary, he went down the rows, turning his head sideways to read titles and authors. Agatha Christie looked intriguing. Among her collection was *The Moving Finger*. He carried the slim book to an empty table in the back of the room. Sitting on his knees in the chair, he began reading. Soon, with the dictionary opened, he started writing.

"What are you doing?" whispered Grayson.

"Vite vords I nicht know," Joe whispered back.

"I am writing down words I don't know," Grayson corrected him.

"Yes. I am viting down vords, words."

After a few minutes, Joe said, "Grayson, you book know?" He held up the mystery novel.

"Yes. I read it a few years ago. Do you know this book? Can you repeat what I just said?"

"Do you know this book? Gut. Bericht erstatten—I vil vite a . . . report for you. Vil you my English look—will you look at my English?" He spoke slowly to get his "w's" pronounced correctly.

"Yes, indeed."

Joe worked on his project for more than an hour. Grayson picked out another book to read for himself. After a while, he got up to stretch his legs and visit the men's room. He asked one of the librarians to keep an eye on his little boy. Joe never wavered from his book; never asked to take a break or get a drink of water; never asked Grayson what time it was. He focused on finding English words to put together that made sense. He copied them carefully, making sure the spelling was correct. The story was interesting. Somebody had been murdered, and a woman detective, Miss Marple, was on the case. He thought he might like to read another book by this author.

He decided to stop after reading sixty pages. When he put down his pencil, he rubbed the side of his left hand on his jeans, trying to clean off the smeary pencil lead. He stood and handed two pages to Grayson for inspection, filled front and back, single-lined, cursive writing. This had been a familiar ritual with his father back in the attic in Berlin. Thank goodness he remembered the cursive lettering. He wanted to impress his guardian.

Grayson took forever reading the papers while Joe stood patiently at his side. Then, the verdict was pronounced.

"Joe, this is exceptionally good. You've not only translated the words, but you've also made out the storyline. How did you learn to write cursive? Okay. Let's go over the grammatical errors."

Joe heard the word "good" and smiled for the first time in a long time. He climbed into the chair.

After checking into a hotel in downtown Albany, Grayson and Joe spent the next several days at the library. Because they came every day, the librarians gave them access to an empty meeting room so they could talk without disturbing other patrons. Grayson worked with Joe's pronunciation, having him read aloud the letters of the alphabet and then numbers. He steered Joe to the young adult section to slow him down, but he had to keep finding more sophisticated books to challenge him.

To add variety, Grayson had him read newspapers and magazines. Much of the news concerned the aftermath of the war in the Pacific theatre. This led to a world map being brought out and geography lessons. Joe's mother had not brought him any books on this subject. At the meeting with the rabbi at Temple Beth-El, Joe remembered being shown the map of Europe and Germany, which he didn't understand at the time. However, with the expansive world map Grayson spread over the entire table, he had a new perspective. Now he knew where the hordes of prisoners had come from with their strange dialects. And he understood he had lived on a different continent in another country. He wrote all this down in a notebook.

What pleased Grayson was Joe's over-enthusiastic interest in everything he read. From the morose, tired, sad-eyed child who only wanted to be left alone under his bed, he had become a cheerful, excited little boy, working diligently to learn his new language. The mastery of English made everything so much easier for him. And he tested his new language skills with the librarians. He fearlessly asked where the water fountain and the restroom were with his guardian keeping him on track with proper pronunciation and the correct placement of the subject and verb. With assurance, he answered questions about his age and where he was from (to be sure, his home was Ithaca, New York). At the hotel, with a bit of coaching from his guardian, Joe asked the concierge where a good restaurant might be and where he could buy a comic book, even though he didn't know what a comic book was. And at the toy section at the Montgomery Ward's department store, Joe paid for a new coloring book, counting out the nickel and pennies.

Grayson inwardly kicked himself repeatedly for past deeds not done, specifically, not considering Joe's lack of basic childhood experiences. He thought about what would have been Joe's upbringing before the concentration camp experience. Common sense told him that the time before would have been when the Nazis had cleaned out the entire Jewish population in Germany. He wondered how Joe and his parents managed to hide for so long during the war. Besides that, the Allies were bombing the country to smithereens. It seemed sheer luck that Joe and his family had survived as long as they did.

Where had he and his parents been living in hiding? Wherever it had been, they still have to have had some access to books for Joe to have had the reading and writing skills he now demonstrated. Joe's exposure to a normal life, with playtime and possible schooling, would have been severely limited or even nonexistent. Maybe he had learned from his parents. Somehow, he had held onto these skills even during the hellacious time at Buchenwald. It was a mystery only Joe could explain.

He decided to give Joe a real test of what he could do. "Joe, write a story about Mr. Henry."

Joe took out a clean sheet of paper. "Story? Geschichte mit Herr Heinrich?"

Grayson stifled a laugh. "Yes. A story about Herr Heinrich, but in German. Describe him. Beschriebung. Write about what he eats, essen, how he sleeps, schlafen. All in German. Alles Deutsche. Understand?"

"Ya, I mean, yes, Grayson." Joe beamed. He liked this assignment.

Grayson studied him carefully. Joe didn't start writing immediately. Wheels of deliberation turned behind that childish knitted brow.

"You know, you're an awfully cute kid,"

Joe grinned sheepishly and bent his head to the paper. He wrote at the top, "Herr Heinrich: Life Eines Konigs."

After twenty minutes, Joe finished the story. Grayson looked at the two pages carefully. He was amazed at the neat, condensed writing. Of course, the essay would have to be translated. When they returned to Ithaca, he would find a German teacher at Cornell University to assess the story. He wanted to know if a professional educator could discern what grade level such writing would reveal.

An unsettling thought came into his head. Joe's apparent ease at reading and writing seemed unusual for a kid he thought was only seven years old. Irene had started first grade before she could master simple sentences, and that had been with much effort. But this essay, with its length and neat, cursive penmanship, looked like the work of a junior high school student. Yet, Joe's baby teeth indicated that he was, indeed, only seven. And he had written down the number "seven" for Rabbi Passow at Temple Beth-El.

The two of them were in a city park one afternoon, taking a break from the library. Joe saw some kids playing on a swing set and a slide several hundred yards away.

"Joe, remember when we visited Rabbi Passow at Temple Beth El?" Grayson spoke slowly for Joe to catch all the words.

Joe nodded.

Grayson studiously ran a fingernail along the rough grain wood of the picnic table where they sat. "He asked you how old you are. And you wrote 'seven.' "

Joe's face darkened with uneasiness. He looked back toward the car. His dictionary was on the front seat.

Grayson took a scrap of paper and a pen from his breast pocket and wrote a date, January 1, 1938, and then wrote the words, "Joe's birthday?"

Joe shook his head. He took the pen and wrote 31 Mai 1938.

Grayson returned the paper to his pocket. "Let's hit the swings." He pointed to the row of swing sets near a couple of seesaw sets. He would save the rest of this conversation for another time.

Another diversion from the rigors of book-learning was going to the movies. *A Tree Grows in Brooklyn* was playing at the Palace Theatre. "This will be another way for you to learn English, and it'll be a lot more fun," said Grayson. Joe had no idea what he was talking about.

The film was more enjoyable than Joe ever imagined. This was way better than just listening to shows on the radio, especially since he had been banished from the music room and had to sit on the bottom of the staircase. But of course, the best part of going to the movies was eating the popcorn. After the movie, he demanded Grayson take him back to the bookstore to buy the novel as soon as possible.

"When we get home, we'll go to the State Theatre and see more movies. But we'll have to take Irene with us," Grayson said as he helped Joe get ready for bed back in their hotel room. "While I'm thinking about it, did you listen to the radio shows at home with Grandma Nina and Aunt Elvie while I was at work?"

"I nicht hear dem gut."

"And why not?"

"Dey not let me listen. I stay on stairs."

With fists on his waist, Grayson shook his head to himself. A mental note: *let the boy sit in the music room during the day to listen to the radio. The nerve of those women!*

CHAPTER TWENTY-THREE

It was a rough night. Joe didn't realize that the moaning was coming from his own mouth. He thought someone other than Grayson was in the hotel room. However, he saw no one in the darkened room. He did not dream of shotgun blasts or corpses lying immobile along the snow-covered electrified fence. His unease had a transparency to it, like fog, that confused him. It was there yet not there.

There was no closet in which to hide. Sitting up in his bed, he heard Grayson still snoring softly in his bed. He barely made out his guardian's white undershirt and shorts. Padding to the bathroom, he lay on the bath mat on the linoleum floor and tried to go back to sleep. But it was too uncomfortable. He kept making little whimpering noises, almost like Irene after being disciplined and feeling sorry for herself.

He got up and went to the big window on the other side of the hotel room. He peeked out the curtain, looking at the street lights three stories below. A few cars rolled by slowly, but he didn't see any people. His head ached.

"Joe? What are you doing?"

Joe turned away from the window, knowing Grayson would be alarmed if he stayed where he was. "Not'ing. I dunt feel gut." He was too tired to cry.

"That's too bad, kiddo. Come lie down next to me." When Joe nestled in, his back snug against the warm, slightly damp chest, Grayson asked, "Did you have a bad dream?" He stroked Joe's head.

"Nein."

"Now, you're supposed to talk in English. Don't revert to German. We had fun today at the park and seeing the movie tonight. You ought to be tuckered out. Why don't you feel well?"

Joe whined again and broke out of Grayson's grasp. He sat on the edge of the bed, his back to Grayson. He rubbed his forehead. "Meine Kopf hurts."

"Does your head hurt? Maybe I can find an aspirin and cut it in half." Grayson got up and turned on the lamp on the hotel dresser. He rummaged through his enormous leather suitcase to find his medical pouch. The bottle wasn't in it. Then he went to the bathroom to look in his shaving kit.

Diese verdammt alten Pyjamas! Joe hated them. He shimmied out of his pajama bottoms, wadded them up, and threw them in a corner, leaving him in his pajama top and undershorts. Crossing his arms, he glowered at the floor, hating everything around him.

He picked up a glass ashtray and began hitting his head with it. Grayson came back into the room with the aspirin tin and a glass of water. "I guess you want to keep that headache," he said mildly as he took away the ashtray. Using a pocketknife, he split the aspirin. While Joe swallowed the pill, Grayson reached for the dictionary. "You are cranky, verruckt. Irritable, reizbar." Joe pushed the glass into his guardian's hand and crossed his arms. His face was a juvenile thundercloud.

As they settled back in bed, Grayson murmured, "I'm too tired to think. You can't be hitting yourself in the head like that. I'll have to deal with you tomorrow." He pressed Joe tightly against his stomach, his substantial leg over Joe's hip, pinning him down.

****

"Wake up, kid. We're gonna blow this town and head north."

Joe opened his eyes groggily. The bedsheet was wrapped three times around his legs, and he couldn't get it untangled. Pushing his messy hair out of his eyes, he vainly helped Grayson pull it away. He turned over and over and ended up on the floor, his temple barely missing the sharp-cornered bed stand.

"C'mon into the shower." Grayson seemed to have no time to wait for him as he headed toward the bathroom.

Joe's eyes stayed tightly closed as the hot shower sprayed pleasantly on his face. When he turned around to reach for the washcloth, there was Grayson in all his nakedness standing there. And not more than one foot away was the biggest male member he had ever seen. At the camp, Joe had seen his share. He had been surrounded by literally hundreds of men of all ages, in their shabby, black and gray-striped uniforms as their only clothing. The new arrivals had to take off their civilian clothes and stand completely naked, save for a thin blanket. They stood in endless lines for several hours, waiting to have their heads shaved. Their genitals had been wormlike appendages buried in heavy pubic hair, their scrotums hanging like bats upside down in dark places. The Nazis had delighted in their cruelty with the Jewish men's private parts, mocking them for their circumcisions. From boot kicks to electrical prods, the prisoners suffered shameful assaults. And their backsides were not overlooked either. Joe had witnessed it all.

But this was by far the most oversized monstrosity he had ever seen. Grayson's penis, also circumcised, was as thick as a chair leg and as long as the man's hand.

"Do not touch!"

Joe jerked back his hand as if from a pot of boiling water on Rose's kitchen stove. He gazed down at his pathetic nub of a wee-wee surrounded by thin, pink scars from the mock orange bush.

"Don't worry. You'll grow. Here's the soap." Grayson held out the card-sized soap and the washcloth. "Normally, I'd let you take your shower first, then I'd get in, but I don't trust you right now to leave you alone."

"Huh?"

"Leave the ashtray alone. Does your head still hurt?"

"I dun't know."

Grayson began scrubbing.

****

They made one last stop at the bookstore. Since Joe knew his numbers, Grayson wanted him to learn some arithmetic, so he selected several workbooks in the children's area and an advanced mathematics book on the adult reference shelf. He also picked up a comic book for a diversion, although it was difficult to find one not dripping with violence. After loading the station wagon, Grayson piled the books and writing instruments into Joe's lap as he sat in the front seat passenger side. "It's going to be a long drive to Niagara Falls," he said as he started the car engine.

The arithmetic was only mildly challenging. The first couple of books were easy--basic addition and subtraction. The second book got into higher numbers and multiplications of fives and twos. Joe figured out how to multiply uneven numbers and fractions, following the directions at the beginning of the chapters. Long division was next. By the time they reached Syracuse, home of Grayson's brother Albert and his family, he had almost finished the third book. Then he began reading his new book, Betty Smith's *A Tree Grows in Brooklyn.* The dictionary lay next to him. The comic book somehow had gotten lost under the seat and was subsequently forgotten.

Joe certainly wasn't in a good mood today. He groused and whined about the boring ride and the mushy, overripe banana he was given for a snack. In the late afternoon, he slept on the backseat.

"Vy we here?" Joe asked as they threw their luggage on the beds in their new hotel room in Buffalo.

"Tomorrow, we're going to see a beautiful waterfall in another state park," Grayson replied as he opened his toiletry bag. "Here. Put your toothbrush and toothpaste and your comb in the bathroom. You'll really enjoy seeing Niagara Falls. There will be more trails we can hike, too. I'll bring my binoculars in case we see some birds."

Joe didn't know what the word "binoculars" meant, but he didn't care. His morose mood settled for the rest of the night.

CHAPTER TWENTY-FOUR

"What do you think?" Grayson had to shout over the roar to Joe as they took stock of the miles of the spectacular vista of foamy waters splashing over the mighty rocks.

Looking down but not seeing the bottom where the water filled into the lake scared Joe. It moved fast and violently, pouring into a cavernous abyss. For security, Joe put his hands on Grayson's knee below his khaki Bermuda shorts and knelt at his guardian's loafers. His small, wet hands held onto the man's leg as he listened to the crashing water. Far beyond the falls to the north lay Lake Ontario, as Grayson had told him. He had shown it to Joe on a map the evening before.

Sightseers crowded the fenced-in viewing area, many of them in light tan military uniforms. Grayson explained that the occasional soldiers in drab, olive-gray uniforms with black berets were Canadian. Families and couples strolled about, watching the glory and taking pictures of one of nature's best aquatic displays.

Grayson put on his sunglasses and leaned over the chain-link fence. He studied the falls through his binoculars. An elderly couple appeared to his right and struck up a conversation, and Grayson chatted with them. Joe couldn't hear what they were saying, but he tightened his grip on that sturdy, well-muscled leg. After a few minutes, they walked away.

Grayson and Joe strolled on the path to see another part of the falls. A young mother with three screaming youngsters bumped into them. Grayson laughed and started talking with her and bending down to say a few words to her daughters. Joe stood beside him with his hands at his sides, trying to listen but losing interest. The family moved on, and Grayson wandered a bit, expecting Joe to follow. Then he backtracked when he didn't see him.

Joe had halted under a white pin oak tree. He thought about what he wanted to ask Grayson. The English words had to be said in the correct order, and the pronunciation had to be perfect. His heart thumped.

"Grayson, vy you ask my birthday?" He spoke slowly, forcing himself to look up. As long as the big man wore those black sunglasses, he wouldn't have to meet his eyes.

But Grayson turned his head as if giving himself time to think of a reply and then looked back to Joe. "To be honest with you, Joe, I wondered how old you were because you seem to know things most seven-year-olds don't."

"Vy? I dun't understand. Thirty-one May, nineteen thirty-eight."

"Yes, you wrote it down yesterday. But when I saw how you knew what to do with that Agatha Christie book, and well you wrote that story about Mr. Henry, I didn't know what to think. Seven-year-old boys don't have the maturity or the schooling to sit and write out notes on a mystery novel."

"But I need to understand das book! I use dictionary!"

"Yes, yes. Then you went through those math books in the car yesterday as though you'd done that work before. Have you?"

"No, Grayson. It vas easy. Please. I tell dis truth!"

"Your mother and father did not teach any of that to you?"

"Nicht fractions oder multi--"

"The multiplication exercises."

"Multiplication exercises. I learned from de books you gave me."

They stood looking at each other.

"Joe, did your parents teach you how to read and write?"

Joe nodded. His little face closed.

"And this was before the camp?"

Joe didn't want to cry. "Grayson, are you angry at me?"

"No."

Tears in his throat gripped his breath. "I not lie. I nicht lie. I am seven." He swept his eyes over the trees and the leaves and the grass and the pebble-covered trail. The great Niagara Falls was forgotten. Fingers of panic squeezed his whole body. "Grayson, vil punish me you? Vil you kill me?" He knew what the SS guards did when they did not get the answers they expected to hear.

The big man said evenly, "No. I will not kill you. Why are you asking that?"

"Vil you hurt me?"

"No."

"Vil you do medical exper . . . tests on me?" He saw Grayson swallow.

"No, Joe. Again, why are you asking me these questions?"

Joe looked at his tennis shoes. "Bad things happen ven you lie."

"Joe, I believe you when you say that you're seven. I believe you."

Joe's eyes rolled up to the trees and then to the cars parked several hundred yards away. He drew back his arm and waved his fist as if he was throwing something. "Dey whip you. Whip you until you are tot." After several thrusts of his arm, he stopped to catch his breath. "Vil you do dat mit me?"

Seeing his guardian's stern face, shadowed by the brim of his New York Yankees baseball cap, he recklessly asked, "Vy you nicht do away with me? Dunt you know dat all de Jews to be Totung und Brand?" He knew he was losing his English as he talked faster. His voice squeaked. "Ich bin ein Jude!"

"But I'm not a Nazi!" Grayson took off his binoculars and grabbed him, and shook him a little too roughly. "I was a United States Army doctor! We went with the American troops to help the Jews at Buchenwald. We were there to give them food and medicine to help them recover from starvation and disease. I was there to find you, to rescue you. I am not going to . . ." His voice cracked.

Joe shook his head, disbelieving.

"Joe, you have hallucinations that get you all confused." He put his large hands on both sides of Joe's head. "When you have these bad thoughts, bring yourself back to reality. Remember that I'm here. Nothing bad is ever going to happen to you. Please listen to me, Joe."

"I get scared. I vil die." Now it was time to cry. "Let me, Grayson. Please. Bitte."

"What? What are you saying?"

Moving back, Joe struck the side of his head with his hand. "Ich wunsche Tod! Understand? Tod! Death!" He beat his fists in the middle of his small chest.

"No, Joe. Don't say that. Don't even *think* it." Grayson took Joe's hands. "Joe, trust me, you're not going to die. You're going to live a long time. You'll see the twenty-first century." His fingers nervously smoothed Joe's shirt, pulling it down. Taking off his cap, he pushed his glasses up on top of his head and sat on his heels. He opened his arms, and Joe collapsed into his arms. "I will love you forever, Joe, and I will protect you with the last drop of blood in my body. God in heaven, I promise you, boy." He bent his head over Joe's back, his great shoulders heaving.

Joe laid his head on the man's shoulder, wrapping his arms around his guardian as best he could. "Grayson, I dunt know vat to do."

He pushed himself back and touched the wetness on his guardian's face. Grayson ran his finger under his dripping nose and wiped the side of his face with his arm. He released Joe so he could sit on the ground to relieve the pressure on his knees. Joe sat in front of him.

Grayson put his hands on Joe's arms, stroking them. He looked intently into his eyes. "You have so much to live for, son. Your whole life is ahead of you. There's a big world of fun and happy times for you. Lots of things to do, like riding a bike and playing baseball and tormenting your sister. I'll teach you how to swim in the ocean when we go down to Florida next Spring, and this winter, I'll put a pair of skates on you, and we'll go ice-skating. There's a big pond on the Cornell campus that freezes over every winter. When you go to school, you'll make new friends and bring them over to the house to play." He went back to fiddling with Joe's shirt, straightening the collar, and pulling out wrinkles. "The books in the library made you happy, Joe. I'll get you a library card after we get home. I'm sure your Aunt Mil will be delighted to take you to Tompkins County Library, and you can read every dad-blasted book in the place."

His pensive face reflected racing thoughts. "I want to watch you enter high school and bring home straight As on your report cards. Maybe you'll play on the basketball or baseball team. We'll go to football games, too. I'll take you to Cornell to watch 'em get beat by

Penn State." His eyes softened. "I'm already imagining you walking across the stage to receive your high school diploma. I'm going to open a bank account for your college fund. I've got one for Irene already. Just don't tell your Grandma Nina. She doesn't think girls should go to college, even though she went to one herself—what a paradox.

"I can't wait to see you graduate from college. I know you'll be at the top of your class. And then the job offers will roll in." His face became somber. "And I'll be there in my best suit on your wedding day. It will probably be in a Jewish temple. Your bride will be the love of your life, and you'll fill my house with kids who will call me Grandpa.

"It almost hurts to look at you." He caressed Joe's face. "Joe, there's a reason why things are as they are for you, why you lost your parents, and now you're with me. Only God knows, and we are duty-bound to accept that and go on." He stopped for a moment and then said, "Will you trust me, Joe?"

Blinking once, Joe said, "Yes."

"Okay," Grayson rose to his feet and pulled Joe up. "I'm hungry. Are you?"

"Oh, ya!"

"There's a snack place by the visitor's center. Would you like some ice cream?"

"Ya, yes. Aber Ersten Sandwich, Brot."

"Oh, you're hungry for a sandwich. All right. Let's go."

Joe brushed away his tears and took Grayson's handkerchief to blow his nose.

CHAPTER TWENTY-FIVE

One nurse slaps gloves over Grayson's hands while another one ties his gown. The same nurse reaches up to tie the strings of his mask at the back of his neck. Already donned in his surgical cap, he inspects the organized array of surgical instruments in the mobile tray station next to the operating table. A medical technician tilts the enormous overhead light over the middle of the table where the doctor wants it. Everything is ready.

But strangely, no anesthesiologist is sitting at the head of the table with his machines and tubes. The gleaming, white room is bare except for six rows of stainless-steel doors with latches along the wall. Grayson knows that the bays are full.

The white double doors bang open. A male nurse wearing a mask, cap, and scrubs wheels in the first patient covered in a white sheet. With another male nurse's help, he lifts the limp, rock-heavy body onto the table and rolls the gurney away.

The sheet is thrown back. An emaciated young male with superficial abrasions on his bald head lies motionless, his blank eyes staring at the ceiling. His body reveals many bones, the result of prolonged starvation.

"Scalpel." Grayson holds out his gloved hand. But before he makes the first incision into the man's midsection, he stops. "This man is dead. Take him away."

Wordlessly the male attendants lift the body and carry it to the steel doors. They lay it not too carefully on top of the other corpses piled up against the bottom bays. As they have worked for Dr. Pierce for years, they do their jobs well.

"Bring in the next one," Grayson orders.

Immediately, another patient is rolled in. This one is a female, well-nourished, brunette, with slanted eyebrows, red lipstick, and a slightly hooked nose. Grayson will perform a hysterectomy on her. But she is also dead. He notices suspicious bruising on her thighs near her groin area, and when he opens her legs to examine the extent of her injuries, he sees the purple, swollen vulva and deep scratches on her inner thighs.

"Next."

Every patient is dead, and the pile in the corner grows. Grayson feels an urgency to move on. At one point, he halts the parade. He goes to the pile and begins counting the feet. He counts forty-seven. Where is the body that's missing a foot? He hadn't noticed any one-legged patient coming in for surgery.

"Here's your missing foot," says the male nurse, wheeling in yet another patient, this one without a sheet covering it. It is a middle-aged male. His right knee is chewed up and bloody, and the rest of his leg is gone. *Probably one of the guard dogs got him*, Grayson thinks. *Now we have all twenty-three bodies.*

"Ah, yes. Now we've got all of them. Put him over there with the others."

The doors open once more. Grayson hears ringing in his ears. The sheet covers a much smaller body. *This should be a child*, he thinks with disinterest.

The sheet is pulled off in a flurry, revealing a male child, about seven years old, so thin that his ribs, sternum, and collar bones are visible. His dull black hair is plastered to his forehead. The closed eyes bear dark, discolored circles in stark contrast to the grayish skin tone of his face. He is naked, but there are no marks on his body except some fresh scars on his groin.

Grayson stands in front of the mock orange bush, his head tilted up to see the body drop in an instant. He feels the swish of air.

He recognizes the boy as his ward but takes up the razor-sharp scalpel anyway. This will be a heart operation. The task is to remove the boy's heart, but he doesn't know why. With the steely precision he has practiced for decades, he begins at the top of the sternum. He presses firmly to start a generous ribbon of blood and draws a straight line down.

The intense heat from the crematorium oven makes him break out in a sweat. He turns to face it. The door is cast iron, surrounded by brick. Above it, a bronze plate is labeled with the manufacturer's name, J. A. Topf and Soehne. An empty-faced prisoner swings open the iron door. The partially burned skeleton rests inside; the skull detached and lying on its side; bits of flesh cling to the ribs.

He caught his breath as he opened his eyes, looking into blackness. He lay on his side, facing the other bed. Although the curtains were closed, lights from the street filtered in to give Grayson enough illumination to know where he was. After a moment, he sat up. The hot room made him sweat, even though he wore only his boxer shorts. He rose to adjust the air conditioner unit, and the fan kicked on, making a loud hum. He turned to see the still body in the other bed.

The dream's details faded in his mind, but the lingering malaise remained. He ran his fingers through his hair and checked the time on his travel clock on the nightstand. Making as little sound as possible, he put on his bathrobe and went to the sliding glass door, which opened to a tiny balcony. He sat in a canvas patio chair after shutting the door, not caring if anyone saw him. It would not be likely at 3:35 in the morning on the sixth floor of this hotel.

He put his face in his hands and then took them away and leaned back, wishing he had his pipe. Since he hadn't wanted to expose Joe to his smoke on this trip, he had left it at home. The wind picked up. He looked up at the starless sky. Perhaps it would rain later, but there was no smell of it in the air.

What the hell had he been dreaming about? Usually, he passed them off as he didn't take much stock in their importance the way some people did. In fact, he always hated to be caught in a conversation with someone who talked on and on about his or her dreams. It was all just tricks of the brain; some neurons firing off during sleep. But this reverie had shaken him. It sucked him down like quicksand.

The sight of the pile of corpses against the side of the gleaming silver bay doors pushed its way into his mind's eye.

Heedlessly, willingly, he had taken the Devil's cold hand and had entered his evil dwelling that was, indeed, Buchenwald. No description from Dante or James Joyce, or John Milton could do justice to this cesspool of suffering and death. Gruesome paintings by medieval artists obsessed with scenes from Hell could not come close to portraying what he had seen. This place had been no macabre image created out of a maniacal artist's mind. It had been unvarnished, sober reality.

Grayson jerked his hand to reach for his Bible. But it was in his suitcase, and he was too tired to get up for it. He needed consolation, spiritual comfort, and courage to deal with his memories of that diabolical place. The most frightening question came to him. How could God have allowed such abominations to take place? His God, his wellspring of assuagement and peace of mind. How could God allow such cruel butchery by one group of human beings onto another? Where was God? Where was God?

Then it came to him. God gave man free will. By choosing to destroy his fellow human beings, man turned away from God and was therefore separated from Him. That was the definition of sin. This holocaust that had taken millions upon millions of men, women, and children was not the direct handiwork of Satan. Human beings *chose* to single out a segment of its populace, deem it a parasite, a blight, and thereby unworthy of existing in this world. Human beings were responsible for this cataclysm.

After the war, Grayson had heard from a few of his religious brethren that when the Jews had rejected Jesus Christ, God withdrew His protection from them. Therefore, they were responsible for the calamities that befell them, even if they were human-made. For those portentous enough to say that it was the Jews' choice to reject Christ as the Messiah, and this wholesale massacre was God's punishment. But Grayson's answer was Hitler didn't exterminate them for that biblical reason. Hitler wasn't beholden to any religious creed other than to himself. Only by accusing the "money-grubbing" Jews of being thieves who had cause Germany's social and financial ruin after the Great War was he able to sway an entire nation-state to cleanse itself of these "undesirables." *That* was man's free will.

As to the war of the past four years, cynics might justify it as nature's way of depopulating the earth, "thinning the herd," so to speak. The world's history was replete with wholesale, mass human death. Wars, famine, disease, and plagues all had kept the human population in check.

But Grayson wouldn't accept any of these reasons. After being driven out of the Garden of Eden, God gave man free will. And with that came culpability of the worst disaster of the twentieth century. The choice to do good or harm lay at man's feet.

The overwhelming comprehension of the bitter scene he had witnessed on April fifteenth, 1945, chained his breath and locked up all the muscles in his body, suffocating him. Would there ever come a time when these terrible memories did not torment him? For all the stiff-upper-lip composure he had been able to keep since that terrible overcast afternoon, he could not keep it now.

He had to force himself to stay in control. By golly, people who depended on him, not the least of all Joe and Irene. Grayson had to keep the Pierce mansion running. The old women expected him to take care of the bills and set up the appointments for the maintenance men and the window-washers and the gardeners. He had to keep four automobiles running. It was his job to make sure the mansion was locked up at night.

On top of that, he had to keep up his practice. His patients needed him. There were meetings and insurance forms and medical reports and new equipment and new procedures to learn. Briefly, he thought about all the paperwork he would have to catch up on after this trip.

Might another visit with the priest at Immaculate Conception be in order? Should he seek help at the veteran's hospital in Canandaigua, a city sixty miles north of Ithaca? Or maybe look up a psychiatrist? He was not too proud to ask for help. Maybe later once Joe settled down.

Grayson wiped his eyes and nose. Sweat dotted his chest and back. With his emotional torment coming up again like another oceanic wave, his tears sprang. He hadn't cried this hard since Margie had passed.

CHAPTER TWENTY-SIX

At the Rochester Public Library, Grayson and Joe spent the afternoon exploring another subject dear to Grayson's heart: science. But first, at the check-out counter, they saw a stack of flyers.

"What does it say, Joe?" Grayson asked, giving one to him.

Joe studied the yellow sheet. There was a picture of a musical instrument he thought was a trumpet and big lettering underneath. He read aloud, "The Rochester Community Band Concert, Saturday, September 29, two-thirty p. m. in front of the Monroe County Courthouse. Join us for a patriotic celebration. Rochester Heritage Days Festival. Bring a lawn chair."

"Very good!" The woman behind the desk clapped. "How did you learn to read so well?" she asked Joe.

Grayson laughed. "Now, the real challenge is if he understands what he just read." He turned to Joe. "Do you know what this is about?" He pointed to the paper.

"Concert? Musik?"

"That's right. And where is it?"

"Monroe County Courthouse. Gerichtgebaude?"

"Yes, Gerichtigebaude, if you say so."

"What's he saying?" asked the librarian.

"He's speaking German. He's from Germany."

"Oh."

Ignoring her, Grayson said, "Do you know what a concert is, Joe?"

"Concert?"

"Let's hit the dictionary again." To the librarian, he asked, "Do you mind if we sit at one of your tables to do some school studies? And perhaps you might be kind enough to tell us where your science section is."

The woman acquiesced, and on the way to a table, pointed to the rows of science books to her right.

When they found a text on biology and sat, Joe said, "Dat is tomorrow, de music."

"The music is tomorrow. Yes, it is. Would you like to listen to it?"

"Oh, ya! I mean, yes, please." Joe grinned and nodded.

"Well, you know we're running out of clean underwear. We can't go to the concert in dirty underwear."

Joe frowned, trying to think how to solve this problem.

Grayson's face broke into a huge smile. "We'll ask at the hotel if they have a laundry service, and if they don't, well, you get to learn how to use a washing machine at the Laundromat. And we should go buy some new shirts so we'll look good on the outside, too."

****

"Oh, my, we'll have to park way over here." After parking two blocks away, Grayson told Joe to hold onto his hand tightly and not let go as they wandered into the crowds in downtown Rochester. It seemed the whole city turned out for this end-of-summer gala. Among the crush of people were young soldiers, some in olive green or tan uniforms, others sporting white uniforms with large black ties and white caps on their heads. Grayson lifted Joe to his shoulders and arranged his legs around his neck. From this giddy height, Joe could take in all the sights—the ever-moving wave of heads, and the colored lights, streamers, and patriotic banners decorating storefront windows and street lamp posts. He heard vendors hawking balloons and flags, and saw booths lining the streets selling everything from handcrafted wooden knickknacks to stuffed animals.

Joe smelled the familiar hot dogs and some other smoky food. He saw kids eating strange, pink, cloudlike things on sticks and women in aprons putting dripping watermelon slices on paper plates. At other booths, attendants could barely keep up with the demand for icy lemonade cups and plastic dishes of melting homemade ice cream. Busy tables covered with red and white gingham tablecloths were laden with pies and surrounded by eager patrons ready to dig in. At one wooden-framed booth, gnarly-faced women donning old-time bonnets sewed on quilts laid across their laps, intentionally or not ignoring the passersby stopping and admiring their finished works hanging over ropes. Other make-shift tents offered games for the kids, and one man in an orange hat and a red rubber ball on his nose entertained them by making animals out of balloons. Other children crowded around another man in a straw hat, waiting to get their faces painted. And zigging and zagging everywhere were the nimble clowns, tickling unsuspecting children and blowing toy horns. Joe couldn't help being reminded of Aunt Elvie in her colorful make-up and weirdly dyed hair. Only these guys went way overboard in their get-ups.

A whiff of popcorn made Joe search where it was coming from, but hands lifted him high again, and his feet landed on the ground. Grayson had spotted two empty folding chairs amidst the gathering audience in front of the gray-bricked courthouse. They hurried to take them.

Grayson found a program on the ground and helped Joe read it—the list of music to be performed, titles on the left, composers on the right. On the opposite page was a somewhat unfocused picture of a serious-looking man in a military-style hat and a lengthy bio below it. Another paragraph described the band's mission and its history. Advertisements from local businesses filled the following two pages. A list of donors and corporate sponsors showed that the band was financially well-supported in this town. On the back of the program was the list of the band members separated by instrument.

The band members, resplendent with colorful red, white, and blue outfits, sat in four rows in a semi-circle, making a racket of musical sounds. Joe counted fifty-six musicians, not including the ones wandering around the drums in the back. Big electrical cords snaking along the concrete patio in front of the group connected to two big black boxes that sat on each side of the podium.

While Grayson pointed to the instrument names and identified them in the band, an obese man in a tight black suit came up to the microphone.

"Good afternoon, ladies and gentlemen." The microphone gave a sharp squeal. He tapped it and went on. "What a glorious day in a glorious country, don't you think?"

The audience applauded. Joe looked around. People filled every chair and sat in lawn chairs around the area, even behind the band on the courthouse steps.

"My name is Raymond Hollinger, and, for you out-of-towners, I'm the mayor of this wonderful city of Rochester. I want to welcome you to this patriotic concert by the Rochester Community Band. Gee, it feels like the Fourth of July again, doesn't it, folks?" More clapping. "We have a lot to be thankful for. Our prayers are with our president and military leaders, and let us keep in our hearts the brave men who fought and gave the ultimate sacrifice for this great nation. We celebrate our victory over Germany and Japan at Rochester Heritage Days Festival. We look to the future to grow and prosper and become the greatest country on the face of the earth!" The audience applauded again, louder and longer.

Joe clapped, too, although he wasn't quite sure what all the man said.

"We will begin our program with the presentation of the colors." Mr. Hollinger motioned to his right.

Five soldiers dressed in military dress uniforms, complete with white gloves, marched shoulder to shoulder, each bearing their service flag. The middle soldier, a marine, carried the American flag. A drumbeat kept them in step as they solemnly made their way to the front of the podium. Servicemen and many civilians, veterans of both this war and the First World War, rose as the colors marched by. They snapped their heels together, puffed out their chests, and held their salute, including Grayson. Joe strained his neck to look up to his guardian; the man's strong, rectangular face was immobile, his eyes never wavering from the American flag.

The drum stopped when the unit faced the silent audience. The four flags drooped slightly at the center soldier's command, allowing his flag to stay erect.

"We will now sing the national anthem," announced the mayor.

Another man, presumably the same one whose picture was in the program, came forward wearing a military-style uniform complete with the hat. Upon standing on the podium, he signaled the snare drum player to begin the drum roll. Everyone stood. Joe listened to the *Star-Spangled Banner* for the first time in his life.

The crowd whistled and cheered after the performance, and the colors marched away. The band concert started with the march, *Semper Fidelis*, in honor of John Phillip Sousa's most famous band, the United States Marine Band.

The conductor, a Mr. Maynard Wilson, talked briefly between each number, explaining how the music fitted in with the celebration of winning the war and showing one's patriotism. Between Aaron Copland's *An Outdoor Overture* and *Commando March* by Samuel Barber, another Sousa march, *The Washington Post*, was played. The audience enthusiastically clapped along and tapped their feet. Then, in honor of the British allies, the band played the first movement of Gustav Holst's *First Suite in E-flat.* After that, patriotic songs more familiar to the audience included *The Battle Hymn of the Republic, When Johnny Comes Marching Home,* and Frank W. Meacham's *American Patrol.*

During the second Sousa march, Joe spontaneously clapped as well, keeping with the beat that felt as natural as breathing. He followed the band leader waving his baton by moving his arm in imitation. There was some counting going on, and it had something to do with the beat. But his poor, pitiful guardian couldn't keep up. Grayson would stay with the music for a few beats, then he'd get behind, and his clapping wouldn't be with everybody else's. He'd give up and then try again and fail again.

All this splendid music brought Joe an elevation of happiness he had never experienced before. This was much better than sitting in front of the radio in the evenings with Frau Dead Fish Eyes. It was absolutely thrilling to listen to live music. And the musicians fascinated him. They sat still and straight, yet the inspirational music they made bounced off the courthouse walls and echoed throughout the nearby streets.

The second to the last number was Carmen Dragon's arrangement of *America the Beautiful.* The band played so sensitively that Joe noticed some ladies in the audience wiping their eyes. Perhaps they were thinking about loved ones who had not come home from overseas to hear this hymn.

During the slow, lyrical piece, Joe sild out of his seat. Grayson watched him slowly move away from the chairs but did not stop him. He used the methodical, careful steps he had practiced to perfection to avoid detection in the camp to get nearer to the band. Crouching near the clarinet section, he scrutinized how the men put their fingers down to press the keys, how they held their mouths to blow into the instruments. He glimpsed the music on the wire stands. Man, he wanted to know how they knew how to play what was on the paper! He stayed in a spot where he thought he wouldn't be noticed, but some in the front row saw him and smiled to themselves. He was just a little boy fascinated by the musicians.

"Our last number is an oldie but a goodie, *God Bless America*, by our great native New Yorker, Irving Berlin." The band leader looked positively drenched in sweat, his sparse brown hair clinging to his head when he momentarily took off his hat.

When the song opened, the audience began to sing the words. Joe hummed along as best he could. When the chorus repeated, he confidently sang the melody. After the song finished, he sneaked hurriedly back to his seat, giggling. His guardian grabbed him and tickled his ribs.

"Well, we can't stop after all this great applause!" the conductor shouted into the microphone over the thunderous clapping at the song's end. "I guess we'll have to play one more." And, of course, that tune was Sousa's *The Stars and Stripes Forever*. Everyone jumped to their feet, waving flags and clapping and whistling.

After the concert, Joe and Grayson enjoyed watching the clowns juggle their rubber balls, playing games at the booths, and eating corndogs, and drinking lemonade for supper. Soon, nightfall approached. More people seemed to pour into the streets, milling around as if waiting for something to happen. And, indeed, something did happen that Joe had never seen before. In the black sky behind downtown buildings, fireworks exploded to the spectators' delight. At first, Joe was startled by the booms and crackles, and he hid behind Grayson's legs. But with some prodding, he came around and stared open-mouthed at the colorful light display, not sure if the falling embers would hit him. The show went on for well over forty-five minutes. When it finally ended, Joe was more relieved than excited about watching it.

He was sad to go back to the hotel. But his seven-year-old body told him the day was done. There were two double beds in this hotel room, and Grayson put him in the one nearest the bathroom. He gave him one last round of tickles and wrestled with him in the bed before drawing up the sheets. It was the first time on their trip that Joe did not protest sleeping alone in his own bed. He dozed off within minutes, clutching the new stuffed giraffe his guardian had bought for him from a street vendor. Grayson turned out the light.

CHAPTER TWENTY-SEVEN

It was after ten o'clock. Joe didn't know what he and Grayson would do today, but shouldn't Grayson be getting up? Holding his math paper in one hand, he shook his guardian's shoulder. Nothing. He fingered the man's large, protruding ear and patted his cheek. Out of curiosity, he ran his finger on his slack jaw, feeling the sand-paperish stubble. He sat on the side of his bed, waiting. When he heard Grayson sniff, he immediately stood. He lowered his face close to Grayson's right eye. It opened, appearing unfocused.

"Grayson, vil you help me vid geometry?"

"Huh?"

"I cannot do geometry. I cannot do the proofs. Vil you help me, please?"

Grayson closed his eye, the other one buried in the pillow. Groaning, he pushed himself up and put his bare feet on the carpet. He squinted at the piece of paper wedged between his fingers.

"What's this?"

Joe grabbed it. "No'ting. I left you Notiz when I vent to get food downstairs." He fetched an apple and a muffin from the small, wobbly table in front of the curtains. "Du bist, wir oder sie oder Sie sind, ihr seid? I bought dis for you. Aber I think der coffee ist cold. I took money from your Briefasche. Sorry."

Still not completely awake, Grayson looked on the night table for his watch. "What time is it?"

"Ten minutes after ten. Please. Vil you help me?" Joe held up the paper.

As the hotel room was still dark from the closed curtains, Grayson turned on the lamp and studied Joe's work. "This is right. Now, these down here. I'll have to look at the directions in your workbook. I want to see how they explained how to do the proofs." He took the apple and muffin. "Did you go down to the coffee shop all by yourself?"

"Ya, Grayson." Joe wasn't sure if he was in trouble.

Grayson smiled tiredly and rubbed the boy's head. "That was very brave of you, Joe. And very thoughtful. Thank you for getting my breakfast."

"You are velcome!"

Joe waited patiently, watching his guardian get ready for the day. As the big man put on his socks and shoes, he asked, "Grayson, vil you teach me music?"

His guardian leaned down to tie his tennis shoes. "I'm afraid you got me stumped there. Music's a mystery to me, except I know what I like. And I can pick out the names of the instruments. I wish I knew how to read music." He collected his things to pack in the suitcase. "Your Aunt Mil could teach you. She knows how to read music. Have you heard her play the piano in the music room?"

"No." Joe worried the corner of his math workbook.

"Are you all packed and ready to go?"

"Vere?"

"I thought we might go to another state park on the way back to Ithaca. We can catch up on some hiking." He unfolded a map of New York and showed Joe the twin set of Seneca and Cayuga Lakes. "This is beautiful country. And I'm thinking about the Finger Lakes National Forest. Sound good? But before we go, I'm going to call home to let everybody know that we'll be back tomorrow evening. And we'll stop at a grocery store to pick up some grub."

A queasy feeling crept into Joe's stomach. Grayson mentioned going back to Ithaca, a place he hoped he'd never see again. He decided not to bring up the subject of music again for fear it might lead to more discussion about Aunt Mil. And what the heck was grub?

During the long car ride, his grave mood attracted Grayson's attention. "Joe, how come you're so quiet? Aren't you excited about seeing the woods again? We'll build another campfire and sleep outside unless it rains. If that happens, I can put up my old Army tent."

Joe shrugged and kept his face toward the window. He didn't want Grayson to see his tears. He hated feeling bad again, especially when he had had such a great time the day before. His guardian mercifully left him alone.

Grayson had visited the Finger Lakes National Forest many times since his boyhood. In these woods, his curiosity about the natural world had led to his study of biology and, ultimately, medicine. When guardian and ward stepped into the cool, tranquil woods, Joe pretended to be interested in the leaves and bugs and listening for the distinct calls of unseen birds high up in the trees. He followed Grayson on the rocky, steep trails, not saying much.

Back at the campsite, worry put knots in his stomach. His palms were clammy, and he had no appetite. He ruminated on how he would tell Grayson that he didn't want to go back to Ithaca. Couldn't they just keep driving around the state?

"Joe, you haven't touched your hot dog, and I have a feeling those marshmallows are going to get stale." Grayson sat on his itchy, Army-issued wool blanket. He looked at Joe, who sat on the ground holding a stick with his hot dog on the end of it.

Joe stared at the blazing fire crackling in the balmy night. Crickets sang duets with the cicadas in the nearby ash trees.

"Are you afraid about going home?"

Joe nodded his head vigorously and then kept his chin down to hide his tears. The stick slipped from his hand. Grayson got up and sat next to him, his big hands clasped together.

"You knew we'd have to go back, didn't you?"

For fear of outright crying, Joe sat motionless.

"There's a more important reason why I wanted to come to this place other than just to hike and look for birds. I don't really care if you learn about mushrooms or butterflies. However, I do want you to learn to identify poison ivy. Do you understand what I'm saying?"

When Joe did not answer, Grayson gently put his finger under his chin and lifted his face.

"Ya, Grayson." Joe had to respect his guardian by answering. He swallowed his tears.

"You're not too happy about ending this trip. You're afraid to go back, and I know why. That's why we're out here without any distractions so we can talk about it."

Joe put his left hand on Grayson's knee.

"Son, when I brought you into my home, I was asking a big job for you to do, namely, getting along with my mother and my sister and my Aunt Elvie. Irene doesn't count because she's a child, and she has to learn to live with you. But these old women! Good heavens, even *I* have trouble getting along with them. This arrangement has been a terrible burden on you, and I am so sorry that I put you through it. And when I jumped right back into working at the hospital and left you to contend with my family, it was the wrong way to get you adjusted to your new life. I will always regret that." He spoke slowly so Joe could understand his words. "Again, Joe. I am so deeply sorry."

Joe nodded again, his tears temporarily forgotten. His little hand pressed on his guardian's knee.

"We went on this road trip because I needed to get you out of the house. We've had to get to know each other and learn to trust each other." He held out his forefinger. "But when we get back home, there are things you need to do to get along with your elders. Remember, they're old and very set in their ways, and they see the world in black and white. It's their way or the highway."

"Like Herr Heinrich?"

Grayson showed slightly tobacco-stained teeth as he gave a laugh. "Yes, but on a much more complicated level. The most Herr Heinrich will do is hiss, show his claws, and off he goes. It's not the same with the ladies. When people get older, it's harder for them to adjust to change. They get fussy and disagreeable. Having a little boy suddenly move in without their approval . . . well, let's say it ruffled their feathers."

Feathers? Ver der birds in the house? He hadn't seen any.

"A big stumbling block was that you didn't know English. But now that you've made remarkable progress in learning it, things at home will go a lot smoother for you. I had expected at least somebody in the house would have helped you with your English, but that didn't happen." Grayson thought for a moment. "Did you use my dictionary? I kept it in my room."

"Nein, Grayson. Aunt Mil would nicht let me."

"What? Why not?"

"I think she said I would tear it up."

Joe's guardian leaned back, trying to compose himself. "You have my permission to touch anything in the house, including the dictionary. Wait, no, anything in my room and my study. There're too many breakable antiques in the other rooms. You can only touch the things that belong to me. You didn't do anything wrong. You just coped the best way you knew how. But things have to be different when we go home tomorrow. Are you listening to what I'm saying?"

"Yes, Grayson." Joe edged closer, putting his whole arm around Grayson's leg.

"First, be brave and talk to these women. Make them talk with you. Ask them questions or comment on what they are doing. Don't show any fear to them. Try not to let them push you around. Be confident with your English and speak up when you want something or don't want something. How else will you get to feel comfortable around them? For heaven's sake, you're going to live with these women for at least the next fifteen years. I won't have you cowering in a corner and hiding from them!

"That brings up the next point. Joe, I don't want you hiding in your closet or under your bed. If you become afraid at night or wake up from a bad dream, you come to me, just as before. And don't worry if you wet your bed. Hopefully, when you relax and settle down during the day, the nightmares will end, and so will the midnight baths. And if I'm not around, you go to Rose. She'll fix you up with a nice cup of hot milk. I'll let her know that's our plan. I'm going to take the lock off your closet door. Will you promise not to go in there except to get your clothes?"

"Yes, I promise," Joe said solemnly. "Vat about Herr Heinrich? If he goes beneath the bed, I can get him out?"

Grayson grinned. "Yes, you can get him out. Just don't pull his tail."

"Nein, nein. He dunt like dat."

"Now, another thing. No more getting into the garbage can in the kitchen to find something to eat." He stopped to watch Joe's reaction.

Joe knew now that sneaking into the kitchen at night to collect food had not been a good idea.

"I know why you did it, and I certainly understand it. You were only doing what you had done in the camp to stay alive. Now it's time to make some changes because that life is over. The garbage is garbage, and it's to be thrown out. You don't need to keep eggshells and empty vegetable cans and lemon rinds." He grabbed Joe around his ribs. "You have some growing to do. As Irene said, you're too skinny. You need to eat nutritious, wholesome food. Rose and Anne will give you all the food you want. Delicious food, hot or cold. All you have to do is ask."

"How I do dat?"

"Just say, 'Rose, I'm hungry. Will you give me something to eat?'"

Joe had to think about that. Everyone in the camp had been hungry. There was never enough food. Men would cry and howl and moan all night in the barrack because they were hungry. He had seen them drop to the ground, too weak to stand anymore for lack of food. And most of the time, they had stayed there unless some other prisoners would be ordered to move them, assuming they were dead.

He made a frown. "How can that be? Vil there be food?"

Grayson replied patiently, "Yes. Rose will show you where the food is. There's some in the cupboards, in the icebox, and in the wall closet we call a pantry. She'll take you to a store where we buy food just like the one we went to yesterday. We won't run out."

"Dey always had food," Joe murmured, thinking about the nasty guards. He recalled the apple core a guard had thrown at some prisoners one time. It had been such fun for that cruel man to watch them fight for it, even picking the seeds out of the mud. "My Vater und me only ate at night."

"My father and *I* ate at night. How did that happen?"

"A fat lady brought us food. We ate fast, behind de Kuchen. Sometimes a fat man came vid she."

Grayson got up to get the dictionary out of the car. Kneeling with a flashlight, he searched for the translation of 'Kuchen.' Joe turned pages with him.

"Dere. Kitchen." Joe pointed to the word.

"Why did the woman give you food? Where did she get it?" Grayson asked.

These questions made Joe sad, remembering the hurried gobbles he had to swallow in the middle of the night. The stout woman with the wavy mouse-brown hair kept diligent eyes for the SS watchmen.

The food had been delicious! She had even brought him milk and cookies, which she said had almonds and cinnamon in them. While he ate, she and his father had moved away and talked in whispers, but he couldn't make out what they had said. The fat woman's velvety voice had been too soft, and she had spoken rapidly. When the heavy-set, angry-faced man accompanied her, Joe had recognized him as who had written his parents' names in a green ledger book when they had been processed upon arrival at the camp. He remembered that he had worn a swastika armband but not the uniform. Peeking out from his mother's skirt, Joe had feared this man would kill him if he looked toward him.

It had been within moments after finishing with this repulsive man at the processing table that his mother had vanished. He had glimpsed her being dragged away by a tall soldier wearing lots of insignia. Even when he started to scream for her, the press of bodies around him took away his breath. Luckily, his father's hand found his hand, and he held on to it for his life.

"Joe? Will you tell me how you were given food? Who was the woman?"

"Can I tell you later?"

Relief flooded his body when he heard the big man say, "Joe, you can tell me later or tomorrow or next week or anytime. When you feel like talking about it, I'll listen."

Joe wiped his cheeks with his shirt collar. He wanted to suck on it but thought better.

"Kiddo, there's one more thing we need to talk about."

Lifting his face, Joe braced himself as he looked at the shadows crossing his guardian's long face.

"When we get back and settled, I want to take you back to the temple, you know, Temple Beth-El. I want you to get to know some Jewish folks in town and begin your studies in Judaism."

Joe hoped the evening was dark enough that Grayson couldn't see the worried look on his face. "Vil you go vid me?"

"Of course. I have every intention of being with you as much as I possibly can. We'll meet with Rabbi Passow again. But Joe, tell me why it was so upsetting to you when we went the first time to Beth-El. Was it because there were all those strange people, or the sanctuary was too big?"

Joe picked up a stick and tapped it on the ground. His heart beat wildly. "I afraid dey vil come to take us," he murmured.

"No, Joe. Do you understand now that that will never happen ever again? We're in America. No more bad people in boots and carrying whips. No more trucks or trains."

Joe nodded, his shoulders slumping from exhaustion. "Grayson, vil you hold me?"

The man put aside the dictionary and picked him up, and embraced him. Joe put his arms tightly around his neck and buried his face in his throat.

"Grayson, I love you." His fingers touched that scratchy jaw.

"I love you, too, Joe. You are the most precious thing in the world to me, along with Irene." He held Joe up higher so he could kiss him on his forehead. Joe kissed him back. His quick fingers found Grayson's ears and began fondling them.

"Vil I sleep next to you tonight?"

"Why wouldn't you? We don't have two beds."

"I mean, vid you sleep, side mit you?" Joe began to feel very tired. Saying words in English took a lot of heavy thinking.

"Yes, boy. You can sleep next to me tonight. But when we get home, you must sleep in your own bed. Even though I said you could come into my room if you have a bad dream, I hope you won't feel you'll need to. We all need our rest." After a pause, he added, "And since I made that phone call this morning to your Aunt Mil, I know you're going to get a big surprise."

"Surprise? Uberraschung?"

"Yes." He held Joe tightly, rocking him from side to side. "Aunt Mil said that everyone misses you, and they hope you're feeling better."

"Even Herr Heinrich?"

"Especially Herr Heinrich. He's been keeping your bed warm."

Joe missed Mr. Henry. The family cat had helped him calm down with his contented, half-closed eyes and his loud, motor-boat purring. Stroking his velvet coat gave Joe much pleasure, and the cat didn't seem to mind his angry, frustrated tears.

Reflecting on the past two weeks, Joe knew now that his greatest hurdle had been conquered, learning the English language. With that, he believed he was ready to meet the challenges ahead. He also knew that this enormous man steadfastly held him securely in his mighty surgeon's hands. Joe was past the rocks of fear and despair that had nearly taken his short life. But still, he would need courage if he were to survive in this new place called America, and specifically the Pierce castle. Armed now with his new language, he was ready.

Joe lay on his side, cuddled up to the big man's broad, comforting chest. Under watchful points of light in the black sky, he closed his eyes.

CHAPTER TWENTY-EIGHT

Forcing down the sour bile in his throat by swallowing hard, Joe mentally steeled himself. The battleship-sized Ford Super Deluxe station wagon turned onto the black-topped road lined on both sides with massive ageless trees. His seven-year-old heart beat fast with dread. He sat on his clammy hands to still them, and he crossed his ankles tightly. Even though the big man driving the car glanced at him with a kindly smile of confidence, Joe didn't meet his eyes. He didn't want Grayson to see the apprehension on his face. Too soon, the castle appeared at the end of the driveway, its slate roof glinting the western son. The car stopped at the front porch. They got out, and after Grayson lifted some luggage out of the back of the station wagon, they walked through the hefty double front doors.

Joe waited in the grand foyer while the women gave Grayson a hero's welcome in the living room. Hearing how they fawned over him, Joe realized now how important his guardian was to this family. He was thankful no one noticed him yet.

But he couldn't stay invisible for long. The three old biddies and Irene peered at him with mistrustful eyes as he cautiously entered the living room, hanging the wall as close as he could without putting fingerprints on it. While his guardian went back and dragged heavy luggage full of dirty clothes, papers, and books into the foyer, Joe had to stand ready for inspection.

He heard some commotion, and the eternally lively cook, Rose, burst from the kitchen with her usual over-the-top enthusiasm. Practically running to him through the family room and into the living room, she was the only genuinely welcoming sight. She took his face in her warm palms and kissed his nose and cheeks. "I'm so glad you're home! I've made your favorite brownies! You know the ones with the white chocolate chunks and the cream cheese frosting? You wait right here." She patted his shoulders and went back toward the kitchen. Joe smelled a delightful, sweet aroma.

Aunt Elvie broke the ice. "Well, how are we doing? Did we have a good time?" She put her age-spotted hands together under her drooping bosom. Joe saw a rubber band around her wrist, possibly from a newspaper. As usual, rouge filled the deep gullies in her wrinkled cheeks, and her eyelashes were coated with blacking. Her dry, thin hair, suffering from overuse of henna and chemical-laced permanents, stood out on her delicate skull like a halo in a medieval painting. And then there was the glint of gold from her capped front tooth flashing through her stoplight-red lipsticked mouth.

"Yes, Aunt Elvie. Ve had a great time." Joe experienced being out of his body, hovering over it.

She tittered to the others, "He's speaking English! How about that!"

Aunt Mil spoke from her perfect-posture stance in front of the newly-acquired Zenith Aztec floor–model radio that stood next to the fireplace. "And where did you go?" The delivery of her question would have made a Catholic school nun proud.

He answered, with shoulders tense, "Ve vent to Albany and Niagara Falls, und ve heard a band concert in Rochester, und den ve vent to the Finger Lakes National Forest."

"You went to Niagara Falls?" yelled Irene. "That's not fair! I've never been to Niagara Falls! You rat!" She charged forward and pushed him.

"Irene, that's enough!" Grayson spoke sharply as he entered the living room.

Before he could take Irene by the arm, Joe stepped up to his sister. "Yes. Vel, dis vas my time mit Grayson. Ve needed to talk, und you vould not let me here!"

Everyone stood with mouths open, including Irene. Joe moved in even closer, looking her straight in the eye. He decided he would not be afraid of her, despite his wildly beating heart. Underneath the display of boldness, he felt a visceral attraction to her. But she turned on her heel and flew upstairs.

"Very good, Joe." Grayson patted his head. "Victoria tua."

Rose came back with a generous piece of chocolate brownies. She kissed him one more time, and he thanked her, remembering to use English words. Joe loved the smooth, deep chocolate taste and the crunchy white chips. As he licked cream cheese frosting from his finger, a lingering push on push leg made him look down. Wiping his hands, he picked up Mr. Henry. He had missed his feline friend and stroked his silky fur. Mr. Henry kneaded his sleeve and head-butted his chin.

"Hump!" Nina Cassandra plopped in her antique rocking chair with the carved wood trim. Joe liked to think of it as her throne. "So, he can speak proper English now?"

Mr. Henry slipped out of Joe's arms and disappeared. Now he had nothing to hold on to during the inquisition.

Grayson replied, "He's getting there. For having studied it only two weeks, he's done exceptionally well." The big man found his pipe in an end table drawer and lit up. He stood at the empty stone fireplace and put an arm on the mantle.

"He certainly looks better. Is he eating now?" asked Aunt Elvie. She sank into the French blue sofa.

"You just saw what he did to that brownie. Why don't you ask him yourself?" Grayson threw a spent match into the fireplace.

Before Aunt Elvie could speak, Mildred cleared her throat. When Joe turned and looked directly at her (as Grayson had told him to do when talking with adults), she shifted her eyes uncomfortably for a split second, then looked back at him. "Joe, what did you eat on your trip?"

"Grayson und I cooked hot dogs over a campfire in de woods. Und den ve roasted marshmallows. But we ate mainly in de hotel restaurant. I liked de sandwich at Niagara Falls. Ve vent to a movie, und I ate popcorn. De movie vas *A Tree Grows in Brooklyn*. We vent to a bookstore, und I am reading de book now."

The women looked at each other with skepticism. "Yes, well, I'm sure you've been looking through the pages," Aunt Mil said. She interlaced her fingers and straightened her well-padded shoulders.

In his peripheral vision to his right, Joe saw a black, patent-leather shoe and a lacy white sock peeking out from the threshold of the living room. However, he kept his attention on the judges.

Grayson said, "Joe, go into the family room and get a newspaper."

Without hesitation, Joe left and returned carrying a folded newspaper.

"Now put it on the floor and find something to read out loud."

Joe sat on the carpet and began reading the front page of *The New York Times.*

"*New York Times*, September sixteenth, nineteen-forty-five. All the news dat's fit to print. MacArthur orders tight censorship; foe's attitude hit. Rigid ban imposed. Allies declare Japanese showed lack of good faith in reports. More suspects give up. Togo, ill, is under U.S. control in Tokyo—Laurel, Filipino puppet, held by de Associated Press Tokyo. Sunday, Sept 16--Arrests, surrenders, suicides und illness accounted today for virtually every member of former Japanese Premier Hideki Tojo's 'Pearl Harbor Cabinet' as Gen. Douglas MacArthur stiffened his policy toward 'a defeated enemy dat has not yet demonstrated a right to a place among civilized nations.' One of de top men sought, Shigenori Togo, de Foreign Minister who carried on de ally negotiations vile Japan's carriers ver moving to the sneak attack on Pearl Harbor, vas located ill at his Tokyo home. He summoned a United States Army doctor, putting himself technically in custody prior to planned surrender. Togo vas reported suffering from a heart ailment."

Joe looked up at Grayson hopefully. "Is dat okay?"

The room was silent. Joe left the paper on the floor and exited the living room, his heart in his mouth. He sat on the bottom step of the staircase and put his head between his knees, collecting himself after the arduous examination. The little girl was gone.

"How did you do it, Grayson?" Mildred finally asked.

"I gave him the dictionary, the one you purposely kept away from him." Not waiting for a reply, he went on. "The kid already knew how to read and write. Once he had my German-English dictionary, there was no stopping him.

"When we went to the public library in Albany, he picked out an Agatha Christie novel and read the first sixty pages using that dictionary to translate the words. He wrote a book report on it, and he never asked me to help him. Of course, I went over it and corrected his grammar and punctuation. Later, I told him to write a story about Mr. Henry in German, just to see how well he could write. He wrote two complete pages in cursive. So he's had some serious schooling. But for him to show us what he could do, he had to have the tool to learn our language. You women kept that away from him." Grayson stared at them. The ladies cast away their eyes.

Mildred spoke. "It wasn't easy to try to navigate through all those foreign words. We simply didn't have the time to translate every word we said to him." She waved her hands in exasperation. "It was just too complicated."

Grayson gave her a skeptical look. Putting his pipe in the ashtray on the end table, he took out two folded pieces of paper from his breast pocket. "Here's the story he wrote." He handed them to his sister. After stuffing and lighting his pipe again, he took a seat on the couch, crossed his knees, and puffed away.

Mildred studied the papers through her silver half-glasses as she sat in a burgundy club chair. They had been filled front and back with neat, cursive writing. "This is in German. I can't make out what he wrote." She dismissively handed the papers back to Grayson, who passed them to his mother.

Nina Cassandra took a cursory glimpse and then held the papers out for someone else to take them. Aunt Elvie obliged her. She scrutinized the strange writing as if it was hieroglyphics.

"That's not the point." Grayson took the papers back. "Do you know any seven-year-old who can write an entire, two-page essay in cursive? In any language? I don't. I counted the words—nearly 500. That's more than what most high school students can write. Irene can barely write a simple paragraph in straight print."

Joe glimpsed Irene racing up the stairs from the family room.

Grayson went back into the foyer to dig through a suitcase. He came back with Joe's math books and handed them to his sister. "Here. If that doesn't impress you, maybe this will."

All three women casually perused through the papers and workbooks, seemingly indifferent to what they saw.

He shook his head. "This is just another example of what the upside-down priorities are in this house. You three women are all highly educated, well-received in the church, and you're pillars of the community. You enjoy first-rate reputations, command respect every time you step outside the house, yet none of you had the common sense to let a little boy use the blasted dictionary to help him learn English! But that's in the past. Now that he's conversant in English, there's no reason for any of you not to talk with this kid."

"Now see here, Grayson--" Mildred half rose.

"Mildred, I want you to get him a library card and let him check out all the books he wants. Don't say no to him even if you think the books are too advanced for him. Oh, by the way, I plan to take his little story about Mr. Henry to a German language teacher, maybe at Cornell. I want an expert to tell me how developed Joe's writing skills are. I want to find out exactly how smart he is."

He collected the papers. He eyed his mother, whose face was a portrait of pure disdain. "And another thing. As I've said over and over, Joe is left-handed. No one will force him to use his right." He held out his hand to stop Mildred's protests. "You can see how neat and precise his handwriting is. It's a little smeary, but that's because he drags his hand across what he's written. And he eats using his left hand. No more arguments at the dinner table about the so-called Devil's hand. He's eating better now, and he's gained a little weight. Joe is a member of this family, and I won't have him getting so scared that he runs and hides and thinks he needs to escape again . . . Mom." The big man bore his fierce gray eyes into his mother.

The old queen bee gave him a menacing look. She grumbled, "We'll see about that." She rocked strenuously on her purple velvet throne.

Grayson almost answered her but thought better of it. He turned to his sister. "Mildred?"

There was an uncomfortable pause in the room. "Whatever you say, Grayson."

Grayson debated whether or not to continue this conversation. "Well, I should go up and help Joe unpack."

That was Joe's cue to scamper up the stairs. He let out a whoop when he saw his bedroom. From the glossy oak floor covered with a navy braided rug to the pine wainscoting and bright red, white, and blue-striped wallpaper above it, the room sported a patriotic cheer. A new brass lamp fastened on the wall above the nightstand would give much better light than the old Tiffany one. Three new teddy bears nestled on the pillows on top of the indigo bedspread. Underneath the windows stood a child's desk, chair, and reading lamp, accompanied by a four-shelf matching bookcase, ready to be filled. A massive globe on a wooden stand stood in the corner, accompanied by a chalkboard on an easel, complete with an eraser and chalk. Navy brocade curtains framed the windows, and white roll shades with red tassels hung over the glass. A mobile of miniature race cars turned lazily from the ceiling. In place of the farm scene painting hung one of a little boy standing on top of a chair inspecting a medical diploma of a doctor who had his back to him. The boy stood in his undershirt and loosened pants, revealing a hint of his rump. Taped up on Joe's dresser mirror was a somewhat crude "Welcome Home, Joe" banner made from red, white, and blue construction paper.

"Well, well," said Grayson as he entered the room. "Now you're living in style, Joe." He turned to Mildred, who stood behind him. "Mil, I couldn't be more pleased with what you've done with the room. It looks so much brighter. I like the Rockwell. What did you do with the other furniture?"

"I gave the old furniture in Rose's room to the Salvation Army, and she got the guest room furniture. It was quite a chore for the movers to get it out the back door to their truck. Rose was thrilled to have the guest room set, and she's been polishing it daily." She turned to Joe, who was trying out the double bed by jumping on it. "Young man, don't you wear out those box springs. They have to last until you graduate from high school. Why don't you look inside the chest?" She pointed to a cedar chest at the foot of the bed.

"Yes, Aunt Mil." Joe jumped off the bed and went to the chest. Slowly he opened the creaking top. "Oh!" He dropped on his knees to rummage through the new toys.

"Mil, I don't believe it. You thought of everything," Grayson said, looking inside the toy box.

"Don't give me that much credit. The toys were Aunt Elvie's idea. She had to take Irene with her. She put up such a fuss about not going with you on the trip that the only way to calm her down was for her to help Aunt Elvie pick out the toys. Be sure to know it wasn't my idea."

Joe turned the adults, his face beaming. "Danke schon. Oder thank you, Aunt Mil. I like dis very much." He rolled the wheels of a yellow toy truck with the palm of his hand.

"You're welcome, Joe," answered Aunt Mil. "And because Rose is benefitting from all this rearrangement too, she's prepared an extra-special dinner just for you. I assume you're hungry."

Joe grinned and nodded. His "aunt" tried her best to smile back but, alas, failed.

"I almost forgot." Grayson search through Joe's suitcase on the floor. "We picked this up in a little gift shop at a synagogue in Buffalo." He pulled out a tissue-wrapped object. With his sister looking on, he leaned over the bed and hung the crystal Star of David where the crucifix had been. It measured a perfect ten inches by ten inches, accented with gold piping. The ornament shone in the waning sunlight from the window, reflecting spots of rainbows on the wall.

"There," he whispered.

Aunt Mil put her hands together and looked away.

Even though this double bed was different, with a sturdy headboard to hold a tissue box, a radio, and several books, the frame was just high enough from the floor for Joe to slide under it if he wanted to. And he did, but only to try to reach Mr. Henry. His efforts usually were in vain as the cat always moved farther against the wall just out of his reach.

True to his word, Grayson replaced the closet doorknob and strike plate. And while he had the hammer, he nailed a 4-inch bronze mezuzah on the bedroom doorframe on the right side. Knowing that Joe would grow taller in time, he set it high but still within his reach. Joe's heart nearly burst with renewed confidence.

During the day, Joe fearlessly walked into the music room and sat with Aunt Elvie and Grandma Nina to listen to the radio. They did not shoo him away. He became fascinated with Aunt Elvie's crossword puzzles. When she pondered over a clue, he helped her, using the dictionary to get the correct spelling. At first, she asserted that she was offended that a little seven-year-old upstart would know words she didn't. After a time, however, she settled down and began relying on his assistance.

A few days after Grayson and Joe had come home, Mildred took Joe to the Tompkins County Library. She held her breath, watching him scamper off, behaving as if he had been in this bibliotheca all his short life. She browsed through the historical romance section for her favorite authors. While reading the first page of a new volume, *Not in Our Stars* by Eleanor Berford, she temporarily forgot about the boy.

A bang perked her attention. She looked between the rows of shelves and found Joe standing on top of a wheeled stool, straining to see more books above his head. "What are you looking for? You better get down or you'll fall."

Joe hopped down and pointed to the top shelf. "Vil you hold me up?"

Before, Mildred had not made an effort to pick up Irene past her fourth birthday. But now, she couldn't very well say "no" to this eager child. Setting her purse on the clean, waxed floor, she awkwardly took Joe around his waist and maneuvered him into her arms. He was surprisingly light. She clasped her arms under his little rear end and walked slowly, letting him look at the volumes on the top shelf.

"Oh, my, this is the European history section. Are you sure you want to read these books?"

Not bothered that his strict, proper aunt was holding him, Joe pulled out a small volume, *The Kings and Queens of Britain*. "Yes. Dis one I start." He thumbed through the pages. "Not too hard. Can I another one get? I mean, get another one, please?"

"One more."

Joe picked another thicker book on the same subject. He nearly burst with excitement. Mildred put him down and watched him sitting on the floor, reading the opening chapter of the heavier book.

"Come along now, Joe." She held out her white-gloved hand to him. "Let's get your library card, and we will go home. You can start reading your books before dinner."

"Can ve come back tomorrow?" Joe asked as he stood.

"You won't have those books finished by tomorrow."

"Yes, I vil. I can read schnell, oder fast."

Mildred gave him an unconvinced look. But Joe was true to his word. Indeed, he and Mildred made more trips to the library in the coming weeks and months. He was a bottomless reservoir, never completely filled by his passion for reading.

CHAPTER TWENTY-NINE

"Let's get you started on some simple Bible phrases," said Aunt Mil.

Joe remembered this scenario from before the road trip with Grayson. It had been a traumatic experience since he hadn't understood the English language and had been subjected to Frau Dead Fish Eyes' infamous wrath.

At the dining room table, she laid out two pieces of paper and another book akin to one of Irene's coloring books. She copied the words "Christ has risen" under a picture of a bearded man in a robe. Several words were printed underneath. She said, "Now, copy the sentence." She pointed to the blank sheet and held out the pencil.

Joe recognized the picture as his sad-faced friend with the long brown hair hanging on the "T" sticks on the wall. Only, in this picture, he wore a white and blue robe, and his pierced hands stretched out toward a yellow sun. He printed the three words, trying to make the writing as neat as possible.

"Very good," his austere aunt said without smiling. "Can you write this in cursive?" She wrote the words in cursive under his and put the pencil again in his right hand.

This is easy, thought Joe as he began. He didn't notice Aunt Mil frowning as he put the pencil in his left hand.

That Joe wrote the words in cursive without effort seemed to impress Aunt Mil enough to fake a brief smile. However, her face was impenetrable to read. "Let's go to the next page," she said, the corners of her thin mouth pursed downward. With fingers that ended with serious red nails, she turned the page. Her gold and emerald necklace clicked as she leaned over to watch him write more sentences. The woman remained calm during the lesson and did not raise her voice. But she still made Joe nervous.

Despite his apprehension, Joe tried as fervently as he could to concentrate. He needed to please this woman. Now that he had mastered English, he could effortlessly answer the religious questions and write them in cursive. From then on, every time Aunt Mil approached him with another set of books, he secretly whispered his thanks to Grayson for helping him learn English during their trip.

Soon, Aunt Mil made out lists of assignments and taped them to his bedroom door. And, like Grayson, she had to keep coming up with more challenges for him because he flew through each task. No subject was too arduous. Moreover, his attention span amazed her. Never did Irene ever sit at the dining room table spending a whole hour on arithmetic problems.

In late October, Mildred took Joe to the Catholic school Irene attended, Immaculate Conception. She informed the principal, Mother Superior Margaret Payne, that her nephew would be enrolling second semester in January. Upon hearing this, Joe started to tell her that Grayson had planned for him to go to East Hill Elementary, a public school. She covered his wet, interfering mouth with her crocheted gloved hand and continued to inform Mother Superior how wonderfully smart and disciplined her new little nephew was.

Later, in the car, she reprimanded him for speaking when nobody had asked him a question. That was a conversation between adults, not children. "And don't you dare tell your father where we went today." Joe shrugged and looked at his new stack of workbooks. Included with the geography, science, and social studies books was a massive book on Catholicism. As if on a dare, she began teaching him Latin. Dutifully, he memorized the words and their meanings. He emboldened her to teach him more, but always with an ear listening for Grayson's Lincoln rolling up the driveway. She told him, "I'll keep these books in my room, and we'll look at them during the day when your father is at work." It always seemed a little strange to Joe that she referred to Grayson as his father when she knew he was his guardian.

Frau Dead Fish Eyes also drilled him on the different parts of the mass and the Catholic calendar. She made him learn about all the saints and the pope in Rome (she had shown him Italy on the globe in his room). As to the crucifixion that hung in every room except his, Joe figured out the unfortunate painted man on the sticks was none other than Jesus Christ, the second most important deity, right after God, the Father.

But he worried about the subterfuge over his Catholic education. He didn't like sneaking around behind his guardian's back and having to hide his Latin books and his missal. Keeping secrets from Grayson made him uneasy. He hated the deception. But the woman displayed her fearsome power, getting in his face so close he could smell her coffee-scented breath and see tiny red veins in her flashing, marble eyes. "Don't you dare say anything to your father about any of this. You will destroy this house if you so much as utter one word in Latin or cross yourself at the dinner table."

One time, Joe sat with Aunt Elvie and asked her why Aunt Mil was so determined to keep his Catholic training a secret from Grayson. From her well-cushioned perch on the davenport in the music room, she wisely said to him, "Let sleeping dogs lie." Joe didn't know where the dogs were and asked where he could find them.

On the last Sunday of October, Grayson took Joe back to Temple Beth-El to get him started in Sunday school learning Judaism with the other tiny group of Jewish kids. Ithaca had only a handful of Jewish families, so few that services were suspended in the summer. Jewish students from the Hillel Center at Cornell University taught the Sunday school classes. Joe went along with learning Judaism with no more interest than learning Catholicism from Aunt Mil. To him, all this was just the adults scuffling over his religious education. He didn't care what his spiritual training was.

Having met one family, the Greens, Joe found a new friend who happened to be his age, Alex. His father was a hematologist at the hospital and knew Grayson. His mother worked part-time at the Cornell library. They were happy to oblige Grayson by taking Joe to Friday evening services and including him in their frequent holiday celebrations. Mrs. Green sometimes took Joe to the Cornell library. It was a real struggle to get him out when it closed.

Joe liked Mr. Hiram Cassel, his Sunday school teacher at Temple Beth-El. The energetic, well-fed instructor always had a joke for his young students, usually a bad pun. Joe also enjoyed his growing friendship with Alex, who lived close enough to visit often. Because Alex also enjoyed reading, they made up extra scenes from their storybooks and acted them out in Alex's or Joe's bedroom. Sometimes, another little friend from the school, Noah Adelman, joined them. Of course, play-acting took work. Rose always had delicious refreshments ready to boost their energy. These were good times.

The Pierce mansion took a respite from the mayhem that had befallen it when Grayson had arrived with his ward back in July. Joe was settling in, but the big black dictionary was never far from easy reach.

CHAPTER THIRTY

Joe missed Grayson during the day. When his guardian came home in the evenings, somehow Irene always managed to beat him, jumping into her father's welcoming arms. One Saturday afternoon, Grayson happened to be home while Irene was at a birthday party. He muttered something about a golf game being canceled because of the weather. Happily, Joe had him all to himself on the family room couch with a thick, heavy photo album while the two old bovines were upstairs napping. Aunt Mil, armed with a pair of scissors, fussed with the newspaper at a corner table.

"Here's Herschel and Virginia Millburn, and this was taken during their honeymoon at Niagara Falls. Virginia is my first cousin on my mother's side. They have three children, Wayne, Evelyn, and Robert. What year did they get married?" Grayson looked up toward his sister.

Frau Dead Fish Eyes clipped a baking soda coupon. "1933. March fourth, I believe."

To Joe, he said quietly, "Your Aunt Mil has always been good with dates."

Joe touched the photograph. He concentrated on listening to Grayson explain who all these people were in the album, trying to get straight the aunts, uncles, grandparents, and cousins. Most of them lived in Buffalo, Syracuse, or Albany.

Grayson turned to a black and white picture of a couple wearing wedding attire. The square-shouldered woman held a large bouquet of roses and sat in a ruffled white, floor-length gown. Her rectangular face was impervious and unsmiling; her light hair swept up and behind her head, fastened with a complicated arrangement of flowers. Her dashing, fair-haired new husband stood with one hand on the back of her chair and held a light-colored top hat in the other. He bore a faint smirk. Grayson mumbled something Joe didn't understand and turned to another page. When Joe tried to push the page back, Grayson whispered "no" and pointed to Irene's baby pictures.

"Look at the time." Mildred checked her watch. "I must pick up Irene at school." She gathered her clippings and headed toward the kitchen.

Grayson waited until she was out of earshot and then turned back to the couple's large photo. In a low voice, he said, "I wanted to wait until Aunt Mil left to tell you about this one. This is Mildred on her wedding day with her husband, Vance Worthington. See the date in the corner, 1927? Vance Worthington came from a wealthy family and owned the Worthington Office Supply Company in New York City. It had been started by his grandfather back before the Civil War. They sold office equipment. Don't worry. I'll explain the Civil War another time."

"Aber I already know about Civil War."

"You do?"

"Ya, between de Union und Confederate States of America. It vas about states' rights--"

"Yes, yes, I don't need a lecture, Joe. How do you know about the Civil War?"

"I in a book read."

"I read it in a book. Watch your subject-verb correlation, Joe." Grayson rolled his eyes and said under his breath, "A pint-sized know-it-all-history professor I'm rearing." Pointing to the picture, he went on. "Well, back to this. Vance and Mildred lived in upper Manhattan in a hoity-toity neighborhood."

Joe wrinkled his forehead upon hearing the words "hoity-toity," but asked, "How did dey meet?"

"Mildred worked in the payroll office. Apparently, Vance fell in love with her on the job." He let the album slide a little, and Joe took hold of it. "That was the happiest I had ever seen her."

Joe looked at the picture again. "She dunt look happy."

"Well, that's about the best she could do. She had quite a life in New York City after she got married. She was what one would call a socialite. That's a person who wears fancy clothes and gives a lot of parties."

Joe asked, "Ver is he now?" He pointed to the suave-looking man in the picture.

"That's a sad story. Eight months after Vance and Mildred were married, he died in an automobile accident. Then her baby boy died under mysterious circumstances in his crib when he was barely three months old. Millie inherited her late husband's entire estate, including the office supply company. Since she knew nothing about business or how to run such a huge company, she sold it. Fortunately, she had good advice from our father's banker, and her timing could not have been better. She sold it before the '29 crash at a particularly good price."

"Crash? De Great Depression ven people out of vork?"

"Yes, the Great Depression. It started in 1929 and affected not only the United States but also Europe. Many businesses went bankrupt, and folks lost their jobs. People had very little money."

Joe was more interested in what happened to Aunt Mil. "Frau tote Fischaugen sold the company," he repeated.

"Who?"

Joe caught his slip. "Aunt Mil. She sold de company."

"Yes. She became a very wealthy woman. She has more money than I will ever see in my lifetime."

"How much wealthy?"

"You mean, how much money does she have?"

"Ya."

Grayson smiled wryly. "Let's just say a lot."

"Vat about Grandma Nina und Aunt Elvie?"

"They're so rich that when they go to the bathroom, there's money in the toilet instead of you-know-what."

Joe giggled. Grayson pulled him into his lap and tickled his sides. Joe put his hands on the man's broad shoulders and returned his gaze.

"Grayson, are you rich?"

His guardian gave a short laugh. "No. I'm comfortable. I make enough money to keep Irene supplied with crayons and new outfits for her dolls. You know they have to wear the latest fashion every season."

Joe sank his knees into Grayson's lap. His guardian pushed his bangs out of his eyes.

"But more importantly, Joe, you will not be wanting . . . ever."

He turned Joe around and opened the album again. He turned it to the back that revealed another photograph. It was a colored, five-by-eight portrait of a young, wide-faced woman, showing even, white teeth behind a red-lipsticked mouth. Her merry blue eyes sparkled. Unlike the somber-looking couple several pages back, this young woman with blonde hair stylishly arranged about her face smiled as if pleased to have her picture taken. Her open, friendly face made Joe wish he could have known her. She appeared in another black and white photograph in a wedding dress in front of a darkened altar and lighted candles. Grayson, dressed in a tuxedo with tails, tilted his head over his petite bride, a proud smile stretching his long, handsome face.

"This was my wife, Margaret. Everybody called her 'Margie.' And over here in this picture is St. Mark's Parish in Syracuse, where we were married. Margie's folks lived in Syracuse, so that's why we had the wedding there. I met her when I was a resident at the Presbyterian Hospital in New York City. She was a recovery nurse. When a patient came out of surgery, she helped him or her wake up and get settled. It is a critical job in the patient's care." He mused over more wedding pictures. "Here are my parents, your grandmother, Nina Cassandra, and your grandfather, William Riley."

But these people were not his grandparents. He had never met his own, as he vaguely remembered his mother telling him that all his relatives had moved to Switzerland shortly before he had been born.

He was about to say this to Grayson but stopped. Grayson's mouth turned down as he looked wistfully at his wedding picture. "She was the love of my life."

Joe studied the couple.

"We got married while I was finishing my residency. We lived in an apartment close to the hospital in Manhattan." He pointed to another picture of a white frame house with shutters, a large tree off to the side. "This photo was taken in front of her parents' house. We had seven happy years together. I may not have told you that she passed away while giving birth to Irene."

"I am sorry, Grayson."

The man absently stroked Joe's back. "I moved into this house so Mildred and my mother could help take care of the baby. After that, my father soon passed away, and I took over his practice. It was supposed to be a temporary arrangement. But as you can see, I'm still here." He forced a smile and turned another page.

"Vat about Aunt Elvie?"

Grayson pushed himself higher on the sofa, making Joe grab his shirt to hang on. "Aunt Elvie is my mother's sister-in-law. Her husband was my uncle Edward, my father's older brother. He was a doctor in Syracuse. They had four children. See this picture? It was taken at his funeral. When he passed on, she didn't want to live by herself, and her kids were grown and scattered around the state. Since this was such a large house, we invited her to stay with us. The more, the merrier, so to speak."

Joe thought about all the people in the pictures. "Are all of dem my new family?"

"Come with me." Grayson rose, and Joe almost tumbled to the floor. He followed his guardian up the broad, oak staircase. They stopped on the landing and turned to the wall.

Above the wainscoting, hanging on the crimson-papered wall in ornate, heavy frames, were numerous old photographs. Joe had seen these pictures from the first time he had climbed the steps back in July, but he had not taken the time to examine them. As he looked at them now, he surmised they were long-deceased relatives. Many pairs of eyes looked back at him. Single portraits of mothers wearing tightly buttoned bodices and cameos at their throats held their cross-eyed babies in front of colorless backgrounds. Their dark, nebulous eyes that stared back at Joe would share no secrets nor reveal any privation of those earlier times. In a long, rectangular photo, a camaraderie of young women dressed in stiff, white lacey blouses, starched facial expressions, and dark skirts stood under a thickly branched tree. Their straight hair of indeterminate colors was parted severely down the middle and stretched back into hidden buns. Perhaps this had been the graduation day at a school. Joe turned his attention to other yellowish pictures. Middle-aged men with their half-turn view away from the camera wore important handlebar mustaches and sparse, untidy beards. One grainy picture was of a group of men in buttoned military uniforms with pushed-in caps on their heads and rifles at their sides, all standing in a field. Tents and horses stood in the distance. The troops looked very unhappy.

Waving his hand at the pictures, Grayson said, "These people are all family members going back four generations, Joe. Look at this one. That's my grandfather, Seymour Herschel Pierce, standing in the mud with some Union soldiers. That was taken during the Civil War. I'm not the only army doctor in the family."

"Oh. Ven?"

Grayson examined the bottom right corner. "Hmmm. It says August 22, 1862."

"Dat vas de Second Battle of Bull Run in Prince William County, Virginia."

His guardian huffed with annoyance. "If you say so."

Dominating the entire wall in the middle was a full-standing portrait of a man in a charcoal gray suit with his hand on a green velvet Victorian parlor chair. On the third finger of his left hand, a bit of red embedded in a gold ring looked like the ruby ring Grayson wore on his left pinky. His other hand tucked in his trouser pocket pushed back the coat, revealing a delicate chain hanging at the waistcoat. Joe's father had a similar chain, with a silver pocket watch on the end of it. This man presented an inviting smile on a clean-shaven, rectangular face with a large nose and narrow set eyes and thinning, chestnut-colored hair. There was also benevolence and compassion in his face, just like in his guardian's face. Joe imagined being held in this man's arms, very much like the man who stood next to him. His tiny shoulders would be pressed against the curved collared shirt, black ascot, and red plaid silk waistcoat. When he looked down, he saw a small brass plate on the burnt gold frame with an inscription, Dr. William Riley Pierce, 1905.

Grayson said, "My father hated to have to stand so long while this portrait was done. I think he had varicose veins and his legs hurt. That's what happens when you're on your feet all day in surgery." He passed his hand over the display. "These are your new relatives, past and present, because you're part of my family now. The ones in the album you'll meet soon. In November, we'll have a big Thanksgiving blow-out."

"Blow-out? Thanksgiving?"

"A big dinner we have in November. It's a holiday to give thanks for all the good things we have in America. Then in August next year, we'll have a big family reunion in the Cayuga Lake State Park."

"Ve missed it!"

"Every other year, Joe. We had the reunion last year. Of course, I wasn't there because I was in the army. During spring vacation, we'll go down to Florida to sit on the beach for a week and do sun damage to our pasty white New York hides. One of the other doctors I work with owns a beach house, and he rents it to us from time to time. Do you know where Florida is?"

"Yes." He had looked up that state in the encyclopedia. He was glad he could now explore that set of matching books, and he had promised himself to read all of them cover to cover.

"Would you like to see the ocean?"

"Ya! Ven can ve leave?"

"Well, we may go in April next year when you and Irene are out of school for spring vacation. But we will definitely go to the reunion next August. And we have Thanksgiving to look forward to." He fell silent momentarily as if thinking about that holiday. "Mildred has been writing letters and making phone calls, telling everybody about you." Grayson stroked Joe's cheek with his finger. "You're getting bigger, you know." His eyes soften.

Joe put his hands in his pockets.

"I will be so proud to show you off to the relatives. They are good people . . . except for maybe one or two."

"Vat?"

"Don't worry about them." He took his hand to lead him back downstairs. "Joe, are you sleeping better now? You seem more rested during the day."

"Ya."

"You're supposed to say, 'Yes.' No more nightmares?"

Joe thought before he answered. "No."

The phone rang in the foyer. After Grayson answered it and talked briefly, he put down the receiver and said, "That was the hospital. I have to go."

Joe knew why he had to leave now. Grayson had explained that sometimes he was "on-call," meaning that he had to be available when the hospital needed him. When the call came at night waking him, Joe would jump out of bed and go to the window to watch the big black car roll out of the driveway. The security lights from the house shone on the car, but he couldn't see Grayson. Then he would crawl back into his bed.

He waited while the big man gathered his things. "Bye, Grayson." His heart skipped as his guardian kissed him again on his cheek.

CHAPTER THIRTY-ONE

Joe couldn't decide who was the harder nut to crack—Grandma Nina or Irene. By careful study, planning, and sometimes the sheer look of cuteness he could make on his face, he had won the hearts of everyone else in the Pierce home (Frau Dead Fish Eyes being questionable). Of course, Grayson loved him and told him so on the nights he was home to tuck him into bed. Rose, the cook, and her assistant, Anne, adored him. They baked special cookies with pecans and chocolate pieces for him and made funny smiling faces of oyster crackers in his tomato soup. He shared with Aunt Elvie her love for the daily radio shows and card games, and he liked to help her with her crossword puzzles. By doing all his schoolwork correctly and remembering his manners, he gained Aunt Mil's silent approval. And finally, Mr. Henry allowed him to hold him for longer than two minutes . . . sometimes.

But the eldest and the youngest were yet to be won over. Joe couldn't swallow his anxiety whenever he had to deal with the hoary dragon lady. It was her indifference that irked him. Most of the time, this old woman acted as if he wasn't even there. She did not praise him for his good behavior nor make any positive comment on his improvement of his English. She had yet even to call him by his name. When she did speak to him, she morphed into an overseer ordering a slave, or worse, the child of a slave. She beckoned to him only when she needed him, and her demands were no less unconditional than the worst SS guards in the camp were.

When they were outside, she would sit in a porch chair under a big, sugar maple tree wearing a rose-patterned silk shawl and a testy disposition. She would shout, "Pinch off the dead flowers in the astilbe bed." Joe broke off the tops of the spent flowers while his knees sank in the dirt. "No, those are gladiolas over there. Pull up that chickweed and the dandelions. And mind the coral bells! Put the weeds in that trash barrel. No, not that one, the one over there on the side of the greenhouse. When you get through with the weeding, I need you to fill up the birdfeeders." And so on.

He brought her a cup of tea and scones in the afternoons in the music room, and sometimes her slippers if her bunions were acting up. As much as he wanted to converse with her while doing these chores, he didn't dare open his mouth. Her grating, croaky voice and her pointed bent finger left him unable to speak.

But when she was on the phone with one of her many friends, the annoying tone in her voice transformed into smoother, higher pitches. She spoke as if she were about to burst into song. Gardening and cooking clubs, card parties, church meetings, and frequent shopping excursions were her favorite topics of conversation. Joe was beginning to think she was like a chameleon, changing her personality when it suited her.

Trips to New York City with Aunt Elvie and her friends from the parish took Nina Cassandra out of the house twice a month. When the two old toddling cows returned, the castle was always in an uproar. Anne was tasked with carrying armloads of packages and boxes up to their rooms on the second floor while they chattered about their visit to Macy's and Bloomingdale's and Gimbels as if they were novice tourists. Joe stayed in his room.

He wondered if Grandma Nina had treated her own children with as much callousness as she did with him. It seemed that Aunt Mil certainly took after her. To get an approving word or an encouraging hand on his shoulder from that woman took more effort than getting a smile on her face. Grandma Nina had to have reared Grayson differently. He wasn't anything like Aunt Mil.

One night as Joe readied himself for bed and Grayson was in his room, he asked him why he was so nice, whereas Aunt Mil was not.

Grayson said, "It's rather complicated. I take after my father. He had a much different personality than my mother. He was very loving and patient with us kids. He made up the love my mother wasn't able to give." He helped Joe climb into bed and pulled the sheet and bedspread over him. "He loved being a doctor because he enjoyed helping people get well and feel better. And that inspired me to go into medicine and continue his practice."

"Vy did dey get married if dey ver so verschieden?"

"What?"

"Umm, nicht same."

"You mean different. Good question. Who knew what the attraction was between them. It was almost an arranged marriage if you ask Uncle Bob. He's my mother's older brother. They were reared in a strict, devout family. Being a female, following the rules was the most important part of her life. That was the way it was back then. Of course, my father's family was Catholic too, but not as, shall I say, dogmatic. I can tell by the look on your face you don't know that word. My family wasn't as strict about Catholicism as my mother's family was. Dad was often criticized by my mother's folks about how he reared me and Mildred and my younger brother Albert. He wouldn't discipline us the way they thought he should. They said he was too sensitive, too tender-hearted. I guess they were right. His heart wasn't very sturdy."

"Vat?"

"He died of a heart attack when he was only fifty-six on June 19, 1935. It happened suddenly, without warning. It was one of the worst days of my life. I loved him very much." He closed his eyes and then opened them. "I learned a lot from him and not just how to be a good doctor. He taught me to respect other people, no matter how different they were. That's important when you're a doctor."

"Irene vants to be a doctor, too."

"Yes. But she's got a-ways to go about learning how to get along with others."

Joe thought, *Ya, she does.* Irene certainly seemed not to appreciate the importance of being respectful or even courteous. This little blonde-headed hellion with a chip on her shoulder was downright mean sometimes. Dealing with her was like handling a two-headed snake. Taking advantage of her good mood was like picking up one head with the risk of being bitten by the other, which would be her bad mood. In the evening, in front of the four-foot-tall Zenith Aztec radio, she would put her arms around him and put her head on his shoulder, giving a convincing demonstration of sisterly affection. When she was in an obliging disposition, they played Candyland and checkers in her room, and he always let her win, hoping to keep her cooperative disposition. Then without provocation, she would change her demeanor in an instant. Her face would become crimson, and her eyes would flash just like her grandmother's. If Grayson was around during these episodes, Joe could fall back on that parental support if he didn't want to play house or Crazy 8's or hold the end of a jump rope. However, if he was on his own with her, he had to cooperate and give into her absurd commands or suffer well-aimed kicks to his shins. When the women were out and Rose was busy in the kitchen, she would chase him from the basement up to the attic and back to the second floor, yelling how much she hated him. Being taller by three inches and outweighing him by several pounds, she easily got him down on his bedroom floor. Then she straddled him and delivered not-too-forceful slaps and punches. He just took the assaults as they came. He would never hit her back.

Still, there were times when the blows turned into tickles, and they would start giggling. And then she would lie on top of him, both catching their breaths. He liked to be close to her and look into her eyes. He often focused on her pouty, strawberry red mouth. He wondered if it tasted as sweet as it looked.

CHAPTER THIRTY-TWO

On Thanksgiving morning, a mighty wind from the northeast brought brisk temperatures and rattled the leaf-barren trees. Joe shivered as he padded into the bathroom to take his bath, his bare feet slapping the cold tiled floor. Feeling a sense of foreboding, he wished he could just stay in the tub soaking in the warm, cozy bubble bath. He played with Daffy Duck and Mickey Mouse, making small talk in German between the two rubber toys while Herr Ente looked on from his perch on the ledge, most likely grateful not to be drowned in the soapy water. But the lump in his stomach did not go away.

Downstairs, Rose and the other two cooks hired to prepare for the nearly forty men, women, and children who would descend on the Pierce mansion in a few hours were toiling in the kitchen. They worked assiduously making vinegar slaw, red bean and macaroni salads, and preparing candied sweet potatoes, vegetable casseroles, baked beans, cornmeal stuffing, giblet gravy, cranberry sauce, and egg noodles. Having come the day before, they had baked three double-layered cakes, dozens of cookies, and apple, pumpkin, pecan, and mincemeat pies, all sitting under plastic wrap on a dessert table in a corner in the dining room along with homemade rolls and nut breads. The kitchen smelled heavenly from the turkey, the clove-studded ham, and the game hens roasting in the two walled ovens. Industrial-sized pots of raw peeled potatoes covered in salted water sat in the sink, ready to be boiled and mashed. Tureens, pie pans, skillets, vegetable plates, mixing bowls, and cutting boards covered every inch of counter space. Covered saucepans sat on the stove, releasing stream from green beans and Brussel Sprouts. More than eighty years old, the kitchen work table nearly collapsed under the weight of the heaps of fresh vegetables, fruits, and cheeses. Mildred cut the crudités and cheese into small pieces and stuck them together with toothpicks. Artfully, she arranged them on the engraved, heirloom silver platters.

In the dining room, Anne and two more hired maids, dressed in starched black uniforms and snow-white lace aprons, sorted silverware and set out linen napkins and condiments. They also counted dinner plates, water goblets, bread and dessert plates, salad plates, and cups and saucers. Anne arranged the wine bottles and glassware. The always-faithful, industrial-sized coffee urn busily percolated on the sideboard. Glass pitchers filled with ice-brewed tea sat next to it.

Joe stood in a corner next to Mr. Henry's food and water bowls.

"Well, are you going to just stand there, or are you here waiting for your breakfast?" asked Aunt Mil, glancing at him. "We're very busy this morning."

"Okay. Ver ist Grayson?"

"He's at the hospital doing an emergency appendectomy."

Joe took one look at the melee and decided not to ask Rose to help him rustle up a bowl of cereal and milk. To avoid getting yelled at for being in the way, he went into the empty music room where he found Mr. Henry washing his fuzzy face beneath the Bosendorfer grand piano in a choice spot of weak sunlight.

The mansion was the largest and oldest home in the Pierce dynasty, so it made sense to have the relatives gather here on Thanksgiving Day. By mid-morning, guests from all over the state began to arrive. A new wave of fear made Joe's hands clammy as he heard car doors bang from outside and a myriad of loud voices resounding in the foyer. Since he did not know any of these people, he worried about how they react to him. Would they be as intimidating as Frau Dead Fish Eyes and the old queen bee? And what about all those children? Would they find his room upstairs, ready to pounce with destructive hands on his favorite toys?

He started to run toward the stairs to retreat to his room. But realizing that would be the first place Aunt Mil would look, he decided to hide in the cramped storage closet under the staircase filled with old candles and dusty red and green stuff. Grayson never said he couldn't hide in here. After closing the little painted door, he strained his ears, listening for his guardian's familiar voice. Instead, he heard Frau Dead Fish Eyes call him.

Cautiously, he peeked through a crack in the miniature storeroom door and saw people taking off their coats, hats, and gloves. The cacophony rose as they yakked with Frau Dead Fish Eyes and the two old bovines who greeted them. The squealing kids' voices reminded Joe of the boisterous children in the library in Albany.

As if caught in a hunter's gun sights, Joe froze as Aunt Mil approached the closet. How did she know he was in here? Nevertheless, she took him by his collar and pulled him out. She dragged him by the hand toward the crowd in the living room. As her lipless mouth pulled back in a laborious, face-breaking smile, she announced, "This is our new little boy, Joe. He's been with us since the second week in July."

Several people spoke at once, greeting him. "We've heard so much about you!" said an overweight woman with dark hair and dressed in an apple-green suit and ivory blouse. She leaned down to Joe. "You're from Germany, aren't you?"

Inexplicably, Joe knew he had nothing to fear from this motherly woman.

"Can he speak German?" asked a plump girl, wearing a taffeta gold skirt and her brown hair pulled back in a ponytail behind a black braided headband. She looked about Irene's age, only a bit taller.

Feeling a sharp knuckle in the middle of his back, Joe said, "Guten tag."

A tall man in a black, single-breasted suit loomed over Joe like a Goliath. He boomed, "Hello, Joe. I'm your Uncle Al. We met back in July in Washington D. C. with your guardian, Grayson. But you probably don't remember. You were a bit under the weather at the time. But you look a lot better now. I heard you know some other languages." He had a big, rectangular face like Grayson's and Aunt Mil, with affable gray eyes and a cleft chin.

Joe had to think fast. "I think you are a loud man," he said in Yiddish.

The adults babbled their approval. The broad-shouldered man shouted over them, "Hey! He knows Polish! Good heavens, Mil, you've worked miracles with this boy! How many languages does he know?"

Sliding up to Joe, Irene whispered in his ear, "Show off!" She and the girl with the ponytail disappeared.

Aunt Mil folded her arms. "More than you know, Albert."

The heavy-set woman with the amiable face said, "Joe, I'm your Aunt Bernice." She pointed to the stairs. "That was Martha. This is Penny and . . ." She hurried to a toddler who was moving dangerously close to a china cabinet in the corner.

"Paul, our oldest," said the loud man, pushing forward a blond-headed boy, who up this point had hung back. He was several inches taller than Joe. "We've got another boy in the family, son. He's your new cousin."

Joe sensed rigid blue eyes taking stock of him. The youth's fair shock of hair, the jutted, aggressive chin, and the defiant thumbs in the belt loops of his pants reminded him of a German boy wearing a swastika armband he once saw on a sidewalk in Berlin. Joe blinked to quiet his heart. The Nazi-teen looked at him with bored indifference.

"Mil, I brought my new camera." Uncle Albert held up a leather case. "I want to take plenty of pictures of my new nephew."

The doorbell rang again. "Just make sure to leave me out of camera range." Mildred waved her hands as she left to greet the next horde of relatives.

An elderly couple stood next to the friendly lady. Aunt Bernice said, smiling, "Joe, this is your new Great Aunt Harriet and Uncle Bob. Uncle Bob is your grandmother's brother."

Grandmother? Grosmutter? He never had a grandmother, at least not the old lizard lady.

Another black-haired lady walked past, holding a glass baking pan with a dish towel covering it. She went on toward the dining room. "Excuse me, Mildred. I brought my cheesecake, and it needs to go into the refrigerator." Joe looked after her.

While watching the maids set out savory hor d'ourves and crudités, icy fingers grabbed him. "C'mere and give your old uncle a hug." The white-haired, shriveled man with a wrinkled forehead and liver spots on his face looked as if he had landed a fish. *Goodness, who is this old geezer?* He reeked of stale cigars and something nasty and unwashed. Joe noticed his brown-stained upper teeth moved and clicked, and his breath smelled sour, like cabbage that had gone to waste in the garden. He and his overweight, blue-haired, equally bizarre-looking wife settled on the sofa in the living room. Joe had to sit on the old man's bony knees and suffer.

Uncle Bob's wife, Aunt Harriet, patted Joe on his leg. "Come, let me hold you." She pulled Joe into her tight lap and wrapped her flabby arms around him. He could feel the rolls of fat underneath her constricted blouse. But at least she smelled better than Uncle Bob. The pretty tin can of talcum powder on Aunt Elvie's dressing table came to mind. "You're as cute as a button." She cooed and pinched his cheek. At least her teeth looked real.

Joe regarded the Nazi-teen as he slumped in an overstuffed chair and carelessly put his feet on the coffee table. He was dangerously close to kicking an antique crystal candy dish. He had the same angry pout that Irene had with her lower lip stuck out. Fortunately for the dish, the kid's father told him to put his feet down.

When another couple with two small children entered the living room, Joe tried to listen to Great Aunt Harriet explain that they were her daughter, Joan, and her husband, Ralph O'Conner. Their two little girls wearing matching checked dresses were her granddaughters, Jill and Audrey. As more relatives and Mildred's best friend, Helen Schlazier, arrived, the racket in the living room rose almost to an unbearable pitch.

Joe managed to steal out of the old woman's lap as she talked to a bespeckled man wearing a too-big brown suit and a funny orange bowtie. On his way back to the little storeroom, he was intercepted.

"Joe, will you take this into the kitchen?" Helen Schlazier carefully handed him a heavy ceramic bowl covered with a tin pie plate. Joe had seen her many times before as she often came over to visit and work with Frau Dead Fish Eyes on various projects. Peeking, he saw pea salad in the bowl. It looked tasty, and his mouth watered. He remembered he had not eaten breakfast.

Mildred kept an eye on the black square clock on the fireplace mantel as the morning wore on. More Pierce relations walked into the living room and spilled into the family and music rooms. Aunt Bernice went around introducing Joe to many of them, holding his sweaty little hand and getting around rowdy children. Keeping up with all these strangers' names was beyond him. Aunt Bernice let go of his hand to talk to another black-haired man, this one young and fashionably dressed in a padded-shouldered wool suit and wearing brown and white oxfords. Joe inched back toward the stairs and sat on the first step. He hugged a white-painted baluster.

Seeing all these people and their out-of-control children, Joe realized that Grayson had many aunts and uncles and cousins, many of whom he hadn't seen in the photo album. They chatted and laughed, having seemed to have forgotten about him. Did they not know how fortunate they were to have the whole Pierce clan together and still alive? These people were not his relatives. Joe wondered if he would have had such a large family before he and his father and mother lived in the attic. He had never met any of his parent's family. Was it possible that they also had been caught by the Nazis and had perished? Throbbing sadness filled his heart. He didn't have anybody.

He looked toward the dining room and saw Anne set out pitchers of ice water. Another maid took off the plastic wrap from the rolls and bread. The coffee urn announced its readiness with a tiny orange light above the spout.

Great Uncle Bob stood and clapped his hands. "Don't you ladies think it's time to get this show on the road?"

His wife, Aunt Harriet, spoke as if to a grandchild, "Just be patient, Bob."

"You're the one who told me not to eat a big breakfast!" The peculiar old guy nearly shouted. "I'm hungry!"

"We're waiting for Grayson," said Nina Cassandra, who sat on her living room throne, holding her cane like a scepter and reviewing her subjects.

"So where is he?" asked Uncle Albert, fiddling with his camera.

The telephone rang from the foyer. The chitchat in the living room died.

Putting down the receiver, Mildred proclaimed, "That was Grayson. He's been delayed at the hospital, and he told us not to wait." She smoothed her polka-dot white and gray Christian Dior dress. "I believe everything's ready. We'll gather in the dining room."

The crowd proceeded.

"Mother, will you say grace?" Mildred asked.

Everyone fell silent and bowed their heads. There was the usual touching of the head, chest, and shoulders. Mothers held their children tightly to keep them quiet. Joe listened to the old biddy say a prayer in the same manner as Grayson at his first meal in this home on that warm, fateful day in July. After the matriarch finished, everyone crossed themselves and murmured, "Amen." Joe almost imitated the gesture but stopped, remembering his promise to Grayson to stay true to his Jewish faith and not make the Catholic sign of the cross. Thankfully, Frau Dead Fish Eyes overlooked him.

Card tables set up in the music and family rooms accommodated the overflow of guests. Joe sat at a table with three other loquacious children nearest the kitchen doorway. He tried to tune out the constant noise as he coped with the large slice of turkey on his plate. Anne and the two maids made him nervous as they flitted about with iced tea pitchers and wine bottles. They moved so fast Joe was getting dizzy. It would have been so much better if he could just sit in the corner of the kitchen next to the icebox and share his meal with Mr. Henry, who at this point was incognito.

The conversation included the latest gossip at local parishes, whose son made it on the basketball team, and the rout by the Army against Notre Dame, 48-0. American GIs were coming back in droves, flooding New York universities on the new G. I. bill, and there was speculation whether President Truman stood a chance at re-election. Lowered voices whispered about the dramatic increase in vandalism and crime on Ithaca's streets since the newly discharged soldiers had returned. Voices raised when electric bills were debated. That led to a favorite topic: money.

Somehow, the discussion at the big dining room table turned to Grayson's plans for Joe's religious training. Joe overheard Aunt Mil tell everyone that, unfortunately, her brother had brought home a Jewish child, and she could not convince him to convert him to Catholicism. Moreover, he intended for the boy to attend the public school. Over the collective chorus of disapproval, Mildred declared that she had already made arrangements for Joe to attend Immaculate Conception after the first of the year. Great Uncle Bob said something about having a sit-down talk with his nephew later. Another male relative, Harold Pierce (Grayson's second cousin on his father's side), loudly declared his concern about whether Joe would be baptized. Nina Cassandra answered him, saying that "the boy had been rescued from the devil's embrace and the ceremony had been executed back in September."

The choir intoned its endorsement.

Joe remembered that afternoon in early September when Frau Dead Fish Eyes, Aunt Elvie, and the old queen bee had rushed him to Immaculate Conception to have this ritual performed. They had planned to do this when they were sure Grayson was in surgery at the hospital. The priest, Father Byrne, had been reluctant to do the baptism without Grayson's involvement. But the women had pushed their case of saving Joe's soul for the afterlife, and the deed was done in the empty sanctuary without fanfare. What Joe remembered most was how cold the water was on the top of his head.

Now, he put down his fork. He wasn't hungry anymore. Before he knew it, Aunt Bernice was at his side. "You want some cake, Joe?"

Joe shook his head. *Wo ist Grayson?*

"Why don't you go downstairs and play? There's a Ping-Pong table down there, right?" She called to her daughter, Martha. "You and Irene take Joe to the basement. He doesn't need to hear all this adult talk."

The girls thundered down the stairs, and Joe listlessly followed.

Tattered chairs, a worn-out sofa, scratched bookcases, old, water-stained boxes, and rusty toys cluttered the basement. Aunt Mil's new Westinghouse washer sat against the painted, concrete block wall; copper pipes hooked up to two water spigots behind it. Next to it sat a matching clothes dryer. A coffin-sized freezer hummed in a corner. The basement smelled damp despite Grayson's efforts to keep the moisture down with a dehumidifier. Irene pulled the strings attached to the bare light bulbs fixed to the unfinished, cobwebbed ceiling. A few weeks ago, Joe had overheard the two cleaning ladies, Phyllis and Valeria, planning to wait until after the Thanksgiving weekend to give the basement a thorough wash-down.

At the Ping-Pong table, Joe did a good job returning the girls' serves. He forgot about the ruckus upstairs, concentrating on hitting the little white ball.

Soon, three more children came down to explore the basement. They found a jump rope missing a handle, a broken rocking horse watching from a corner, and a pair of bent roller skates. A scuffed, beat-up toy box contained metal racing cars sans wheels, tiny plastic planes with broken wings, deflated rubber balls, puppets without strings attached, headless dolls, board games missing pieces, and old, used-up coloring books and broken crayons. "You guys be careful with my stuff. Don't break anything," Irene warned.

The stuck-up Nazi kid, Paul, sauntered down the stairs. With thumbs hooked on his belt loops, he surveyed the basement like a sheriff upon entering a saloon. "What's going on down here?"

No one answered him. Irene, Martha, and Joe kept playing Ping-Pong. Paul grabbed a paddle and began taking the girls' volleys. Joe gave way as the taller youth swung his arm wide, smashing the ball so recklessly that it flew across the room and hit Debbie, a four-year-old youngster, on the arm. She began to cry.

"Now, see what you did!" Martha shouted as she walked over to pick up the ball. "You're supposed to leave it on the table!"

"Aw, she's just a baby. C'mon, let's play."

Debbie followed the other children back up the stairs when she realized no one here would address her tears. The game resumed, but Paul still could not control the ball. After a few minutes, he gave up. "Hey, do you know how to play marbles?" he asked Joe.

"Yes." Joe didn't want to play marbles.

"You got some here?"

"Bag ist upstairs in meinem dresser."

"What about cowboys and Indians?"

Joe hadn't played cowboys and Indians before.

"It stinks down here," said Martha. "Let's go upstairs to your room, Irene." The two girls put their paddles on the green wooden table and ascended the stairs.

"Stay here," Paul said. "I got somethin' we can use." He stomped back up the steps.

Joe wiped perspiration from his forehead. He put down his paddle and collected the wayward toys to put back in the toy box. Above his head, he heard voices and the floor creaking as heavy feet tramped on it.

"I just saw Daddy's car in the driveway, Joe," Irene said as she and Martha came pounding back down the stairs. "Let's go."

Before Irene turned around, a hand pushed her roughly on the shoulder. Paul stood behind her, holding a rifle. The girls halted, aware that he blocked their escape.

All color left Joe's face. Certain he would wet himself, he slowly backed away. Paul went around the girls and pointed the weapon at him.

Grinning, he said, "What's the matter? Haven't you ever seen a Red Ryder air rifle before? My dad got this for me for my birthday last week. Ain't it somethin'?"

He still aimed the gun at Joe, high toward his chest.

"Put it down, Paul," Martha said.

"We don't keep guns in the house." Irene moved closer to Joe.

"Shut up! We're gonna play cowboys and Indians, and we need the gun." To Joe, he said, "I'll be the cowboy. You'll be the Indian."

Joe heard the click. With a scream stuck in his throat, he pushed past the girls and the Nazi teen and flew up the stairs. Through the kitchen, knocking over a chair, he ran through the dining room and family room just as fast as if a SS guard was on his heels. Grayson, standing in the foyer holding a flat paper bag and talking with his brother, Albert, saw him fleeing for his life. He dropped the package to go after him. Joe bounded the stairs just as his guardian reached out to grab him. But, as once before in a foyer closet, the man snatched nothing but air.

Thank God, the closet door in his bedroom was open. Joe slammed it shut and, in a frenzy, pushed shoes and boxes out of the way. He found a woolen blanket to cover himself. Closing his eyes and wrapping his arms around his sides, he mouthed in Hebrew, "The Lord is my shepherd, the Lord is my shepherd . . ." Hot tears slid down his face. He tried to curl himself up as tightly as he could, protecting his stomach. But Joe couldn't protect his mind from that terrorizing moment. He saw the rifle. He heard the familiar click and the ear-splitting report following it. He saw the prisoner who had bravely tried to make a run for it slump over without a sound at the barbed-wire fence, the fast spurt of blood coming out of his neck. Joe moaned and rocked himself. His stomach weakened, and his dinner came up.

The closet door opened, and he heard Irene. "He's in here, Aunt Mil."

"What? What's he doing in there?" Aunt Mil's voice floated from farther away.

"You're in trouble, Joe," Irene whispered. "You're not supposed to be in here." She pulled away the blanket. In the light from the opened door, she saw his face. "Aunt Mil, he threw up."

"Bring him out." Frau Dead Fish Eyes opened a dresser drawer for a clean shirt.

There was ferocious shouting going on downstairs. Someone began mounting the stairs with aggressive steps. Joe heard more agitated voices talking all at once and then retreating footfalls. A boyish voice, shrill and whiney, kept interrupting the thunderous manly voices, but it was utterly defenseless against the verbal onslaught. Aunt Mil shut Joe's bedroom door, and when she took him into the bathroom, she closed that door as well.

"My goodness, you're shaking like a leaf!" Aunt Mil said as she wiped his face and neck. The damp washcloth felt good against his burning cheeks. She took off his soiled shirt.

Irene held the clean shirt. "I was scared, too. That was a real gun, and I heard a click like he pulled the trigger."

"Well, your father's talking with that naughty boy and your Uncle Albert. How did he get that gun into the house?"

Irene shrugged. "He must have sneaked it in, maybe through the kitchen door." She handed the shirt to her aunt.

Joe put out his arms like a toddler, and his aunt put them through the sleeves. She led him by the hand back into the bedroom. When they sat on his bed, Joe wrapped his arms around her neck and pushed his face into her generous bosom, sobbing. Her black onyx bead necklace made imprints on his forehead. Aunt Mil briefly patted his head as if he were an exotic animal. Irene lightly stroked his back.

"I-I heard das click. He vas going to shoot me."

Aunt Mil tilted his chin up to look into his red eyes. "No, Joe, he wasn't going to shoot you. He was just acting irresponsibly. He should have never brought that gun into the house in the first place." She stood him on the floor. buttoned his shirt and stuffed the tail into his pants. "You're going to be in many different circumstances in your life, and you have to act properly. You can't just run off and hide in the closet every time you feel threatened."

Joe fidgeted. "But I get afraid again."

"Well, you are just going to have to get over it."

"Ya, doch--"

"Look at me, Joe, and stop talking in German." Aunt Mil put her hands on both sides of his face. Her fish-dead eyes were unsympathetic cold orbs. "You are not in the camp anymore. No one is going to shoot you or harm you. Trust me, Joe. No one in this house will ever allow anything bad to happen to you."

Joe looked at the wet spots of his tears on the front of her Christian Dior dress. Grayson had asked him to trust him, too.

She crossed her arms. "Joe, you have to concentrate on living in the present. The past is in the past, and it's not going to come after you. If you feel like you're going to cry, just buck up. Keep saying your prayers. The Lord will always protect you."

"He's got stuff on his shoes." Irene pointed to Joe's feet.

"Well, get the washcloth."

"Aunt Mil, I did something wrong." Joe took off his Poll Parrot shoes and gave them to Frau Dead Fish Eyes. He hated the babyish tone in his voice, but he was at this woman's mercy. She had complete power over him. She could and would do anything she wanted to with him. He had to confess his transgression and be ready to receive his punishment.

As she wiped his shoes, she said, "What did you do?"

He glanced at Irene for support. But his sister only stood there in her crinoline-lined plaid Thanksgiving dress with the velvet bows in her hair, her placid face an unreadable mask.

"I-I promised Grayson I wouldn't go in the closet anymore."

Aunt Mil examined the bottom of his left shoe and wiped it one more time. "You did? When?"

"Ven ve vent on our trip in de summer. He told me I should not sleep in dere or under de bed because I needed to face my bad dreams and nicht anymore hide. I have to sleep on top of de bed."

Frau Dead Fish Eyes folded the rag and set it in the wash pan on the floor. "Irene, hand me a brush. We have to get Joe looking presentable before the relatives see him again." She moved closer to Joe. "That's exactly what I'm talking about, Joe. Face your fears. Own up to them and then be done with them. Don't let them control your life."

Irene handed the brush to her aunt.

Aunt Mil brushed Joe's hair. "Now, if you've broken your promise to your father, then you have to make it right. When you commit a sin, no matter how small or insignificant you might think it is, God knows about it. The Lord knows everything. He watches your every move. He hears every thought in your brain. The wrongful act you did separates you from Him, and that is what sin is all about. When we go to confession, we tell God about our wrongdoings, and we ask for forgiveness. We say our Hail Mary's and pray and take communion to be full of God's grace. We become one again with Jesus Christ. Don't you want that, Joe?"

He nodded eagerly. He'd agree to anything Aunt Mil said if it would help relieve his guilt.

"By confessing our sins and asking for Jesus's forgiveness, we're on our way to Heaven." She tried to stretch back the corners of her seashell pink-lipsticked mouth into a smile, but it was too much effort. "But it starts with your decision about dealing with the sin you committed right now, young man. You broke a promise you made to your father. What are you going to do about it?"

Joe drew up his brows. "Go to confession?"

"Yes. We'll arrange a time next week to meet Father Byrne to hear your confession. I'll go over with you how it's done and what to say. You may borrow my rosary beads." She looked at her niece. "And not a word to your father about it from either of you." She rose.

"Aunt Mil, can I stay here for a vile?" Joe asked.

The stern woman stopped. "Young man, what did I just say about your fear? You can't run and hide from it. If you stay up here in your room, how will you ever be able to face Paul and Uncle Al and Aunt Bernice and all the other relatives again? I would be disappointed if you stayed in your room. That would be impolite of you. We have a house full of guests. Don't you want to play with your new cousins? I know your father bought a special board game just for today."

Joe said nothing.

"Well, I hope you will come to your senses and come downstairs."

CHAPTER THIRTY-THREE

Joe's emotional exhaustion overwhelmed him, and he slept after his aunt and sister left. Even though the overcast sky glared through the window, his slumber was deep and without dreams. He awoke to the sound of disembodied voices and jazz music floating from far away, perhaps the music room. Looking at the clock on his bed stand, he figured he had slept more than an hour.

He remembered to run the brush through his "bed" hair, and he slapped his cheeks to wake himself up. He steeled himself to face the snake pit downstairs.

As he descended the stairs, the voices stopped. They knew he was coming. Entering the living room, he hugged the wall, leaving dull fingerprints. He observed a very stormy-faced Uncle Albert and a sullen Paul standing between the French blue davenport and the matching armchair. Relatives with their coffee cups and roaring stares surrounded them. Grayson stood in rolled-up shirt sleeves and tie next to the fireplace, an elbow on the white granite mantel, puffing brusquely on his pipe. The children were gone, apparently banished to another part of the castle.

"Paul has something to say," said Uncle Albert. He stubbed out a cigarette and pushed the boy forward.

Joe scanned the room for the rifle. Then he faced Paul squarely, making his face a stoic mask, trying not to let the youth's bigger size frighten him. He forced himself not to cry. Not in front of these shallow, clueless people.

"Sorry about the BB gun. I won't bring it again," Paul mumbled. He jerked his head to get his blond bangs out of his deep-set eyes.

Joe noticed freckles on his stuck-out nose.

"Where is it now?" demanded the kid's father.

Paul replied, again in a mumble, "It's locked in the trunk of the car."

"Speak up, boy!"

"I said it's locked up in the trunk." Defiant anger made him raise his voice.

Joe thought, *But maybe you will steal the car keys later and get it out again. You look like you want to finish the job.* He squeezed his eyes shut so he wouldn't see this ruffian in a Hitler Youth uniform, complete with a swastika armband.

Feeling a hundred pairs of judgmental eyes on him, Joe inched his way over to a straight-backed side chair between two plump female relatives whose names he didn't know. He saw his guardian confer with Uncle Albert and Paul by the fireplace. Uncle Albert then put his hand on son's shoulder and patted it. Joe made a face. *Why is that cruel boy getting a pat on the back? Good job for an impudent, insincere apology?*

Joe looked at Grayson, still standing at the fireplace mantel. He could tell that he was trying to calm his breathing. "Please, Grayson. Can we go somewhere?" He took his guardian's big hand and pulled him out of the living room and into the foyer. They went into Grayson's study, and the big man closed the door partway. Leaning on the front of his massive, ninety-year-old cherry desk and folding his arms, Grayson waited.

Joe stood with his hands at his sides; his small chest bravely pushed out. "Grayson, I have to confess to you. I did a bad thing today." He brushed a tear out of his eye. He would be a man about this.

Grayson tilted his head.

"I broke my promise to you. I hid in de closet. I ran in dere und shut de door und put de blanket over my head because I vas scared. I made a mess, too, because I threw up. I am sorry, Grayson. I know I should not have done dat, but I vas nicht thinking." The guilt came up to his chin, and he wanted the old, creaky wooden floor beneath his feet to part and swallow him whole. He lowered his head and shut his eyes, waiting for the wrathful blow to his head. When it didn't come, he fearfully looked up.

The big man was motionless, not even blinking, just staring at him.

"Grayson, vat vil you do to me? Vil you punish me?" Joe's voice rose to a shrill pitch. This was worse than having that gun pointed at him.

Unbeknownst to him and Grayson, Uncle Albert had seen the two of them go into the study. He lingered in the foyer to hear the conversation through the half-opened door. His son, Paul, joined him.

Joe saw the big man's whitened knuckles as he gripped the edge of the desk. "Joe, I'm not going to punish you. Whatever would make you think that I would?"

"You're nicht beat me?" He thought about the whipping post, the usual twenty-five lashes with the merciless bullwhip. "Vil you send me back to de east to camps in Poland? I vil die there, Grayson! De other kinder vent there, und ve knew dey ver going to get toten."

"No, Joe. Why are you talking about getting sent to Poland?"

Joe swallowed a catch in his throat. "Auschwitz," he whispered.

Grayson may not have heard him. "Look here. Paul pointed a gun at you, and you thought he was going to shoot you. You did what you had to do. It was only natural to run away." He took out his white handkerchief and wiped Joe's nose and cheeks. "Kiddo, let me tell you something. If that boy would have pointed that BB gun at me, and here I am, six foot five, two hundred twenty-five pounds, I would have run into my closet and shut the door, too. Anybody who has a gun pointed at them is going to be scared, even terrified. You don't have to confess anything. You didn't do anything wrong."

"Aber I zebrocken my promise to you, und Aunt Mil said it vas a sin, und I am not going into Heaven get!" He put his fists up to his eyes to block out the sight of the men hanging from the scaffold with their arms tied behind their backs. They had been punished, too, for some infraction. He started sobbing in sympathy with their blinding agony.

"Come here, boy."

Grayson let Joe cry loud and hard as he held him, relieving an unendurably long day of stress. Outside the study, another father glowered at his son.

"Joe, listen to me. You didn't break your promise."

"Aber Aunt Mil--"

"Don't listen to your Aunt Mil. What happened to you today was different." He turned Joe's face back to him. "Listen carefully, son. You had a real reason to hide in the closet. You thought you were going to get hurt, and you had to protect yourself. When you go into the closet at night because you had a bad dream, you're not in any real danger. It's all in your head. You're scared because of what you're imagining, not because you're going to be harmed. And I'm asking you not to hide in your closet or under your bed because you must find a better way to cope with these hallucinations and nightmares. I want you to stop having these bad dreams. I know they make you lose sleep. Then you're cranky in the morning, and everybody else gets in a bad mood."

"But I try, Grayson! Ich will nicht die schlechten Traume!" Tears renewed. "I—I--"

"English, Joe. I don't have my dictionary here."

"I--I dunt vant bad dreams."

"That's why I want you to come to me, and we'll talk about it. Remember when we had that talk on the last day of our trip in August? We were camping in the Finger Lakes National Forest."

Joe nodded. He tried to put his collar in his mouth to suck on to cope with his anxiety, but Grayson put his hand down.

"And I said when we got back home, you have to have courage and stand up to the womenfolk because you knew how to talk with them in English. You have the tools to gain confidence in yourself. Unfortunately, today has been a setback. But you don't have to be scared. Things are still just as they have been."

Joe pushed his fists against Grayson's dampening shirt. He coughed and nearly choked on his sobs. "Grayson, I need to tell you something more." A strange, light-headed floating sensation came over him. He imagined jumping off a cliff, plummeting to his death in the perilous rocky chasm below, just as if he would if climbing over that chain-link fence at Niagara Falls.

"I'm listening." His guardian's voice was deep and reassuring. Joe wanted to grab onto that mighty voice that had the strength of a centuries-old oak tree in a storm.

But he held onto Grayson's collar, pulling at it without realizing it. He looked deeply into his guardian's grey eyes. "De prisoners. Dey had roll call in de middle of de night. Dey had to because more prisoners came. De Nazis could nicht keep track of all dem, so dey began shooting anyone who didn't fall into line fast enough. I saw dem." He stopped before slipping into German. "Dey use rifles und pistols, Grayson. Mostly dey made dem bend down on der knees und shot them behind de ears. I saw de blood come out." He held his breath.

Grayson had seen the bodies, the bullet wounds behind the ears, the dark stuff already coagulated and dried on the necks. There were so many of them that they were just part of the scenery. Bodies lined the barbed wire fences, and others lay haphazardly in the middle of the dirt streets. No one seemed to be bothered by them. They could just as well have been potted plants.

Joe buttoned and unbuttoned the top of his guardian's dress shirt underneath his tie to keep his fingers moving. "Dat's why I ran into das closet. I vas afraid dat boy vud shoot me like de Nazis shot other Jews." He lowered his head.

"I have a confession to make to you, too." Grayson pulled Joe right up to his face, his small, upturned nose pressed against his much larger nose. Joe could see the dark rings around his gray irises and the tiny red veins in the whites of his eyes. "I still have nightmares, too. I can't sleep, Joe," he whispered. The big man let go of him and pushed him back. He stared at the rows of dusty, out-of-date medical books tightly packed in the bookshelves on the wall behind Joe. "As a doctor, I've seen my share of dead bodies. In medical school, I practiced on cadavers, cutting on body parts to learn how to perform surgery on living patients. When I was in the army, I had to dig bullets and shrapnel out of boys who should have lived their lives here, going to college, or starting families. This war, this humongous waste! But nothing, nothing prepared me for what I saw in that camp, son. My life changed forever, just as it had for all the other soldiers and medics who walked into Buchenwald. I . . . feel like I've got a curse on me. Like . . ."

Joe saw Grayson's face darken. The big man looked away as if talking to himself. "Why couldn't it have been just a dream? God playing a nasty prank? I would have even accepted it as a poke in the eye by Lucifer himself, not an invitation to actually stand at the very gate of his kingdom of Hell."

He turned to Joe. "I shouldn't be talking like this to you, but here you are. You've seen so much more than I have. So how can I even begin to understand what you went through? What audacity do I have to try to help you get over that awful place! I have no spiritual wisdom, no hand to guide you out of that Hell." He held Joe against his chest and rocked him. "All I can do is love you, Joe. All I can do is love you as your father did. I owe that to him. *I owe that to him.*"

Despite being pressed so tightly, tears still slipped down Joe's neck. He didn't want to think about his father. It would just make a bad situation very much worse.

"We're in this together, boy. I'm telling you again that I love you. And if I have to, I will tell you every day until I die to make you believe me."

Joe put his hand on his guardian's face. "Ich liebe Dich, Grayson." He thought and then said, "Can I just stay here by myself?" He let go of his guardian and stood before him.

Grayson sighed and composed himself. "What makes you think you can't?"

"Aunt Mil told me to go out und be with de relatives. But I'm still afraid of dat boy."

Grayson rubbed his hands on top of his thighs. "Joe, you don't have to go out and entertain the riff-raff. You've done enough for today. But you need to eat something. Let me fix up a plate for you. Would you like some turkey, maybe some apple slices, and celery sticks with some peanut butter?" He knew the latter were Joe's favorite treats.

Joe dropped into the cracked, well-worn leather couch against the wall opposite the desk. He folded his arms in the rebellious disposition of a young Pierce daughter. "Ich bin nicht hungrig."

"Joe Kaufmann, we're not going to argue about this." Grayson also crossed his arms; his feet set apart. "If you don't eat and end up losing weight again, I'll put you back in the hospital, and that I. V. line will go right back in your arm."

"Und I rip it right out again."

The two stared at each other, waiting to see who would call the other's bluff first.

Sometimes living is just too hard to do, Joe wanted to say. *Least of all, eating when you're too upset.* But he knew if he said this aloud, Grayson would still not give in. He said nothing and put his head down on a stiff, uncomfortable needlepoint pillow that had the word Mother stitched on it. His guardian cracked his knees as he bent to put his hand on his arm.

"Everything's okay now?"

Joe had to think. "Vel, I guess. Does dis mean I dun't have to go see de priest for Beichte?"

"What?"

"Aunt Mil said I have to confess my sin to a priest, you know, for breaking my promise to you. Dat way, I'll be ready to go to Heaven to meet Jesus. Ve are supposed to see der Priester next week, und she's going to let me borrow her rosary beads, und oops, I vasn't supposed to tell you about dat. Ow! You're squeezing my arm, Grayson!"

CHAPTER THIRTY-FOUR

The two Pierce brothers decided to unwind in the gloomy, outmoded parlor after all the guests had departed earlier in the evening.

Al looked inside the liquor cabinet. "What kind of booze you got in here, Grayson?" Ash from his drooping Camel cigarette threatened to drop and burn a hole in the carpet, which already was spotted with a few scorches.

Sitting in an armchair in an ugly faded flower pattern, Grayson said, "Use an ashtray, Al. There's one on the bar." He twisted his hips in the chair. It was so old the stuffing had been worn down to almost nothing.

"Oooo. 1926. What are you saving this for, Gray?" Al examined the dusty bottle of cabernet he found in the back of the lower shelf. He remembered his smoldering cigarette and found a tin ashtray just in time. "Is this leftover from your wedding?"

"Probably. Where are the kids?" Grayson rubbed his temples and pulled off his tie after carefully putting his silver tie clip decorated with a golf club on the mahogany end table. He forgot to think it might disappear because some furry, four-legged beast might regard it as a new toy. His head pounded behind his eyes.

"Last time I looked, they were headed upstairs to their rooms. Rose was with them. Oh, here's the scotch. You want some?" He found two tumblers from a cabinet under the pink marble counter.

Holding them up to the dim light from the ruby-colored shell-topped chandelier, he searched for a dishcloth to wipe them.

"No. Yes. Goddammit, this has been a helluva day, and I deserve it. Relatives wear me out."

Al blew out the dust from the glasses and poured three fingers straight. "Yeah, me, too. Thank God Thanksgiving's only once a year." After handing the drink to his brother, he sat in a scratchy matching chair and took a sip. "Ah, Gray, are we okay about my kid? I'm not going to sleep too well if there're any hard feelings about that fracas with the BB gun." He loosened his tie and rolled up his sleeves.

Grayson set his glass on a "See Niagara Falls" coaster on the drop-leaf end table. "Don't worry about it. The storm is over, I hope. We'll see."

"You mean about Joe having nightmares?"

"How do you know about that?"

"Well, it's confession time for me. Paul and I overheard your talk with him in your study. I had no idea, Gray. You've got an intense little boy on your hands."

Grayson said nothing and studied his drink. He debated about getting up to search for an aspirin tin. There might be one in the half bath off the foyer.

Al said, "If there's a silver lining in all this, Paul's learned a lesson. I have, too. What that kid described about the camp he came from makes my hair stand on end. Good heavens, man, what did you go through over there?"

"Maybe we'll talk about it another time, Al. My head hurts, and I'm dead tired." Grayson took a sip of the scotch, thinking it might take the edge off his headache. He wouldn't mind getting drunk, but he pushed that foolish idea out of his mind.

"Don't think Paul's off the hook. He'll get his punishment when he gets home. It'll start with taking that air rifle back to the Sears store." The man relaxed his shoulders and twisted his neck to get out the kinks. He had the same features as his brother—large gray eyes, big, straight nose, handsome square jaw. But his brown hair was a shade lighter and had a tidy part on the right side. He pondered his liquor glass. "It doesn't seem fair, does it? We were both in the Army, yet I stayed stateside, and you had to go overseas to see the real action. Guess that's what happens when you pick your profession."

"Oh, it was fair enough. You never could stand the sight of blood. A little splinter in your finger and you'd scream like a girl. The only blood you tolerate is what comes out of the turnip you squeeze when you bill your clients."

"Hey, that's about to change, Gray."

"Huh?"

"I'm going over to the other side. I'm throwing my hat in the ring for district attorney."

"No! When?"

"Next summer. Will you come up to Syracuse and help me lick a few envelopes?"

"I will if my schedule works out. Make sure Millie knows. She'll run your campaign. In fact, she'll probably win the race for you." He took a generous swallow of scotch.

"Will your little boy go to school soon?"

"Yes. He'll go to East Hill Elementary after Christmas."

"Really?"

Grayson stared at his brother.

Al cocked his head. "That ain't what I heard around the dining room table."

"What are you talking about?"

Twisting his mouth in skepticism like his mother, Al replied, "Mil announced to everybody that he's going to Immaculate Conception."

"Oh, she did, huh? Well, she's living in a fantasy world. And she knows better." Grayson exhaled. "I guess that'll be another argument."

"Joe seems to know English well." Al rose to refill his glass.

"Joe is an extraordinary kid. He has more smarts than you, me, and the whole damn world put together." Grayson began to feel warm and unbuttoned the top two buttons of his shirt. "If Rose is up there with him, he's probably reading one of my college chemistry textbooks to her and putting her to sleep."

"What?"

As if Grayson had extrasensory perception, Joe was, indeed, reading to Rose in his room. She loved to sit in a rocking chair with him in her cozy lap, his little legs spread over her wide knees. When Joe and Grayson had returned from their upstate New York trip, she had read to him before bedtime when Grayson was at the hospital.

At first, she had chosen a Mother Goose nursery rhymes book and *A Child's Garden of Verses* by Robert Lewis Stevenson. But soon, he was reading to her. When he had learned she liked paperback romances, he indulged her by picking out new books by her favorite authors from the library. Sometimes he'd surprise her with a whodunit or a memoir of a current celebrity.

Tonight was no different. After only a few minutes, however, Rose was softly snoring. Joe carefully slid off her lap, turned out the light, and shut the door soundlessly. He headed toward Irene's room to crash the girls' party. But her room was empty except for the toddler, Penny, asleep in Irene's bed. He wandered downstairs and found the two girls nestled just outside the parlor.

"We're watching our daddies getting drunk!" Irene whispered, giggling.

"Shhh!" Martha put her hand over her cousin's mouth, barely containing herself.

Joe peered into the cavernous, darkened room. Decades of dust that had wafted up to the polished cedar wood ceiling and the faded red velvet wallpaper had given it a shabby ambiance. The air in the turn of the century-styled room was bathed in smoky blue.

Resolute heels clicked on the floor. Aunt Mil was coming. The children ran to hide in the small storage closet under the staircase.

Mildred walked into the parlor. "Oh, there are the two of you. I've been looking for you, Grayson, for the last half hour. Have you locked the house?"

The children cautiously edged back into the hallway.

"No, I haven't gotten that far yet, Mil."

"Well, it's getting late. I don't know how long Mother and Bernice and Aunt Elvie will be up. They're still in the music room."

"It was a great Thanksgiving, Millie," Al's baritone voice filled the parlor. "The food was great. I wish I could hire your cook away from you."

"No deal. Rose is staying right here."

"I was asking Gray about little Joe's smarts. What were you sayin' that he's got more brains than God?" Al nudged his brother's knee, drawing a smug grin.

"Humpf!" Mildred disappeared from the children's view. They tiptoed back to their spot out of sight just beyond the wide doorway framed with decorated latticework.

Mildred went to the liquor cabinet. "He's intelligent. I'll say that much. Where's the sherry?" She opened the doors and looked inside.

Grayson snorted. "That's like saying the Pope's an altar boy. Al, once he settled down and started learning English, there was no stopping him. I couldn't give him anything that stumped him. When I took him on that trip this past summer, we went to the library in Albany, and as soon as we started going down the aisles, he grabbed a mystery novel by Agatha Christie and started reading. Then he took a piece of paper and wrote a book report on it."

Al shook his head. "No!"

"Of course, he had my German-English dictionary to help him." Grayson threw an accusing look at his sister.

"But how could he have had enough schooling? How long was he in Buchenwald? He couldn't have learned anything there."

"That's the mystery, Al." Grayson forgot his headache as he got up to pour another drink. A second wind rejuvenated his body. "I have no idea how long he was in the camp. It could have been six weeks or six years. But he definitely knew how to read and write before I brought him to the States."

The children relaxed on the floor as they listened to the adults. Irene kept eyes on Joe as the subject of Buchenwald was discussed. She needed to keep him quiet if he got upset.

Grayson said, "I want to get him tested for his I.Q. I'll have to make some phone calls to see where to take him. Maybe Cornell's education department can test him." He looked around the room for a pipe, but he didn't find one. "Al, can I have one of your cigarettes?"

His brother threw him a half-crushed pack. He lit up and enjoyed that rush of nicotine. "I had him write a little story about the family cat. He wrote it single-spaced, in German, on both sides of two papers, and in cursive. I've been meaning to get it translated. I'll do that when I get him tested. Damn, he's got some brainpower." He sat back in his chair.

"Yes, and once he finds out his I. Q., he'll expect special attention," snipped Mildred.

Al thoughtfully swirled the remaining scotch in his glass. "Gray, tell me again where Joe's going to school after Christmas." He glanced at his sister from the corner of his eye. He loved getting under her pretentious skin. Would she take the bait?

Mildred lowered her tiny glass to her lap. She squared her padded shoulders just like her mother, Nina Cassandra.

Grayson left his chair and stood in front of the bar. He drank the entire two fingers of scotch in one big gulp. It burned all the way down. Setting the glass on the bar counter, he decided that would be all the drinking he would do tonight. "East Hill Elementary." He dragged on his smoke.

Still watching Mildred, Al said, "Yeah, but wouldn't he be better off at Immaculate, with Irene going there, and you know, keeping with the family tradition and all? Wouldn't you agree, Millie?"

"I suppose," replied Mildred. She took a seat at the end of the davenport, sipping her sherry.

After stubbing out his cigarette, Grayson walked to the other side of the room and began checking the rusty latches on the massive, iron-framed windows to make sure they were locked. It was a needless task, as they hadn't been opened in years. A wave of vertigo hit him as he tilted his head up to look at the vine and grape leaf patterns in the creamy plaster molding in the ceiling. Damn that alcohol!

"You're taking him to mass, aren't you? Pretty soon, the priest will want him as an altar boy, just like his old man. Huh, Gray?"

Steadying himself, Grayson returned to the middle of the room, wiping sweat from his forehead with his arm. "Joe attends the Jewish temple. You know it, Beth-El. They have services on Friday evenings, and he attends their Judaism classes on Sunday mornings." Moving to the billiards table, he began rolling balls around on it.

"Oh, really?"

"It's a sore subject around here, Al. Let's not get into it." Mildred stood and put her finished glass on the counter. She returned to her seat and pushed around the arrangement of fake pink lilies sitting under the cut glass table lamp.

"Yes, it's a sore subject, but let me rub some salt in the wound." Grayson raised his voice as he turned to his sister. "I heard from Joe about borrowing your rosary beads for a visit to Father Byrne next week. Something about going to confession. What's that all about?" He lost interest in the billiard balls and walked back to the couch.

Mildred brushed an imaginary strand of hair from her temple. "I don't believe I know what you're talking about, Grayson. That child has a wild imagination. Perhaps he overheard something from Irene."

"Millie, that's not something he would make up. What did you tell him up in his room?"

"Nothing, Grayson. Nothing you need to be concerned about."

"Well, I'll either hear it from you, or I'll hear it from Irene. Wasn't she up there with you?"

Mildred retorted, "How dare you! You would turn your daughter against me. That would be cruel and thoughtless to put her between us." Her voice was steady, but not her hands.

"Not half as cruel and thoughtless as the guilt trip you laid on Joe about hiding in his closet after a loaded gun was pointed at him! The kid was so traumatized he vomited!" Oh, how the scotch threw open the well-secured gates of his outrage. "Joe needed you to tell him he wasn't going to get shot. He needed an adult telling him he was safe and that he wasn't going to get hurt! But all you said was he committed a sin because he broke a promise to me about hiding in the closet. Dammit, Millie, where's your common sense? That little boy didn't need a lecture. He needed someone to hold him and calm him down."

The dead-fish eyes staring back at him strengthened his resolve. "Millie, you need to take a warm bath to melt the ice in your veins. I should never have let you go up there to his room. I should have been there with him, not carrying on downstairs with Al and his boy."

"Oh, poppycock! You're making too much of this!"

Grayson slapped a fist into his hand. "Do you know what I was doing after he came down from his room? Did you see where I was?"

"No, but whatever you were doing, it could have waited. It was very rude of you to disappear from all the guests."

Grayson leaned closer toward his sister. "Let me fill you in. I was in my study, cleaning up the emotional mess you left with the boy."

"What are you talking about? What mess? Did he throw up again? What's the matter with that child?"

Grayson so much wanted to grab his sister by her sharp, pompous shoulders and shake her that he walked away. He clutched the edge of the marble countertop of the bar.

"Maybe he's catching the stomach flu. I'll call Dr. Abernathy tomorrow. Did anybody see him eat any dinner? Where's Rose?" She looked about as if desperate to find a way out of this conversation.

Grayson waited until she finally stopped blathering. Sarcasm laced his voice. "Joe apologized to me for hiding in the closet. He believed hiding in his closet to run away from a gun pointed at him was wrong." He raised his voice. "Mil, you made him think that. Then you laid on the good old fashion Catholic guilt by telling him he sinned, and he has to go to a priest to confess." He moved forward again, his head shaking. "Millie, I told you before. Joe is a Jew. I'm rearing him as a Jew. Don't confuse him with Jesus Christ and your rosary beads. He doesn't need to be told that the only way into Heaven is through going through the motions in a confessional stall. You will *not* take him to Father Byrne. I don't want him ever to step into Immaculate Conception." The scotch beckoned. He lit up another cigarette. "And furthermore, he's going to East Hill Elementary School. You had some nerve announcing to everybody that he's going to Immaculate."

Mildred's dead fish eyes came to life and blazed. "I won't apologize for how I handled him. Can I help it if he can't behave himself? I've tried my best to teach him manners, especially when we have guests. But he won't learn. I don't care how smart you think he is. He's got problems, Grayson. Admit it."

"Aw, no, Millie," said Al. "He's a sweet boy. Gray's right. The kid was just scared."

"Oh, you don't know anything about what's going on with that child. You weren't here this past summer finding the garbage can upside down and the grapefruit rinds and the eggshells and the potato peelings in his closet."

"What? Did you have an animal in the house?"

"No, it was that little boy. He wouldn't eat the meals Rose put in front of him at the dinner table. No, he had to sneak around at night and take garbage out of the kitchen trash can. He'd stash it in his closet and then eat it days later. The smell was worse than a city dump. My housekeepers had a horrible time cleaning it all up. And the bedwetting! He kept us up all night! Then there was that business with the window."

The children were slumped on the floor, staying very still. Irene put her arms around Joe, who kept his head down.

As Grayson listened, he stood with his back to them, smoking irritably. He poured another drink. He knew he should pour it right down the drain in the metal sink in the bar instead of his throat. Growing ire accelerated his pulse.

Al smoked his cigarette thoughtfully. "Yeah, well, Gray called me about that in September. He fell out of his bedroom window, didn't he?"

"No, he jumped out. He tore the window screen."

"Well, that was a tough time for him. But he's okay now, isn't he? To me, he acts like he behaves himself pretty well."

Mildred countered, "Think again. Running through the house like that this afternoon! Why, everyone thought we couldn't handle him, that he's unmanageable and wild. I was absolutely humiliated!"

Grayson closed his eyes, trying to stay calm.

Even Martha put her arms around Joe, stroking his shoulder.

"Well, who the hell cares what the relatives think?" Al's voice boomed.

"I care! We have to get along with these people." Mildred's voice matched her brother's in volume. She turned back to Grayson. "And for your information, Grayson, there has been a lot of whispering going on about Joe."

"I don't want to hear it," Grayson answered through gritted teeth.

"Things that are being said behind your back. That little incident with his bedroom window has been difficult to keep under wraps. Yes, I know it's no one's business but . . ."

Grayson paced.

Mildred went on. "All I'm saying is he's got to learn to act more mature." She got off the couch to refill her glass. "Grayson, I implore you. This child is begging for structure and discipline. He has to know his boundaries. I've said that before about Irene. You indulge her and spoil her to the point where she thinks she can get away with anything. She expects to get whatever she wants."

Irene's tears dripped onto her Thanksgiving dress.

Mildred waved a hand. "And you give in to her. That little boy will be the same way if you don't start disciplining him." Crossly, she opened a new bottle of brandy started pouring. "Just like today with the gun. You mollycoddled him all afternoon. After all, it was just a toy gun. It wasn't going to hurt him."

"God blast it to Hell! It was a real BB gun!" Grayson splashed liquor on his shirt as he finally turned to face her. "And it was loaded!

Joe heard the click. Paul took the safety off! Do you have any idea what could have happened to him if he got shot at that close range? He could have lost an eye or gotten hit in the neck or, worse, in the head. The girls could have been injured, too. No matter what a gun salesman tells you at a gun store, these blasted BB guns are dangerous! Mil, I've taken birdshot out of too many kids of well-intentioned hunters, and let me tell you, it's a damn ugly sight. Teenaged boys are given those guns to go out and practice shooting tin cans in the backyard. Then the family comes into the ER with a gunshot wound in their kid's stomach because nobody thought the kid's little brother or sister would pick up a loaded weapon!"

Neither Grayson nor Mildred noticed their younger brother Al sinking in his chair, tears coursing down his cheeks.

"Joe knew he was about to get shot, and he did what he had to do to survive. He ran! He had a lot of practice doing that at Buchenwald. He told me how he saw the Nazis shoot Jewish prisoners, seeing them just drop where they stood and leaving them there. I saw them piled up, hundreds of them. This kid knows exactly what guns do. They put holes in people's heads, and their brains splash out, and they die! And that little boy was witness to that!"

"Oh, God!" Al put his face in his hands.

"Grayson, we don't need to hear--" Mildred started.

"Yes, you do! How else are you going to know what Joe went through?" Shaking, Grayson poured a half glass of scotch. His rage blurred his vision more than the booze. After a swallow, he banged the glass on the bar counter. "When he came to me this afternoon, he was a basket case. I have tried so much to help him adjust and s-s-settle into his new life with us. These last couple of months, he started to sleep all through the night. I could tell he was getting along better with Irene. And when you finally laid off about him using his left hand, he's-s-s-s beginning to eat and gain some weight." He weaved about. "And I *told* you back in July to leave the discipline of my kids to me. Do you *not* remember me coming into your room and telling you that? Do you?"

His sister would not reply.

"Then this sh-sh-shit had to happen." His head rolled on his neck. "It's like one of Mom's best dishes-s-s smashed with a hammer. There're a million pieces, and I've got to put the damn thing back together again, and I don't even know where to s-s-s-start!" He caught his breath. The floor threatened to hit him in the face.

"God, Grayson, what can I do so you'll forgive me? What can I say?" Al pushed himself out of his chair with much effort. He wiped his teary face with his pocket handkerchief. "I'm so sorry what my kid did. I should have never given him that gun!"

Grayson went to his weeping brother. They embraced, swaying in a tipsy fog. Al was a good three inches shorter than Grayson, and he put his face on his brother's shoulder and sobbed. "It's okay." Grayson sighed and patted the other man's back. They let go, and both rocked a little in an alcoholic haze.

"Oh, you two make a fine pair!" Mildred poured another brandy.

"Hey! At least I'm not afraid to show some feelings!" Al pointed a wandering finger at her. "I'm a human being, unlike you! You act like you got a broomstick up your ass!" Al smoothed his perspiration-soaked hair on top of his head.

"I know how to control my emotions. Evidently, they didn't teach that in either law school or medical school."

Grayson passed his hand over his head in the same gesture as his brother. "We have cons-s-s-ideration of what other people feel and what they're going through when they're hurting and need our help. We couldn't do our jobs if we didn't show some empathy. And it wouldn't hurt you one bit to sh-sh-show some too, especially to those smaller and weaker than you, like little children." He weaved about and grabbed the top of a bar chair. "It would be the C-r-r-r-ristian thing to do."

Mildred retorted, "You are such a hypocrite! You can't tell me about being a Christian when you won't even convert that boy! That boy whom you claim to love as if he were your own son! It's a disgrace to the family! All day today, I had to answer to everybody about him--when's he going to Immaculate Conception? What parish did he come from? Is he baptized yet? I just about choked when I had to say he was Jewish! I've never been so embarrassed in my entire life! And Mother was right there trying her best to keep the wolves at bay, too. What's the matter with you, Albert?" She glared at her younger brother who was shaking his head.

"I don't understand why you are making this all so difficult, Grayson. The least you can do is get him to stop acting like a stray dog that needs some obedience training."

"He's my kid! How dare you say that!" Grayson clenched his fists.

"And you can't get it through your thick head that he's running around like a wild animal and upsetting this whole house. For the love of Christ, Grayson, take off those rose-colored glasses, and see the child for what he is!"

"Goddammit, Millie, the kid is scared out of his FRIGGIN' MIND!"

"Don't you shout at me, William Grayson Pierce!"

The children fled.

All three adult siblings looked toward the room's entrance. Nina Cassandra, Bernice, and Elvie stood like statues staring at them.

"I'll go check on the children." Bernice slipped away. Elvie followed her.

"I'll be up soon, honey," called Al weakly.

CHAPTER THIRTY-FIVE

The Pierce matriarch pressed forward with a speed that belied her age. "What's the meaning of this? What's going on?" She surveyed the room, sniffing. "It smells like a dance hall in here." She shook a crooked finger at Grayson. "I'll not tolerate any foul language in this house, you hear me, boy?"

Grayson replied through clenched jaws, "I'm sorry, Mom. It's been a long evening." He meandered back to the bar.

His mother eyed him closer. "Why, you're as drunk as a skunk! And there are children in this house! Shame on you, Grayson!" She stepped back to examine her brood again. Turning to her youngest child, she said, "Al, your face is red. Are you drunk, too? Whatever for? You're a grown man. Are those tears? For heaven's sake. Stop acting like a baby!" To her daughter, she said, "And it looks like you've been hitting the booze, too, Mildred. My goodness! You three have been having quite a party in here."

Holding her brandy, Mildred lowered herself on the divan, clutching the arm to steady herself. Al lit a cigarette and went back to his uncomfortable armchair. Grayson wandered around the parlor, empty tumbler in hand.

"Well, somebody has to have the presence of mind to keep one's wits about oneself, and I suppose that would be me." Nina Cassandra sat in an outworn mustard-yellow loveseat and carefully hooked her cane over the scratched mahogany coffee table. She pulled out a wadded pink handkerchief she always kept under her dress belt and dabbed the folds in her neck. "My, it's warm in here! It's been a terrible day, and I'm tired. Grayson, while you're over there, see if there's any ice in that icebox under the bar and pour me some water."

Grayson did as he was told and handed the pressed glass tumbler to his mother. True Hell would be seeing two of her in his drunken state. He wandered back toward the billiards table.

Nina Cassandra enjoyed her cool drink in the silent room. She gulped it noisily, smacking her nearly non-existent lips that had the outline of smeared pink lipstick from earlier coffee cups. She looked around for a coaster.

The Pierce clan dowager was sixty-eight years old. Age had thinned and loosened her facial skin, and gravity had pulled down her sagging cheeks into the corners of her mouth, and her fragile eyelids drooped behind her gold-rimmed glasses, giving her a perpetual scowl. A splatter of age spots dotted her face near her stretched, flabby ears, and a mole hid deeply in the crease along the side of her blue-veined, sharp nose. The slack layers of skin under her chin often shook as she talked or turned her head. Once a stunning shade of amber, her hair was completely white, brushed up, and held in place with jeweled metal combs. Snowy pin curls crowned the top of her head.

She wore her diamond earrings and her choker necklaces as proudly as did an elder member of a European royal family. She wore her clothes well, having them fitted at the same alterations shop on the corner of Fifth Street and Harvard in downtown Ithaca for the past fifty years. When she bought her dresses and separates at Saks Fifth Avenue in New York City, she would have them altered while visiting friends or attending the Museum of Art. She never left the house without a hat and gloves. Her purse always matched her shoes. No one could say that Nina Cassandra Pierce did not look her best no matter what the occasion.

Although she was a big woman, osteoporosis had shrunk her by a few inches. Weight gain about her stomach did not slow her down as much as increasing arthritis that roamed around her joints, hence the cane. Migratory arthritis put her in terribly irritable moods. Grayson worried about her health and often checked her blood pressure, which was always high. However, despite her son's admonitions, she refused to see a physician who would likely put her on medication.

"We heard shouting from the music room. Why can't the three of you get along? Every time we have a family get-together, you all end up at each other's throats, especially when there's alcohol involved." She opened a drawer in the end table and found a coaster, another Niagara Falls advertisement.

Grayson lit a cigarette and began taking balls out of the billiards table pockets.

"We've just been talking, that's all," said Al.

"Grayson, I'm astonished at you. I've never seen you behave this badly. You don't drink like this. What's come over you?" She saw the half-empty scotch bottle on the bar counter.

"I always drink more around Al."

"Hey, don't blame it on me, you big galoot!" Al said half-jokingly. He eyed the bottle.

The billiard balls softly clicked as Grayson rolled them across the green worsted cloth table. With the cigarette in the side of his mouth, he unbuttoned his perspiration-stained shirt, revealing thick, dark chest hair beneath his undershirt. Still uncomfortable, he pulled out the tail.

"We were just talking about his boy, Joe," Al offered. "I was apologizing again to Gray about Paul and the BB gun."

"Yes, that was an unfortunate event, Albert. How did he sneak that gun into the house to begin with?" Nina Cassandra slurped her water.

"He hid it in the car trunk without us seeing him. Somehow, he must have gotten my car keys during the dinner and took it out and went down the basement with it. He said he wanted to show it off and play cowboys and Indians with Joe. I guess I've taken him to too many Gene Autry movies."

"I hope he's learned his lesson. What will you do with the gun?"

"It'll go back to the store."

"Sneaking around like that. You'd better keep a closer eye on him, Albert. Before you know it, he'll be doing worse things, and you'll have a juvenile delinquent on your hands. That won't reflect well for you if you run for district attorney."

"Humpf! As if that's all that matters," Grayson said under his breath.

Nina Cassandra spoke louder. "What did you say over there? You've got some snide comment to make?" She took another sip of her water, the ice cubes clinking. She burped and frowned. "I couldn't keep those old busy-body relatives at bay. They kept asking me about the little rapscallion. Where did he come from? Is he in school? Did Grayson adopt him? Is he going to be confirmed? I felt like I was on trial!"

Grayson gave up on the billiard balls and sat with his family. Mildred's eyes pinned him like switchblades.

"What'd you tell 'em?" asked Al.

"I said Grayson picked up the child this past summer after he got out of the Army. He hasn't been in school, and I didn't know why Grayson made the foolish decision to keep him at home. He should have started in September. And he's too young to be confirmed, but at least we've got him baptized." She dabbed her neck again.

Her last comment Grayson's attention. "When did this happen?"

Nina Cassandra ignored him. "I was so mortified by that little imp running through the living room this afternoon I thought I'd die." The old woman folded her handkerchief. "Grayson, this child is getting to be too much to handle. And it's only going to get worse as he gets bigger and older. He'll turn into a delinquent like Paul."

"Paul's not a delinquent, Mother," Al said defensively. "He's a good kid. He just made a bad decision today. Give him a break, will you?"

Nina Cassandra tilted her head up and looked down her blue-veined nose. "Well, you're pretty soft with him. If it weren't for Bernice, he'd be more spoiled than he already is. You've got a good wife, Albert. *Her* daughter is well-behaved." She waited, tapping a finger on her cane.

"Go ahead and s-s-say it, Mom," Grayson snapped. "Irene is-s-s-s spoiled and misbehaves all-l-l-l the time."

"She is disrespectful and headstrong."

In his heart of hearts, Grayson could not disagree.

But the matriarch had more to say. "She needs a mother, Grayson. Mildred, Elvie, and I can only do so much. She needs the security and structure of a real family. We can't give that to her. We have busy lives, and we can't be looking after her all the time. The older she gets, the more attention she'll need, particularly in her teenage years.

And when you're at the hospital working so many hours, she doesn't get the parenting she requires."

"You mean to tell me that amongst the thhhrrr-ee of you, with the experience of rearing seven kids, you can't help me raise one little girl?"

"Grayson, you need to find yourself a wife and settle down. It's unseemly for you to be forty years old and not married again."

Grayson grimaced, embarrassed and not a little annoyed at his mother's acerbity. "I haven't wanted to get married, Mom. I've been busy with my practice, and then I joined the army. And now that I have Joe, it's just not on my agenda."

Nina Cassandra seemed not to have heard her son. "Never in my fifty years as a mother did I ever expect my children to turn out as miserable as you three. I've worked my fingers to the bone rearing all of you. And you were difficult, difficult to carry, difficult to birth, difficult to bring up. Such quarreling you three did! It was a good thing Will and I had this big house with all these rooms to separate you children. I'm surprised it's still standing." She clasped her handkerchief tightly and sighed loudly. "All I'm asking for is some peace! Some normalcy in this house. Is that too much to ask? Look at the sorry lot of you. Sometimes when I pray to the Lord, I ask where have I failed? Where did I go wrong?"

"What the hell are you talking about, Mom?" Al snarled.

"A grandson on his way to delinquency. He'll end up in prison before he's twenty-one."

"Oh, for God's sake!" Al got up and went over to the bar again to pour yet another drink.

"My eldest son, trying to rear a rebellious daughter by himself and then being a total fool by bringing home a backward child from some God-forsaken place overseas, expecting the rest of us to rear him. Oh, mercy!"

Grayson put his head in his hands. The only thing worse about this vituperation was that a clear-minded sixty-eight-year-old mother was delivering it.

Nina Cassandra stopped. Her daughter, Mildred, waited.

"And poor Mildred."

"Stop it, Mother! Don't bring it up!"

"God brought down His wrath on you, Mildred. Your unfortunate husband, the baby."

"You promised me you'd never bring that up again, Mother!"

"All the millions Vance left you won't make up for the loss of that little boy. How old would he have been now?"

"Mother! Did you not hear what I just said?" Mildred stood. "That's in the past. Please stop talking about it!"

"Let's see. The car accident was in '28, and it's 1945 today."

"Mom, will you just change the subject? You're upsetting Millie," said Grayson.

"That would make him seventeen. My, to think about what he could have been! How handsome he would have been. I bet he would have had his father's eyes. Vance had the most beautiful green eyes." She shook her white-haired head in false pity. "Such a terrible misfortune. I never thought the police figured out exactly how the accident happened. Somebody wasn't watching at the steering wheel." She looked back at Mildred. "It was a smart thing he had a will, although I'm certain he had a life insurance policy, didn't he, Mildred? I don't remember."

Mildred wiped her face before anyone could see her wet eyes.

"We should plan a trip down to Manhattan in the spring, perhaps on Memorial Day, Grayson. Mildred needs to put flowers on his grave."

This statement caused Mildred to shake her head violently. She collapsed on the divan.

"Mom, I don't think that's such a good idea. Let Millie do that when she's ready to." Grayson's face softened in sympathy for his sister.

"Well, she needs to pay her respects sometime. And there's no reason why you couldn't have found another good husband, Mildred. With your talents and wealth, you could have had the pick of the New York social scene."

Mildred shrieked in frustration. Folding her arms under her bosom, she rose and turned her back.

"Yeah, Mom. And that would be all you'd need to brag to your nosy friends here in this little provincial town." Al batted his eyes in an effeminate way as he waved his cigarette. He raised his voice to a girlish pitch. "My daughter, the princess of high society, the diva of downtown New York, the eye of the Big Apple."

"Shut up, Al." Grayson sat in a shabby percale-covered wing chair.

"Oh, to think of all the grandchildren I could have had! I'm grateful for the four I have, except only I don't see three of them as often as I'd like."

"Good job, Mom. You're batten' a thousand." Al opened and closed drawers to see if he could find anything to eat.

"What? I'm just saying I seldom see the grandchildren. But since you seem to be so busy with your law practice, I guess you just don't have the time to bring them down."

"There you go, pushin' everybody's buttons again. All right. I'll talk to Bernice about bringing the kids more often. You know, when they're in school, it's not easy to come down just on Saturday and Sunday. We have a lot of catching up to do ourselves on the weekends, with Bernice teaching school and all. But you barely pay any attention to them while they're here anyway."

"Can I help it if they run to the basement or up to Irene's room the moment they get here? I can't chase after them as I did thirty-five years ago with you."

Martha, Paul, and now Penny (as long as her mother held her hands) hated having to stand rigidly like troops ready for inspection in front of the old queen bee sitting in her royal purple rocking chair in the living room. She inspected them from head to toe, examining them for warts or dirt under their fingernails or a crooked part in their hair. She would inquire if they were taking their daily dose of mineral oil—two tablespoons—which Bernice would answer in the affirmative (they never really took it). "Regularity is next to godliness and cleanliness," she would declare to the children. "Don't you forget it!"

"Children should be well-behaved and well-groomed. I tried my best with all of you, but your father always thwarted me. Will was too soft on you boys. He should have made men out of you. Mildred was always stronger than both of you put together." She eyed her daughter.

Mildred did not move. Stoically, she seemed to have fortified her emotional loins.

"Mildred, you never let your feelings get out of control as your father and those two miserable brothers of yours did. That's an essential part of one's character. It shows maturity and good breeding." Her wrinkled face uncharacteristically opened with a saccharine smile. "Come sit next to me." She patted the divan cushion.

"Mother, I want to go to bed. I've had far too much brandy and too much conversation tonight," Mildred turned around and smoothed non-existent creases in her dress.

The matriarch shifted her body toward her elder son. "Oh, there's another thing. Grayson, now I remember why I came into the parlor in the first place. It's time to put an end to this little adventure you've had with that boy."

Her son's red-rimmed eyes widened as he looked at her. Mildred and Al stared.

"Grayson, you've had this little brat for almost half a year now, and, frankly, it's been the worst five months we've ever had in this house. He's been under my feet long enough. And there has been nothing but uproar and fighting ever since you brought it here, and I'm done with putting up with it. You and Mildred keep bickering over his religious upbringing. I don't understand what the squabbling is about. He is supposed to go to mass with the rest of the family. And he was supposed to enroll at Immaculate Conception. But it's so late in the school year now I doubt they would still take him."

The heat under the pot of outrage turned up in Grayson's pounding head.

"There will be peace in this house, and since I am the owner, I set the rules around here, and that child has got to go." She waved her hand. "He's ruined my bedsheets with his bedwetting, broken the window in his room, put food stains on the closet floor, and on top of everything else, ruined a perfectly good Thanksgiving dinner by getting upset by a toy gun.

"You must find a good home for him; the sooner, the better. Perhaps there's an orphanage in New York City that will take him. You know Mavis Swenson, don't you? She has connections with the diocese in Manhattan. I'll give her a call next week. I'll even pay to take him down there."

Al interjected. "Mom, it's more complicated than that. There's a court petition to be filed. You just can't hand the kid over to a bunch of strangers."

Grayson's mouth stupidly hung open. His shock was so great he forgot to close it. Finally, he spoke, blinking his eyes. "Mother . . . he's my boy."

"Hogwash! You're just his guardian. It can all be changed. Al just said it's all a matter of filling out some papers. Grayson, I understand how much you want children. I know how much pain you endured when Margie died. She was the sweetest, courteous, most wonderful girl I have ever met. She was a perfect match for you, and she would have given you many children. Unfortunately, however, the Lord had other plans." She rested, letting settle the meaning of the Lord's "other plans."

"But if you just find yourself another wife, you could have lots of children. Goodness sakes, you're still young! And handsome, and you have a good career. You ought to be able to find a respectable, good-looking woman who would be willing to adopt Irene and start a new family."

Her eyes narrowed, and she leaned forward. "But you have to get rid of this other child first. He's a liability. No decent woman would be willing to take a rug rat with the problems he has, least of all with the fact that he's Jewish and he's foreign, German of all things. He barely speaks English, and he's sickly. When you were over there in Europe, couldn't you at least have picked a boy with a better constitution?"

Al gave a short, tense laugh. "Mom, you make it sound like he brought home an unwanted puppy from the dog pound. You don't really mean for Gray to give him up, do you? Yeah, he's got some problems, but hell, we all had problems too when we were growing. And we turned out okay."

Grayson scowled at him.

"Well, I mean what I say." Nina Cassandra set her omniscient profile. "Grayson, be practical about this. The child would be better off with his own people. You've been taking him to that Jewish place. Haven't they offered to take him off your hands? They have their own culture, their own way of doing things and rearing their young, which I believe would be more suitable for this child's temperament."

"The only temperament Joe has had been molded from the experience he had living in that hellhole called Buchenwald!" Grayson stood, lifting his weighty, emotional sword. "What exactly do you mean by 'their own way of doing things?'" His acrimony swelled like a fast-growing tumor in his gut.

The old woman studied the diamond-encrusted rings on her bent fingers. "You know. After all, they are from exotic and less civilized places, and they choose not to believe in Christ."

"Christ was a Jew," Al offered.

"You know what I mean."

"What you mean is you think they're primitive heathens," Grayson spat. When his mother did not deny it, he said, "That's your explanation for Joe's behavior? That because he's Jewish, he acts like a savage because Jews are savages because they don't worship Christ?"

"Well, I wouldn't go so far as to say that."

Grayson shook his head and set his fists on his waist. "God, you don't have a clue, do you, Mother? Next to Irene, that boy is the most important person in my life. You have no idea, no concept of my relationship with him. But even if you did, I don't think you would care because all that matters is what suits you in your own little world. All that's important is your comfort and tranquility. Well, I suppose at your age, after working your fingers to the bone rearing three children and taking care of a weepy husband, you deserve your peace and quiet."

"I have no idea what you're talking about, Grayson. You're not making any sense. Sit down. You're so drunk you'll likely topple over."

Grayson could barely breathe. He had never thought that his mother had such a racist, vile attitude toward the Jews. And knowing full well how fervently his sister wanted to convert Joe, she most likely had the same obscene view. The topic of Jews and Judaism had never been mentioned in the family as he had grown up. There had been no discussion on the subject, as there had been no contact with Jews or any other minority. Ithaca was a small, lily-white upstate New York community with maybe a couple of Italian families from New York City and a few blacks who lived on the south edge of town. He never knew how his father regarded other people, other cultures. Grayson hoped that he would have been open-minded and tolerant. Of course, he would have! His father had loved everybody.

Seeing that white-haired old biddy sitting placidly on the divan, spinning the melting ice cubes in her water glass, made Grayson feel revulsion toward her. He considered his mother with her unbelievable disregard for his relationship with Joe. How could she not see the complete devotion, the absolute commitment he had to his ward?

The floor would stay level under his feet, so long as he held on to the chair. He looked at his right hand. Where did he put his glass of scotch?

Facing her, Grayson said, "Mother, all my life, you have never taken me seriously. You have n-n-never listened to me. You've never paid any attention to my needs or my interests. I can't tolerate the blatant lack of res-s-pect you have demonstrated toward me. I will not tolerate it. Thank God, Father never held to that. I don't think I could have made it through medical school if it weren't for his support and en . . . couragement. All the while, you seemed to take my years and years of study and hard work for granted. I will never take that attitude with Irene and Joe. You have been treating them with the same callous indifference you've treated me. Is that how you want your grandchildren to remember you? That you were distant and unloving, more interested in your garden flowers-s-s- than your own flesh and blood?"

"That child you brought into this house is not my flesh and blood, and neither is he yours!"

Grayson staggered out of the parlor and headed for his study. He returned with a small black and white photograph in his hand. He shoved it under his mother's face. "Here. Look at this."

She drew away her eyes.

"I said, look at this! This is Joe sitting on a cot in the make-shift hospital a few hours after I dragged him out from under those wooden slats the Jews used for beds in one of the stinkin' barracks. Look at it!"

"I don't need to see it." She pushed away his hand.

He held the picture inches from her rheumy eyes. She couldn't help but see it.

"A photographer from one of the American newspapers took this along with some others because he wanted to show back here in the States the suffering the Jews endured at these concentration camps. He mailed me this copy. I have more in the wall safe. Do you want to see those too?"

Mildred and Al stood behind their mother to look at the picture.

Joe sat wrapped in a blanket, but his upper chest was bare, showing his protruding collar bones and sternum. Most of his black hair had fallen out, exposing a fragile, almost transparent skull. Ugly sores spotted his mouth, nose, and cheeks. The worse to look at was the abject vacuousness in his huge eyes.

"Do you not feel at least some pity for this boy?"

They met each other's eyes. Then Nina Cassandra looked the other way.

Mildred took the photo from Grayson to study. Al shook his head.

Grayson said to his mother, "I couldn't leave him. He would have for s-s-s-sure died a miserable death from starvation. I have chosen to rear him as my own son. And if you refuse to accept him as such, so be it. I won't live with anyone, not even my own family, who thinks this child is little more than an unruly pet that needs to be housebroken. He wasn't a puppy that I brought home!

"Joe is not your little servant boy, Mom. I've seen how you order him around, telling him to fetch a pair of sewing s-s-s-scissors or your newspaper or to pull weeds in your flower beds. Those seem to be the only times you ever interact with him. And if he tries to stay in the same room with you and Aunt Elvie to listen to the radio, you can't stand it! You shoo him out as if he's going to infect the room! Is it that uncomfortable for him to be around you?

"And you, Mildred! Since you have been s-s-s-sneaking behind my back, exposing Joe to the Church, which I have specifically told you not to, then I have no choice but to get him away from you and take him out of here. Give it up! You're not going to win this fight! Joe is a Jew. He will be brought up in the Jewish faith! And if you believe he will go to Hell, then fine! Stop meddling in the affairs of my children!"

Mildred fired back, still holding the photograph. "Grayson, do you not love the church where you were born and reared? Do you not love the Lord? If you believe in Christ, then you are duty-bound to bring this boy into His bosom. If you love Joe as your son, which I believe you do, then convert him. You've saved his life. Now you are compelled save his soul!" Her impassioned face reflected her unwavering stance on the issue.

"Are you implying that rearing Joe in the Jewish faith means I'm less of a Christian? You are questioning my faith because I choose to respect the religion my boy was born into? Mildred, how twisted can your thinking be! My children will not be reared with small-minded people who are racists, no, dare I say, anti-Semitic. I know my children better than any of you, and I am responsible for their upbringing. When it comes to my children, what I say goes!"

He took the photo and put it in his shirt breast pocket. "I've made my decision. My kids will be better off with me in my own home. I'm m-m-m-moving out. I'll find another house, maybe closer to the hospital."

"What?" Mildred and Al exclaimed.

"See here, boy! You're talking nonsense!" shouted Nina Cassandra.

"Irene will finish out the school year at Immaculate, and next fall, she'll join Joe at East Hill Elementary." He considered the bottle of scotch on the counter. "I'll ask around at the hospital for a nanny. Anne's a pretty good cook. She'll jump at the chance to be in charge of her own kitchen."

"Are you serious, Gray?" Al put his hands on the arms of his chair.

"Yes-s-s. You want to go with me tomorrow to s-s-s-scout out the real estate?"

"Well, okay. But it's not the right season, with winter coming on, you know."

"Oh, that's just the liquor talking." Nina Cassandra waved a dismissive hand. "Don't worry. He'll be singing a different tune tomorrow when he reaches for the aspirin bottle."

Grayson picked up his glass on the matching end table on the other side of the divan and finished his scotch. He weaved about as he scratched the back of his sweaty neck and pulled at his shirt. "Yeah, you go ahead and think it's just the booze talking. I'll admit I'm drunk, and I can barely stand. But I have the presence of mind to know I mean exactly what I say. I'll hire a nanny and bring on Anne." He rubbed his forehead, wishing he could just lie down and go to sleep right there on the threadbare carpet.

"How could you think of allowing a perfect stranger to rear your daughter?" said Mildred. "Mother is right. You're out of your mind to think you can just pick up and leave us. You're not being practical about this. With your job, you'll be away from Irene and Joe eight or even ten hours a day. Who will be there when they come home after school, helping them with their homework, taking them to activities and club meetings, birthday parties, buying clothes and shoes for them? Pretty soon, they'll be calling their nanny 'Mother.' Have you thought about that? At least here they have family looking after them, a family who loves them. And on top of that, what makes you think you can afford to hire Anne and a nanny and make a big mortgage payment every month? You're not making that much money as a doctor."

"Yes," Nina Cassandra agreed. "Grayson, your children would be better off here with us."

Grayson put his fists up to the sides of his head.

Aunt Bernice pulled the wool blanket up under Joe's arms and smoothed the end of the sheet over it. She had helped him get into his new flannel pajamas (alas! they were still too big, like all the other sets). She had rubbed his feet to warm them and had tickled his legs up to his sides to get him giggling. They both heard the shouting from downstairs. Joe's face grew somber.

"They're just doing some serious talking. It doesn't mean anything," said Aunt Bernice, taking his fingers into her soft hand and sitting next to him.

"It's about me. Dey always argue about me."

"Oh, you don't know that, honey. Why, I bet they're arguing about things like who overate at dinner or who's going to have the Christmas party this year."

Joe shook his head. "Grayson is shouting at Aunt Mil because I told him about confessing to a priest next week und using her rosary beads. I vasn't supposed to tell him dat, und he got mad. Ver's Paul?"

"Oh, he's sleeping in the bedroom at the end of the hall. That's where he likes to sleep when we come over to visit. Joe, you don't need to worry about Paul. He's learned his lesson. Your Uncle Albert talked to him again earlier this evening." Aunt Bernice leaned closer, almost whispering. "I'll tell you a secret. Paul was bawling his eyes out. He's very sorry about that BB gun. Tomorrow he's going to make it up to you." She patted his arm. "You know we're supposed to get some snow tonight. Would you like to build a snowman in front of the house?"

"Vat a snowman?"

"You've never built a snowman?"

"Nein. Is it hard to do?"

"Joe Kaufmann, you are going to have the best time of your life tomorrow. You'll have so much fun building it you'll forget all about what happened today."

He didn't believe her, nor was he convinced of Paul's remorse. All the tears that dangerous boy could shed would not guarantee Joe's safety from him. The only time he would truly be at ease would be when the mean Nazi kid was in the family car heading back to Syracuse.

CHAPTER THIRTY-SIX

Scrape, scrape, scrape, scrape. Stop. Scrape, scrape. Stop. Scrape, scrape, scrape, scrape, scrape, scrape, scrape, scrape. Stop. *What the Sam hill is rubbing on my hair? Ow! It's biting my scalp!*

Scrape, scrape, scrape, scrape, scrape. Stop. *Is that a needle poking my eyelid? What's that fuzzy thing on my forehead? Oh, hell.* Scrape, scrape, scrape, scrape. Stop. Knead. Knead. Knead. Purrrr . . .

His shoelaces were halfway pulled out of his size fourteen, triple-A, ox blood-polished black dress shoes, his brown silk socks thrown carelessly beside them. Circling the shoes like a garter snake lay his stiff leather belt with a solid gold buckle, a birthday gift from Mildred he had received before entering the Army. A stained, hand-croqueted doily from the divan lay on the floor. When he had situated himself on the faded mustard-yellow Victorian sofa to sleep, he had wanted to straighten out his legs, but since he was so tall, his ankles hung well over the arm. Lying on his right side, his head rested uncomfortably on the minuscule bolster pillow. His arms folded around a brown and yellow teddy bear. He'd have a sore neck this morning, along with a headache from the past evening of heavy drinking. Before collapsing on the couch the night before, he had taken off his shirt, stained with sweat and liquor, and had tossed it on the ugly, flower-printed armchair. Sometime during the night, he undid the clasp at the waistband of his trousers, exposing red and black diamond-patterned boxer shorts. Before him, a full ashtray sat on the scratched mahogany coffee table, along with two empty Depression glass tumblers.

Joe, still in his gargantuan-sized pajamas, lay on top of Grayson. His legs straddled his guardian's hips to keep his balance, and his arm draped over the big man's neck. His cheek rested on Grayson's bare upper arm. He slept soundly.

True to his nature to find the perfect spot in which to bathe, nap, or just keep watch over his "territory," Mr. Henry saw the dull-witted kid's back as the ideal place to nest. It was relatively high up, warm, and soft. He didn't even need to use his claws to get a foothold. Then cautiously padding to the big man's head, he washed the "fur," not caring about the odorous smell. The inside of his front leg needed a quick lick. Some kneading was required in the pliant neck, plus contented purring. Seeing all was as it should be, he jumped to the kid's back and then settled on his side. He stretched out his legs and put his head on the idiot boy's shoulder. The tip of his tail moved ever so slowly. Closing his avocado green eyes, he purred some more.

Rose whispered excitedly to Aunt Elvie and Bernice to come and look when she saw the three of them on top of one another in the parlor divan: Grayson and Joe sleeping, and Mr. Henry lying on Joe, eyes half-closed. Irene and Martha also saw them and sniggered.

"Shhh! You'll wake them!" whispered Aunt Elvie.

"I'll get Al's camera," said Bernice in a low voice. "I think it's still in the living room. We've got to get a picture!"

Mr. Henry was having none of this. He jumped off the divan at the first flashlight explosion and sprinted toward the kitchen and his food bowl. By the third shot, the explosion from the flashbulb woke up the giant and his elfish sidekick. Bleary-eyed and not entirely sure where he was or why he was holding a teddy bear, Grayson inadvertently shoved Joe off, sending the poor kid to the floor, his head barely missing the edge of the coffee table.

The epic Pierce family battle resumed at the breakfast table over Rose's waffles, bacon, and orange juice. Without any regard to their houseguests, Mildred and her mother, Nina Cassandra, resumed their harangue on Grayson. Surely, he had come to his senses about moving out. "It's impractical, too much work! This house has been your home for years! It's simply out of the question!"

Grayson ignored them as he studied the real estate section in the morning paper. He took a pen and circled some prospects. He said to his brother, Al, "I'll make some calls this morning, and then let's go take a look at some houses."

Al still seemed somewhat reluctant. "This isn't a good day to go out driving around town when there're five inches of snow on the ground." He spread another pat of butter on his waffles.

Grayson folded the paper and put it aside. "Well, I suppose you're right. And being the day after Thanksgiving, the realtor offices might be closed. I guess I can wait until Monday." He heard a strange "crunch" under his foot. Looking under the table to see what he had stepped on, he saw his tie clip, the golf club slightly bent. He picked it up. "Hmmm. I wonder how this got here."

"Daddy, can we go outside to play in the snow?" Irene asked, waving a fork of dripping waffle.

Mildred spoke over her niece. "Don't forget about that new package, Grayson."

Bernice added, "Oh, yes. Paul wants to show Joe how to play, don't you, Paul?" She looked at her son, who was too busy gulping his orange juice to pay any attention.

While everyone talked at once, Joe tried to figure out what had started the breakfast conversation, that is, something about Grayson moving out. Was his guardian leaving? He seemed serious about it, looking at houses for sale in the paper. Was he moving because of him? Maybe he had gotten tired of dealing with him and his problems. If Grayson left, what would happen to him? Undoubtedly, the old biddies wouldn't put up with him. Dread filled his chest. Maybe he would be sent to another concentration camp if there was one here in this country.

Joe put down his fork, letting it slide in the syrup of his waffles. Worry made his insides shake, and he hunched his shoulders, trying to make himself small. He wished he was a turtle so he could hide in his shell.

"Huh? Don't you want to go out and play in the snow, too?"

He didn't realize everyone was looking at him. He had no idea who had asked him about the snow. The adults were smiling at him, except, of course, Grandma Nina and Aunt Mil. When he met Paul's face, he saw carefully veiled malice in those deep-set washed-out eyes under the longish bangs. *You leave me alone!* was the non-verbal message Joe tried to give him. He inched out of his chair as if trying to escape a rabid dog without drawing its attention.

Upstairs and into his room he ran. He wished he had a lock on the door. All these relatives were too much. He even hoped Grayson wouldn't come up. But he would not go under the bed or into the closet. Mercifully, no one came after him, and he was left to himself. Because the room was chilly, he put on another shirt. At the set of bookshelves, he chose a book he had recently checked out at the library, *Gone with the* Wind by Martha Mitchell. A big chunk of a book to read, but Joe loved this historical novel. He sat at his desk and began on page 127.

After a while, there was a jarring knock on his door. "Hey, we're going outside to build a snowman, Joe. You coming?" said Irene from the other side.

"No. I dunt like snow." Joe had too many bad memories of the unbelievable severe Arctic weather of the past winter at the camp. He nearly got frostbite.

He heard shouting and laughter, and he went to the window, the same one he had jumped out of last summer. He stood on his desk chair and watched Irene and Martha rolling a ball of snow in the front yard, making it bigger and bigger. But Paul kept interrupting their hard work by kicking it. He also made snowballs and threw them repeatedly at the girls. Little Penny sat off to the side, singing to herself and making her little pile of whatever three-year-olds could make out of snow. Joe heard a door slam, and out came Grayson and Uncle Al, bundled in their heavy coats, boots, and wool caps. The snowballs began to fly. Paul never stood a chance.

Irene and Martha persevered in building their snowman, lifting the second and third balls onto the first big one with help from their fathers, and adding more snow to give it a better shape. Martha went inside, followed by her father, who carried Penny. Grayson sneaked up behind Irene and grabbed her, throwing her over his shoulder and swinging her. She squealed like the little girl she was. He played with her in a fresh patch of snow, tickling her. Then Joe saw him kiss her cheek and laugh with her.

After a short while, Grayson and his daughter went into the house. But before Joe stepped off the chair, he heard a noise from behind the castle, which he thought was a garage door, and he saw Grayson and Uncle Al carry wide, curved shovels to begin moving the wet snow off the front porch and steps. Paul appeared with a broom and pretended to help.

Joe got down and pushed the chair back under his desk. Sorrow hit him like the riding crop used so often on the newly arrived camp prisoners.

But he didn't have the entire day to feel sorry for himself. After lunch, Grayson took a paper bag from a closet in his study and put it on his desk in front of the youngsters. "I brought you all something. I've been keeping it in my office at the hospital and was planning to give it to you kids yesterday." He took out a long, thin, white box.

"It's a Monopoly game!" Irene shouted, clapping her hands. "Look, Martha!"

"Now, you kids can practice fighting over money and real estate just like the rest of the Pierce family."

"C'mon! Let's play!" Irene took the box. Then she stopped. "Thank you, Daddy." She and Martha went to the dining room to set up the game on the table. Joe trailed behind them.

Paul had to be coaxed into joining the board game. He voiced his impatience as Irene explained the game to Joe. His sister, Martha, told him twice to shut up. Nonetheless, whether by luck of the dice or thoughtful planning, Joe bankrupted the others in less than three hours.

The children played other games for the rest of the afternoon. The adults sat in the family room, trying to stay awake after the heavy lunch of Thanksgiving leftovers. Grayson succumbed to slumber in his easy chair, breathing noisily through his mouth.

Joe's revenge came later when he and Paul played checkers with Paul's father looking on. He took his time planning his strategy while Paul impulsively moved his pieces regardless of the consequences. After Joe beat him three games in a row, Paul gave up and resigned himself to an overstuffed armchair, his face showing resentment and thinly veiled animosity. Relieved, Joe went into the dining room to embark on new conquests over the girls' board games.

Al and his family stayed for one more day to wait for the state roads to be cleared. The subject of Grayson's moving out had been dropped, yet an uncomfortable malaise hung about the mansion like an unwelcomed ghost. New and old family wounds that had been so brutally sliced open on Thanksgiving Day were forcefully closed in unsaid thoughts. That Saturday evening, everyone attempted to get into the holiday spirit by having a go-round at the piano with Christmas carols while Mildred pounded out the chords. It was a postcard-perfect New England scene, complete with the hot chocolate, the popcorn, and the marshmallows roasting over the crackling blaze in the fireplace.

After lunch the next morning, while Bernice was bundling her children and packing the suitcases, Al took Grayson aside in the parlor.

"We need to talk about Thanksgiving evening," he started. They stood at the bar, which summarily had been closed after that historic family war three nights prior.

Grayson crossed his arms.

"This impasse between you and Millie over Joe, it's not doin' the kid right. You know it's hurting him when he hears you two fighting like that. Bernice told me when she put the kids to bed Thursday night, Joe said he heard you and Mil arguing over him. You're not considering how it's affecting him."

His brother shook his head angrily.

"Have either of you thought about how Joe wants? Have you ever asked him?"

"He's a Jew. His family was Jewish."

Al caught his arm and his eyes. "Are you sure? Have you asked him?"

"Of course, he's Jewish. The prison shirt he was wearing had the yellow star on it and his father's shirt. And now that I'm thinking about it, when I took him to see the rabbi at that temple a day after he arrived at the house, he had written his name in Hebrew." Grayson looked toward the tall windows on the east wall. The late fall sunlight shone sparkling frost on the glass. He remembered the first time he had taken Joe to Temple Beth-El for a Friday evening Shabbat service back in July before he had jumped out of his bedroom window. He had fidgeted and cried so much that he had to take him outside to the front steps. After the service, Grayson had made his apologies to the rabbi and had taken Joe home. After their excursion around the state, Joe was still recalcitrant about going back to Beth-El. But return he did.

Now, Al questioned him about Joe's religious background. At Buchenwald, there had been a lot of confusion in the overwhelming crowds. It was nearly impossible to know who was a Jew or a gypsy or a homosexual or a Communist or just a war prisoner. Perhaps Joe had worn that shirt not because he was Jewish but because someone had given it to him, or maybe he had found it.

But the boy's father was Jewish. He had seen the Star of David on the bloodied shirt and had matched the serial number to the man's name in the ledger book he had found in the administration building. His name was Hans Kaufmann.

"You're sure?" asked Al.

"Yes. He's Jewish, all right." He shook his head again. "Mil wants to mold him into what she thinks he ought to be. But darn it, he's my child. I'm in charge of his religious training. I keep saying that, but she's not listening!"

"Gray, the two of you are so much alike it's as though you're beating your head against a mirror. She's not going to give in any more than you are. Stubbornness runs in the family, you know."

"That's why I have to move out."

"Hell, you'd have to move to Timbuktu to get away from her. Don't you get it? She's got an investment in this kid, too."

"What?"

"She loves that kid."

"You lost me there, Al. All I see is a middle-aged matron trying to suffocate a helpless little boy. She hasn't the faintest idea about what he's been through. She has no concept of what he's seen. By golly, *I* don't know what all happened to him at that Buchenwald camp. I'm dying to find out, but I can't ask him. I don't want to upset him. He gets that way so easily. I have to take things slow with him, let him decide when he wants to talk." Grayson collapsed on the aged, musty couch. "But these self-satisfied old broads just push and push. That's why I took him on that road trip this past summer to get away from them." He rubbed his big hands. "I've got to get him out of here."

Albert sat beside his brother and put an understanding hand on his shoulder. "As I said, Millie loves that boy. Otherwise, why would she put up such a fuss about getting him converted? She's accepted him into the family. I bet she went right to work getting him set up with clothes and his toothbrush and a haircut and dentist appointments when you brought him home. Am I right?" Grayson nodded. "And she'll stand by him just as much as you will, in her own sanctimonious way. If there's any virtue in this family, it's commitment to a cause, especially one that's about ready to swirl down the toilet."

He lit a cigarette. They both heard voices and bumping around in other rooms. Rose's sing-song voice floated from the kitchen, something about packing snacks for the children.

Al went on. "Yep, she'll be as much a mother to him as she is to Irene. Can't say that about Mom. I just hope to God he didn't hear what she said about him." He dragged deeply and exhaled slowly. "Shit. I can't believe her wanting to put him in a damn orphanage. That's cold, just plain cold."

Grayson watched his brother smoke, fighting the urge to ask for a cigarette. "Mom and Aunt Elvie haven't lifted a finger for him, not even a pat on his head. You're right. Millie does care for him if you can get past her stiff neck."

"Then build on what you have. Gray, let me do some arbitration here. I propose you work with Millie instead of butting heads with her. Compromise with her. I'm not saying to give in, just allow her some wiggle room with Joe."

"What exactly do you mean?"

"Let her take him to mass on Saturday evenings." He held out his hand as Grayson shifted his big body in rigid disagreement. "And let him study a little bit out of his Baltimore Catechism."

"Joe's been going to Friday evening services and attends their Sunday school classes to learn Judaism. He spends the Jewish holidays with the family of a hematologist I work with at the hospital, and he plays with their son. With Saturday mass thrown in, that'll make for a busy weekend for him."

"Then plan so he doesn't have any other activities on the weekend. For sure, the kid's got to have time for play and goofing off."

"And don't forget he's starting school after the first of the year." Grayson studied the edge of the end table with his thumbnail. "I'm apprehensive about that. It's going to be stressful for all of us."

"Then take the pressure of you and Millie bickering out of the picture."

"Al, I'm not sure Millie will go halfway on this. How do we know Joe won't get confused learning about two completely different religions?"

"Are they so different, Gray? It's still about God." Al shrugged. "Talk to Joe about it. I bet he'll go for it. He's got a lot of brains. I could tell the way he played Monopoly with my kids. He beat the hell out of Paul at checkers. I'd like to teach him chess sometime." He stubbed out his cigarette. "In ten or fifteen years, he'll decide on his own which way he'll go. It's his life, you know. It should be his decision about how he chooses to worship God. Maybe he'll just chuck it all and become a Protestant!" He narrowed his eyes. "This moving out would be a big upheaval for both Joe and Irene, although they would eventually adjust to it. I think you should think about this. Give it some time. Maybe in the spring, see how things stand with Mil and then decide. Besides, it'll be a lot easier to find a house and move when the weather's better."

Grayson nodded. "All right, Al. You win. Let's bring our sister in here and have it out."

"That's the spirit!" Al patted his brother's back.

Mildred was beckoned to hear Al's proposal.

"Take a seat, Mil. Grayson and I want to talk with you." Al motioned to one of the worn-out armchairs.

Mildred crossed defensive arms. "What's this all about?"

"Please, just sit, Mil." Grayson looked out the doorway to make sure no one was eavesdropping.

The two men sat on the couch. Reluctantly, Mildred perched on the edge of a chair.

Al, ever the lawyer, began. "Now hear me out, Mil. This house's foundation is in serious danger of being destroyed with all the brawling and sniping and shouting going on. Joe is getting stressed out about it. I've only seen it these past few days, but I suspect he's been ducking the bullets between you two for quite a while. Right?"

Mildred chose to look away and start toying with her gold Cartier necklace.

"You and Grayson need to compromise about which religion Joe's going to be brought up in." To Mildred's rolling eyes, he raised his palm. "I want to help you two come to a settlement of sorts. This for the boy's sake. Grayson has agreed not to move out if you and he can settle how Joe will be taught his religion."

Grayson forced himself to look at his sister. Twisting his mouth in the manner of a true-blooded Pierce, he said, "Yes, Mil. Al is right. Let's come to an agreement on this. Al, can I bum a cigarette?" After lighting up, he said, "Okay. Here's what I will do. Joe can study his missal and Baltimore Catechism here at home, and you can help him with his Latin. However, he still attends Beth-El services and goes to Sunday school. And he will celebrate the Jewish holidays with the Greene family as he has so far."

Mildred shot back, "What about mass? What about confession? And when he is old enough to be confirmed and take communion, are you going to let him?"

Grayson said, "No. When Joe is thirteen, he will have his bar mitzvah."

To this, Mildred put on a sour face.

Al jumped in. "Millie, Gray will let you take Joe to Saturday night mass. That way, he can still go to the Beth-El school on Sunday mornings. But no trips to the confessional stall. He'll continue observing the Jewish holidays with that Jewish family he talked about, but he'll still celebrate Christian holidays too. You know, Christmas and Easter."

Grayson smoked thoughtfully. Mildred folded her hands in her lap, her face showing concentrated deliberation.

She finally spoke. "I'll have to think about this."

"No," said Al. "The decision has to be now. You both have to agree to this new arrangement."

Grayson put out his cigarette.

"Here's an idea," said Al. "You two come to a verbal agreement now. Then, over the next couple of days, you both write a list of all the religious things you want Joe to study. Write down specifically what rituals and observances you want him to participate in. Mail the lists to me, and I'll draw up a contract. After hammering out the details and making any changes, I'll have my secretary type two copies. Then, Bea and the kids and I will come down for another visit in a week or so. You both will read it and sign it, and that'll be it."

Grayson and Mildred stared ahead, their minds and emotions turning. Silence filled the old parlor.

After a moment, Mildred asked, "What about Mother?"

Al replied, sighing, "Yes, we have to deal with Mom. She's a brick wall none of us can climb over."

Grayson said, "I say we'll just have to humor her and agree with what she says and then stick to the contract."

Al turned to Mildred. "Will that be okay with you?"

"Well, all right, then. I don't like this, but if it's for the boy's sake."

Al's face broke into a broad smile. "What do you say, brother?"

Standing, Grayson fingered the loose change in his pants pocket. "I don't like it either, but I'll agree." He looked daringly at his sister. "As long as we don't slide into arguing. And Joe goes to East Hill in January."

Mildred gave a grudging nod. Her mouth was that flat line again.

Explaining all this to Joe almost seemed an afterthought. Grayson and Aunt Mil and Uncle Al sat with him at the dining room table to tell him about his future dual religious education. Although he thought he understood, he just shrugged. As long as the grown-ups didn't fight over him, that's all he really cared about. The more pressing dilemma was whether to start setting up his Lincoln logs in the basement or playing with his Slinky on the back staircase behind the old servants' quarters next to Rose's room.

A week later, after much correspondence, Al and his family came back to the Pierce mansion. While Aunt Bernice minded the kids in the family room, the adult Pierce children sat at the same dining room table, official-looking papers in front of them. Much care was taken studying the contract.

"You've got Joe attending Sunday school at the parish before mass," Grayson observed, pointing to the first paragraph on page two. "That's too much time for him to get exposed to Catholicism."

Mildred countered, "He needs to attend Sunday school to learn what goes on in the mass. It will mean nothing to him if he doesn't understand the holy sacraments. How will he learn our relationship to God?"

"He will learn about his relationship with God at the temple. He goes there for Sunday school." Grayson's voice rose a little.

Al raised his hand. "Wait a minute. We had this all ironed out in your letters. This contract has been drawn up after you both agreed to the final draft. Don't start having afterthoughts now. Okay, Grayson?" He eyed his brother's frown. "Just keep reading."

Grayson and Mildred pressed on examining the three-page contract in silence. After a few minutes, that silence was abruptly shattered.

"Well, well. Here we are, negotiating a silly contract as if it were a treaty between two countries at war!" Nina Cassandra lowered her substantial body into a chair. "This is just rich. Why is it necessary to bother with this nonsense? I thought it was decided that the child would remain in the Church. This is all poppycock!"

Nina Cassandra's youngest son glared at her. "Mom, please stay out of this. For once, this doesn't concern you."

"Everything in this house concerns me! I own it, you know!"

The success of the contract was dubious at best.

CHAPTER THIRTY-SEVEN

Now that Hanukkah was over, having spent the first week of December at the Greene's house for celebrations, Joe could look forward to the big Christian holiday, Christmas. He had figured out from listening to the commercials on the radio that December 25th was the birthday of the skinny, nearly naked man on sticks hanging on the dining room wall. He couldn't quite understand why this holiday was so important. Nothing was ever said about it or Jesus Christ himself at his Sunday school classes at Beth-El. These past eight days of Hanukkah were filled with songs, dreidel games, lighted menorahs, and delicious jam-filled donuts. How could this Christian holiday top that?

When Joe accompanied Rose on shopping trips, he observed Ithaca's holiday pageantry at its best. Garlands of fake pine branches and oversized plastic red bells hung on wires across the downtown streets. While passing storefronts, Joe saw open-mouthed angels holding red music folders while protecting the latest, state-of-the-art radios and phonographs. In Holly's Clothing Store, he observed a plastic Santa Claus in a red, wooden sleigh attached to eight reindeer in bell-clad harnesses sat on a women's hats counter. Powdery fake snow spread around the display. In Ithaca's bakery establishments, puffy cotton snow and Christmas ornaments decorated display cases filled with frosted cookies, fruitcakes, muffins, and marzipan. At the Sears store entrance, delicate toy reindeer, a giant, mechanical Santa Claus, and his tiny, red-suited minions greeted the customers.

Styrofoam snowmen in tartan scarves and shiny top hats sat in strategic places, looking on with blind, charcoal eyes. A blanket of glittery, fake snow covered the floor, and Christmas bells of all colors hung with wide, slick ribbons hung from the ceiling.

Such opulence held Joe in awe as he had never seen any of this in his life. At the JC Penny store, shoppers moved up and down the aisles, too busy looking for that perfect gift to notice Joe, who held Rose's hand tightly. Three-foot-tall gold-wired reindeer, standing on top of display cases filled with sterling silver flatware, ceramic knick-knacks, and shiny tea sets, looked up at the wrap-around balcony that also brimmed with customers. They White, sparkling angels blowing soundless fanfares on papier-mache' herald trumpets shared space with poinsettias and ten-pound boxes of Whitman's Sampler. In the center of the main floor stood a thirty-foot tall Christmas tree, overloaded with gaudy decorations and colored lights and surrounded by empty, gift-wrapped boxes. A scantily clad, pink cherub huddled in a bottom branch, holding a white ribbon with "Welcome, 1946" painted on it, a nod to the coming New Year. And Christmas tunes intoned from the ceiling loudspeakers endeavored to keep everyone in the holiday spirit.

Joe had his first meeting with a barrel-chested Santa Claus at the Montgomery Ward store. Not exactly sure about this red-suited fellow with the obvious fake white beard, he sat on his slippery knee and listened to the question: "And what do you do want for Christmas?"

Joe replied, "I vant *You Can't Go Home Again* by Thomas Wolfe. Und vile you're at the bookstore, I vud also like *Darkness at Noon* by Arthur Koestler. I've already finished *Gone mit the Wind.* I thought I vud read something a little lighter over Christmas."

Standing nearby holding her packages, Rose stifled a chortle at the obese man in a red cap in total astonishment. Santa forced a smile and almost pushed Joe off his lap. He held out his fleshy hands to the next child who looked utterly terrified.

One day, Grayson took Joe to Tompkins County Hospital to hand out Christmas cards, candy canes, and small bags of Rose's homemade peppermint fudge to the staff, the doctors, and the nurses. Joe knew that was his guardian's excuse to show him off wearing a ridiculous elf costume, complete with a stupid felt hat with annoying bells sewn on it. When Joe complained that he was getting lost in the way-too-big outfit, Grayson smiled and said, "Don't worry. You'll eventually grow into it." Joe sighed. This was not going to be the only time he would have to endure this humiliating chore.

At the castle, lively Christmas songs on the radio continuously filled the music room during the day. While Rose did her Christmas baking, her joyous but off-key singing could be heard throughout the kitchen and adjacent rooms. Joe sang along with her but couldn't get her to match pitches. However, to his delight, she kept overflowing plates of sugary goodies everywhere, tempting anybody who walked past them. Baskets of big navel oranges and grapefruit from Florida, an annual gift from Grayson's doctor partner, Stan Madison, sat on the coffee tables in the family and music rooms, accompanied by tins of mixed salted nuts. Hot cider in carafes was on hand to wash it all down. The perennial twenty-pound box of Russell Stover candies took center stage on top of the Bosendorfer piano next to a wooden manger scene.

On top of the miniature shed, a blue glass star sparkled. Three white-robed porcelain angels bowed their heads and prayed over the resting donkey and sheep. When Joe had watched Irene unwrap the newspaper protecting the manger pieces, she had to explain who the Joseph and Mary statues were, and the infant glued inside the little brown box she had called the manger was none other than baby Jesus. She and Joe played with the shepherds and the dark-faced wise men until some old biddy yelled at them to put them back.

Although Joe could appreciate everyone else's excitement about the upcoming holiday event, inwardly, he shrugged it all off. The only part of this brouhaha he got excited about was crunching the chocolate chip cookies decorated with red and green sprinkles, picking out stuck caramel popcorn from his back molars, and sinking his teeth into the pecan maple fudge, all while listening to Fibber McGee and Molly on the radio with Aunt Elvie.

****

Early on Tuesday morning, Joe heard a rustling noise coming from the living room. Curious, he went into the room to find Mr. Henry clinging to the Christmas tree trunk halfway up. Several frosted balls, two of them broken, lay amidst the piles of wrapped presents underneath. Unbeknownst to Joe, this was Mr. Henry's annual ritual. The shiny "cat toys" and the tree itself were too appealing to resist. As Joe carefully pulled him out, trying not to topple the ten-foot spruce tree, he overheard conversation in the foyer.

"Yes, I know you two are working in the basement today. But I want you to do something else first." That voice belonged to the old queen bee, and she was talking to Val and Phyllis, the cleaning ladies. "Go upstairs to the boy's room and pack a suitcase. You'll find it on the top shelf in the closet."

"Going on a trip, Mrs. Pierce?" asked Valerie.

"Yes. Pack enough for two days. That should be enough."

"Oh, where is he going?" Joe recognized Mrs. Clown Face's shaky voice.

"We are going to New York City, Elvie. I've arranged for Helen Schlazier to drive us there. She'll be here at eight-thirty. We've got to hurry."

"I didn't know we were going. Are we doing more Christmas shopping?"

"Yes, in a way."

"But we've so much--"

"I'll leave a note for Grayson saying we'll be back the day after tomorrow."

The voices faded. Alarm made Joe drop Mr. Henry. What was going on? That old dragon woman had never taken him on a trip. Whenever she went to New York City, Aunt Elvie and one or two of her friends from the parish went with her to shop for clothes and perhaps take in a Broadway show. And these outings always took place in the spring and early fall. To drive on snowy roads for hours to a dirty, overcrowded city was not her modus operandi (Joe had learned that phrase in one of Agatha Christie's detective novels).

There was no one in the castle he could ask about this. Grayson was diligently cutting into somebody's guts at the hospital. Aunt Mil was busy at the parish bossing the other volunteers preparing for the Christmas Bazaar this weekend, and Irene was waiting for an opportunity to push some kid in the snow on the school playground. Rose had left earlier to pick up some laundry soap.

Joe thought about grabbing his coat and running. But it was upstairs in his bedroom closet. Maybe he could snatch somebody's wrap in the foyer closet. The boots wouldn't fit, but he knew all about thrashing about in three-foot snowdrifts in feet bound only in cloth strips in the Nazi camp. He knew he was in danger.

Before he could turn around, sharp, painful fingers seized his upper arm.

"You there. Put on your coat and stand at the front door. Go on!"

Feeling his face draining of blood, Joe raced upstairs. He didn't speak to the cleaning ladies as they were too busy looking through his sock drawer. He got his coat and slowly descended the wide staircase. His stomach shook, and he clenched his jaws to keep down his breakfast of cornflakes and milk as he waited at the front doors.

The cleaning ladies came down carrying his suitcase. The doorbell rang, and Phyllis pulled open the left-side door.

"Hello, Phyllis! Hello Val!" The tall woman in her mink coat stepped over the threshold. She clapped her leather-gloved hands. "My, it's brisk this morning!" Her cheeks were red from the cold. She stamped her rubber rain boots on the throw rug laid down to catch snow tracked in from the porch.

"Please come in, Mrs. Schlazier. Mrs. Pierce and Mrs. Platt will be here-"

"Helen, it's so good to see you!" Aunt Elvie came into the foyer wearing her coat and hat. "How are the roads?"

"They're fine in town," replied Helen. "But I don't know about the state roads."

The queen bee approached, tapping that threatening cane on the floor. "They'll be all right. We've got a long drive ahead of us, so we have to go. We have to get to Manhattan by this afternoon."

What's in Manhattan? Joe only knew of that place because Grayson had told him he had done his residency at a hospital there many years ago. And he had lived in an apartment with his wife, Margie. They had talked about that when Grayson had shown him the big photo album months ago.

The cleaning ladies helped carry everyone's luggage to Helen Schlazier's brown, 1944 Fisher Fleetwood Cadillac. Joe followed the cackling women to the car. Before he climbed into the roomy backseat, Rose rushed out with two small boxes. Just as she was handing them to him, the old dragon lady intercepted and took them.

"Thank you, Rose. We will eat these on the trip." She put them next to her on the front seat.

After more folderol, all the car doors were finally shut. Helen slowly rounded the turn in the Pierce castle driveway and headed out toward the city street.

Aunt Elvie sat in the back with Joe. Her presence gave him a little bit of comfort, and he allowed himself to relax. As he had done when Grayson had brought him to the castle in a taxi for the first time back in the summer, he kept his eyes on the passing landscape. Today, whiteness covered the fields, the trees, and the occasional barn.

After a couple of hours of driving, Aunt Elvie asked, "What did Rose put in the boxes, Nina?"

"Let's see," replied the queen.

Both Joe and Aunt Elvie leaned over the seat to see Nina Cassandra taking iced sugar cookies under the red tissue paper. "Here you go," she said, giving Elvie two of them. "Helen, do you want a cookie?"

"No, not now. I need to keep my hands on the steering wheel." Helen looked straight ahead, bracing for another curve in the slick road.

"Joe, this is yours." Aunt Elvie held out a cookie.

Before Joe took it, the hoary dragon lady snapped, "No, don't give him any cookies, Elvie. He'll spoil his appetite."

"But it's another two hundred miles yet. He'll go hungry."

"He'll have enough to eat where we're taking him."

"What do you mean? Are we taking him somewhere? I thought he was going with us to do Christmas shopping."

The old white-haired woman turned back around to watch the road. "Never mind. You'll know soon enough." She opened her big leather handbag, searching for something.

Aunt Elvie gave the cookie to Joe.

Helen said, "I'd like to know, too, Nina. Just exactly where are we going in Manhattan?"

Nina Cassandra opened a letter. "I have the address and the directions right here. When we get to the Park Avenue Viaduct off Hudson Boulevard, I'll tell you where to go."

Apprehensive rheumy eyes met Joe's fearful ones. Joe saw worry in the clown lady's loose, rouged face.

Traffic became heavier as the car entered the thoroughfare going into the city. Joe had never seen so many cars and buildings and people. The ubiquitous Christmas decorations put the Ithaca street decorations to shame. After about twenty minutes, Helen drove under the Park Avenue viaduct.

Nina Cassandra opened the letter again. "Now look for East 35th Street. Then turn right."

As they drove away from the downtown streets, they left the skyscrapers and department stores and hurried Christmas shoppers and entered city blocks filled with squat, one and two-story shops and businesses. Going farther south, they came into a quieter residential area. Houses were neat and well-maintained, with long front yards and various sizes of snowmen sporting frozen carrots and button eyes. They drove several blocks. Finally, a sprawling, red brick church appeared with an enormous white steeple. Behind it stood two-story brick buildings with rows of windows, plus what looked like garages and sheds that seemed about to fall over. Around the property, lonely bare trees stood like neglected statues in the snow.

As they rolled onto the paved road leading to a side door, Joe glimpsed a white and black marquee, *St. Mark's Parish and Children's Home.* Dirty snow sat in piles around it.

Aunt Elvie saw the sign, too. "Nina, this is a parish! I've never seen this church before. Are we going to mass?"

Nina Cassandra replied, "Do you remember Mavis and John Swenson? They used to go to Immaculate. They moved down here to Manhattan five years ago. This is their parish."

"Well, all right." Aunt Elvie sounded unsure.

Helen parked the Cadillac in one of the open spots that wasn't covered in ice and snow. She and Elvie took Nina Cassandra's lead, exiting the car. But Joe gripped the door handle, hoping the women wouldn't pry his hand away.

Nina rapped on the car window with her cane. "Get out!"

Joe heard her tell Helen to fetch his suitcase from the trunk. There was some discussion.

Banging a storm door behind him, a priest wearing a black coat over his cassock approached. Joe watched him greet the old dragon lady, shaking her hand. She, in turn, introduced Helen and Aunt Elvie. Then he and the queen bee came to his side of the car. The priest opened the car door, letting freezing winter air rush in.

"Hello, little boy. Can you come out of the car?"

Joe looked into this cleric's sallow face. His eyes were slits behind his rimless glasses, and he had a low forehead and a crooked nose as if he had broken it sometime in his life. Joe couldn't take his arm away as the older man pulled him out. The priest took his hand in his icy one, and on numb legs, Joe walked with him into the dreary building followed by the women. Inside, they stopped at a low-ceilinged lobby. Joe wrinkled his nose at the odor of bleach, mildew, and stale urine. A nun who looked like she had lived most of her life in the previous century sat at a scuffed wooden desk overladen with files, envelopes, ledgers, and a beat-up typewriter.

With Helen and Aunt Elvie watching in sheer confusion, Nina Cassandra said to the priest, "Thank you, Father Gregory, for taking the boy. I've packed his suitcase with clothes for two days. And here are his papers. Now let me write you that check."

Everyone waited as she bent over the old nun's desk. She wrote a check in a flourished script and then handed it to the nun, who promptly put it in a metal box. Nina Cassandra turned to her companions. "Well, that's it. Look at the time. I reserved three rooms at the Warrick Hotel. I thought we'd go there first to freshen up, and then we'll have supper at Keens. I'm hungry enough for a nice, juicy steak. I'll tell you how to get to the hotel, Helen."

The other woman couldn't find her words. But Elvie did. "Nina, what about Joe? Are we leaving him here? What about Gray--"

Nina Cassandra said in a firm voice, "Now, don't you worry about Grayson. I'll take care of him."

Helen asked, "What about Mildred? Did you discuss this with her?"

"Oh, she's been complaining about that little monster from the day Grayson brought him into my home. She'll be glad he's out of her hair."

"But she talks about him all the time. She's enormously proud of him. I still don't understand why we're here."

"Don't worry about it. Everything's been arranged. We should go now." The old white-haired cow headed toward the door.

Joe knew what this place was. He saw the puke-green walls, the weary linoleum, and the inadequate overhead florescent lights. He recognized the nun's black robe and the wrinkled man's white collar.

He had seen it before in the orphanage in Zurich after he had been taken out of Buchenwald. Although that children's home had been warm and comfortable, and the nuns and staff had been good to him, he had no idea if that would be the case here. He heard echoes of children's voices down the corridor decorated with hand-drawn Christmas artwork on what looked like paper sacks. He blinked his eyes as waves of dizziness overcame him. As he slumped to the thickly waxed brown and white checkered floor, he tried to stifle his sobs. All he could do was make desperate moans deep in his throat.

What he didn't hear was the animated talking going on outside.

Smiling benignly, a sister of indeterminate age led Joe by the hand, carrying his suitcase. They walked to the end of the hall and climbed a set of concrete stairs. "Here is the dormitory room where you'll sleep," she said as she opened a set of metal double doors.

They entered a vast, poorly lit room filled with two long rows of neatly made single beds with no partition or curtains between them to provide any privacy. Over each bed's rickety metal frame lay a six-inch thick mattress, a flat pillow, and a paper-thin cotton blanket. Joe remembered similar blankets handed out to the Buchenwald prisoners, one for two or three of them. Gun-metal grey lockers lined the walls, and the gritty windows above them rattled in the winter wind, threatening to come apart and crash to the floor. He shivered under the mold-scented draft coming down from vents in the dull white plaster ceiling. He looked up and saw large water spots that dotted the cracked walls.

The nun showed him his bed and his locker, which was almost unreachable. She made him get out of his clothes and into a strange uniform of white pants, a shirt, scratchy wool socks, and too-big canvas shoes. His suitcase went into the locker. Then she showed him the communal shower room, with six rusty shower heads and hard-water stains under them on the brick wall. After allowing him to use one of the dingy toilets and washing his hands in an orange-stained sink, they went out of the dormitory room and into another part of the second floor.

A paneled door with the word "CHAPEL" carved above opened to a quiet, tiny room. Four rows of pews and a small wooden altar took up almost the entire space. On the left was a blue and green stained-glass window with a yellow cross. A gold chalice and three purple candles plus a white one stood on the altar covered with a white cloth. And overseeing the room was a hefty-sized statue of that brown-haired man, his face turned down and his body attached to a stone cross. He wore the same headdress full of prickly things, and his outstretched hands and bound feet dripped painted blood.

Joe knew immediately what this room was. He followed the nun's lead by genuflecting at the pew closest to the altar, lowering himself on the kneeling bar, and putting his hands together. He was supposed to pray, but he didn't have any rosary beads to help him. He heard the sister's murmurs as she tightly closed her eyes. They both stayed there for a long time.

This was wrong. He wasn't supposed to be here. Grayson would get angry if he knew that he was making these Catholic motions. What was going on?

Supper was a plate of rice and some unidentifiable piece of meat swimming in slimy gravy, plus a cup of room-temperature milk and a meager piece of bread. The other boys sitting around him at the long table ignored him as they greedily ate. Looking at the paltry food, Joe imagined the tasty meal Rose would be serving at the castle tonight. Maybe roast chicken, buttered parsley potatoes, honeyed carrots, and hot buttermilk biscuits with butter and grape jelly. And since she knew he had a sweet tooth, she always had a dessert, maybe strawberry ice cream with chocolate syrup and whipped cream. Thinking about that made this food tasteless.

After the meal, Joe followed a group of youngsters as they were escorted to a cramped room that contained several beat-up chairs, a dumpy, soiled couch, and grubby, broken toys blackened with fingerprints. Joe stood in a corner to stay out the way of the others playing and screaming their heads off. He noticed several toy pistols and moved out of the way when a couple of the boys fought with them. After a long time, nuns pushed everyone into the vast sleeping room on the second floor.

When he got on his knees at the side of his bed, pressing his hands together and pretending to say his Catholic prayers, Joe knew he was paying for his sins now. He had upset the whole castle, running and hiding under the big double bed in his room, waking his guardian with his crying and wetting his bed in the middle of the night, stealing leftovers from the kitchen garbage can, and worst of all, cutting that window screen. Even fighting and playing with the little girl and making a ruckus stomping up and down the stairs was enough bad behavior to exile him to this gloomy place. Guilt crushed him.

Grayson had finally given up on him. And Frau Dead Fish Eyes had gotten her way by banishing him to a Catholic orphanage, permanently cutting him off from his "pagan" Jewish roots. He would have to convert or at least go through the motions. She was most likely busy with her charity work and had given the job of bringing him here to her most compliant mother. He had lost the privilege of living with a wealthy, highly respected family, enjoying hot baths and warm, clean clothes, good food, and a bedroom full of toys and books. Indeed, the Pierce family had had enough of him and had dumped him just like a dog that had refused to be housebroken at the city pound.

Hopelessness draped his small shoulders like a blanket of chain mail. It was the same desperate abandonment he had felt when he had seen his mother disappear into the throngs of people at the camp entrance. And the searing memory of witnessing his father's death was too much to bear. Oh, how he longed to crawl back into that dirt hole under the wood slats in that filthy, stinking barrack! It would have been a slow death by starvation, but death it would be. How had his life taken such a tragic turn to become so miserable? What did he do to deserve these calamities?

He had an epiphany as he stared at his new, shabby bed. His only real sin was having been born a Jew. It was the foundation of his misfortunes. Being in this run-down, odious place was God's sentence on him. And he hadn't the strength to overcome such judgment on his soul. He couldn't stand up for himself. He didn't know how.

Worst of all, he had failed the only champion who steadfastly had been at his side. On their camping trip in August, Joe remembered how many times Grayson had to tell him that he was safe, that no one was going to harm him, that the concentration camp life was over, and that he would have a new life, full of promise and hope. Even while enduring the nightmares and the bedwetting and the hallucinations, Grayson had been patient with him, soothing and comforting him.

But Joe had known all along that it was all nothing but a ruse. He always had pushed back on his guardian's promises to keep him safe. He couldn't allow himself to trust that big, broad-shouldered man. And because that life had been too good to be true, he had now landed in his actual home, a loveless, cold prison that was as stark and demoralizing as the dirt hole in the barrack at Buchenwald. Sadness filled his heart. His guardian had forsaken him.

Joe took his blanket and quietly crawled under the flimsy bed. He covered his head, hoping that if he fell asleep, he would not wake up in the morning.

****

The next day started at 6:30 am with an icy shower in the community shower room with nine other boys. Joe focused on his tiny cake of soap and did not react to the shouts and laughing around him. He had to wash quickly as a strange older boy kept shouting from the doorway to "hurry up." When he went back to his bed to put on his clothes, his suitcase was not in his locker. He put on his "uniform."

The nuns ushered the boys into the long dining room. Joe didn't mind the oatmeal sans sugar, but he'd rather have had his bowl of corn flakes. After the quick, 15-minute meal, the sisters led him and the rowdy, juvenile "inmates" down a poorly lit hallway to a classroom. Joe had never stepped foot in such a room, and when the other fifteen boys took their seats, he hesitantly chose an empty, scarred student desk in the middle. He saw a much larger desk at the front with neat stacks of paper, books, a ruler, and a full pencil can. A wall-to-wall chalkboard hung behind it with an American flag on a pole nailed on the right side. Above the chalkboard was the ubiquitous, suffering figurine hanging on the predictable sticks. On another wall hung a picture of a white-garbed, middle-aged man wearing a white cap that looked like a yarmulke over a seriously receding hairline. He wore glasses and a red cape, and had a robot-dead look on his clean-shaven face. Joe had to rack his brain to remember his name—Pope Pius XII.

Also in the room was a floor stand globe, and under a set of windows on the north wall a bookshelf full of tattered books and a dated encyclopedia. Joe noticed rain falling on the snow that clung to bare tree branches outside. The sky was overcast--typical New York winter weather. The room was cold, so he sat on his hands to keep them warm.

A nun wearing cat's eyes glasses rushed in carrying folders and books. Her manner was identical to Frau Dead Fish Eyes, looking neither left nor right and certainly not wearing a smile. Joe knew this sister meant business. The students got to their feet and stood at attention.

"Good morning, class."

"Good morning, Sister Angela."

"We will start with our opening prayer and then the Pledge of Allegiance."

Joe mouthed the words. He didn't know what the "Pledge of Allegiance" was, and the hand over the heart was a new gesture.

Everyone, including the nun teacher, sat. Students took out their papers, pencils, and books. Joe followed along and found his supplies in a compartment under his seat—a copy of the Baltimore Catechism, a math book, an English text, and a geography book. Putting the math book on top of his desk, he eagerly watched to see what would happen next.

"Open your math book to page ninety-seven."

More shuffling. Joe was ready. Suddenly, his heart jumped. He was holding the pencil in his left hand. *Oh, no!*

"Mr. Johnson, come to the blackboard. Copy the exercises and complete the answers."

An emaciated, white-headed kid wearing oversized pants held up by a belt approached the board with the enthusiasm of a tired dishrag. He struggled to hold his math book. The slowness of his hand was painful to watch, but the room stayed quiet. The boy managed to copy three exercises on long division, but then he stopped.

"Now write the answers."

The boy stepped back, his head down.

The nun rose, a ruler in her hand. "Did you not complete the homework assignment?"

The poor kid shrugged.

Joe couldn't stand it. He popped up and blurted out, "I can do it!"

The sister turned to him as if noticing him for the first time. "You are supposed to raise your hand, young man. Who are you?"

Before Joe could respond, the black-robed woman looked at a paper on her desk blotter. "Hmm. You're the new student, Joseph Kaufmann."

"Yes, ma'am."

"Well, you need a refresher course in proper classroom manners." After a pause, the sister said, "Come up, and let's see what you can do." Her mouth turned down with impatient distrust.

With confidence he didn't know he had, Joe went up to the board. He waited for the dour-faced boy to step aside. Taking the chalk from him, he wrote the answers with confidence. Then he took the other kid's math book and wrote out more exercises and answers. The students quietly copied what he wrote. Just like Aunt Mil and Grayson, the nun seemed astounded by his mathematical prowess, although her reaction was well concealed. Frowning, she observed him skipped several pages to the text's very back, copying the last exercises on fractions and writing the answers. Thankfully, she didn't seem to notice his left-handedness.

After finishing, Joe turned to Sister Angela, meeting her dark eyes. He held his breath. Did he see a slight hint of confusion?

"Return to your seats, both of you. Class, get out your English books."

As the students followed her instructions, the sister studied the blackboard. She picked up an eraser, then put it down. She faced the class with her teacher's manual in hand. "Charles, read Chapter Eight starting on page sixty-one."

Using his finger as a guide, Charles began reading the big-printed passage. But he stumbled over several words. The story was about a sea captain and his crew preparing to sail across the Atlantic Ocean from Manchester, England. Growing bored at the child's struggling pace, Joe turned the page to look ahead. *This book is too easy.*

"Mr. Kaufmann! Why aren't you on the same page? You think you can't follow along?"

"No--"

"Stand up when I'm talking to you."

Joe rose and stood by his desk, knowing he had to speak English without his German accent. "No, ma'am. I just read the rest of that page and was reading the next one." Someone snickered behind him.

The sister said sternly, "Who's that?" She scanned the room. The students were as still as marble statues.

With irritation in her voice, Sister Angela said, "There is no talking or laughing in this room." She returned stony eyes to Joe. "I suppose you can read the next paragraph."

Joe began. "Captain Victor took the money from the merchant and put it in his waistcoat pocket. He looked at his men to see if they were ready to set sail."

Joe went on for several lines, never missing a word, and pausing at the end of each sentence. He didn't hear the classroom door open, nor did he notice the grey-faced priest entering.

But the nun saw him. The priest waved his hand and nodded his head, gesturing her to continue the class.

Joe looked up. "Would you like me to read it again in Latin?" He had practiced his Latin with Aunt Mil by translating parts of his library books out loud. She had told him he needed to know the language to understand what was happening during mass.

"What did you say? In Latin?" Sister Angela scoffed, "You don't know Latin. You're wasting my time."

Joe held the book closer to his face. He started at the beginning of the chapter. "Kessinger et maritimam urbem, et est semper plena erat nautis gregem operarios." He continued with four more sentences, taking no heed of the surprised, open mouths of everyone around him. When he got to the bottom of the page, he halted, thinking that he could translate all this again in German, Hebrew, and mostly Yiddish. But wisely, he decided not to offer to do so.

A short-lived moment of disbelief shadowed Sister Angela's face. However, she straightened her back and her composure. "That will be enough from you, young man. I won't tolerate a show-off. That would be an offense in the eyes of the Lord. Sit."

Crestfallen, Joe put down the text and slowly took his seat. He wasn't trying to show off. He was trying to get in good graces with this puritanical woman. But he realized she was cut from the same uncompromising cloth as Aunt Mil. Nothing he did would change this teacher's opinion of him. Defeated, he put his head down in his folded arms.

A light finger tapped his shoulder. He looked up through wet eyes to see the black-suited man he recognized from yesterday. The priest wore an amiable, bemused smile. He pointed to the half-opened door, and Joe followed him. Standing right outside in the hall were Grayson and Aunt Mil.

Joe bounded into Grayson's arms and wrapped his arms around his neck. "Grayson! You're here!" Joyful tears sprang in his eyes.

While Aunt Mil awkwardly touched his back, his guardian kissed him over and over. "Yes, I'm here, Joe. I missed you terribly."

In a croaking voice, Joe said, "I thought you ver gone forever! I thought you left me--"

"Shhh," said Aunt Mil in a low voice. "Let's move down the hall so we don't disturb the class."

The priest said, "We can go into my office. This way, please."

Carrying Joe, who still clung to his neck, Grayson followed the priest toward the front entrance with Mildred behind him. At the receptionist's desk sat the same moldy nun. She gave a disapproving look as they walked past several desks and filing cabinets to a back room crammed with office furniture and boxes. Grayson and Mildred sat in folding chairs with Joe in Grayson's lap. He looked up at his guardian's tired face. Did he see a hint of bags under his eyes?

"There seems to be a misunderstanding, Mr. Pierce," started the priest, taking a thin, brown file from a wire basket on his desk.

"That's *Doctor* Pierce," Aunt Mil corrected him. She leaned over to take Joe and put him in her lap. Joe's heart beat fast, for she had never done this before. She seemed entirely comfortable holding his arm with a gloved hand. She met his eyes. But, true to her nature, she didn't smile. She looked tired, too.

"I want to get to the bottom of this, Father," Grayson spoke aggressively. "What happened yesterday? How did my boy end up here? I've never heard of this parish or this orphanage."

The priest opened the file. "A few weeks ago, one of my parishioners, Mrs. Mavis Swenson, told me about a seven-year-old boy who needed a good home. She said she had a long-time friend from when she and her husband had lived in Ithaca many years ago, a Mrs. Nina Cassandra Pierce. A child war refugee from Germany had been staying with Mrs. Pierce temporarily and asked if there was a possibility of bringing him here to St. Mark's. I told Mrs. Swenson to tell Mrs. Pierce that we would have to wait for an opening. We've been over-burdened taking in other orphans, you see, plus young mothers who had lost their husbands in the war and had no means to support their children. But just last week, another child had been boarded out to a foster home. I told Mrs. Swenson we could take this one." He gestured to Joe.

Mildred snapped, "This one has a name, Joseph Kaufmann."

The priest took in her terse words and then held out some papers for Grayson. "These are the birth certificate and naturalization papers Mrs. Pierce left with him."

Grayson took the papers without looking at them. "Yes, I am quite familiar with these documents. I should be as I was the one who had them drawn up." He folded the papers and gave them to Mildred, who put them in her purse. He said quietly to his sister, "She must have rummaged through my drawers in the study." Aunt Mil nodded, that almost non-existent, unforgiving line of a red-lipsticked mouth set hard as usual.

The priest said, "Mrs. Pierce donated a thousand dollars to help with the costs of running our orphanage. We are very grateful for that."

"Just like her," Grayson said under his breath. To the priest, he said, "Look here, Father. I am this boy's legal guardian. The papers are right here." He motioned to Mildred, who went through her purse to retrieve them. She handed them to the priest.

The priest squinted at the documents. He turned on a dusty metal lamp on his desk and looked at them for a long time. Then he spoke. "This is most confusing."

"You don't believe what you're seeing?" asked Mildred. She set Joe on the floor. "My brother brought this boy back from an orphanage in Switzerland this past summer. Joe was an orphan from the Buchenwald concentration camp in Germany. Doctor Pierce was a surgeon with the 102nd Evacuation Hospital when the army opened that horrible place in the middle of April. He saw Joe and had the God-given charity to bring him back to live with us in Ithaca. He already has a good home." The dark purple hat on her head quivered. "How do you think he knew Latin well enough to translate that textbook? *I* taught him that, plus a good deal more."

The priest still did not look convinced.

Grayson dug in his wallet and threw his driver's license and his Tompkins County Hospital employee card on the desk. "There. Do you believe who I am now?"

The man in the white collar slowly handed the cards back to Grayson. "I am baffled about this situation, Dr. Pierce. Why would Mrs. Pierce bring the boy here yesterday? And it appears that you didn't know about this. How are you related to her?"

Grayson exhaled to muster patience. "Mrs. Pierce is our mother. We certainly had no idea she had been arranging this behind our backs."

"And obviously doing this for weeks," added Mildred.

"Why would she do this? Had you not discussed this with her before?"

Grayson and Mildred eyed each other. Who would go first to answer these uncomfortable questions?

Joe wandered about, looking at the walls of books. He had never seen so many versions of the Bible. There were also volumes on Christian philosophy, canon law, and theology. As he knew no one was paying attention to him, he took a book from a set of six, *Confessions of St. Augustine*. He sat on the floor in a corner and began reading.

Grayson said, "This shenanigan she's pulled, which is almost a kidnapping, is understandable knowing her attitude toward my ward. She couldn't stand the fact that I brought home a Jewish child to rear in our home. She is as intolerant and cold-hearted as a piece of concrete." His face shook with simmering indignation.

"Perhaps she believed a Catholic environment would be best for his soul. Wouldn't you agree?"

"Joe's religious upbringing is my business, not hers." He glanced at his sister. "It's an internal family affair that we are dealing with. But the bottom line is she had no business taking Joe away from me and bringing him here. She has done terrible emotional damage to him by uprooting him from the only stable home he's known since Buchenwald. But, of course, his welfare has never been of any concern to her. Having a little boy running around in her big old house disrupts, as she has said, her peace and tranquility."

Joe could no longer keep his attention on the tiny print of the second page. Shame made him put down the book.

The conversation stopped. Then Grayson narrowed his eyes. "Oh, I think I know what's going on. You're wondering about that check."

The priest kept a blank face.

"You're afraid Mrs. Pierce will stop payment on it once she sees Joe is back home with us. Well, you'll have to work that out with her. I'll even give you our phone number so you can call her and discuss the matter."

Grayson stood. He dug into his wallet again. He wrote down a phone number on the back of a business card and dropped it in front of the priest. "Here."

"Well, this has been most perplexing." The priest almost looked disappointed.

"Where's Joe's coat?" asked Mildred. She pulled Joe to his feet. "Whose shoes are those? Why, these aren't his clothes! What kind of orphanage are you running here?"

The priest opened the door. "Let me get one of the sisters to look for his coat." He would not answer her other demanding questions.

Grayson, Mildred, and Joe waited in the lobby for an indeterminable amount of time. They could hear children's high-pitched voices from behind walls. The dowdy old nun at the desk typed away, pretending to be unaware of their presence. Other younger nuns and women in street clothes rushed about, doing whatever they did to keep this orphanage running smoothly. None of them acknowledged them.

Grayson sighed and weaved back and forth, his eyes on the polished floor.

"You're tired, Grayson. I'll drive back." Mildred put a hand on his arm.

Joe took his guardian's thumb. "Grayson, I need to tell you something," he whispered.

"Not now, son. Wait until we get in the car."

Joe then tried Frau Dead Fish Eyes. "Can we stop to get something to eat? I'm hungry."

His aunt looked down at him. "Didn't they feed you breakfast?"

"Ya, but it vasn't very much."

Mildred shook her head in exasperation. "This is the worst place for children!" She didn't care that the busy body nun at the desk looked at her.

A stout, panting nun Joe had not seen before appeared. "We've seemed to have misplaced his coat. But we have this one."

Upon inspection, Mildred said, "You sisters are incompetent. This garment is in tatters. It's probably not even clean. Joe, you'll have to make do. I guess this means you'll get one of your Christmas presents early. I bought a new coat for you at Holly's."

Joe sniffed the coat. It smelled of old mildew. He didn't want to put it on, but he knew not to argue with Frau Dead Fish Eyes when she was perched her moral high horse. He took Grayson's hand when they exited the depressing, bleak place.

While Mildred guided the big Lincoln Town car out of the snow-packed driveway, Joe was ready to burst. "Grayson, how did you know I vas here? Grandma Nina never said anything about coming here. I'm hungry. Did you hear me talk Latin in dat room? I did all de math problems on de chalkboard. I knew how to do de long division because you taught me on our camping trip. I dunt think dat nun teacher liked me. She said I vas showing off."

"And were you?" Grayson slumped in the back seat; his fedora dropped to the floor. "Mil, do you know how to get back to the main road from here?"

"Yes, I think so." She looked in her rearview mirror to catch Joe's eyes. "Joseph Kaufmann, you leave your father alone. He was at the hospital until one o'clock this morning, and we drove straight from the house to New York. He hasn't had any sleep."

Joe straightened his legs and sat away from Grayson. But he couldn't resist putting his head on the big man's shoulder. "Ya, Grayson, I guess I vas showing off."

"Good for you. That sister saw what an intelligent kid you are even if she was too obstinate to admit it."

Joe screwed up his face. "Grayson, I'm sorry for causing so much trouble. I . . ."

He saw that his guardian's eyes were closed. He scooted over and looked out the window.

CHAPTER THIRTY-EIGHT

Mildred decided to get back to the Pierce castle as soon as possible, so they only stopped once for gas. Grayson slept all the way. When they walked through the family room and into the dining room, Joe noticed that there was nothing on the long, cherry-wood table except a display of fake roses and evergreen twigs entwined with a red ribbon in a gold-plated urn. He didn't even smell anything cooking from the kitchen, and he was still hungry.

"Is Rose here?" he asked.

"She might be downstairs doing laundry," replied Aunt Mil. She took off her ermine-trimmed car coat. "Now, don't eat so many of those cookies. You'll spoil your appetite for dinner."

Joe had found a plate of crispy ginger cookies on the sideboard. Not his favorite, but they had to make do for now.

Mildred opened the basement door in the kitchen and called for Rose. She returned to the dining room.

"I'm coming!" The cook tramped up the stairs carrying a straw basket full of freshly laundered sheets and towels.

"Oh, my sweet little Joe! You're home!" Rose set down the basket and threw her arms about Joe. She kissed him over and over. "Are you all right?"

"Vel, I vasn't dere long enough. But I helped in de class mit some math problems. I'm hungry. Vil you give me something to eat, please?" Joe remembered what Grayson had told him on the last night of their road trip. If he was hungry, all he needed to do was ask

Rose for food. There was always plenty of it in the pantry and in the icebox.

In the dining room, Grayson took off his fedora and unbuttoned his coat. He sat and took a wadded piece of paper from his pants pocket and unrolled it. "According to this note, Elvie went with her and Helen Schlazier to New York to do some shopping." He frowned as he studied the fluid, perfect cursive writing. "And she didn't bother to say she was taking Joe with them. What the hell did she expect us to think? She knew we'd know he was gone."

Mildred said. "Yes, and she didn't seem to care what reaction we would have." She carefully took off her purple Cloche hat and put it on the sideboard. She looked at herself in the matching wood-framed mirror above it to pat her ash-blonde curls. Then she said to Joe, who stood at the table, crunching cookies and getting crumbs on the crimson and gold Persian rug, "Joe, we are going upstairs to get those clothes off and you in the tub. And leave that cookie here."

Joe put the partially eaten cookie on the table and ran to the staircase. Grayson looked at it and ate the rest of it. He liked ginger cookies.

In Joe's bedroom, Aunt Mil set out a flannel shirt, brown socks, and jeans. Joe was glad to get the orphanage garbs off. As he went into the bathroom to start the tub, he said, "Grandma Nina told Valerie und Phyllis to pack a suitcase before ve left."

"What? You had your own clothes?" Aunt Mil carried a clean pair of undershorts and a white T-shirt into the bathroom. She went to the closet to retrieve a fresh towel and a washcloth. "What happened to them?"

Joe shrugged as he took off the ill-fitting pants. "I dunt know. De suitcase vas gone dis morning. I had my best shoes in der, too." He put the white "uniform" in a pile.

Mildred put her hands on her hips. "Well, no wonder you were wearing those dirty clothes and those shoes that were too big for you. They probably gave your good ones to some other child. Those rags you wore are going in the trash. I don't think the Salvation Army will take them."

Joe had had enough experience to take his bath on his own. The nightly bed-wetting occurrences back in the summer had given him practice. But Aunt Mil stayed and helped him. She even washed his hair. Strangely, Joe sensed a calm, almost conciliatory manner from this otherwise forbidding woman. He would not go so far as to say she was affectionate toward him, but there were noticeable cracks in her glacial face. However, he knew better than to let down his guard. Her eyes were still as immovable as an insensitive fish's. As Aunt Elvie once told him when he was helping her with her *New York Times* crossword puzzle, a leopard doesn't change its spots. Joe had wondered at the time if the leopard was with the sleeping dogs who lay undisturbed.

After giving him his bath and helping him put on warm, familiar clothes, Aunt Mil said, "Since you said you were hungry, Rose can make you a peanut butter sandwich. Your father will want one, too."

She took Joe's hand as they went back down the wide stairs. He thought, *she still thinks Grayson is my father. She calls him that all the time.* Then it came to him. This woman had accepted him as a member of the family from the beginning. She had bought his clothes, had taken him to the library and the bookstore, and had taken him to his haircuts and dentist appointments while Grayson was at the hospital. She had even made plans to enroll him at that parish school after Christmas, even though Grayson didn't know about it at the time. Under the intimidating, unbending exterior, she did care about him. She was very much involved in his life, even if she had the disposition of a Nazi Gestapo.

After Joe and his guardian ate peanut butter sandwiches and gulped the requisite glasses of milk in the kitchen, Grayson looked at the wall clock above the stove: 3:10. "I've got to pick up Irene at school."

"I can do it," countered Aunt Mil.

"No, you're tired, Mil. My goodness, you've been up longer than I have. Why don't you take a nap? It's been more than a long day."

"Yes, I think I will." She sighed.

"C'mon, Joe."

Riding shotgun in the gargantuan Lincoln town car, Joe asked, "Grayson, vy did you let Grandma Nina und Aunt Elvie take me to dat orphanage?"

"Son, I didn't. I had no idea she planned this. I'm so sorry you had to go through that. I can't imagine how you felt being left there." He shook his head. "She'll have a lot of questions to answer when she gets back."

Painful, familiar fear spread in Joe's chest. "But vil I have to go back? I didn't like it dere. I thought--I thought you didn't vant me anymore." He looked out the car window and observed the rows of houses with their unlit Christmas lights wrapped around shutters and porch beams and wreaths hanging on front doors. He would not cry.

Grayson parked the car halfway down the block on Buffalo Street where Immaculate Conception School stood. He left the engine running to keep the heater on. Sliding to the passenger side, he pulled Joe into his lap, who buried his head in the big man's thick wool overcoat. "Son, you are not going anywhere. I will never abandon you. You have to have faith in me. This will never happen again. Do you believe me?"

They met eyes. A silent moment of truth drowned out the distant shouts and laughter of children. Before Joe could answer, the back car door opened, and Irene hopped in and threw down her school books.

"Oh, boy! Joe, you're back! I missed you!" She tried to climb over the seat to reach him.

"Irene, sit down in the backseat." Grayson let go of Joe and slid back to the driver's side ad put the car in drive. "Did you have a good day at school, sweetheart?"

"Yes, Daddy. We made rings out of construction paper and put them on the Christmas tree in the hall. And we learned a new Christmas song in music class."

"And how many of your classmates did you push in the snow on the playground?" Grayson drove slowly as the streets were slushy.

"Let me count. One, two, three. Only three this time. We had a snowball fight, too. I won."

As he put the car in drive, Grayson muttered under his breath, "Another phone call from Mother Superior."

Rose reached for her coat on a kitchen chair. "Dr. Pierce, everything appears under control here. I need to buy some more groceries for dinner." She looked at him and then Mildred uneasily.

"Take your time, Rose."

Everyone settled in the music room. Mildred closed the curtains to block out the early-evening cold, and Grayson built a fire in the fireplace. Then he sat in his easy chair with his feet resting on the ottoman and a smoldering pipe in his mouth. He perused the pages of the *Ithaca Journal* without much success at reading the articles. Giving up, he folded the paper and practically threw it on the floor. He stood and paced in front of the huge, age-old Bosendorfer piano.

Likewise, Mildred tried to work on her cross-stitching but seemed unable to concentrate on the Christmas wreath pattern in the dismal light of the floor lamp. She put away the waste canvas and the embroidery thread and stared into space with creased brows and folded arms. And, unusual for her, she seemed not to notice Joe and Irene on the floor in front of the six-foot Balsam Fir Christmas tree. Its branches bowed to the multitude of ornaments, red plaid bows, colored lights, and icicle strands. They played with Mr. Henry, who pawed a piece of ribbon that kept slipping away.

The grandfather clock chimed from the family room six times. The tension in the music room was so thick one could cut it with a dull knife.

A door opened and closed several times. Grayson and Mildred listened as they looked at each other.

"Thank you, Helen, for a wonderful trip. I can't tell you how much fun we had. And here's a little thank-you gift I picked up at Macy's."

"Well, thank you, Nina. I-I really don't deserve it. Do you and Elvie have all your packages and suitcases?"

"My, it's good to be home! So warm, and it smells like there's a fire burning in the fireplace."

"Helen, thank you for driving us. It's been an unusual two days. Well, goodbye and Merry Christmas."

"Merry Christmas, Elvie."

"Oh, yes. Merry Christmas, Helen! And thank you again!"

There was scuffling in the foyer. A stick tapped on the black and white tiles. "Take these gifts, Elvie. We can put them under the tree in the living room."

"I wonder where everybody is. I don't smell dinner cooking. Did you give Rose the day off today?"

"Yes, I did. I thought for once, for all the baking and decorating the house she's been doing, she deserved a day's rest. I'm sure she left a casserole and some vegetables in the ice-box."

"Did she say where she was going?"

The elderly female voices faded. There was silence, and then the disembodied voices from the living room grew louder.

"Wasn't that a marvelous chorus singing carols on the sidewalk on Fifth Avenue? They sounded like professionals."

"Yes, they did, Nina."

The two old women, resplendent in their newly-purchased holiday dresses and Christmas tree pins attached, entered the music room. They stopped as Grayson and Mildred stood before them, staring at them.

Mr. Henry ran off. When Joe started to go after him, he stopped and slid into the corner with Irene, almost hiding behind the Christmas tree.

Aunt Elvie took a sugar-coated gumdrop from a plate on the end table and sat in her well-worn place on the red and blue-flowered sofa. Groaning, the queen bee dropped herself into the couch on the other end and hooked her cane over the edge of the coffee table. She busied herself straightening the cream-colored doily on the sofa arm. Then she turned and saw Joe. Startled, she cried, "What's *he* doing here?" Her rheumy eyes flashed like the diamond necklace around her turkey-wattled throat. "St. Mark's reneging on keeping him? I took two days out of my busy schedule to go all the way to New York to drop him off. And I paid that priest good money to keep him!"

"I don't even know where to begin." Grayson clenched his fists while struggling to keep his voice under control. "Why did you take my ward to that orphanage in Manhattan?" He boldly walked to the sofa and stood less than two feet from his mother.

"Because that's where he belongs! I had to wait almost three weeks before there was an opening to get him into St. Mark's. Now, I see you've brought him back. I left a note telling you that Elvie and Helen Schlazier and I were going to New York City to do some shopping. How did you know to find the orphanage?"

Mildred stepped up. "When I came home yesterday after meetings all day, I saw that Joe was gone. I asked Rose where he was, and she said he had gone with you and Elvie to New York. I never saw the note. But all the same, I was suspicious. Since when would you take Joe anywhere, least of all to New York City? When I questioned Rose about it further, she said she had overheard you talking on the phone with someone about St. Mark's in Manhattan, something about children. I went straight to the library and looked up that parish in a New York City phonebook and found there was an orphanage connected to it."

Outrage intensified in her voice. "At first, I couldn't believe it, that you would take our little boy to some strange orphanage and leave him there. And you had the audacity to do it behind our backs! I was fuming. I called Grayson at the hospital several times, but he was in surgery. He didn't get home until one o'clock this morning. He and I jumped in the car in the middle of the night, and we rushed to that church in New York to fetch Joe. We were worried sick about him. What was he to think? That he'd been abandoned one week before Christmas?" Her dead eyes came alive with infuriation. "Mother, your cruelty is breathless."

"And I was looking forward to a nice, relaxing Christmas. Well, I supposed we'll have to make another trip. What a mess you've made, Grayson. Now, what are you going to do about it?" Looking annoyed at having her six-foot-five-inch son hovering over her, she took her cane for want of holding on to something.

Mildred came forward and shook her finger at her mother. "You did a terrible, selfish thing taking Joe away like that!"

"I put him in a Catholic orphanage, Mildred, so that he could be converted. Isn't that what you wanted? You kept arguing with Grayson all these months about needing to save the child's soul. Well, I solved that problem for you."

"We had a contract, and it was--"

"Balderdash! That harebrained scheme Albert cooked up wasn't worth the paper it was written on. Now get away from me!"

Neither of them stepped back. Grayson leaned into her closer than he ever had in his life. He looked directly into her watery eyes. "The only problem you solved by dumping him in a smelly, run-down children's home was alleviating your own discomfort of having my ward living under the same roof as you."

He backed away, almost tripping over the coffee table. Wiping his perspiring brow, he paced the room, tapping his fists against his legs. Joe stood rooted next to the Christmas tree.

Grayson turned back to his mother. "It's bad enough that you have no sympathy, no compassion, not even any acknowledgment that this little boy came out of a Nazi concentration camp. You have no benevolence, no kindness, no respect for him or anyone else. You pride yourself on being a devoted Catholic, but you certainly don't abide by Christian values."

"What? You have no right saying those things to me! How dare you!" Nina Cassandra pushed on her cane to stand.

Grayson inhaled deeply while debating his next words. He summoned his mettle. "Let's get this out in the open. You are a contemptuous, bigoted anti-Semite! You think Jews are filthy pagans who deserve all the suffering they've had to endure for centuries. You said as much on Thanksgiving evening when Millie and Al and I were boozin' it up in the parlor room. Do you remember that?"

Nina Cassandra pulled her mouth down. In the room's deathly silence, she held her tongue as if thinking of an apt reply.

Joe knew what the phrase "anti-Semite" meant. Panic roared through his body.

The back kitchen door opened and then slammed shut. There was a commotion as if bags were being carried into the dining room. Rose inadvertently walked into the music room, still in her brown coat and gloves. Alarm stopped her. "Oh, my," she said softly.

Nina advanced toward the cook swiftly. "Aren't you supposed to be on your day off? Why are you here now?"

"I . . . I . . ." Poor Rose trembled. She looked back and forth between her employer, Nina Cassandra, and Grayson. Her mouth opened, but she couldn't speak. Joe desperately wanted to go to her to protect her.

Nina pointed a wrathful finger at the cook. "*You're* the one who started all this! You had no business listening to my phone conversations, and it was certainly inappropriate for you to tell Mildred where I had taken the ragamuffin. It's not your place to interfere in our family business." She waved a contemptuous hand. "Your employment ends the day after Christmas." She turned away.

Rose gasped. Joe ran to her and put his arms around her thick waist.

"Don't be ridiculous," said Mildred. "Rose has been with us for twenty years. She's not going anywhere."

"And who are *you* to have any say about this? *I* pay her salary, not you!"

"Fine. You go ahead and terminate her. I'll hire her right back."

Nina Cassandra sagging jowls quivered with self-serving fury. "I own this house. It's my business as to how it is run. The cook goes, and that grimy little hoodlum will be sent right back to St. Mark's as soon as I can arrange it. I just hope they'll still take the little trouble-maker."

One could almost see Grayson's blood pressure rising in his crimson face. "Now, you listen here, old woman. You may hold the deed to this house, but you share it with the only three people in this entire Pierce family who are willing to tolerate you. And you will *not* take Joe back to that dad-blasted orphanage. His home is here with us!"

Nina Cassandra wobbled with her cane as she sat back on the sofa. She took out her customary pink handkerchief from underneath her dress belt and dabbed her neck. Her heavily lined face was pink with exertion. "Grayson, I've told you before. That child is not part of this family. He is not a Pierce, nor is he your son. He is a foreign child who came from the country we just defeated in this terrible war. On top of that, he is not of the faith. He has been nothing but a nuisance since the first time he sat at our dinner table. I am worn out over your stubbornness."

"Joe is my ward! I am his legal guardian! And I will rear him as my son!" Grayson passed a frustrated hand over the top of his head. "How would you like it if Mildred and I decided to take *you* out of this house and stick you in a nursing home? And doing it without even telling you beforehand!"

Nina Cassandra shot back, "You wouldn't dare!"

"That's *exactly* what you did to Joe yesterday." Fatigue made Grayson clutch the back of his easy chair. Trying to scale this white-haired, fortified stone wall drained his stamina.

Nina turned to Elvie. "Have you ever heard such arguing? Did any of your children defy you like this?"

Elvie, batting her blackened eyelashes, did not answer at first. Licking sticky sugar off her fingers, she looked around the music room nervously. In a tentative voice, she said, "Well, Nina. I do think Grayson has a point. He did rescue the little boy from whatever that place was in Germany. It's his business if he chooses to adopt him. Far be it from us to tell him what he can and cannot do. After all, he is a grown man. He can make decisions for himself."

Nina gaped at her sister-in-law, her mouth dropping in complete surprise.

Elvie added, "And Mildred has been doing her part helping Joe with his schoolwork and buying his clothes and taking him to the library. And don't forget she did a lot of work in his bedroom getting the walls repapered and buying new furniture and a new rug."

The room stilled. Emboldened, Joe inched toward the evil queen. It took courage that he would never have had in the camp in approaching a Nazi guard. With his heart in his throat, he stepped forward and put his hand lightly on her dress over her arthritic knee.

"Grandma Nina, I'm sorry I've been so naughty. I didn't mean to do bad things dat made you mad. I am sorry I broke de window screen. Maybe I do chores, und Grayson can give me an allowance. Den, I vil save money und pay you for fixing it. I promise to behave und not run through de house, und I'll pick up my toys on de floor. Und I'll help you in the garden. I like to pull weeds."

The queen bee had no choice but to look back at him. Her mouth was a perfect upside-down "u."

"Bitte, vil you let me stay? I didn't like it at dat orphanage. It smelled funny, und dere vas dis draft in de sleeping room, und it vas cold all de time. Und I dunt think de nun teacher liked me."

Joe turned to Frau Dead Fish Eyes. "Aunt Mil, I am sorry I ran into de closet on Thanksgiving. I know I should not hide under de bed. I know I should not put garbage food in my closet. I'll be good from now on. I promise. Do you forgive me?"

The tall woman blinked as she stared down at him. She bent and uncharacteristically put his face in her hands. "I forgive you, Joe," she whispered. Stroking his silky black hair, she said again, "I forgive you. We won't ever abandon you. Your place is right here in this home."

Was there a glint of compassion in her cast-iron face?

As Grayson observed this interaction, he felt a tug on his belt. Irene practically jumped into his arms. He smooched her noisily and then lowered her to the floor. Noticing that the fire in the fireplace had shrunk to embers, he went to it and put two pieces of ash wood in it. Then he turned and faced his mother. All other eyes were on her as well.

Nina Cassandra looked back with annoyance. "Why are you all staring at me? As far as I'm concerned, the discussion is closed. There's nothing more to say about it."

Joe looked up at his guardian. Was this it? Was he to resign himself to the tyranny of the Pierce matriarch? Were his pleas and promises in vain? Would there be no leniency for him?

He crumpled at his guardian's feet, feeling exactly like the pathetic, starved inmate who also had collapsed in the excrement-filled pothole at "Little Camp." Joe had witnessed the wretched man succumb to the razor-sharp whip of the ruthless SS guard. There was no mercy for this man's life, no reason for him to fight for his life. Joe had watched him die on the spot.

His heart squeezed in pain. He'd known that his demise had been imminent the moment the enormous American soldier had pulled him out from the dirt hole where he had safely hidden in the barrack. His mother had been gone for months, his father was dead, and he was alone. Since then, that feeling of abandonment had always been with him just beneath the surface of his consciousness. Rejection had consumed him at the orphanage. Now hopelessness swept through his little body again, defeating him.

He put his face in his hands and wept. His guardian gently picked him up, and Joe buried his face in his sweaty neck, trembling with fear. He wanted to suck his collar again.

All that could be heard in the music room was his muted sobs.

Grayson faced the tyrannical queen while holding Joe, his eyes burning. In a lethal voice, he said, "Mom, did you really think you'd get away with taking my boy from me? Did you believe that by putting him away in an orphanage, this house would be set right? Are you so locked in your own universe that you can't see how the rest of us feels? Why would you be so, so mean-spirited as to create such turmoil in the lives of your family? "You don't rule the roost anymore. Your bullying must end.

"This child stays here in this house until he is of age. If you can't or won't accept that, then you have chosen to drink from that bitter cup of unhappiness."

Nina Cassandra's face went white.

Grayson spoke in a calmer voice. "Just think how Dad would have thought about Joe. He'd have been thrilled to have another grandson." He tilted his head slightly. "He loved kids."

Mildred murmured, "Yes. He loved us all." She crossed herself.

Grayson sat wearily in his chair and settled Joe in his lap, who put his head under his guardian's neck, wanting to sleep. To everyone, he said, "This is Joe's first Christmas. This is a children's holiday. It's about Joe and Irene, not us."

Elvie said mildly, " 'But Jesus called the children to him and said, "Let the little children come to me, and do not hinder them, for the kingdom of God belongs to such as these.' Luke 18:16." She covertly looked toward Nina Cassandra.

Grayson noticed the Pierce cook still standing in her spot. "Rose, will you please fix dinner?"

"Yes, Dr. Pierce. I'll make sure it's ready in an hour." She left the room.

"Irene, see if you can find Mr. Henry. He needs some attention, even if he wouldn't admit it."

Irene dutifully started looking under the furniture.

Mildred sat in a wing-backed chair and put on her half-glasses. She reached for her cross-stitching in the basket. Her shoulders sagged.

For want of something to do, Elvie piped, "Let's hear what's on the radio. Maybe we can find a station with Bing Crosby singing some Christmas songs. I love it when he sings *White Christmas.* That would be just peachy!" She leaned over to pick up the remote on the coffee table.

Nina Cassandra sat motionless, staring at Grayson. One could almost see the white-hot steam of fury billowing around her.

****

" 'Scrooge was better than his word. He did it all, and indefinitely more; and to Tiny Tim, who did not die, he was a second father. He became a good friend, as good a master, and as a good man, as the good old city knew, or any other good old city, town, or borough, in the good old world. Some people laughed to see the alteration in him, he let them laugh, and little heeded them; for he was wise enough to know that nothing ever happened on this globe, for good, at which some people did not have their fill of laughter in the outset; and knowing that such a these would be blind anyway, he thought it quite as well that they should wrinkle up their eyes in grins, as have the malady in less attractive forms. His own heart laughed; and that was quite enough for him.' "

Grayson took the book from Irene. "My dear, you read that very well." He handed it to Joe, who had just licked the last grains of salt from his popcorn bowl. "Your turn, Joe."

" 'He had no further intercourse vid the Spirits, but lived upon Total Abstinence Principle, ever afterwards; und it vas always said of him, dat he knew how to keep Christmas vel if any man alive possessed de knowledge. May dat be truly said of us! Und so, as Tiny Tim observed, God Bless Us, Everyone!' "

Joe closed the book and asked, "Grayson, can ve read another one?"

Grayson glanced up at the square ebony clock sitting on the mantel above the living room fireplace. Tonight, the fire blazed hot, filling the room with a sweet, woody aroma. The ten-foot Christmas tree decorated with cranberry strands, glass ornaments, and lights stood safely on the opposite side of the high-ceilinged room. Gifts in satin bows and colorful ribbons overflowed around it. A clumsily wrapped present that had the outline of a bicycle leaned against the wall next to it.

"Joe, it's nearly ten-thirty. You and Irene need to go to bed so you can get up tomorrow at an ungodly hour to wake me up. Tomorrow's going to be a big day. We'll have work to do opening all those presents and eating Rose's Christmas dinner. And don't forget, Uncle Al and Aunt Bernice and their family and Great Aunt Harriet and Uncle Bob will be here in the afternoon. We're going to have a full house. Now, off you go!"

He grabbed his kids and tickled them before they dashed up the wide, oak stairs.

BIBLIOGRAPHY

Biber, Jacob. *Risen From the Ashes.* Borgo Press, 1990.

Black, Edwin. *IBM and the Holocaust.* Crown Publishers, 2001.

Confino, Alon. *A World Without Jews.* Yale University Press, 2014.

Dwork, Deborah. *Children With A Star.* Yale University Press, 1991.

Dwork, Deborah, and Robert Jan Van Pelt. *Auschwitz.* W. W. Norton, 1996.

Gilbert, Martin. *The Boys.* Owl Books, 1996.

Gilbert, Martin. *The Righteous.* Owl Books, 2004.

Gross, Leonard. *The Last Jews in Berlin.* Open Road, 2015.

Harran, Marilyn, et al. *The Holocaust Chronicles.* Publications International, 2000.

Helman, Peter. *When Courage Was Stronger Than Fear.* MJF Books, 1999.

Hemmendinger, Judith, and Robert Krell. *The Children of Buchenwald.* Gefen Publishing House, 2000.

Hughes, Matthew, and Chris Mann. *Inside Hitler's Germany.* MJF Books, 2000.

Johnson, Eric A. *What We Knew.* Basic Books, 2005.

Kaplan, Marion A. *Between Dignity and Despair.* Oxford University Press, 1998.

Klee, Ernst, Willi Dressen, and Volker Riess, editors. *The Good Old Days.* Translated by Deborah Burnstone, The Free Press--Simon and Schuster, 1988.

Kogon, Eugen. *The Theory and Practice of Hell.* Berkley Medallion, 1966.

Konigseder, Angelika, and Judith Wetzel. *Waiting for Hope.* Translated by John A. Broadwin. Northwestern University Press, 2001.

Koonz, Claudia. *The Nazi Conscience.* Belknap Press, 2003.

Levi, Primo. *Moments of Reprieve.* Translated by Ruth Feldman. Penguin Books, 1995.

Lichtblau, Eric. *The Nazi Next Door.* Mariner Books, 2014.

Lower, Wendy. *Hitler's Furies.* Houghton Mifflin Harcourt, 2013.

Mullally, David S. *Order in the Court.* Writer's Digest-F & W Publications, Inc., 2000.

Novick, Peter. *The Holocaust in American Life.* Mariner Books, 2000.

Rosenberg, Maxine B. *Hiding to Survive.* Clarion Books, 1994.

Shirer, William L. *The Rise and Fall of the Third Reich.* Gallery Books, 1990.

Toland, John. *Adolph Hitler.* Vols. I and II. Doubleday and Company, 1976

Wiesel, Elie. *After Darkness.* Schocken Books, 2002.

Wiesel, Elie. *Night.* Hill and Wang, 2006.

Zelizer, Barbie. *Remembering to Forget.* University of Chicago Press, 1998.

"Historic WW II Nazi Concentration Camps." Quality Information Publishers, 2006. DVD

"Holocaust Ravensbrook and Buchenwald." ArtsMagic LTD, 2006. DVD

"Night and Fog." Criterion Collection, Janus Films, 2003. DVD.

"Naked Among Wolves." Dir. Frank Beyer. IceStorm, 1963. DVD.

ABOUT THE AUTHOR

Anita Tiemeyer was born and raised in Columbus, Indiana. She has been a writer for over fifty years. Ms. Tiemeyer received her Bachelor of Music degree from Western Illinois University in 1980. She entered the Air Force in 1983 and served at Lackland Air Force Base in San Antonio, Texas, until 1991. She was awarded her Master of Music degree in 1995 from Butler University in Indianapolis, Indiana. As a music educator by profession, she has maintained a private music studio in Central Indiana for over thirty-five years. *The Guardian's Son* is her second published novel, Book I of a series of six. Her first book, *A Brother for Sorrows,* is the fourth book. Both are available for purchase on her website and at Amazon and Barnes and Noble.

Connect with the author at:

Website: www.anitatiemeyer.com

Email: ast4586@gmail.com

Facebook: Anita Tiemeyer, author